The Liminal Line – Daybridge Chronicles: Tales from the Nexus

INTRODUCTION

The Liminal Line represents a departure from my usual storytelling style and themes. While set in the same universe as the Daybridge Chronicles and Ethan Reeves Werewolf Detective Series, this novel explores more cerebral science fiction concepts and metaphysical themes than the urban fantasy elements readers may expect from my other works.

This standalone story delves into quantum physics, parallel realities, and existential questions about the nature of consciousness—offering a different kind of adventure while still maintaining connections to the broader Daybridge universe.

Readers looking for my typical urban fantasy elements will find those aspects subtly woven throughout but should approach this particular journey with an openness to exploring new territory alongside familiar characters.

CHAPTER ONE: AN UNREMARKABLE DISCOVERY

Robert North's eyes burned as he stared at his laptop screen, the midnight glow illuminating his face in the otherwise darkened physics lab. Three empty coffee cups stood like sentinels around his keyboard. The simulation had failed again—quantum tunneling calculations refusing to stabilize across his model.

"Dammit," he muttered, running his fingers through his disheveled black hair.

Rain pattered against the windows of Daybridge University's Kepler Building. Robert checked his phone: 2:37 AM. He'd promised his adviser results by morning, but the equations kept spiraling into nonsensical values.

He saved his work and shut down the computer. Sleep deprivation wouldn't help in solving advanced quantum mechanics. The walk home to his apartment in Westhill would take forty minutes—if he hurried.

Outside, the rain had intensified. Robert pulled his hood up and trudged down the marble steps of the science building. The campus was deserted, streetlamps creating halos in the mist. His shoulders slumped under the weight of his backpack and exhaustion.

He turned onto Thornfield Avenue, a shortcut through the old part of town. The wet cobblestones gleamed under the amber lights. Something caught his eye—a subway entrance nestled between two brownstones. Iron railings curved downward into warm light below.

Robert stopped. Had that always been there?

He'd walked this route hundreds of times in his three years at Daybridge. He couldn't recall ever seeing a subway entrance on Thornfield. But his tired brain wasn't exactly reliable tonight.

Rain trickled down his neck. The prospect of getting home in ten minutes instead of forty was too tempting.

"When did they extend the Blue Line this far north?" he wondered aloud, descending the stairs.

The station below felt like stepping into another era. Brass fixtures gleamed alongside worn marble tiles. The ceiling arched higher than modern stations, adorned with mosaics depicting constellations. A single bench sat empty beneath a large analog clock reading 2:43.

No ticket booth. No turnstiles. No other passengers.

Robert pulled out his phone to check the transit app, but found no signal. The screen showed only the time—2:44—and his battery at 17%.

"Great," he sighed.

A distant rumble grew into a metallic screech as warm air rushed up from the tunnel. The approaching train's headlight cast long shadows across the platform.

The train that emerged wasn't the sleek silver model of Daybridge's modern system. This was something older—burnished copper with rounded edges, windows trimmed in dark wood, interior lights glowing amber rather than fluorescent white.

The doors slid open with a pneumatic hiss. Empty.

Robert hesitated. Something felt off, but exhaustion clouded his judgment. Home was just a few stops away, and his bed called to him.

"What the hell," he muttered, stepping aboard.

The doors closed behind him with surprising gentleness. The car smelled of polish and faint ozone. Wooden seats lined the walls, worn smooth by decades of passengers. Above them, old-fashioned advertisements for products he didn't recognize—Thornton's Tooth Powder, Mayfield's Ready-Made Suits, Petersen's Fountain Pens.

The train lurched forward, gaining speed smoothly. Robert slumped into a seat, his backpack heavy on his lap. The rhythmic clacking of wheels on track had an almost hypnotic quality. He leaned his head against the cool window, watching the darkness punctuated by occasional lights rush past.

His eyelids grew heavy. The quantum equations that had tormented him all night faded from his mind. The gentle rocking motion lulled him deeper into exhaustion.

He didn't remember closing his eyes.

"Westhill Station. End of the line."

Robert jerked awake. A voice—distant and tinny through speakers—had announced his stop. He blinked momentarily disoriented.

The train had stopped. Through the windows, he could see a platform similar to the one he'd boarded from, though this one had a small wooden bench and a different constellation mosaic overhead.

He grabbed his backpack and stumbled to the doors, which opened silently at his approach. The platform was empty. No station attendant, no late-night travelers. Just Robert and the distant drip of water from somewhere in the ceiling.

The train doors closed behind him, and the strange copper car pulled away, disappearing into the tunnel with surprising swiftness.

A single exit led upstairs. Robert climbed, legs heavy with fatigue, emerging onto a rain-slick sidewalk. The familiar outline of his neighborhood greeted him, streetlights shimmering on wet pavement.

Three blocks to his apartment. He could make it.

As he walked, something nagged at the edge of his awareness. The bakery on the corner—hadn't it been a bookstore yesterday? He paused, staring at the storefront. "Sweet Crumb Bakery" read the sign in flowing script. But Robert could have sworn Rosewood Books had occupied that space since before he moved to the neighborhood.

"I need sleep," he mumbled, continuing on.

The maple trees lining Elmwood Drive seemed taller somehow, their branches reaching higher than he remembered. And wasn't Mrs. Agarwal's house blue, not pale yellow? Robert squinted at the building, trying to reconcile his memory with what stood before him.

Even his apartment building looked slightly different—the brick a shade darker, the front door's brass handle replaced with a silver one. He fumbled for his keys, finding the right one by touch rather than sight.

The lock turned smoothly, and he entered the familiar lobby. The elevator was still out of order—that hadn't changed—so he dragged himself up three flights of stairs to apartment 3C.

Inside, he dropped his backpack by the door and kicked off his shoes. The layout was as he remembered—kitchen to the left, living room straight ahead, bedroom down the short hall to the right. But something felt subtly wrong, like furniture shifted an inch in every direction.

"Hello?" he called out, suddenly aware that his roommate might be home.

No answer. The digital clock on the microwave read 3:17 AM. Noah was probably asleep.

Robert shuffled to the bathroom, splashing cold water on his face. In the mirror, his reflection looked exactly as he expected—dark circles under tired eyes, black hair sticking up at odd angles, three-day stubble shadowing his jaw.

He dried his face with a hand towel—blue, not green like he thought it had been—and headed to his bedroom.

His room appeared normal at first glance. Bed unmade, desk cluttered with textbooks and papers, laundry hamper overflowing. But as he collapsed onto the mattress, he noticed his quantum mechanics poster had moved from the wall beside his desk to the one above his bed.

"Did Noah come in here?" he wondered. But that didn't make sense—his roommate knew better than to touch his things.

Robert's eyelids grew heavy again. Whatever strangeness he was noticing could wait until morning. He was too exhausted to think clearly.

As sleep claimed him, one final incongruity registered: the smell of his sheets. They should have smelled like the lavender detergent he always bought. Instead, they carried a subtle scent of something citrusy.

His last conscious thought was that he must have grabbed the wrong detergent at the store.

Morning came with harsh sunlight through blinds Robert didn't remember opening. He groaned and rolled over, fumbling for his phone on the nightstand. 10:23 AM. At least he didn't have class until afternoon.

The events of the previous night came back in fragments—the failed simulation, the rain, the strange subway that had gotten him home so quickly. He sat up, rubbing his eyes.

In daylight, his room looked normal, though the relocated poster still hung in its new position. Robert stared at it, trying to remember when he might have moved it. He couldn't.

He shuffled to the kitchen, where he found a note from Noah:

Had early clinical rotation. Leftover pizza in fridge. Don't forget rent due Friday. -N

The handwriting was Noah's, but the paper was yellow instead of the blue Post-it's his roommate usually used. Robert opened the refrigerator—sure enough, half a pizza sat on the middle shelf in a clear container.

Pepperoni and black olives. Noah hated olives.

Robert closed the refrigerator, a chill running down his spine that had nothing to do with the cold air. He moved to the living room window and looked out at the street below.

Westhill looked like Westhill, but with subtle differences he couldn't quite articulate. The Korean grocery store across the street had a different awning. The bike rack on the corner held three bikes instead of the usual five or six. The stop sign at the intersection seemed closer to the crosswalk than he remembered.

"I'm losing it," he muttered, pressing his palms against his eyes.

The lack of sleep, the stress of his thesis project—they were making him notice insignificant details and assign them importance. There was a perfectly rational explanation for everything.

The subway, though... that was harder to dismiss.

Robert pulled out his phone and opened the transit app. The map showed the familiar lines—Blue, Red, Green, Orange—but none extending to Thornfield Avenue. According to the official map, the nearest subway station was fifteen blocks from where he'd entered last night.

He switched to his browser and searched "Thornfield Avenue subway station, Daybridge."

No relevant results.

He tried variations—"historic subway Thornfield," "hidden subway entrance Daybridge," "old copper train Daybridge transit,"—but found nothing suggesting the station he'd used existed.

A knot formed in his stomach. He couldn't have imagined it—he'd gotten home somehow, and it wasn't by walking for forty minutes in the rain.

Robert poured himself a bowl of cereal, noticing the box design seemed slightly different, though he couldn't pinpoint how. As he ate, he decided he would retrace his steps that evening. He'd find the subway entrance again and prove to himself he wasn't going crazy.

His phone buzzed with a text from Professor Liang: *Any progress on the simulation?*

Reality crashed back. His thesis. The failed calculations. The real world demanded his attention.

Robert texted back: *Not yet. Going back to lab now.*

Whatever was happening with the subway and these strange inconsistencies would have to wait. His academic career wouldn't.

He showered quickly, dressed in clean clothes, and gathered his materials. As he was about to leave, he hesitated at the door, then turned back to grab a small notebook from his desk. On its first blank page, he wrote:

Possible differences observed:
- Sweet Crumb Bakery (was Rosewood Books?)
- Taller trees on Elmwood
- Mrs. Agarwal's house yellow not blue
- Apartment building brick darker
- Door handle silver not brass
- Blue towel not green
- Poster moved
- Sheets smell citrus not lavender
- Yellow note not blue
- Noah ordered olive pizza (he hates olives)
- Korean grocery different awning
- Fewer bikes at rack
- Stop sign position

Looking at the list, Robert felt ridiculous. Most could be explained by faulty memory or simple changes he hadn't noticed before. But the subway—that was different. He added one more item:

- Subway station on Thornfield that doesn't exist on maps

He tucked the notebook into his backpack and left the apartment, locking the door behind him. As he descended the stairs, a neighbor he'd never seen before nodded in greeting.

"Morning, Robert," the elderly man said casually.

Robert returned the greeting automatically, then froze on the next step down.

How did a stranger know his name?

He turned to ask, but the man had already disappeared into his apartment, the door closing with a soft click.

The knot in Robert's stomach tightened. Something was wrong—really wrong—and he couldn't shake the feeling that it had begun when he stepped onto that impossible subway train.

CHAPTER TWO: SHIFTING REALITY

Robert spent three hours in the physics lab that afternoon, running the simulation again with adjusted parameters. The results still made no sense. Quantum particles shouldn't behave this way—at least not according to any theory he'd studied.

"Your boundary conditions must be wrong," Professor Liang said, peering over his shoulder at the screen. Her silver-framed glasses reflected the dancing numbers. "The wave function is collapsing too rapidly across multiple potential states."

"I've checked them five times," Robert said, rubbing his temples. "It's like the particles exist in multiple states simultaneously, even after observation."

Professor Liang frowned. "That violates basic quantum principles. Something's wrong with your model."

Robert nodded, but a strange thought nagged at him. What if the problem wasn't his model, but reality itself?

He dismissed the idea immediately. One weird subway ride and some minor discrepancies in his neighborhood didn't mean quantum physics was breaking down. He was overtired and overthinking.

"I'll recalibrate and try again tomorrow," he promised.

Dusk settled over Daybridge as Robert left campus. The rain had stopped, leaving puddles reflecting the amber streetlights. His feet carried him automatically toward Thornfield Avenue.

He needed to know if the subway entrance was real.

The cobblestone street looked exactly as it had the night before. Robert walked slowly, examining the facades of buildings, searching for the iron railings that had led him underground.

There—between Thornfield Antiques and a narrow apartment building—stood the entrance. Iron railings curved downward, lights glowing warmly below. It existed.

Robert felt both relieved and unsettled. He hadn't imagined it.

He descended the stairs, finding the same vintage station with its constellation mosaics and brass fixtures. This time, he noticed details he'd missed in his exhaustion: the mosaics depicted constellations he didn't recognize, arrangements of stars that didn't match any in Earth's night sky. The analog clock read 6:17, matching his watch precisely.

A distant rumble announced an approaching train. Robert stood back from the platform edge, heart beating faster. The burnished copper train emerged from the tunnel, slowing with a metallic squeal.

This time, Robert wasn't alone. A woman in a burgundy coat stood at the far end of the platform. She boarded the front car without looking in his direction.

The doors of the middle car opened before him. Robert hesitated only briefly before stepping aboard.

The interior was identical to his previous journey—wooden seats, vintage advertisements, the smell of polish and ozone. The woman in burgundy was nowhere to be seen, despite having entered the car directly in front of his.

"Westhill," he said aloud, as if the train might respond to his destination.

The doors closed, and the train began to move. Robert took a seat, keeping his backpack on his lap. This time, determined to stay awake, he pulled out his notebook and pen.

October 3, 6:18 PM - Second journey on the Thornfield subway.

Train appears identical to first trip. No other passengers visible in my car.

Woman in burgundy coat entered front car but isn't visible now.

No conductor or transit staff present.
No route map or station listings inside train.

The train picked up speed, swaying gently on the tracks. Through the windows, Robert saw only darkness punctuated by occasional flashes of light—tunnel maintenance lamps, perhaps, or reflections from unknown sources.

After about five minutes, the train began to slow. No announcement came, but a station platform appeared outside the windows. The doors opened automatically.

"Westhill Station," Robert muttered, gathering his things.

He stepped onto the platform, which appeared identical to the one he'd arrived at the previous night. The same constellation mosaic overhead, though tonight he noticed it depicted stars in impossible formations—patterns that couldn't exist in Earth's night sky.

The copper train pulled away as soon as the doors closed, disappearing into the tunnel with remarkable speed.

Robert climbed the stairs to street level, emerging onto what should have been his neighborhood. At first glance, everything seemed normal—the same buildings, the same street layout. But as he walked toward his apartment, the differences accumulated.

The Sweet Crumb Bakery was now Cardiff Books & Tea. The maple trees on Elmwood were their normal size again. Mrs. Agarwal's house was back to blue but now had a red door instead of white.

His apartment building's brick was the familiar lighter shade, but the number above the door read "357" instead of "355." The lock still accepted his key.

Inside, the lobby had the same layout but different furnishings—a modern glass coffee table replaced the wooden one he remembered, and landscape paintings hung where there had been abstract art.

Noah was in the kitchen when Robert entered their apartment, stirring something on the stove that smelled like curry.

"Hey," Noah said without looking up. "Dinner in twenty."

"Thanks," Robert replied, watching his roommate carefully.

Noah looked the same—tall, lanky, with curly brown hair and the perpetual shadow of a beard he could never fully grow. He wore the green Daybridge Medical scrubs Robert had given him for his birthday last year.

"How was your day?" Robert ventured.

"Brutal. Three emergency surgeries back-to-back." Noah sighed. "Dr. Patel says I've got good hands, though."

Robert frowned. Noah was studying pediatrics, not surgery. And who was Dr. Patel? His supervisor was Dr. Goldstein.

"Surgery rotation this month?" Robert asked casually.

Noah gave him an odd look. "Very funny. I've been on trauma surgery since August, you know that."

Robert felt a chill run up his spine. "Right, sorry. Brain's fried from lab work."

He retreated to his room, heart pounding. Noah was different—or rather, this version of Noah was different. Robert's roommate had never expressed interest in surgery, but had always been passionate about pediatrics.

His bedroom looked mostly the same, though the quantum mechanics poster was back in its original position beside the desk. His laptop sat where he'd left it that morning, but the sticker on its lid—normally the Daybridge Physics Department logo—was now for something called "Quantum Futures Initiative."

Robert sat heavily on his bed, pulling out his notebook. Under today's date, he wrote:

Changes after second subway journey:

- Cardiff Books & Tea (was Sweet Crumb Bakery yesterday, Rosewood Books originally)

- Mrs. Agarwal's house blue again but with red door (was yellow yesterday, blue with white door originally)

- Apartment number 357 not 355

- Lobby furniture different

- Noah now in trauma surgery (was pediatrics)

- Mentions Dr. Patel (was Dr. Goldstein)

- Laptop sticker different

He stared at the list, a theory forming in his mind. It seemed impossible, yet it was the only explanation that fit the evidence: each time he rode the subway, he arrived in a slightly different version of Daybridge.

Not a hallucination. Not misremembered details. An actual different reality.

The implications made him dizzy. If parallel worlds existed and he was somehow traveling between them, what happened to the Robert North who belonged in each world? Was he temporarily displacing his counterparts? Or were these worlds that diverged only at the moment of his arrival?

"Food's ready!" Noah called from the kitchen.

Robert closed his notebook and went to join his roommate—his altered roommate—for dinner. As they ate, he casually probed for information, trying to determine how different this version of his friend might be.

Noah was still a medical student, still lived in the same apartment, still complained about his workload. But small differences emerged: he'd grown up in Chicago, not Philadelphia; he played guitar, not piano; he was allergic to shellfish, not peanuts.

"You're being weird tonight," Noah said eventually, narrowing his eyes. "Everything okay?"

"Just tired," Robert replied. "And struggling with that quantum tunneling simulation."

"The one for Professor Williams? Didn't you finish that last month?"

Another difference. In his world, Robert worked with Professor Liang, not Williams.

"Different project, similar concept," Robert said vaguely. "I'm going to crash early."

Back in his room, Robert added to his notes, mapping the differences between this Noah and his Noah. Then he pulled out his laptop and searched for information about parallel universes.

The many-worlds interpretation of quantum mechanics suggested that every possible outcome of every event spawned a new universe. In theory, there could be infinite versions of Daybridge, each differing in ways large and small.

But how was he moving between them? And why him?

Robert searched next for information about the Daybridge subway system. As before, no station was listed on Thornfield Avenue. Historical transit maps showed no evidence of a line ever being planned for that street.

He dug deeper, searching city archives that were accessible through his university credentials. In the Planning Commission records from 1943, he found a single reference to a "Thornfield Line Extension" that had been proposed but apparently abandoned.

The document noted: "Project discontinued due to unexpected geological anomalies and severe equipment malfunctions. Chief Engineer M. Hanover reports unusual temporal distortions in the tunneling area. Recommendation: seal the existing excavation and reclassify the project documents."

Robert stared at the screen. Temporal distortions. In 1943.

He searched for more information about M. Hanover but found nothing. The Thornfield project seemed to have been erased from official records.

Another search revealed that 1943 was the year Daybridge had housed a classified government research facility—part of the war effort. Details were scarce, but there were references to experiments in "advanced physics applications."

Robert closed his laptop, mind racing. Had wartime scientists accidentally created some kind of dimensional rift? Could the subway he'd discovered be running through that rift, connecting parallel versions of Daybridge?

It sounded absurd. But so did everything else that had happened.

Over the next five days, Robert rode the subway three more times. Each journey brought him to a slightly different version of Daybridge.

After the third trip, he found himself in a city where the university's physics department specialized in something called "quantum membrane theory" rather than traditional particle physics. Professor Liang didn't exist, and Robert's own research focused on "interdimensional energy transference."

The fourth journey brought him to a Daybridge where his apartment building had a working elevator, Noah was engaged to a woman named Clare (whom Robert had never met), and Robert himself apparently played in a local band on weekends.

After the fifth trip, he discovered that Daybridge had a Democratic mayor instead of a Republican one, the university's science building was called "Tesla Hall" instead of "Kepler Building," and coffee shops served something called "aurora beans" that Robert had never heard of.

With each shift, the differences became more pronounced. Robert meticulously documented everything in his journal, creating maps of each version of Daybridge and noting the variations in his own life circumstances.

The constant changing began to wear on him. He never knew which version of his friends he would be talking to, which version of his research he was supposed to be conducting, which version of himself he was supposed to be.

After a week of dimensional jumping, Robert had filled nearly half his notebook with observations. Patterns emerged: the changes seemed to radiate outward from Thornfield Avenue, with nearby locations showing more significant alterations than distant ones. His own personal history remained largely consistent, though his professional focus varied considerably between realities.

Most significantly, no version of Daybridge acknowledged the existence of the Thornfield subway in its official records. The entrance appeared only when Robert specifically sought it out, and no one else seemed to notice it—or at least, no one mentioned it.

At the university library in the fifth version of Daybridge, Robert finally found something substantial. A book titled "Quantum Fractures: Theoretical Models of Multiversal Bleed" by Dr. Eleanor Kwan contained a chapter on "transit anomalies"—locations where the boundaries between parallel realities had supposedly weakened.

The book described precisely what Robert was experiencing: hidden transit systems that appeared inconsistently and transported travelers to alternate versions of familiar locations. Dr. Kwan theorized that these anomalies often resulted from "technological interference with quantum fields"—exactly the kind of experiments that might have been conducted in wartime Daybridge.

The book listed several historical examples of such anomalies, including one in "northeastern America during the 1940s" that was never officially documented but had generated persistent local legends.

Robert checked the author's biography. Dr. Eleanor Kwan was listed as a professor at Miskatonic University—an institution he'd never heard of. When he searched for information about her online, he found nothing.

That night, back in his apartment (version five, with the working elevator and Noah's fiancée), Robert compiled everything he had learned into a single cohesive theory:

1. In 1943, wartime experiments in Daybridge created a fracture in the multiverse.
2. This fracture manifested physically as a subway system that traversed parallel realities rather than physical space.
3. The subway appeared only to certain people—perhaps those with particular quantum sensitivity.
4. Each journey shifted the traveler to a progressively more divergent reality.

The final point troubled him most. If each reality was more different from the last, how far might the divergence go? Would he eventually find himself in a Daybridge he couldn't recognize at all? And more importantly, could he ever find his way back to his original reality?

Robert stared at his journal, at the carefully documented changes across five different versions of his city. He needed more information, more data. But he also needed help.

In the morning, he would try to find someone who understood what was happening. Perhaps there was a version of Dr. Kwan in this Daybridge, or someone else who studied quantum fractures.

As he prepared for bed, Robert glanced out his window at the unfamiliar skyline of version-five Daybridge. The city lights seemed to blur and shift as he watched, as if reality itself was becoming unstable.

Or perhaps it was just his perception that was changing.

Either way, he knew he couldn't continue jumping between realities indefinitely. Eventually, he would need to find his way home—his real home, in his original Daybridge.

If such a place still existed for him at all.

Across town, in a cluttered bookshop called "Steinman's Rare Editions," Jake Steinman looked up from his antique radio equipment. The needle on one of his modified gauges had jumped suddenly, registering an energy fluctuation unlike anything he'd seen in years.

"That's not good," he murmured, adjusting dials and checking readings.

The pattern was unmistakable: someone was crossing between realities, creating ripples in the dimensional fabric of Daybridge. Jake had been monitoring such anomalies for decades, ever since he'd discovered his own unusual connection to the city's hidden infrastructure.

He tracked the disturbance to its source: somewhere near Thornfield Avenue. The old subway line was active again after all these years.

Jake sighed and closed his ledger. Whoever was riding those trains didn't understand the danger they were in—or the danger they posed to Daybridge's fragile multiversal stability.

He would need to find them before they wandered too far from home to ever return.

CHAPTER THREE: THE ECHO EFFECT

"Robert? You planning to explain this anytime soon?"

Robert looked up from his notebook to find Noah standing in his bedroom doorway, holding something in his hands. With a jolt, he recognized his dimensional mapping notes—pages he'd torn from his journal and taped to the wall behind his desk.

"It's for a... creative writing project," Robert said, the lie sounding hollow even to his own ears.

Noah stepped into the room, examining the papers more closely. The maps of six different Daybridge variations were arranged in sequence, with notes detailing the specific differences between each reality. Red strings connected key locations that showed the most significant alterations.

"Creative writing," Noah repeated flatly. "So you're not actually keeping track of whether my coffee shop is called 'Morning Brew' or 'Rise & Grind' depending on the day of the week?"

Robert winced. He'd forgotten that this version of Noah—version six, the one he'd arrived at last night—was more observant than most. This Noah was pursuing forensic psychiatry rather than surgery or pediatrics.

"It's complicated," Robert said.

"No kidding." Noah tapped one of the notes. "According to this, I'm engaged to someone named Clare in one version of your... story. And I'm a trauma surgeon in another." He turned to Robert, concern evident in his eyes. "You've barely slept in days. You mumble about 'versions' and 'shifts' when you think I can't hear you. And yesterday you asked me if I remembered growing up in Chicago, which I've never mentioned because I grew up in Baltimore."

Robert sighed. He'd been getting careless, losing track of which details belonged to which reality. The constant shifting was wearing him down.

"You wouldn't believe me if I told you."

"Try me." Noah sat on the edge of Robert's bed. "I've got clinical training in psychiatric evaluation, remember? I know the difference between creative eccentricity and concerning behavior."

Robert hesitated. Would telling Noah help or hurt? Would this Noah even believe him? After a moment's deliberation, he decided the truth couldn't make things worse than they already were.

"I've been traveling between parallel versions of Daybridge," he said simply. "Each time I ride a certain subway line, I emerge in a slightly different reality."

To Noah's credit, he didn't laugh or immediately dismiss the claim. He merely raised an eyebrow and asked, "What subway line?"

"The one that appears on Thornfield Avenue. The entrance is between an antique shop and an apartment building."

"There's no subway on Thornfield."

"Not officially. Not on any map. But it's there—at least, sometimes it's there. I can show you."

Noah studied Robert's face, then nodded slowly. "Okay. Show me."

They walked to Thornfield Avenue in silence, the autumn evening wrapping around them with unusual warmth for October. Streetlamps cast pools of light on the cobblestones as they approached the spot where Robert had repeatedly found the subway entrance.

"It should be right here," Robert said, gesturing between Thornfield Antiques and the narrow apartment building beside it.

Noah frowned. "That's a brick wall."

Robert stared in disbelief. Where the iron railings and stairs should have been, a solid brick wall stood, weathered and covered with ivy as if it had been there for decades.

"That's impossible," he whispered, approaching the wall and placing his hands against the rough surface. "It was here yesterday. I rode the train last night."

"Robert..." Noah's voice held a mix of concern and skepticism.

"I'm not making this up!" Robert pressed his palms harder against the bricks, as if he could force them to reveal the entrance through sheer determination. "It exists. I've used it six times now."

"Maybe we should head back," Noah suggested gently. "You're clearly exhausted, and—"

"It's real," Robert insisted, turning to face his roommate. "The subway is real. The parallel Daybridges are real. Everything I've documented is real."

Noah raised his hands in a placating gesture. "I believe that you believe it's real. But Robert, this sounds like a stress-induced—"

"Don't psychoanalyze me!" Robert snapped, immediately regretting his tone. He ran a hand through his hair, trying to calm himself. "Sorry. I just... I know how it sounds. But I'm not hallucinating or having a breakdown. Something genuinely strange is happening in Daybridge, and I'm caught in the middle of it."

Noah studied him for a long moment, then sighed. "Let's get some food and talk about this rationally. When's the last time you ate anything?"

Robert couldn't remember. The constant reality shifts had disrupted his normal routines.

"Fine," he conceded. "Food first, then we talk."

As they turned to leave, Robert glanced back at the brick wall. For just a moment—so briefly he might have imagined it—he thought he saw the outline of the subway entrance shimmer into existence, then fade away.

At a nearby diner, Robert picked at a plate of fries while Noah worked through a burger. The vinyl booth creaked whenever they shifted position.

"Start from the beginning," Noah said, wiping ketchup from his mouth. "When did you first find this subway?"

Robert recounted his initial discovery—the late night at the lab, the rainstorm, the unexpected entrance on Thornfield. He described the vintage station and copper train, and how he'd arrived home to find subtle differences in his neighborhood.

"Each time I use it, I end up in a slightly different version of Daybridge," he explained. "The changes are small at first, but they accumulate. In the original Daybridge—my Daybridge—you're studying pediatrics under Dr. Goldstein. In the second version, you're in trauma surgery with Dr. Patel. In this version, you're doing forensic psychiatry."

Noah frowned. "I've always wanted to be a forensic psychiatrist. Since undergrad."

"In my reality, you've always wanted to work with kids. You volunteer at Children's Hospital every summer."

"I hate children's hospitals," Noah said flatly. "They depress me."

Robert nodded. "Exactly. You're different in each version. So is the city. So is everything."

"And you think you're what—sliding between parallel universes like in some sci-fi show?"

"I know how it sounds. But I've found research suggesting it's possible. There was a book by Dr. Eleanor Kwan—"

"The quantum physicist from Miskatonic? She's brilliant."

Robert stared. "You know her?"

"Of course. Her work on dimensional boundaries is groundbreaking, if controversial. But Robert, her theories are largely mathematical models, not proven phenomena."

This was new. In none of the previous Daybridges had Noah known anything about quantum physics or Dr. Kwan.

"Could you introduce me to her?"

Noah laughed. "She's not exactly local. Last I heard, she was doing fieldwork somewhere in the Arctic, studying anomalous energy patterns."

Robert slumped back in the booth. Another dead end.

"Look," Noah said, his voice softening, "I'm not saying you're crazy. Strange things happen in Daybridge—everyone knows that. But what you're describing... it's extreme, even for this city."

"I know," Robert admitted. "But it's happening, Noah. And I don't know how to stop it or get back to my original reality."

"Assuming this is real," Noah said carefully, "have you considered that continuing to use this subway might make things worse? Each jump takes you further from your starting point, right?"

Robert nodded. "But it's the only lead I have. Maybe if I ride it enough times, I'll circle back to my original Daybridge."

"Or maybe you'll end up somewhere so different you'll never find your way back."

The words hung between them, heavy with implication. Robert had considered this possibility but had been avoiding it. What if each journey took him irrevocably further from home?

"I need to try one more time," he said finally. "Tomorrow. And I need you to come with me—to see if the entrance appears when I'm actively looking for it."

Noah hesitated, then nodded. "Fine. But if we don't find anything, you promise to see someone professional about this? The university has good mental health services."

"Deal," Robert agreed, though he had no intention of keeping that promise.

That night, Robert dreamed of trains. Not the copper subway cars he'd been riding, but every kind of train imaginable—steam locomotives, bullet trains, antiquated trolleys, futuristic monorails. They all converged on a massive central station, their tracks interweaving impossibly.

In the dream, he wandered the platforms, each one labeled with a different version of Daybridge. Some names he recognized from his journeys: "Daybridge-Patel," "Daybridge-Williams," "Daybridge-Forensic." Others were unfamiliar and unsettling: "Daybridge-Abandoned," "Daybridge-Submerged," "Daybridge-Inverted."

A station announcer's voice echoed through the dream: "All realities are experiencing delays due to interdimensional congestion. We apologize for any inconvenience to your existence."

Robert woke with a start, heart pounding. Sunlight streamed through his window—he'd overslept. A quick check of his phone showed three missed calls from Professor Williams. He was late for lab work.

The day passed in a blur of apologetic emails and rushed simulations. The quantum tunneling model continued to produce impossible results—particles existing in multiple states simultaneously, refusing to collapse into single positions even after observation.

"The mathematics are sound," Professor Williams insisted, reviewing Robert's work. "But the results violate Copenhagen principles. It's as if..."

"As if the particles are existing in multiple realities at once," Robert finished the thought.

Williams looked up sharply. "That's an unorthodox interpretation."

"But theoretically possible under Many-Worlds, isn't it? If every quantum state spawns a new universe, maybe our equipment is somehow detecting particles across multiple branches."

"That would require a fundamental breach in dimensional boundaries," Williams said, but his expression was thoughtful rather than dismissive. "Fascinating hypothesis, though not one I'd present at a conference without substantially more evidence."

Robert wanted to tell him that he had evidence—personal, experiential evidence of multiple realities. But that would sound insane, even in a field as speculative as theoretical physics.

Instead, he simply said, "I'll continue refining the model."

By evening, Robert's anticipation had built to an almost unbearable level. Noah met him at their apartment as promised, though his expression remained skeptical.

"One visit," Noah reminded him as they walked toward Thornfield Avenue. "If we don't find your magical subway, you're talking to Dr. Levine at the counseling center."

Robert barely heard him. As they approached the spot between the antique shop and apartment building, his pace quickened. The wall had to have returned to a subway entrance. It had to.

It hadn't. Solid brick greeted them, just as it had the previous night.

"No," Robert whispered, pressing his hands against the cool surface. "No, it was here. It has to be here."

Noah placed a hand on his shoulder. "Robert—"

"It changes," Robert insisted. "Sometimes it's visible, sometimes it's not. We just need to wait."

"It's getting late. We should—"

"Just thirty minutes," Robert pleaded. "Let's wait thirty minutes and see if anything changes."

Noah sighed but agreed. They sat on a nearby bench, watching the unremarkable wall as pedestrians passed by, giving them curious glances.

Twenty-eight minutes later, nothing had changed. Robert stared at the wall with such intensity that his vision began to blur. The bricks seemed to waver, like heat rising from pavement.

"Time's almost up," Noah said gently.

"Just a few more minutes."

"Robert, you promised—"

"Look!" Robert pointed at the wall, where the outline of the subway entrance had suddenly shimmered into view, iron railings materializing as if emerging from fog. "Do you see it?"

Noah frowned, squinting at the wall. "See what? The bricks?"

"The entrance! It's right there!" Robert stood, moving toward the now-visible stairs leading down to the station. "How can you not see it?"

"Because there's nothing there," Noah said, rising to follow him. "Robert, stop. You're walking toward a solid wall."

But to Robert, the entrance was perfectly clear—more solid and real than it had ever been. He descended the stairs, hearing Noah call after him from the street.

The station below looked different this time. The brass fixtures were tarnished, the marble tiles cracked in places. The constellation mosaics overhead seemed to shift subtly, stars rearranging themselves as he watched.

A rumble announced an approaching train. This time, the copper car that emerged was noticeably weathered, its once-gleaming surface dulled with age and wear. The doors opened with a strained wheeze rather than their usual smooth hiss.

Robert hesitated. Something felt wrong—more wrong than usual. But he needed answers, and this train was his only path to finding them.

He boarded, and the doors closed behind him with a sound like a sigh.

The journey started normally enough. The train accelerated smoothly, carrying Robert through darkness broken by occasional flashes of light. But after five minutes—longer than any previous trip—the train had not slowed for a station.

Ten minutes passed. Fifteen. The train maintained its speed, the rhythmic clacking of wheels on track the only sound.

Robert checked his phone. No signal, as expected. The screen showed the time as 7:43 PM, though he was certain more than twenty minutes had passed since boarding.

At what should have been the thirty-minute mark, the train finally began to slow. Through the windows, Robert could see a station platform approaching—but not the familiar Westhill Station he expected.

This platform was longer, wider, with multiple benches and elaborate tilework covering the walls. The sign above read "CENTRAL NEXUS" in ornate lettering.

The doors opened. Robert stepped out cautiously, finding himself in a station unlike any he'd seen before. The ceiling soared at least thirty feet above, supported by marble columns wrapped with intricate metalwork. The air smelled of ozone and something else—something like old books and brass polish.

"Pardon me, sir," said a voice behind him. "You'll want to clear the doorway for other passengers."

Robert turned to find an elderly man in a transit uniform—navy blue with gold buttons and trim. His white hair was impeccably combed, his posture military-straight despite his apparent age.

"Where am I?" Robert asked. "This isn't Westhill."

"Indeed not, sir. This is Central Nexus, the primary interchange for all lines." The man gestured to a large board mounted on a nearby wall, displaying dozens of destinations arranged in columns. "Your connecting train will depend on your ultimate destination."

Robert approached the board, studying the listings. Each entry consisted of "DAYBRIDGE" followed by a modifier: Daybridge-Prime, Daybridge-Altered, Daybridge-Historic, Daybridge-Modern, Daybridge-Academic, Daybridge-Mercantile. Dozens more filled the columns, many with designations he didn't understand.

"I want to go home," Robert said. "To my original Daybridge."

The station attendant raised an eyebrow. "And which would that be, sir? We have many versions available."

"The... the first one. Before I started riding these trains. Daybridge where my roommate Noah is studying pediatrics, where I work with Professor Liang on quantum tunneling simulations."

"Ah." The attendant consulted a pocket watch. "Daybridge-Prime, then. I'm afraid that line is currently experiencing technical difficulties. Multiversal track maintenance. You might try Daybridge-Academic in the meantime—it's quite similar in most respects."

"When will the Prime line be running again?"

"Difficult to say, sir. Temporal distortions make scheduling somewhat approximate." The attendant gestured toward a different platform. "The Academic line departs in seven minutes from Platform 3. You might find it satisfactory until Prime service resumes."

Robert felt a surge of hope. This station attendant understood what was happening—could explain the system of reality-shifting trains. And he'd confirmed that Robert's original reality—Daybridge-Prime—actually existed.

"Who are you?" Robert asked. "What is this place, really?"

The attendant smiled thinly. "I am merely a transit facilitator, sir. As for Central Nexus, it is exactly what it appears to be—the convergence point of multiple reality tracks. Now, if you'll excuse me, I have other passengers to assist."

The man turned away, approaching a woman in the 1940s attire who had just emerged from a different train. Robert wanted to follow, to demand more answers, but the attendant and woman suddenly seemed very far away, though he hadn't seen them move.

Disoriented, Robert made his way to Platform 3 as directed. A train waited there—copper like the others, but with "ACADEMIC LINE" stenciled on its side in gold lettering.

He boarded, finding the interior similar to his previous trains but more polished, with leather seats instead of wooden ones. The advertisements overhead featured university events and academic publications.

As the doors closed and the train began to move, Robert felt a strange doubling of his vision. The car seemed to exist in two slightly different configurations simultaneously—one with the leather seats he was sitting on, another with wooden benches glimpsed like a superimposed image.

The sensation intensified as the train accelerated. Through the windows, Robert saw not darkness but brief flashes of different Daybridges—skylines shifting, buildings appearing and disappearing, streets rearranging themselves.

His head began to pound. The doubled vision worsened until he could see three, four, five overlapping versions of the train car. In each version, different passengers sat in different positions, all ghostly and translucent.

"Echo effect," said a voice beside him—a voice that seemed to come from multiple sources at once.

Robert turned to find an elderly woman sitting next to him—or rather, several versions of an elderly woman overlapping in the same space, like multiple exposure photographs.

"Excuse me?" he managed, his own voice sounding distant and distorted.

"You're experiencing the echo effect," the woman—women—said. "Happens when you ride too many lines too quickly. Your perception begins to span multiple realities simultaneously. Quite disorienting at first."

"How do I make it stop?" Robert asked, closing his eyes against the nauseating multiplicity.

"You don't," the woman replied simply. "Once it starts, it tends to progress. The boundaries between realities become more permeable to you with each crossing."

Robert opened his eyes, immediately regretting it as the overlapping images swam in his vision. "Are you experiencing it too?"

The woman smiled—several smiles, all slightly different. "I've been riding these trains for forty-three years, young man. I see all versions at once now. You learn to sort them eventually, to focus on the reality you want to perceive."

"Forty-three years?" Robert echoed in horror. "You've been trapped in these trains for decades?"

"Not trapped. Traveling. There's a difference." The woman adjusted her purse—purses—on her lap. "I'm a dimensional tourist. The multiverse is infinitely more interesting than any single reality."

Before Robert could respond, the train began to slow. The station appearing outside the windows seemed to flicker between multiple versions, settling gradually into a single configuration.

"Your stop, I believe," the woman said. "Daybridge-Academic. Mind the gap between train and platform—it's wider in this reality than most."

Robert stood unsteadily, the echo effect making the simple movement challenging. "Thank you for the explanation. I hope I find my way home before forty-three years pass."

The woman's smile turned sad. "Home is relative when you've seen as many realities as I have. Good luck, young man. And do try to limit your jumps from now on—the effect becomes permanent after a certain threshold."

The doors opened, and Robert stepped onto yet another version of Daybridge.

Daybridge-Academic looked much like the versions Robert had visited before, with some notable differences. The university campus dominated the city center, its buildings more numerous and imposing than in his original reality. Streets were named after scientists and philosophers rather than local historical figures.

But the most disorienting aspect was the persistent echo effect. As Robert made his way to his apartment—located in the same place but now part of "University Faculty Housing"—he saw multiple versions of each building and person. Most strongly visible was the current reality, but ghostly overlays of other Daybridges flickered in and out of his perception.

In his apartment, he found a version of Noah surrounded by medical textbooks. This Noah acknowledged him with a distracted wave, apparently accustomed to Robert's comings and goings. The apartment itself seemed to shift subtly as Robert moved through it—furniture rearranging, colors changing, dimensions expanding and contracting.

In his bedroom, Robert collapsed onto his bed, head pounding. The echo effect made even this simple space disorienting. His desk appeared in three different positions simultaneously. His bookshelf contained volumes that faded in and out of existence as he watched.

He closed his eyes, but the multiplicity persisted in his mind's eye. He could see—or sense—versions of himself in other Daybridges, going about different lives. Robert the physicist, Robert the musician, Robert the doctor, Robert the teacher.

His phone chimed. Somehow, in this reality, it had signal. A message from Professor Liang—not Williams—appeared on the screen:

Meeting tomorrow canceled. Equipment malfunction in lab. Quantum particles exhibiting unprecedented dimensional instability. Will discuss when you return.

Even the physics was being affected by his reality jumping. Or perhaps it was the other way around—the physics anomalies were causing the dimensional breaches.

Robert managed to type a response with trembling fingers:

Experiencing similar anomalies. Will explain tomorrow.

He set the phone aside and tried to focus on a single version of his room, to anchor himself in this reality until he could figure out his next move. But the echoes persisted, growing stronger rather than weaker.

In the bathroom mirror, he saw not one reflection but several—each Robert North slightly different. One had longer hair, another glasses, a third a small scar above his eyebrow.

"Focus," he told himself—selves. "You need to find Jake Steinman."

The name came to him suddenly, though he wasn't sure from which reality. Jake Steinman, owner of a bookshop called "Steinman's Rare Editions." Someone who might understand what was happening to him.

Robert didn't know how he knew this, but the knowledge felt certain, as if planted in his mind by his experiences across multiple Daybridges.

Tomorrow, he would find Jake Steinman. But tonight, he needed to rest, to try to stabilize his fragmenting perception before the echo effect became permanent.

As he drifted into uneasy sleep, Robert saw trains in his mind's eye—dozens of them, all converging on a single point in space and time. And standing at that convergence point was a figure watching the trains approach with calculating eyes.

A figure who looked remarkably like the old station attendant from Central Nexus.

CHAPTER FOUR: JAKE STEINMAN TAKES NOTICE

The antique radio in the back room of Steinman's Rare Editions crackled with static at precisely 3:17 AM. Jake Steinman's eyes snapped open in the darkness of his apartment above the bookshop. He'd been expecting the alert but had hoped it wouldn't come.

Another boundary breach. The sixth in eight days.

Jake swung his legs over the side of his bed, not bothering with the lamp. He navigated the familiar space by memory and the faint glow of street lights filtering through his curtains. The wooden stairs creaked under his weight as he descended to the bookshop below.

The store was a carefully curated maze of towering bookshelves, reading nooks, and display cases filled with curiosities. Moonlight slanted through the high windows, casting long shadows across the hardwood floors. Jake moved with practiced ease through the labyrinth of literature to the unmarked door at the rear.

The back room appeared, to casual observers, to be nothing more than storage and a modest workshop for book restoration. Antique radios lined one wall—Atwater Kent, Philco, Zenith, RCA—their wooden cabinets gleaming with decades of careful polishing. Vintage measuring instruments occupied another wall: barometers, astrolabes, chronometers, seismographs.

None of them measured what they appeared to measure.

Jake approached the crackling Philco cathedral radio, its vacuum tubes glowing amber in the darkness. The needle on its modified dial had swung far to the right, into a section marked with symbols rather than numbers. He adjusted a brass knob, and the static resolved into a pulsing tone—steady, then erratic, then steady again.

"Location?" Jake asked the empty room.

In response, a map of Daybridge illuminated on the wall, projected from a modified magic lantern. A pulsing red dot marked a point near the university's Kepler Building.

"Subject identity?"

The projection shifted, showing a young man with dark hair exiting the science building, head down against the rain. The image was grainy but clear enough to make out his features.

"Robert North," Jake murmured, recognizing the physics graduate student from previous monitoring. "Again."

He moved to a different instrument—an altered seismograph that measured dimensional tremors rather than earthly ones. The paper strip showed increasingly dramatic spikes corresponding with each of North's crossings.

The pattern was troubling. The first breach had been minor, barely registering on Jake's equipment. But each subsequent crossing created larger disturbances, as if the multiversal boundaries were deteriorating with each transit.

Jake had been monitoring Daybridge's dimensional stability for nearly three decades. In all that time, he'd only seen this pattern once before—in 1998, when a teenage girl had accidentally discovered the old maintenance tunnels beneath Riverside Park. She'd made seven crossings before Jake could intervene. By the seventh, entire city blocks were experiencing reality slippage. It had taken months to repair the damage.

North had already made six crossings. The seventh could be catastrophic.

Jake turned to a leather-bound ledger on his desk, opening it to a fresh page. In precise handwriting, he noted the date, time, location, and intensity of the breach. Then he added:

Subject: Robert North (PhD candidate, Quantum Physics)
Pattern: Increasing amplitude, decreasing interval
Estimated window before critical threshold: 36-48 hours

Intervention priority: Immediate

Closing the ledger, Jake considered his options. Direct confrontation was risky—subjects experiencing reality slippage were often disoriented, sometimes paranoid. But observation alone might not be sufficient given the accelerating timeline.

He would need to monitor North closely, establish the exact nature of his dimensional access point, and intercept him before the seventh crossing.

Jake glanced at the wall clock: 3:42 AM. Too early to begin the pursuit, but too late to return to sleep. He made himself tea and settled into the worn leather chair behind his desk.

From a drawer, he removed a thin file labeled "Thornfield Anomaly - 1943." The yellowed papers inside documented the original breach—the wartime experiment that had fractured reality along Daybridge's dimensional fault lines.

Jake had inherited this knowledge from his mentor, Margaret Steinman, who had been one of the original researchers. When the government abandoned the project and sealed the records, Margaret had recognized the need for ongoing monitoring. She'd established the bookshop as a cover for her real work: guarding the boundaries between realities.

"The Thornfield Subway," Jake murmured, studying a faded blueprint. "Of course."

The transit system had been designed to move troops and equipment quickly between research facilities. But when the dimensional experiments went awry, the subway tunnels had become conduits between parallel realities—physical manifestations of quantum connections.

Officials had sealed the entrances, demolished the stations, and buried the evidence. But they couldn't erase the tunnels themselves. They existed in a state of quantum superposition—both present and not present, appearing only under specific conditions to specific people.

People like Robert North, apparently.

Jake closed the file. At first light, he would begin his search for the young physicist. Time was running short.

By nine o'clock the following morning, Jake had positioned himself near the university's science complex. His tweed jacket and leather messenger bag helped him blend in with the academic crowd. At 61, with salt-and-pepper hair and reading glasses, he could easily pass for a visiting professor.

He didn't have to wait long. Robert North emerged from the Kepler Building looking distinctly unwell. Even from a distance, Jake could see the signs of advanced reality slippage: the slight doubling of North's outline, the momentary hesitations as he navigated a landscape that appeared differently to his compromised perception, the way his gaze tracked objects others couldn't see.

The young man moved with the cautious deliberation of someone walking on unstable ground. Twice he stopped suddenly, blinking hard as if trying to clear his vision. His hands trembled slightly as he checked his phone.

Jake followed at a discreet distance as North made his way to the university library. Inside, the student headed directly to the history section, pulling books on Daybridge's development and architectural evolution.

Interesting choice. Not quantum physics or dimensional theory, but local history. North was trying to understand the physical context of his experiences.

Jake selected a book from a nearby shelf and pretended to read while observing the young man. North's reality slippage was more advanced than he'd initially assessed. The doubling effect was pronounced, and occasionally North would reach for something that wasn't there—at least not in this reality.

After an hour of research, North gathered his notes and books and headed to the rare document section on the third floor. Jake followed, maintaining his cover as a casual researcher.

In the climate-controlled rare document room, North requested city planning records from the 1940s. The archivist returned with several boxes, which North began to sort through methodically.

Jake positioned himself at a table with a clear view of the young physicist. From his messenger bag, he removed a small device disguised as an antique pocket watch. When opened, its face displayed not time but dimensional stability readings. The needle hovered in the yellow zone—not yet critical, but concerning.

North's presence was affecting local reality, causing minor fluctuations in the very fabric of the room. Books momentarily displayed different titles, furniture shifted slightly in position, light fixtures alternated between styles. Most people wouldn't notice these subtle changes, but to Jake's trained perception, they were glaring evidence of deteriorating boundaries.

After two hours of research, North appeared to find something significant. He photographed several documents with his phone, made extensive notes, and returned the materials to the archivist. As he gathered his belongings, his expression showed both excitement and apprehension.

Jake closed his "watch" and prepared to continue the pursuit. But as North stood to leave, a wave of dimensional instability rippled through the room. The young man swayed, gripping the edge of the table for support. His outline blurred dramatically, momentarily showing three distinct versions overlapping.

The dimensional monitor in Jake's pocket vibrated in alarm. This wasn't good. North's condition was accelerating faster than anticipated.

Jake abandoned discretion and approached the struggling student.

"You need to sit down," he said calmly, taking North's arm. "The echo effect is intensifying. You're experiencing a cascading perception collapse."

North stared at him, confusion giving way to recognition. "You're Jake Steinman."

"I am. And you're Robert North, PhD candidate in quantum physics, currently experiencing severe reality slippage due to unauthorized dimensional transit." Jake guided him back to the chair. "How many crossings have you made?"

"Six," Robert admitted, his voice unsteady. "How do you know about—"

"I've been monitoring the breaches. The subway on Thornfield, I presume?"

Robert nodded, then winced as the movement seemed to cause him pain. "Everything's overlapping. I see multiple versions at once."

"The echo effect. It happens when you cross too many boundaries too quickly." Jake checked his dimensional monitor again. The needle had edged closer to the red zone. "We need to get you somewhere stable. My shop has shielding that can temporarily dampen the effect."

"Your bookshop," Robert said. "Steinman's Rare Editions. I was coming to find you."

"Oh? And how did you know to look for me?"

"I don't know exactly. The information was just... there in my head this morning. Like I'd always known it."

Jake nodded. "Quantum information bleed-through. You're picking up knowledge from your counterparts in other realities." He helped Robert to his feet. "Can you walk?"

"I think so."

They made their way out of the library, Jake supporting Robert when the echo effect intensified. Outside, the autumn air was crisp, leaves spiraling down from the massive oaks that lined the university paths.

"Your condition is affecting local reality," Jake explained quietly as they walked. "Notice how the leaves are changing color as they fall? Red to gold to green and back again?"

Robert watched the impossible color changes with horrified fascination. "Is that my fault?"

"Not fault. Consequence. Each dimensional crossing weakens the boundaries between realities. Your perception is bleeding through, and reality itself is responding to the instability."

They turned onto Merchant Street, where Steinman's Rare Editions occupied a Victorian townhouse with bay windows displaying carefully arranged books and curiosities. The shop stood at the intersection of several major ley lines—a dimensional nexus point that Jake's mentor had chosen deliberately for its natural stability.

As they approached the entrance, Robert suddenly stopped. "Wait. I need to know—can I get back? To my original Daybridge?"

Jake considered the question carefully. False hope would be cruel, but so would unnecessary despair.

"Potentially," he said finally. "But it becomes exponentially more difficult with each crossing. The path back is never as straightforward as the path away."

He unlocked the shop door, the bell above it chiming softly. The interior was cool and dim, smelling of old paper, leather bindings, and furniture polish. Customers browsed quietly among the shelves or sat reading in comfortable chairs tucked into alcoves.

Jake led Robert through the maze of bookshelves to the unmarked door at the rear. Inside the back room, he directed the young man to the leather chair behind his desk.

"Sit here. The shop is built on a convergence of stable ley lines. It exists in nearly identical configurations across multiple realities, which makes it a natural anchor point."

Robert sank into the chair gratefully. "The echo effect—it's less intense in here."

"As I said, natural stability." Jake moved to a cabinet and removed a small brass device resembling an astrolabe. He adjusted its rings and placed it on the desk near Robert. "This will help further. It generates a localized field that reinforces the boundaries between realities."

As the device began to hum softly, the doubled images surrounding Robert seemed to fade slightly. His outline became more defined, less blurred by overlapping versions.

"Better?" Jake asked.

Robert nodded. "The multiple versions are still there, but... quieter somehow. Like they're in the background instead of competing for attention."

"Good. That should help you think more clearly." Jake took a seat opposite him. "Now, tell me exactly how you discovered the Thornfield Subway, and what happened during each of your crossings."

Robert recounted his experiences—the rainy night, the unexpected station, the vintage copper train. He described the progressively more divergent realities he'd encountered, and his most recent journey to Central Nexus where he'd met the elderly station attendant.

"Central Nexus," Jake repeated, his expression grave. "That's troubling. The hub usually doesn't reveal itself until much later in the progression."

"Progression of what?"

"Dimensional dissolution. The process by which a traveler becomes untethered from their origin reality." Jake opened his ledger and made several notes. "The fact that you've reached Central Nexus after only six crossings suggests you have an unusual sensitivity to multiversal structures. Are you working on anything related to quantum observation or parallel theories?"

"Yes, actually. A simulation modeling quantum tunneling effects. The particles in our model refuse to collapse into single states even after observation. They maintain multiple potential positions simultaneously."

"Of course they do," Jake said grimly. "Your research is bleeding into reality, or perhaps reality is bleeding into your research. Causality becomes circular in these situations."

Robert leaned forward, wincing as the movement triggered another wave of echoes. "I need to understand what's happening. The archives mentioned a project in 1943—something about temporal distortions during subway excavation. Was that the origin of all this?"

Jake hesitated. How much should he reveal? The full truth might overwhelm the already struggling physicist. But partial information could lead to dangerous assumptions.

"The Daybridge Containment Initiative," he said finally. "A classified project during World War II. The government believed that manipulating quantum fields could create weapons of unprecedented power—or defenses against such weapons. They conducted experiments in tunnels beneath the city, taking advantage of Daybridge's natural dimensional permeability."

"Something went wrong," Robert guessed.

"Catastrophically wrong. They tore a hole in the fabric of reality itself—a multiversal breach that couldn't be repaired, only contained. The subway system you discovered was originally meant for transporting personnel and equipment between research sites. After the breach, the tunnels became physical manifestations of interdimensional pathways."

"And you're what—the caretaker of this information?"

"Guardian would be more accurate. My mentor, Margaret Steinman, was part of the original research team. When the government abandoned the project and sealed the records, she recognized that someone needed to monitor the breach. She established this bookshop as both cover and headquarters for that work. I inherited the responsibility when she passed."

Robert absorbed this information, his gaze drifting to the modified instruments lining the walls. "These all measure dimensional stability, don't they? Not weather or seismic activity."

"Correct. They allow me to detect boundary breaches and intervene when necessary." Jake leaned back in his chair. "Which brings us to your situation. Your repeated crossings have created a cascading effect that threatens local dimensional stability. If you make a seventh crossing, the damage could become irreparable."

"But I need to get home," Robert insisted. "To my original Daybridge."

"I understand. But continuing to use the subway randomly will only take you further from your origin point. Each reality branch creates exponentially more branches, like a tree with infinite limbs. Finding your specific branch becomes nearly impossible without guidance."

"The station attendant mentioned Daybridge-Prime. He said that was my original reality but that the line was experiencing 'technical difficulties.'"

Jake's expression darkened. "The Station Master. Another troubling development."

"Who is he?"

"Not who—what. The Station Master is a manifestation of the system itself—a quantum construct created to maintain order within the interdimensional transit network. If he's interfering directly with your journeys, the situation is more serious than I thought."

Jake stood and moved to the modified seismograph. The paper strip showed increasingly dramatic spikes, with barely any return to baseline between them.

"The boundaries are failing," he said quietly. "Your crossings have weakened them to a critical point. One more transit might create a cascading collapse—a multiversal convergence event."

"Meaning?"

"Multiple versions of Daybridge could begin to merge uncontrollably. Overlapping realities occupying the same space-time coordinates. The echo effect you're experiencing, but on a city-wide scale."

Robert paled. "That sounds apocalyptic."

"It would be... chaotic," Jake admitted. "Potentially survivable, but fundamentally altering the nature of local reality. Daybridge would become a dimensional anomaly—a place where multiple versions exist simultaneously, where causality breaks down, where history becomes fluid rather than fixed."

"How do we prevent that?"

Jake noted the shift from "I" to "we" with approval. The young man was beginning to understand the gravity of the situation.

"First, no more subway rides. Not until we've developed a plan for controlled transit." Jake moved to a bookshelf and selected a volume bound in faded blue leather. "Second, we need to identify your exact origin point. The multiverse contains infinite variations of Daybridge, but only one is truly yours."

He opened the book to reveal not pages but a complex three-dimensional model that seemed to hover above the binding—a fractal pattern of interconnected lines forming a tree-like structure.

"This is a partial mapping of the known Daybridge variations. Your origin point is somewhere in this network." Jake traced a path along one branch. "If we can identify specific divergence markers in your home reality, we can potentially navigate you back through controlled transit."

Robert stared at the impossible book with its hovering multidimensional map. "How would we do that?"

"You need to document everything you can remember about your original Daybridge—not just physical landmarks, but events, people, details that might be unique to that reality branch."

Jake closed the book and returned it to the shelf. "But first, we need to stabilize your condition. The echo effect is progressing rapidly. Without intervention, you could become permanently untethered—existing across multiple realities simultaneously, unable to fully perceive or interact with any single one."

"That sounds... horrific."

"It is. I've seen it happen." Jake's expression grew distant. "The woman becomes known as the Wandering Lady in most Daybridge variations. She exists partially in dozens of realities, appearing and disappearing seemingly at random. Most people can only see her briefly before their perception filters her out as an impossibility."

Robert's face showed recognition. "The homeless woman who talks to pigeons in Riverside Park? I've seen her flicker in and out of existence."

"That's her. Martha Craine. Former physics professor at Daybridge University, 1988. She discovered the tunnels by accident and made too many crossings before anyone could intervene."

The gravity of his situation settled over Robert like a physical weight. "How do we stabilize my condition?"

Jake moved to a cabinet and removed a small wooden box inlaid with copper wire in intricate patterns. Opening it revealed a pendant—a simple disk of dull metal on a leather cord.

"This is stabilized neutronium from the original 1943 experiment. It exists simultaneously across multiple realities and can help anchor your perception to a single dimensional track." He handed the pendant to Robert. "Wear this at all times. It won't cure the echo effect, but it will slow its progression and help you maintain your connection to this reality."

Robert slipped the cord over his head. The pendant felt unexpectedly heavy against his chest, and strangely warm. Almost immediately, the overlapping images surrounding him seemed to recede further, becoming ghostly impressions rather than competing realities.

"That's... better," he said with relief. "Much better."

"It's temporary," Jake cautioned. "The pendant buys us time, nothing more. We still need to find your origin point and develop a controlled method of return."

Robert nodded, then suddenly looked alarmed. "What time is it?"

Jake checked his actual watch. "Nearly three."

"I have a meeting with Professor Williams—or Liang, depending on which reality I'm perceiving most strongly right now."

"You should maintain your normal routines as much as possible," Jake advised. "Continuity helps stabilize your dimensional perception. But avoid the Thornfield area entirely. The entrance will call to you, especially as the echo effect progresses. The system wants to complete the cycle it began with your first crossing."

"What cycle?"

Jake hesitated again. "There's a pattern to multiversal transit. Seven crossings complete a dimensional octave—a full spectrum of reality variations. The seventh crossing typically returns the traveler to their origin point, but with a fundamental change: they become permanently connected to the system, able to perceive and traverse multiple realities at will."

"That sounds potentially useful," Robert observed.

"It's dangerous," Jake countered. "The human mind isn't designed to perceive multiple realities simultaneously. Most who complete the cycle eventually lose their grip on any single reality. They become like Martha—fragmented across the multiverse, never fully existing anywhere."

He moved to his desk and wrote something on a card. "My private number. Call immediately if the echo effect intensifies or if you feel compelled to seek out the subway. Day or night."

Robert accepted the card, tucking it into his wallet. "Thank you. For explaining all this, and for the pendant."

"Don't thank me yet. We've only begun to address your situation." Jake's expression was somber. "And the clock is ticking. The dimensional instability you've created will continue to grow until we resolve it, one way or another."

As if to emphasize his point, the modified radio on the shelf crackled with sudden static. Jake glanced at it, concern crossing his features.

"You should go to your meeting," he said. "Maintain normalcy. I'll continue researching your specific case and potential solutions. Return here tomorrow morning, and we'll begin the process of identifying your origin point."

Robert stood, steadier now with the pendant's influence. "One more question—how did you know to find me today?"

Jake smiled thinly. "Guardian, remember? I've been monitoring the dimensional breaches since your first crossing. When they began to approach critical levels, I knew I needed to intervene."

"You've been following me."

"Observing," Jake corrected. "From a respectful distance. Until today, when your condition deteriorated more rapidly than anticipated."

Robert nodded slowly. "I'll see you tomorrow, then."

"One final warning," Jake said as Robert reached the door. "The echo effect can manifest in unexpected ways. You may experience time slips, memory bleed-through from other versions of yourself, even physical objects appearing or disappearing. Try to remain calm if these occur. Panic accelerates the dimensional dissolution process."

"Wonderful," Robert muttered. "Anything else I should worry about?"

"Just one thing. The Station Master you encountered—he's not a benevolent guide. He serves the system's purpose, not yours. If you see him again, outside the subway context, be extremely cautious. His appearance in conventional reality would indicate a severe breakdown of dimensional boundaries."

Robert absorbed this final warning with a grim nod. "Tomorrow morning, then."

As the young physicist left the shop, Jake returned to his instruments. The dimensional readings were still critical, but no longer accelerating as rapidly. The pendant was working, at least temporarily.

He opened his ledger and made detailed notes of their conversation, adding observations about North's condition and the unprecedented speed of his progression through the system. Then he turned to the back of the book, where a list of names was written in different hands—Margaret's elegant script at the top, followed by Jake's own entries over the decades.

Names of those lost to the multiverse. Those he had failed to save.

With grim determination, Jake vowed that Robert North would not be added to that list.

CHAPTER FIVE: THE MISSING STUDENT

Robert left his meeting with Professor Williams feeling marginally better. The pendant Jake had given him continued to dampen the echo effect, allowing him to focus primarily on a single reality—this current Daybridge-Academic version. The ghostly overlays of alternate realities had receded to the periphery of his perception, visible only when he specifically looked for them.

Williams had been surprisingly understanding about Robert's distraction. "Quantum research affects people differently," the professor had said. "Sometimes the mathematics gets under your skin, makes you see the world through probability functions rather than certainties."

If only he knew how literal that statement was in Robert's case.

As evening approached, Robert decided to walk back to his apartment rather than taking the bus. The exercise helped clear his head, and he deliberately chose a route that avoided Thornfield Avenue. Jake's warning about the subway's pull echoed in his mind.

The autumn air carried the scent of fallen leaves and wood smoke. Students hurried across campus, bundled against the growing chill. Everything seemed normal—as normal as things could be when you were experiencing quantum reality slippage.

Robert touched the pendant through his shirt, grateful for its stabilizing effect. Tomorrow he would meet Jake again, and they would work on identifying his origin point—his true home reality. The prospect gave him hope.

His phone buzzed with a text from Noah:

Heading to emergency rotation. Leftover pasta in fridge. Don't wait up.

At least this version of Noah was consistent—the surgical resident who worked impossible hours and communicated primarily through food-related notes. Robert had almost grown accustomed to him.

As he approached his apartment building, fatigue washed over him suddenly. The mental strain of maintaining focus against the echo effect, combined with the emotional weight of his conversation with Jake, had left him exhausted.

He climbed the stairs to the third floor, unlocked his door, and went straight to his bedroom. Sleep would help. Everything would seem clearer in the morning.

Robert didn't even bother undressing fully, just kicked off his shoes and collapsed onto the bed. The pendant pressed against his chest, warm and reassuring.

His last thought before drifting off was a silent promise: *No more subway rides.*

The dream began normally enough. Robert was walking through campus, late for an exam he hadn't studied for—standard anxiety dream territory.

But as he hurried across the quad, the buildings began to shift and change. Kepler became Tesla became Einstein became structures he didn't recognize at all. The sky cycled through colors—blue to violet to a sickly green. Students passing by spoke in languages that changed mid-sentence, their faces morphing from familiar to strange and back again.

A train whistle sounded in the distance.

Robert tried to run away from the sound, but the campus rearranged itself around him, paths looping back on themselves impossibly. No matter which direction he fled, he found himself approaching a subway entrance that hadn't been there before.

Iron railings. Warm light from below. The smell of ozone and brass polish.

Don't go down there, he told himself. *Jake warned you.*

But his dream-self descended the stairs anyway, drawn by an irresistible pull.

The station below was Central Nexus, but warped and distorted. The constellation mosaics depicted stars in violent motion, rearranging themselves into faces that watched him with knowing eyes. The departures board listed destinations that made no sense: "Daybridge-Inverted," "Daybridge-Hollow," "Daybridge-Abandoned."

The Station Master stood on the platform, his uniform now blood-red instead of navy blue.

"Your connecting train is waiting, sir," he said, his voice echoing strangely. "Final boarding call for Daybridge-Threshold."

A copper train idled at the platform, its surface rippling like liquid metal. The doors stood open, revealing an interior that seemed to extend far deeper than physically possible.

"I don't want to go," Robert protested. "I'm trying to get home."

"This is the only way home," the Station Master replied, his face suddenly very close though he hadn't appeared to move. "The seventh crossing completes the cycle. You must balance the equation."

Robert backed away. "No. Jake said—"

"Jake Steinman is a custodian, nothing more. He maintains what he cannot understand." The Station Master's eyes reflected the shifting constellations overhead. "The system requires completion. You have begun the sequence; you must finish it."

The train whistle sounded again, urgent and demanding.

"Last call for Daybridge-Threshold," the Station Master announced. "Mind the gap between worlds."

Robert turned to flee, but the stairs back to the surface had vanished. The Station Master's hand closed around his arm with surprising strength.

"The train awaits," he said, pulling Robert toward the open doors.

Robert struggled, but his feet moved against his will, carrying him into the waiting car. The doors closed with a sound like a sigh.

As the train began to move, Robert caught a final glimpse of the Station Master through the window. The old man smiled, his teeth too numerous and too sharp, his uniform now writhing with subtle movement as if alive.

"Transit complete," the Station Master called after the departing train. "Enjoy Daybridge-Threshold, where all possibilities converge."

The train plunged into darkness.

Robert woke with a gasp, heart pounding. His bedroom was dark, moonlight filtering through the blinds. For a moment, he thought it had been just a nightmare—a processing of his anxieties about dimensional travel.

Then he noticed the ceiling.

It was at least twenty feet high, not the standard eight feet of his apartment. And it appeared to be made of some crystalline substance that refracted the moonlight into prismatic patterns.

"No," he whispered, sitting up abruptly. "No, no, no."

This wasn't his bedroom. The proportions were all wrong—too large, too tall, the corners at slightly non-perpendicular angles. The furniture was similar to his but constructed of unfamiliar materials that gleamed with a subtle inner light.

Robert scrambled out of bed, nearly falling as his feet hit the floor farther down than expected. The floor itself felt wrong—slightly yielding beneath his weight, almost membranous.

He stumbled to the window and yanked open the blinds.

The Daybridge outside was fundamentally wrong.

Buildings stretched impossibly tall, their architecture defying conventional physics with spiraling forms and gravity-defying overhangs. The sky—visible despite it being night—had a distinctly greenish tinge, with three moons of different sizes hanging above the horizon.

People moved along the streets below, but their proportions seemed distorted—limbs slightly too long, heads slightly too small. Vehicles that resembled cars but had no visible wheels glided silently along the roads.

Robert backed away from the window, panic rising in his throat. "This is a dream," he told himself. "Just another dream."

But he knew it wasn't. Somehow, despite his best intentions, he had made the seventh crossing. He had arrived in what the Station Master had called "Daybridge-Threshold."

Robert reached for the pendant Jake had given him, but it was gone. His fingers found only bare skin where it should have hung. Without its stabilizing influence, the echo effect would accelerate unchecked.

As if triggered by this realization, his vision began to split. Not into the manageable overlays he'd experienced before, but into a kaleidoscopic fragmentation that made the already-alien room nearly incomprehensible. Every surface divided into multiple versions, each shifting and changing independently of the others.

Robert pressed his palms against his eyes, trying to force his perception to stabilize. When he lowered his hands, the room had settled somewhat, though ghostly afterimages still flickered at the edges of his vision.

He needed to find the subway entrance. If he had arrived here via a seventh crossing, perhaps he could return via an eighth. It wasn't much of a plan, but it was all he had.

Robert moved cautiously to what appeared to be the bedroom door. It slid open at his approach, revealing a living space that bore only a passing resemblance to his apartment's layout. The ceiling soared even higher here, at least thirty feet, with floating globes of light instead of conventional fixtures.

"Noah?" he called out, not really expecting an answer.

"Temporal designation 'Noah' is not currently registered in this dwelling," replied a voice from nowhere in particular. "Would you like to submit a visitation request?"

Robert nearly jumped out of his skin. "Who said that?"

"Dwelling Intelligence Interface," the voice responded. "This unit is designated to assist residents and authorized guests."

"I need to leave," Robert said, moving toward what he hoped was the front door. "How do I exit this... dwelling?"

"Egress point is located on the southern perimeter. Current environmental hazard level is moderate. Protective measures are advised."

"What kind of hazards?"

"Dimensional flux storm approaching from the west. Probability of perceptual dissonance: sixty-seven percent. Recommended protection: reality anchors or perception filters."

Robert had neither of those things, whatever they might be. But he couldn't stay here.

The front door—a tall, narrow oval—opened at his approach. The hallway outside was similarly distorted—too wide, too tall, the walls curving subtly inward near the ceiling.

Robert made his way to what appeared to be an elevator, though it had no buttons, just a smooth panel that glowed faintly.

"Ground level," he said experimentally.

The panel flashed, and the elevator began to descend without any perceptible motion beyond the changing numbers on the display: 47... 46... 45...

Forty-seven floors? Robert thought with dismay. *How tall is this building?*

When the doors finally opened on the ground floor, Robert stepped into a lobby that resembled a cross between an art museum and a botanical garden. Massive sculptures of impossible geometry stood amid plants with bioluminescent flowers. The ceiling was a dome of the same crystalline material as his bedroom, refracting the green-tinged light from outside.

People—or entities that approximated people—moved through the space, their clothing flowing and shifting like liquid fabric. None of them paid Robert any attention, despite his conventional appearance among their otherworldly forms.

He made his way cautiously to the main entrance, a towering arch that opened onto the street. Outside, the alien nature of this Daybridge became even more apparent.

The buildings weren't merely tall—they were impossibly so, stretching up until they disappeared into low-hanging clouds. Their forms twisted and curved, sections floating separate from the main structures with no visible means of support. The streets were broader than any in his Daybridge, paved with a material that seemed to ripple slightly underfoot.

And the people—the residents of this threshold reality—moved with fluid grace that suggested different joint structures, different relationships to gravity. Their faces, when Robert could bring himself to look directly at them, featured subtle differences in proportion that registered as profoundly unsettling: eyes slightly too large or too widely spaced, mouths that extended farther than they should when speaking.

Their language, when he overheard snippets of conversation, contained familiar words arranged in patterns that made no linguistic sense: "Temporal folding exceeds yesterday's prediction cycle." "Have you filtered your perception since the convergence?" "The boundary thinning makes transit so convenient."

Robert tried to orient himself, to find landmarks that might correspond to familiar locations in his Daybridge. He needed to locate Thornfield Avenue, to find the subway entrance that had brought him here.

But nothing was recognizable. The street layout followed patterns that seemed to deliberately avoid right angles. Buildings that might have been familiar were distorted beyond recognition.

Robert approached someone who appeared marginally more human than the others—a woman with only slightly elongated limbs and nearly normal facial features.

"Excuse me," he said, his voice shaking slightly. "Could you direct me to Thornfield Avenue?"

The woman turned to him, her eyes shifting color as she focused on his face. "Thornfield? That designation was phased out during the third convergence. Are you referring to Liminal Boulevard?"

"I... I'm not sure. I'm looking for a subway entrance."

The woman's expression shifted to something that might have been sympathy or amusement—it was hard to tell with her alien features. "The Central Transit Nexus is seventeen blocks eastward, but you won't need dimensional insertion there. This is already Threshold reality."

"I need to get back to my original Daybridge," Robert explained, desperation creeping into his voice. "My home reality."

"Origin realities are rarely accessible after convergence events," the woman said, as if explaining something obvious. "But you might consult a Boundary Technician. There's an office in the Probability Tower." She gestured toward a spiraling structure that dominated the eastern skyline.

"Thank you," Robert managed, backing away from her uncanny gaze.

He began walking eastward, toward the tower she had indicated. As he moved through this alien Daybridge, the echo effect intensified. Buildings flickered between multiple configurations. People shifted appearance mid-step. The sky cycled through shades of green, then blue, then colors that had no names in his reality.

Robert's head pounded with the effort of processing the shifting perceptions. Without Jake's pendant, the dimensional dissolution was accelerating rapidly. Soon he wouldn't be able to perceive any single reality clearly enough to navigate it.

He needed to find a way back. Back to Jake's bookshop, back to a Daybridge he recognized, back to any reality more stable than this threshold world where physics itself seemed negotiable.

As he approached the Probability Tower, a distant rumble shook the ground. People around him looked westward, their expressions showing concern.

"Flux storm intensifying," someone nearby said. "Perceptual anchors activated."

The greenish sky darkened abruptly, clouds swirling in patterns that hurt Robert's eyes to follow. Lightning flashed—not in jagged bolts but in expanding rings that rippled outward like stones dropped in water.

Robert felt a pressure building inside his skull, as if his brain were swelling against his cranium. The echo effect worsened dramatically, his vision fragmenting into dozens of overlapping perspectives. He stumbled, falling to his knees on the rippling pavement.

"Help," he gasped, but his voice seemed to split into multiple versions, each speaking different words in different tones.

No one stopped to assist him. The residents of Threshold Daybridge hurried for shelter, many of them touching devices on their wrists that caused their forms to shimmer and stabilize against the growing dimensional disturbance.

Robert crawled toward the nearest building, seeking any kind of shelter from the storm. As he moved, his perception fractured further. His hands seemed to multiply before his eyes—five, ten, twenty versions overlapping, each in slightly different positions.

He reached the building's entrance just as the first wave of the flux storm hit. It wasn't rain or wind but a ripple in reality itself—a visible distortion that rolled down the street like a tsunami, transforming everything it touched. Buildings briefly became their architectural blueprints, then exploded into their component atoms, then reassembled in new configurations.

Robert pressed himself against the building's wall, praying it would provide some protection. As the wave approached, he closed his eyes and braced for impact.

The sensation when it hit was indescribable—as if every atom in his body were being simultaneously pulled apart and compressed. His consciousness seemed to expand beyond his physical form, stretching across multiple realities at once. He perceived versions of himself in countless Daybridges: Robert the physicist, Robert the doctor, Robert the musician, Robert the criminal, Robert the corporate executive, Robert the homeless man, Robert the child, Robert the elder.

For one terrifying moment, he was all of them simultaneously, experiencing thousands of lives in parallel.

Then, merciful darkness.

In Daybridge-Prime—the original reality from which Robert had first departed—Noah Thompson sat in the campus security office, frustration evident in his posture.

"I'm telling you, something's wrong," he insisted to the officer taking his statement. "Robert wouldn't just disappear like this. He's missed classes, lab sessions, meetings with his adviser—that's completely out of character."

Officer Chen reviewed the information on her tablet. "According to the department secretary, Mr. North hasn't attended classes for eight days. But you say you saw him yesterday?"

"Yes, at our apartment. He was acting strange—talking about different versions of the city, mapping changes in neighborhood businesses. I thought he was having some kind of stress breakdown."

"Did he mention going anywhere? Taking a trip, maybe?"

Noah shook his head. "No. He wanted to show me some subway entrance on Thornfield Avenue, but when we got there, it was just a brick wall. He seemed really confused about that."

Officer Chen made a note. "Any history of mental health issues? Drug use?"

"No! Robert's the most stable person I know. He's a quantum physics PhD candidate, for God's sake. His whole life is organized around his research."

"Sometimes academic pressure can trigger—"

"This isn't a breakdown," Noah interrupted. "Something happened to him. When I woke up this morning, his bed hadn't been slept in. His phone goes straight to voicemail. His laptop is still on his desk. It's like he just vanished."

Officer Chen sighed. "We'll file a missing persons report and check local hospitals. Since he's an adult with no known medical conditions, there's not much else we can do at this point. He might have just needed to get away for a few days."

"He wouldn't do that without telling me," Noah insisted.

"People surprise us sometimes," the officer replied, her tone suggesting this conversation was one she'd had many times before. "Leave your contact information, and we'll call if we learn anything."

Noah provided his details, frustration turning to worry. As he left the security office, he pulled out his phone and tried Robert's number again. Straight to voicemail, as expected.

"Robert, it's me again. I'm really worried, man. Just... call me back, okay? Let me know you're alright."

He ended the call and stood in the crisp autumn air, uncertain what to do next. Campus life continued around him—students hurrying to classes, professors engaged in animated discussions, tours of prospective students following guides with practiced enthusiasm.

None of them seemed to notice that something fundamental had gone wrong with reality. That someone was missing who shouldn't be.

Noah decided to retrace their steps from the previous evening. Robert had been fixated on that supposed subway entrance on Thornfield Avenue. Maybe there was something there after all—something Noah had missed.

The walk to Thornfield took fifteen minutes. The street looked exactly as it had the night before—historic brownstones, cobblestone pavement, antique shops and cafés catering to the university crowd.

Noah found the spot Robert had indicated—between Thornfield Antiques and a narrow apartment building. Just as before, a solid brick wall stood where Robert had insisted there should be a subway entrance.

"This is crazy," Noah muttered, examining the wall more closely. The bricks were weathered, covered with decades of grime and patches of ivy. There was no indication that an entrance had ever existed here.

As Noah turned to leave, his gaze fell on the antique shop. STEINMAN'S RARE EDITIONS, read the elegant gold lettering on the window. Below that: BOOKS • CURIOSITIES • KNOWLEDGE.

On impulse, Noah pushed open the door, a small bell announcing his entrance. The interior was dimly lit and labyrinthine, shelves of books creating a maze that extended deeper into the shop than seemed possible from the outside. The air smelled of old paper, leather, and furniture polish.

"Can I help you find something?"

Noah turned to find an older man watching him from behind a wooden counter. Silver-gray hair, reading glasses on a chain around his neck, tweed jacket with leather elbow patches—he looked like a professor emeritus who had decided to surround himself with books in retirement.

"I'm not sure," Noah admitted. "I'm looking for my roommate, actually. He disappeared last night after becoming obsessed with finding a subway entrance that doesn't exist."

The man's expression shifted subtly. "This entrance—where exactly did he believe it to be?"

"Right outside your shop. Between you and the apartment building next door."

The man removed his glasses, polishing them with a handkerchief in a deliberate motion that seemed designed to buy time for thought.

"Your roommate's name?" he asked finally.

"Robert North. He's a PhD candidate in quantum physics at the university."

The glasses stopped moving. "Robert North. Yes, I see." The man replaced his glasses and extended his hand. "Jake Steinman. Owner of this establishment and... someone who might be able to help you."

Noah shook the offered hand. "You know something about Robert?"

"Perhaps. Though the situation is... complicated." Jake glanced around the shop, where a few customers browsed among the shelves. "Why don't we continue this conversation in my office?"

He led Noah through the maze of bookshelves to an unmarked door at the rear of the shop. The room beyond was unlike anything Noah had expected—less an office than a laboratory filled with antique equipment. Radios, barometers, seismographs, and devices Noah couldn't identify lined the walls. A large desk dominated the center, covered with maps and open books.

Jake closed the door behind them. "When exactly did you last see Robert?"

"Last night, around 9 PM. We went to Thornfield Avenue looking for this subway entrance he kept talking about. When it wasn't there, we got dinner at Marlowe's Diner, then headed home. I went to bed around midnight. Robert was still up, working on something. This morning, he was gone."

Jake moved to one of the modified radios, adjusting dials with practiced precision. "And in the days before his disappearance, did Robert mention multiple versions of Daybridge? Different realities where details had changed?"

Noah stared. "Yes. Exactly that. He had maps taped to his wall showing different versions of the city. He claimed our relationship was different in each one—that in some version I was a trauma surgeon, in another a pediatrician."

"I see." Jake noted something in a leather-bound ledger. "And you thought he was experiencing some kind of breakdown."

"Wouldn't you? He was talking about parallel realities, invisible subway stations, versions of me with completely different career paths. It sounded delusional."

"Not delusional," Jake corrected. "Accurately perceptive, in fact. Just of phenomena most people aren't equipped to notice." He turned to face Noah directly. "Robert did find a subway entrance on Thornfield Avenue. He's made at least six dimensional transits using that system. And now, it appears, he's made a seventh—with potentially catastrophic consequences."

Noah blinked. "You're saying his delusions were... real?"

"They weren't delusions. Robert was experiencing reality slippage—perceiving multiple versions of Daybridge simultaneously due to repeated dimensional boundary crossings." Jake gestured to his modified instruments. "I've been monitoring the situation for days. Yesterday, I intercepted him and provided a temporary stabilizing influence. But it appears he's made another crossing despite my warnings."

"You're serious," Noah realized, studying Jake's expression. "You actually believe all this."

"I don't merely believe it—I know it with absolute certainty. I've been guarding Daybridge's dimensional boundaries for nearly thirty years." Jake opened a drawer and removed a file labeled "Thornfield Anomaly - 1943." "The subway your friend discovered is a physical manifestation of interdimensional pathways created during a classified government experiment during World War II."

Noah struggled to process this information. It sounded like science fiction, yet Jake's matter-of-fact delivery and the room full of monitoring equipment suggested he was deadly serious.

"If what you're saying is true, where is Robert now?"

Jake's expression darkened. "Based on the readings I'm getting, he's crossed into what we call a threshold reality—a version of Daybridge where the laws of physics operate very differently from our own. It's a dangerous place for someone without proper preparation or protection."

"Can we get him back?"

"Potentially. But the situation is complicated by temporal inconsistencies." Jake consulted one of his instruments. "According to my readings, Robert has been gone from this reality for approximately eight days, though you saw him yesterday."

"That's impossible. I had dinner with him last night."

"In this reality, yes. But time flows differently across dimensional boundaries. The Robert you saw last night had already been traveling between realities for days from his perspective." Jake made another note in his ledger. "The fact that you witnessed his final departure is actually fortunate—it gives us a precise fix on his last known position in this reality."

Noah sank into a chair, overwhelmed. "This is insane."

"Reality often is, when you examine it closely enough." Jake removed a pocket watch from his vest and consulted it. "We have perhaps 36 hours before Robert's connection to his origin reality—this Daybridge—becomes too attenuated to restore. After that point, he'll either remain trapped in the threshold reality or, more likely, become permanently untethered—existing partially across multiple realities without fully manifesting in any of them."

"Like the Wandering Lady," Noah murmured.

Jake looked up sharply. "You know of her?"

"The homeless woman in Riverside Park who seems to flicker in and out of existence? Robert mentioned her yesterday. Said she was in all his versions of Daybridge."

"Martha Craine. Former physics professor. Lost to the multiverse in 1988." Jake closed his ledger with a decisive motion. "We won't let Robert share her fate."

"What can we do?"

"I can attempt to locate him using my equipment, then establish a controlled dimensional transit to retrieve him. But I'll need something with a strong quantum entanglement to his home reality—this reality."

"Like what?"

"An object he values highly, something uniquely associated with his identity in this version of Daybridge."

Noah thought for a moment. "His grandfather's fountain pen. Robert always keeps it on his desk—uses it to sign important documents. Says it brings him luck."

"Perfect. Can you retrieve it?"

Noah nodded. "I can go to our apartment right now."

"Do so and return here as quickly as possible." Jake handed him a business card with a number scrawled on the back. "Call this number if you notice anything unusual—particularly any signs of reality instability. Flickering objects, momentary architectural changes, people appearing or disappearing suddenly."

"You think that might happen?"

"Robert's seventh crossing has created a significant dimensional disturbance. The effects could manifest throughout Daybridge, especially in locations he frequented regularly." Jake moved to a cabinet and began removing equipment. "We'll need to act quickly once you return with the pen."

As Noah turned to leave, Jake added: "One more thing. If you encounter anyone who seems to know too much about Robert's situation—particularly an elderly man in a transit uniform—do not engage with him. Contact me immediately."

"Who would that be?"

"The Station Master. A manifestation of the system itself. If he's appearing in conventional reality, the situation is even more dire than I feared."

Noah nodded, though he understood perhaps half of what Jake was telling him. The important part was clear: Robert was in danger, and they had limited time to find him.

As he hurried out of the bookshop, Noah glanced back at the brick wall between the buildings. For just a moment—so briefly he might have imagined it—he thought he saw an outline of iron railings shimmering against the bricks, and warm light spilling up from below.

Then it was gone, and the wall was solid once more.

In a version of Daybridge that shouldn't exist—a threshold reality where physics bent to accommodate impossibility—Robert North lay unconscious on the rippling pavement as the flux storm raged around him.

And standing over him, untouched by the dimensional chaos, was the Station Master. His uniform had changed again, now a shimmering material that seemed to absorb rather than reflect light. His face remained elderly and dignified, but his eyes contained impossible geometries.

"The seventh crossing is complete," he said to the unconscious physicist. "The cycle progresses as designed. Soon, the boundaries will fail completely, and all versions will merge into one magnificent convergence."

He knelt beside Robert, placing a white-gloved hand on his forehead.

"Rest now, Catalyst. Your work is nearly done."

CHAPTER SIX: BETWEEN WORLDS

Consciousness returned to Robert in waves, each bringing a new sensation: the hard surface beneath him, the distant sounds of unfamiliar voices, the lingering disorientation of the flux storm. When he finally opened his eyes, he found himself lying on a bench in what appeared to be some kind of park.

But not any park he recognized.

The trees—if they could be called trees—spiraled upward in impossible helixes, their foliage shifting colors as he watched. The sky above had settled into a more tolerable blue-green, though occasional ripples of darker color moved across it like clouds. The three moons had faded to ghostly outlines, visible even in daylight.

Robert sat up slowly, his head pounding. The echo effect remained intense but had stabilized somewhat. He could see five or six versions of his surroundings simultaneously, though one—this alien Daybridge-Threshold—dominated his perception.

"You're lucky to be alive," said a voice nearby. "Most untethered travelers don't survive their first flux storm."

Robert turned to find a man sitting on the ground nearby, his back against a spiraling tree trunk. At first glance, he appeared to be just another homeless person—ragged clothes, unkempt beard, weathered skin. But as Robert's vision adjusted, he noticed that the man seemed more substantial than his surroundings, less subject to the echo effect's distortions.

"Who are you?" Robert managed, his voice hoarse.

"Name's Gil. Gilbert Harmon, technically, though titles don't mean much between worlds." The man gestured at the alien landscape around them. "Welcome to the edge of reality, kid. Threshold Daybridge, where all versions blur together."

Robert stared at him. "You're... from my reality? Original Daybridge?"

Gil chuckled, the sound surprisingly warm in this unsettling environment. "No, not yours. Mine was... different. I was a physicist at Daybridge University, specializing in quantum field theory. Back in 1979, at least from my perspective."

"You've been here since 1979?" Robert asked incredulously.

"Not here specifically. I've been riding the rails between realities for... well, time gets slippery when you cross dimensions frequently." Gil scratched his beard thoughtfully. "Maybe forty years by my internal clock. Could be more in absolute terms."

Robert tried to stand but found his legs unsteady. He settled back onto the bench. "The subway. The Liminal Line. That's what brought me here."

"Ah, so you know its name already. Took me years to piece that together." Gil's eyes—a startling clear blue against his weathered face—studied Robert with scientific precision. "You're experiencing severe echo effect. I can see at least seven versions of you overlapping. Recent crosser, aren't you?"

"Seven trips," Robert confirmed. "The last one brought me here."

"Seven." Gil nodded gravely. "The dimensional octave. That explains the flux storm—they always intensify during octave completions."

Robert leaned forward, hope kindling. "You understand what's happening. Can you help me get back? To my original Daybridge?"

Gil's expression softened with sympathy. "That's the question, isn't it? The one all of us ask at first." He sighed, pulling a flask from inside his tattered coat. "Want a drink? It's just water, but it helps with the dimensional vertigo."

Robert accepted the flask gratefully, taking a small sip. The water tasted slightly metallic but refreshing. "Thanks."

"To answer your question," Gil continued, "finding your way back becomes exponentially more difficult with each crossing. After seven? Nearly impossible without specialized knowledge and equipment." He gestured at himself. "As you can see, I never managed it, and I was a leading expert in quantum field theory."

"There has to be a way," Robert insisted. "I met someone—Jake Steinman. He seemed to understand what was happening. Said he was a guardian of dimensional boundaries."

Gil's eyebrows rose. "Steinman? Margaret's protégé?"

"You know him?"

"I knew Margaret. She was part of the original Containment Initiative in '43—the project that accidentally created the Liminal Line." Gil took back his flask. "If her successor is involved, your situation might not be hopeless after all. The Steinmans have resources most travelers don't."

Robert felt a surge of hope. "So, there is a way back?"

"Potentially. But first, you need to understand what you're dealing with." Gil stood, offering Robert a hand. "Can you walk? We should move before another flux storm hits. They're coming more frequently now, with the boundaries weakening."

Robert accepted the help, rising unsteadily to his feet. "Where are we going?"

"Somewhere safer than open space. I have a... well, calling it a home would be generous, but it's a stable location in this unstable reality."

They made their way through the alien park, Gil setting a deliberate pace that allowed Robert to adjust to the disorienting environment. The paths shifted subtly as they walked, sometimes branching where no branch had existed moments before, sometimes reconnecting in impossible loops.

"Focus on me," Gil advised, noticing Robert's struggle. "I've been here long enough to develop a certain dimensional consistency. I don't shift as much as the native architecture."

Robert fixed his gaze on Gil's back, using the man's relative stability as an anchor for his perception. It helped somewhat, though the echo effect continued to overlay multiple versions of their surroundings.

"What is this place?" Robert asked as they navigated the ever-changing landscape. "The Station Master called it 'Daybridge-Threshold.'"

"Ah, you've met the conductor of this metaphysical train wreck." Gil's tone carried complex emotions—bitterness, respect, fear. "Threshold is exactly what the name suggests—a boundary state between defined realities. It's where the multiverse is thin, where parallel worlds bleed into one another."

"But it seems so... solid, despite the strangeness."

"That's because it's not a transitional space—it's a reality unto itself, formed from the bleed-through of countless Daybridges." Gil gestured at the impossible architecture around them. "Every building you see is a composite of thousands of potential versions, every resident a being who exists simultaneously across multiple realities."

They exited the park onto a broad avenue lined with structures that resembled commercial buildings, though their functions were impossible to determine. People—or entities approximating people—moved with that same fluid grace Robert had noticed earlier, their features shifting subtly as he watched.

"Don't stare at the natives too long," Gil warned. "Your brain isn't adapted to process their multidimensional nature. It can trigger seizures in newcomers."

Robert quickly averted his gaze. "They seem to ignore us."

"Threshold residents perceive reality differently than we do. To them, we're the strange ones—flickering, inconsistent beings who don't fully exist in their perceptual framework." Gil turned down a narrower side street. "They've learned to filter us out as sensory noise, mostly."

The buildings grew smaller and more irregular as they moved away from the main avenue. Eventually, Gil led Robert to a structure that seemed more stable than its neighbors—a modest two-story building with a façade that remained consistently brick despite the echo effect.

"Welcome to my humble interdimensional abode," Gil said with a hint of irony. "It's not much, but it maintains consistent internal physics, which is rare in Threshold."

Inside, the building contained a single room that defied its external dimensions—much larger than should have been possible, yet not overtly supernatural in appearance. It resembled a combination of living quarters and research laboratory. Bookshelves lined the walls, filled with volumes in various languages and alphabets. Tables covered with equipment—some recognizable as scientific instruments, others utterly alien—occupied the center space. A simple bed and kitchenette stood in one corner.

Most notably, every vertical surface was covered with equations, diagrams, and maps—some drawn directly on the walls, others on paper pinned in overlapping layers. Robert recognized quantum field equations, probability matrices, and what appeared to be attempts to map the structure of the multiverse.

"You've been studying this," Robert said, examining the nearest wall of calculations.

"For forty years," Gil confirmed, moving to a hotplate where a kettle sat. "Tea? It's a blend I've developed that helps stabilize perception across realities."

"Yes, please."

As Gil prepared the tea, Robert circled the room, studying the decades of research. The mathematics was far beyond even his graduate-level understanding—incorporating principles and notations he'd never encountered.

"This is incredible," he murmured. "You've mapped the entire multiversal structure of Daybridge."

"Not entirely. The complete structure would require infinite dimensions to represent properly." Gil handed Robert a steaming mug. "But I've managed to identify the major branch points and probability clusters."

The tea had an unusual flavor—herbal with subtle metallic undertones—but almost immediately began to ease the disorientation of the echo effect. The overlapping realities receded slightly, allowing Robert to focus more clearly on the threshold reality.

"Thank you," he said, genuinely grateful. "This helps."

"Certain molecules exist in quantum superposition naturally. The tea contains several." Gil gestured to one of the chairs at a cluttered table. "Sit. We have much to discuss, and your dimensional anchoring is deteriorating rapidly."

Robert sat, cradling the warm mug between his hands. "Anchoring?"

"Your connection to your origin reality." Gil took the seat opposite him. "Each crossing weakens that connection. After seven, most travelers begin to lose coherent memories of their original world."

A chill ran through Robert that had nothing to do with the tea's temperature. "I... I can still remember my Daybridge."

"Can you? Try to recall specific details—the exact color of your apartment building, the pattern of cracks in the sidewalk outside your favorite coffee shop, the sound of your roommate's voice."

Robert concentrated, trying to conjure these details. To his horror, they seemed frustratingly vague—approximations rather than precise memories. He could remember that he had a roommate named Noah, but couldn't recall exactly what his face looked like. He knew he lived in an apartment near campus, but the specific layout had become indistinct.

"This can't be happening," he whispered. "I've only been gone for a day."

"Time flows differently between realities, especially in Threshold." Gil's expression was sympathetic but unflinching. "What feels like a day to you might be weeks in your home reality, or mere minutes. The asymmetry makes return navigation exponentially more difficult."

Robert set down his mug, hands trembling slightly. "Tell me about the Liminal Line. What exactly is it?"

Gil leaned back in his chair, his eyes growing distant with recollection. "In 1943, the government established the Daybridge Containment Initiative—a classified project researching quantum field manipulation for military applications. They were trying to create a weapon that could... well, the specifics aren't important. What matters is that they accidentally tore a hole in the fabric of reality."

"The subway tunnels," Robert guessed.

"Not initially. The tunnels were conventional infrastructure, built to connect various research facilities across Daybridge. But when the quantum breach occurred, the tunnels became... something else." Gil's hands sketched shapes in the air as he spoke. "They transformed into physical manifestations of probability paths—connections between parallel versions of Daybridge that had diverged at key historical moments."

"So, the Liminal Line doesn't travel through space, but through probability?"

"Precisely. Each station connects to a version of Daybridge where history took a slightly different turn. The tunnels themselves exist in a state of quantum superposition—both present and not present, appearing only under specific conditions to specific people."

Robert thought about his experiences on the subway. "But why me? Why was I able to see the entrance when others couldn't?"

"Some individuals have a natural sensitivity to quantum fluctuations—usually those already working with related concepts." Gil gestured to the equations covering the walls. "Your research in quantum tunneling likely primed your perception. You were subconsciously looking for evidence of the phenomena you were studying."

"And the Station Master? What is he?"

Gil's expression darkened. "Not what—who. He was Dr. Maxwell Hanover, Chief Engineer of the original project. When the breach occurred, he was at the epicenter. Instead of dying, he became... integrated with the system itself. A quantum ghost, existing across all versions simultaneously, maintaining the infrastructure of interdimensional transit."

"He doesn't seem interested in helping travelers find their way home," Robert observed.

"The Station Master serves the system's purpose, not individual travelers. And the system..." Gil hesitated. "The system wants to grow. To connect more realities, to facilitate more crossings. It's like a living organism expanding into available ecological niches."

Robert considered this disturbing information. "What about the octave? The Station Master mentioned a seventh crossing completing some kind of cycle."

Gil stood abruptly, moving to a particular section of wall covered with circular diagrams. "The dimensional octave is a fundamental pattern in multiversal structure. Seven crossings complete a full spectral circuit, returning the traveler not to their origin point but to a threshold state where all potential variations converge."

He pointed to a diagram showing seven concentric circles connected by spiral patterns. "In music theory, an octave represents a doubling of frequency—a higher iteration of the same fundamental note. In dimensional travel, the octave represents a complete cycle through probability space, theoretically returning you to your starting point, but at a higher level of dimensional perception."

"But I didn't return to my starting point," Robert pointed out. "I ended up here, in this... threshold reality."

"Because the system is broken," Gil said simply. "The 1943 experiment damaged the natural order of dimensional boundaries. The octave that should return travelers home instead strands them at the threshold, where the Station Master can... harvest their perceptual energy."

"Harvest?" Robert felt a new wave of unease. "What does that mean?"

Gil sighed heavily, returning to his seat. "The Station Master requires quantum observers to maintain the system. Travelers who complete the octave become permanently entangled with the dimensional infrastructure. Their perception—their consciousness—becomes part of the mechanism that keeps the boundaries permeable."

Robert recalled the Station Master's words in his dream: *You must balance the equation.*

"So I'm being... recruited? Consumed?"

"In a manner of speaking." Gil took a sip of his tea. "Though the process isn't immediate. It requires your conscious participation—your acceptance of the role. That's why the Station Master appears in dreams, why he tries to persuade rather than simply taking."

"But what's his ultimate goal? Why maintain this system at all?"

Gil's expression became troubled. "That's the question that's kept me searching for forty years. The Station Master is planning something—something beyond maintaining the status quo. The increasing frequency of flux storms, the weakening boundaries between realities... it's all building toward some kind of convergence event."

"What would that mean?"

"A collapse of multiversal barriers. A merging of all possible Daybridges into a single, impossible configuration." Gil gestured at their surroundings. "Threshold reality would become the only reality—a place where all possibilities exist simultaneously, where causality itself breaks down."

The implications were staggering. "And that's what he wants? To destroy reality as we know it?"

"Not destroy—transform. The Station Master believes this convergence is the natural evolution of existence—many becoming one, all possibilities realized simultaneously." Gil's voice lowered. "And he's been working toward it since 1943, collecting travelers, weakening boundaries, preparing for a critical mass of dimensional instability."

Robert struggled to process this revelation. "And I'm part of that plan somehow? My seventh crossing contributing to this... convergence?"

"You're not just part of it," Gil said gravely. "Based on the intensity of that flux storm, I believe you're the catalyst—the final component needed to trigger the event. Something about your specific dimensional signature is amplifying the instability exponentially."

Robert felt ill. His innocent discovery of the subway entrance had apparently set in motion catastrophic consequences—not just for himself, but potentially for all versions of Daybridge.

"We have to stop it," he said firmly. "Find a way to reverse what I've started."

Gil's expression showed both surprise and approval. "Most travelers at this stage are concerned only with finding their way home. You're thinking more broadly."

"If what you're saying is true, there won't be a home to return to if this convergence happens." Robert stood, moving to examine the equations covering the walls more carefully. "You've been studying this for decades. Have you found any way to counteract the process?"

"Theoretical approaches only." Gil joined him at the wall, pointing to a particular cluster of equations. "The most promising involves using the Liminal Line itself as a conduit for a counter-resonance wave—essentially canceling out the dimensional instability by generating its precise opposite."

"Like destructive interference in wave physics," Robert said, understanding dawning. "We'd need to generate a dimensional wave exactly out of phase with the current instability."

"Precisely. But the mathematics are... challenging. And we'd need access to specific equipment that exists only in certain versions of Daybridge." Gil tapped a different section of the wall. "I've identified three potential realities where the necessary technology might exist, but I've never been able to navigate to them precisely. The Liminal Line doesn't respond to directional inputs from ordinary travelers."

"But Jake might know how," Robert suggested. "If he's a guardian, if he has specialized knowledge about the system..."

"If we could reach him, yes." Gil returned to the table, lifting a device that resembled a modified radio. "I've been attempting to establish quantum communication across realities for years, with limited success. Occasionally I can pick up transmissions from various Daybridges, but sending messages back is nearly impossible due to dimensional attenuation."

Robert joined him at the table. "What about the subway itself? Could we find an entrance here in Threshold?"

"The Liminal Line manifests differently in Threshold. There are no conventional stations, only... access points that appear unpredictably during periods of relative dimensional stability." Gil adjusted dials on his modified radio, which emitted bursts of static. "I've mapped several potential locations, but they shift with each flux storm."

Robert's mind raced with possibilities. Despite the deterioration of his memories, his scientific training remained intact. "If the Liminal Line is a physical manifestation of probability paths, and Threshold is a convergence point for multiple realities, then theoretically there should be a central hub—a nexus point where all lines intersect."

"Central Nexus," Gil confirmed. "I found it once, decades ago. But it's not fixed in Threshold's geography—it moves, hiding itself from those who seek it directly."

"But the Station Master can access it."

"The Station Master is part of the system. He exists wherever the system needs him to be." Gil's expression turned speculative. "Though perhaps... yes, we might be able to use that connection. If we could attract his attention without accepting his offer, he might inadvertently lead us to Central Nexus."

Robert recalled his dream encounter with the Station Master. "He seems to communicate through dreams. Could we use that somehow?"

"Possibly. Dreams in Threshold are highly permeable to dimensional influence." Gil moved to a cabinet and removed a small device that resembled a circlet of woven copper wire. "This is a perception amplifier I developed. It enhances natural quantum sensitivity, allowing the user to perceive and potentially influence dimensional boundaries even while unconscious."

"A dream manipulator," Robert said, examining the device.

"More a dream navigator. It won't give you control over the dreamscape, but it might allow you to establish a more equal footing with the Station Master—to resist his influence while maintaining awareness of your actual goal."

Robert hesitated. "This sounds dangerous."

"Extremely. Confronting the Station Master in the dream realm means exposing yourself directly to his influence. If you accept his offer, even unconsciously, you'll become permanently bound to the system." Gil placed the circlet on the table. "But it may be our only option for finding Central Nexus quickly enough to matter."

"How much time do we have? Before this convergence event?"

Gil consulted a device on his wrist that resembled a watch with multiple overlapping dials. "Based on the current rate of dimensional degradation... less than forty-eight hours. Possibly much less."

The weight of responsibility settled heavily on Robert's shoulders. "And if we fail?"

"Then all versions of Daybridge collapse into a single, chaotic reality where causality itself breaks down." Gil's blue eyes held Robert's gaze. "Where every possible history happens simultaneously, where people exist in multiple contradictory states, where physics becomes merely suggestive rather than binding."

Robert thought of Noah, of Jake, of all the people in his original Daybridge—and all the people in every other version. Countless lives disrupted, countless minds unable to process the impossible new reality.

"I'll do it," he said, reaching for the copper circlet. "I'll confront the Station Master, find the way to Central Nexus."

Gil stopped him with a gentle hand. "Not yet. First, we need to prepare you. Your dimensional anchoring is too weak for such an encounter." He pointed to the tea. "Finish that. Then we'll begin the stabilization process."

Robert nodded, returning to his seat and the cooling tea. As he drank, a question occurred to him. "Gil, you've been here for decades. Why haven't you tried this approach before?"

A shadow passed over the older physicist's face. "I have. Three times. Each attempt... damaged my connection to the dream realm. I can no longer reach the level of awareness necessary to navigate effectively." He gestured to a faded scar that ran along his temple. "The Station Master doesn't appreciate interference with his plans."

The implications were clear: this was dangerous not just in theory but in demonstrated practice. Robert might succeed where Gil had failed, or he might suffer the same fate—or worse.

But the alternative was unthinkable. A collapsed multiverse, endless chaos, the end of reality as anyone understood it.

"Tell me what I need to do," Robert said, setting down his empty mug. "How do we prepare?"

Gil nodded with approval and perhaps a touch of sadness. "We begin by reinforcing your most fundamental memories—the core details of your identity that transcend specific realities. Then we practice perception focusing techniques that will help you maintain awareness during dream navigation."

He moved to a shelf and selected several small vials containing powders of various colors. "And we'll need these—compounds that enhance quantum perception while promoting dream lucidity. A delicate balance between awareness and receptivity."

As Gil mixed the compounds with practiced precision, Robert tried again to recall specific details of his original Daybridge. The effort was frustrating—like trying to remember a book read long ago, where the general plot remained but specific passages had faded.

He could recall that he was a physics graduate student researching quantum tunneling effects. He remembered Noah as his roommate, though the specifics of their relationship remained blurry. He knew Jake Steinman had tried to help him, had given him a pendant that stabilized his perception—a pendant now lost.

But the texture of his life—the sensory details, the emotional connections, the daily routines that defined his existence—those had begun to slip away, replaced by a generalized awareness of having been Robert North in some version of Daybridge.

"I'm losing myself," he said quietly.

Gil paused in his preparations. "Not yourself—just your specific contextual history. Your core identity remains intact." He approached with a small bowl containing a paste-like substance. "This will help anchor your essential self, even as peripheral memories fade."

"What is it?"

"A mnemonic stabilizer. Compounds that promote quantum coherence across neural pathways." Gil offered the bowl. "Apply it to your temples and the base of your skull."

Robert hesitated only briefly before dipping his fingers into the cool paste and applying it as directed. The sensation was immediate—a tingling that spread across his scalp and down his spine, followed by a sudden clarifying of thought.

"My research," he said, memories crystallizing. "I was modeling quantum tunneling effects, but the particles in my simulation refused to collapse into single states. They maintained multiple potential positions simultaneously, even after observation. That's why I was able to perceive the Liminal Line—my research was already interacting with the multiversal structure."

Gil nodded. "Excellent. Focus on those professional memories first—they tend to remain more stable across realities than personal connections."

"Professor Liang was my adviser," Robert continued, the details returning with surprising clarity. "We were preparing a paper for the

Quantum Physics Symposium in December. The simulation results were troubling her because they violated Copenhagen principles."

"Good. Now try to recall your apartment—the physical space, not the emotional associations."

Robert concentrated. "Third floor. Two bedrooms. The elevator was always broken, so we had to take the stairs. Kitchen to the left when you enter, living room straight ahead, bedrooms down a short hall to the right. My room had a window that faced east, so the morning sun would wake me if I forgot to close the blinds."

With each detail recalled, Robert's sense of his original reality strengthened. The echo effect remained, but his perception of the threshold reality became more stable, less disorienting.

"The stabilizer is working," Gil observed, mixing another compound in a different bowl. "Now we need to prepare you for dream navigation. The Station Master will attempt to disorient you, to make you forget your purpose. You must maintain focused intent throughout the encounter."

For the next several hours, Gil guided Robert through a series of exercises designed to strengthen his mental discipline and dimensional perception. They practiced techniques for recognizing reality distortions, for maintaining coherent thought during perceptual shifts, for resisting subtle manipulations of memory and desire.

As they worked, the light outside Gil's dwelling shifted from day to night, though the transition seemed to involve more colors than should have been possible. The three moons rose again, casting prismatic light through the windows.

"It's time," Gil said finally, handing Robert the copper circlet. "You should rest now. When you dream, the Station Master will come—he can sense your presence in Threshold, especially with your enhanced perception."

Robert accepted the circlet, turning it nervously in his hands. "What exactly do I do when he appears?"

"Do not accept any offer he makes, no matter how tempting. Do not agree to 'join' or 'serve' or 'complete' anything." Gil's expression was deadly serious. "Your goal is to follow him—to allow him to lead you to Central Nexus without realizing your intention. When you discover its location, you must wake immediately."

"How do I wake myself from a dream?"

"The circlet has a built-in mechanism. Intense pain—real pain, not dream pain—will trigger consciousness." Gil pointed to a small, sharp projection on the inner surface of the copper band. "Press your thumb against this if you need to wake quickly."

Robert nodded, placing the circlet carefully on his head. It fit snugly, the copper warm against his skin.

"One last thing," Gil said, pressing a small object into Robert's hand. "Keep this with you, both in the dream and after you wake."

Robert examined the item—a smooth stone disk with intricate symbols carved into both sides, suspended on a leather cord. "What is it?"

"A dimensional anchor, similar to what Jake gave you but calibrated specifically for navigation through Threshold reality. It won't stabilize your perception as effectively, but it will help you maintain your direction once you find Central Nexus."

Robert slipped the cord around his neck, the stone disk settling against his chest with surprising weight. "Thank you, Gil. For everything."

"Don't thank me yet." Gil led him to the simple bed in the corner. "The hard part is still ahead. Remember—find the location, then wake immediately. Don't linger in conversation with the Station Master."

Robert lay down, the copper circlet cool against his forehead, the stone disk heavy on his chest. Despite the danger ahead, he felt a strange calm—the clarity of purpose that comes with full commitment to a necessary course of action.

"If I don't make it back," he said quietly, "find Jake Steinman. Tell him what we've learned about the convergence."

Gil nodded solemnly. "Rest now. Focus your intent as you drift toward sleep: Central Nexus. Location. Direction. Nothing else."

Robert closed his eyes, repeating those words in his mind as consciousness began to fade. The last thing he heard was Gil moving about the room, adjusting equipment, preparing for whatever might come next.

Then sleep claimed him, and the dream began.

CHAPTER SEVEN: THE PATTERN IN THE NOISE

Jake Steinman's back room had transformed from a simple office into a command center for interdimensional crisis management. Maps covered every available surface, marked with timestamps and energy readings. Modified instruments hummed and clicked, monitoring dimensional stability across Daybridge. A chalkboard displayed a complex timeline of Robert's known movements across realities.

Noah Thompson sat at the edge of this organized chaos, turning Robert's fountain pen between his fingers. The antique Parker Duofold had belonged to Robert's grandfather—a prized possession that he'd never willingly leave behind.

"How long has he been missing in this reality?" Jake asked, adjusting dials on what appeared to be an antique radio but was actually a quantum fluctuation detector.

"Eight days according to campus records," Noah replied. "But I swear I saw him yesterday. We had dinner together at Marlowe's Diner."

Jake made a note on his timeline. "The temporal inconsistency is widening. Robert's crossings have created significant chronal displacement."

After Noah had returned with the fountain pen, Jake had insisted they visit the university. Using his surprisingly effective credentials as a "historical consultant," he'd gained access to campus security footage, class records, and even Robert's research data.

The evidence painted a disturbing picture of a man gradually losing his tether to conventional reality. Security cameras showed Robert appearing and disappearing at impossible intervals—entering buildings but never leaving, or appearing in locations without having been recorded en route. His research notes became increasingly erratic, filled with marginalia about "quantum persistence across observation" and "parallel state maintenance."

Most telling were the timestamps on his digital files. Robert had apparently been modifying research data at times when Noah clearly remembered him being elsewhere—asleep, at dinner, even once while they were watching a movie together.

"He was existing in multiple timestreams simultaneously," Jake had explained. "His consciousness moving between realities while his physical form maintained a semblance of continuity in each."

Now, back at the bookshop, Jake was attempting to synthesize all this information into a coherent picture—one that might lead them to Robert's current location.

"What about his journal?" Noah asked. "Did it tell you anything useful?"

Jake glanced at the notebook they'd recovered from Robert's room—a detailed chronicle of his journeys through parallel Daybridges. "More than he realized, I think. His observations of the variations between realities follow a specific pattern."

He moved to the largest map on the wall—a vintage street plan of Daybridge with multiple overlays of translucent paper, each marked with colored lines and symbols.

"Each crossing took him to a reality that diverged from the previous one at a specific historical juncture." Jake traced a path across the overlays. "First crossing: a reality where urban renewal in the 1980s followed a different architectural philosophy. Second crossing: a reality where the university expanded eastward instead of northward in the 1990s. Third crossing: a reality where the medical school emphasized surgical specialties over research medicine."

Noah stared at the map, recognition dawning. "Those are all changes that would affect me or my environment. The coffee shop I use, the campus layout, my medical focus."

"Precisely." Jake made another notation. "The variations centered on points of personal significance to both Robert and his immediate social connections. The Liminal Line wasn't taking him to random parallel Daybridges—it was following a deliberate progression through increasingly divergent personal timelines."

"But why? What's the purpose?"

Jake turned to his monitoring equipment, checking readings before answering. "The system is intelligent, in its way. It creates paths of least resistance for travelers—routes that feel almost familiar, despite the differences. It eases you into dimensional displacement gradually, so you don't immediately reject what you're experiencing as impossible."

"Like boiling a frog slowly," Noah murmured.

"An apt if unpleasant metaphor." Jake returned to the timeline on the chalkboard. "But there's something else happening here—something I've never seen before. The pattern of Robert's crossings forms a geometric progression when mapped across dimensional coordinates."

He drew a spiral pattern on the board, marking seven points along its curve. "Each crossing took him not just to a different reality but to a specific harmonic of his origin point. The spiral tightens with each transit, eventually reaching what we call a 'threshold reality'—a boundary state where multiple versions converge."

Noah tried to follow the complex mathematics. "And that's where Robert is now? This threshold place?"

"Almost certainly. His seventh crossing occurred during your dinner at Marlowe's, though you perceived it as him simply going to bed afterward." Jake consulted one of his instruments. "The energy signature of that final breach was massive—nearly ten times the intensity of his previous crossings. It created ripple effects throughout Daybridge's dimensional structure."

"Is that bad?"

Jake's expression was grim. "Catastrophic, potentially. Each crossing weakened the boundaries between realities. The seventh completed what we call a dimensional octave—a full cycle through probability space. That completion has triggered a cascading destabilization that could lead to total boundary collapse."

"Meaning what, exactly?"

"Meaning all versions of Daybridge could begin to merge uncontrollably. Reality as we understand it would break down. Causality, continuity, even basic physics would become... negotiable." Jake ran a hand through his silver hair. "We're already seeing early signs. Have you noticed anything unusual today? Momentary shifts in your surroundings, objects appearing or disappearing, people seeming briefly unfamiliar?"

Noah hesitated. "The coffee shop where I stopped this morning... for a second, I thought it was a bookstore. The barista called me 'Doctor' instead of by name. And on my way here, I could have sworn the stoplight at Maple and Fifth was on the wrong corner."

"Reality bleed-through," Jake confirmed. "Your perceptions are more accurate than you realize. That coffee shop is a bookstore in several adjacent realities. You are a practicing physician rather than a medical student in at least three versions I've documented. And that stoplight was indeed moved in 1998—but only in realities where Councilman Rivera won the election instead of Councilwoman Patel."

Noah rubbed his temples. "This is giving me a headache."

"That's your brain attempting to reconcile contradictory sensory information." Jake checked another instrument. "The effect will worsen as the boundaries continue to deteriorate. We have perhaps thirty-six hours before the collapse reaches critical mass."

"And what happens then?"

"A convergence event. All possible Daybridges merging into a single, impossible configuration." Jake's voice grew quiet. "I've never witnessed one personally, but the theoretical models are... disturbing. Imagine a city where every possible version of history happens simultaneously. Where you might turn a corner and find yourself in a Daybridge from fifty years ago, or one that never existed in our timeline at all."

Noah tried to process this apocalyptic scenario. "Can we stop it?"

"Possibly. If we can locate Robert and bring him back to his origin reality—this Daybridge—we might be able to stabilize the dimensional boundaries." Jake moved to a cabinet and removed an old leather case. "But first, we need to find him."

From the case, he extracted what looked like a brass sextant modified with additional lenses and dials. "This is a dimensional resonance locator. It can detect objects or persons with strong quantum entanglement across realities."

He placed Robert's fountain pen on a small platform attached to the device. "The pen shares quantum states with both Robert and this specific reality. It should allow us to triangulate his current position in the multiversal framework."

Noah watched as Jake made delicate adjustments to the instrument. "Even if we find him, how do we reach him? I can't see these subway entrances like Robert could."

"You won't need to. I have other methods of dimensional transit." Jake aimed the sextant at the pen and peered through its eyepiece. "Though they're considerably less pleasant than riding a train."

After several minutes of careful calibration, Jake stepped back from the instrument with a troubled expression.

"What's wrong?" Noah asked.

"His quantum signature is... fragmented. Distributed across multiple probability coordinates." Jake made a notation in his ledger.

"It's as if he exists in several places simultaneously, though his primary concentration is indeed in a threshold reality."

"Can you reach him?"

"Not directly. The threshold state is too unstable for conventional transit." Jake considered the problem. "But there might be another approach. If Robert has encountered a Station Guide, he may attempt to reach Central Nexus."

"Station Guide? Central Nexus? You're losing me again."

Jake set aside the sextant. "The interdimensional transit system has caretakers—entities that were once human but have become integrated with the system itself. They appear as transit officials to travelers. Central Nexus is the hub where all probability lines converge—the one location that exists across all versions of the multiverse."

"And you think Robert will go there?"

"If he's received proper guidance, yes. It's the only way out of a threshold reality." Jake moved to another cabinet and removed a small wooden box. "We need to establish a quantum communication link. If we can reach Robert, even briefly, we can coordinate our efforts."

The box contained what appeared to be two identical pocket watches. Jake opened one, revealing not a clock face but a small circular screen surrounded by tiny dials and buttons.

"Quantum entanglement communicators," he explained. "Created by Margaret Steinman in the 1960s. They maintain connection regardless of dimensional location, though the signal degrades with distance across probability space."

He handed one of the devices to Noah. "Keep this with you at all times. If it activates—if we receive any communication from Robert—I need to know immediately."

Noah accepted the strange device, studying its intricate mechanism. "What do we do in the meantime?"

"We continue gathering data and preparing for retrieval." Jake turned to his wall of maps. "I need to identify the exact probability coordinates of Robert's original reality—the precise version of Daybridge he came from. Otherwise, even if we find him, we won't be able to return him to his proper dimensional alignment."

"How do you determine that?"

"By mapping the pattern in the noise." Jake gestured to the overlapping transparencies on the wall map. "Each reality has a unique dimensional signature—a specific configuration of historical divergence points that distinguishes it from all other versions. By analyzing the variations Robert documented in his journal, I can extrapolate backward to identify his origin point."

Jake moved to the chalkboard, erasing the previous timeline and beginning a new, more complex diagram. "I need you to tell me everything you remember about Robert. Not just recent events, but his entire history as you understand it. Family background, academic career, personal habits—everything that might help establish his baseline reality."

For the next hour, Noah recounted his knowledge of Robert's life—his childhood in Seattle, his undergraduate work at MIT, his graduate research at Daybridge University. He described Robert's meticulous nature, his preference for fountain pens over digital notes, his habit of working late in the lab when facing difficult problems.

Jake recorded it all, occasionally asking clarifying questions or checking details against Robert's journal entries. As the information accumulated, he began to identify inconsistencies—places where Noah's memories diverged from Robert's written observations.

"You say his parents live in Seattle, but his journal mentions visiting them in Portland," Jake noted.

"That's wrong. They've always lived in Seattle. His father teaches at the university there."

Jake made a note. "And you're certain he attended MIT for undergraduate study?"

"Absolutely. He has the diploma framed in his bedroom."

"Interesting. His journal references 'my time at CalTech' on several occasions."

Noah frowned. "That's definitely wrong. He's never even been to California as far as I know."

"These discrepancies are crucial," Jake explained. "They help us identify which reality variations affected Robert's memories during his journeys. The more recent the crossing, the more significant the memory alteration."

By the time they'd finished, the chalkboard was covered with a complex web of divergence points and probability vectors. Jake stepped back, studying the pattern with intense concentration.

"There," he said finally, circling a specific intersection of lines. "That's our Robert. Daybridge-Prime, Variation 3.7. A reality where the 1943 experiment occurred but was successfully contained, where urban renewal followed the Patel Plan rather than the Rivera Initiative, where the university expanded northward, and where the medical school emphasizes research over surgery."

Noah blinked. "That's... our reality, right?"

"Precisely. Which confirms my suspicion that Robert's origin point is indeed this specific version of Daybridge." Jake made a final notation in his ledger. "That simplifies our task considerably. We don't need to navigate to an adjacent reality—just retrieve him from the threshold state and return him here."

"How do we do that?"

Before Jake could answer, a sharp knocking sound came from the front of the shop. Both men froze, listening. The bookstore had been closed for hours, a "Research in Progress" sign posted on the door.

The knocking came again, more insistent.

"Stay here," Jake said quietly, moving toward the office door. "If I'm not back in five minutes, take the communicator and go to the university library. Find Dr. Eleanor Kwan's book on quantum fractures in the restricted collection. It contains emergency protocols."

"Wait—" Noah began, but Jake had already slipped through the door, closing it firmly behind him.

Alone in the cluttered office, Noah cradled the quantum communicator in his hand, uneasiness building. Through the door, he could hear the muffled sound of Jake's footsteps moving through the bookshop, then the creak of the front door opening.

Voices drifted back—Jake's and another, older-sounding voice that somehow carried despite its quiet tone. Though Noah couldn't make out the words, something about the second voice raised the hair on the back of his neck.

Unable to contain his curiosity, he moved to the office door and cracked it open slightly. Through the narrow gap, he could see Jake standing in the shop's entrance, facing an elderly man in what appeared to be an old-fashioned transit uniform—navy blue with gold buttons and trim.

"... not your concern, Guardian," the elderly man was saying, his voice carrying that same unsettling resonance. "The sequence progresses as designed. Intervention will only increase the probability of catastrophic disjunction."

"Your 'sequence' is destabilizing the entire dimensional framework," Jake replied, his tone controlled but tense. "The convergence you're facilitating will destroy ordered reality across all probability vectors."

"Not destruction—transformation." The uniformed man smiled, the expression eerily symmetrical. "All possibilities realized simultaneously. The ultimate expression of quantum potential."

"At the cost of coherent existence. You were human once, Maxwell. You must understand what's at stake."

The elderly man's smile faded. "Maxwell Hanover ceased to exist in 1943. I am the Station Master now, and I serve the system's purpose." He gestured toward the back of the shop—toward the office where Noah watched through the cracked door. "Your assistant has recovered the catalyst's temporal anchor. An admirable effort, but ultimately futile."

Jake shifted position, blocking the man's line of sight to the office. "Robert North is not your 'catalyst.' He's a human being who stumbled into something he didn't understand. His actions were not willing participation in your convergence agenda."

"Intent is irrelevant. Effect is all that matters." The Station Master's form seemed to flicker slightly, as if not entirely present in the room. "The seventh crossing is complete. The threshold breach has been established. The catalyst now serves his function in the probability matrix."

Noah felt a chill at the clinical way this strange man discussed Robert, as if he were merely a component in some vast machine rather than a person.

"Where is he?" Jake demanded. "What have you done with him?"

"He rests at the threshold, where all possibilities converge." The Station Master adjusted his white gloves with mechanical precision. "Soon, he will accept his role willingly. They always do, in the end. The human mind cannot resist the allure of infinite potential."

"I won't let you use him to trigger a convergence event."

The Station Master's expression hardened, his eyes reflecting light in a way that seemed wrong—too bright, too uniform. "You cannot prevent what has already begun, Guardian. The boundaries fail even as we speak. Reality bleeds into reality. The walls between worlds grow thin."

As if to emphasize his point, the surrounding bookshop briefly... shifted. For an instant, the shelves rearranged themselves, books changing color and position. The floor plan altered, windows appearing where none had been before. Then everything snapped back to normal, leaving only a faint afterimage of the alternate configuration.

Noah gasped involuntarily at the disturbing sight. The Station Master's head turned sharply toward the sound, his gaze fixing on the partially open office door.

"The catalyst's anchor," he said, his voice suddenly eager. "Yes, I sense its resonance now. A direct connection to his origin reality."

Before Jake could react, the Station Master made a gesture that seemed to bend space itself. His form elongated impossibly, stretching across the intervening distance to materialize directly in front of the office door.

Noah stumbled backward as the door swung open, revealing the Station Master in all his uncanny wrongness. Up close, the man's appearance was even more disturbing—his features too perfectly symmetrical, his movements too precise, his eyes reflecting impossible geometries.

"Noah Thompson," the Station Master said, his voice resonating at a frequency that made Noah's teeth ache. "Roommate, friend, anchor point in the probability matrix. Your quantum entanglement with Robert North is most useful."

Jake appeared behind him, a strange device in his hand that emitted a pulsing blue light. "Step away from him, Maxwell."

The Station Master ignored the warning, his attention fixed on Noah—or more specifically, on the fountain pen and quantum communicator he still clutched in his hands.

"Perfect dimensional resonance," the Station Master observed. "A direct channel to the catalyst across probability space."

He reached for the items with white-gloved hands that seemed to elongate unnaturally. Noah backed away until he hit the desk behind him, nowhere left to retreat.

"Don't touch him!" Jake raised the blue-light device, which emitted a higher-pitched hum.

The Station Master paused, glancing at Jake with mild annoyance. "Your dimensional disruptor cannot harm me, Guardian. I exist across all probability vectors simultaneously."

"Not harm—contain." Jake adjusted a dial, and the blue light intensified. "This office sits at the convergence of three major ley lines. Combined with a properly calibrated disruption field, it creates a localized dimensional isolation effect."

The Station Master's confident expression faltered slightly. He looked down at his own form, which had begun to lose definition around the edges, becoming slightly translucent.

"A temporary inconvenience," he said, though his voice carried less certainty than before.

"Long enough for our purposes." Jake stepped forward, the disruptor held steady. "Now, I'll ask again—where exactly is Robert North?"

The Station Master's form continued to fade, his outline blurring. "Where you cannot reach him, Guardian. The catalyst rests in the dream realm between worlds, guided by one who should know better than to interfere with the system's purpose."

"Gil," Jake breathed, recognition in his tone. "Gilbert Harmon is with him?"

The Station Master's face showed genuine surprise for the first time. "You know of the Wanderer? Interesting. Perhaps your understanding of the system is more complete than I estimated."

"Gil has been riding the rails for over forty years," Jake said. "I've tracked his movements across multiple realities."

"The Wanderer resisted integration, as your catalyst now attempts to do." The Station Master's form had faded to a ghostly outline, his voice becoming distant. "But resistance merely delays the inevitable. The convergence approaches. Reality itself grows thin."

As if to demonstrate, the surrounding office briefly phased out of existence, replaced by a different configuration—a laboratory filled with strange equipment, walls covered with equations. Then it shifted again, becoming a storage room filled with dusty boxes. Finally, it returned to Jake's office, though subtle differences remained—books on different shelves, instruments slightly altered in design.

"You see?" The Station Master's voice echoed as his form became nearly transparent. "The boundaries fail. All possibilities converge. The catalyst fulfills his function."

With those final words, he vanished completely, leaving Jake and Noah alone in the suddenly silent office.

Noah released a breath he hadn't realized he was holding. "What the hell was that?"

"The Station Master. Once Dr. Maxwell Hanover, now a quantum ghost integrated with the interdimensional transit system." Jake lowered the disruptor, which had begun to smoke slightly from overuse. "And confirmation of our worst fears. Robert is indeed at the center of a planned convergence event."

"But we learned something useful, right? This Gil person is with him."

Jake nodded, returning to his desk and opening his ledger to a specific page. "Gilbert Harmon, a quantum physicist, disappeared in 1979 after reporting 'unusual transit phenomena' on Thornfield Avenue. I've detected his quantum signature across multiple realities for decades but could never establish direct contact."

"Is he helping Robert or hurting him?"

"Helping, I believe. The Station Master seemed displeased by his involvement." Jake turned to his instruments, making rapid adjustments. "Gil is what we call a 'Dimensional Wanderer'—someone who has been riding the rails between realities for so long that they've developed a unique relationship with the multiverse. Neither fully integrated with the system like the Station Master, nor bound to a single reality like most humans."

"Can he get Robert back to us?"

"Possibly, if he can guide him to Central Nexus." Jake activated several devices simultaneously, creating a complex harmony of electronic tones. "But they'll need our help. The Station Master will do everything in his power to prevent Robert from escaping the threshold reality."

Noah held up the quantum communicator. "Can we use this to reach them?"

"We can try." Jake took the device, making minute adjustments to its dials. "But first, we need to understand exactly what Robert has been experiencing. His journal contains the key to the pattern—the specific sequence of dimensional transitions that led him to the threshold state."

He moved to the desk where Robert's journal lay open, its pages filled with meticulous notes and hand-drawn maps of various Daybridges. "Each crossing followed a specific quantum harmonic—a frequency of probability that resonates with particular historical divergence points."

Jake traced the progression with his finger. "First crossing: minimal divergence, primarily architectural differences. Second crossing: moderate divergence, institutional variations. Third crossing: significant divergence, personal history alterations."

As he analyzed the pattern, Jake's expression shifted from concern to dawning realization. "This isn't random. The Liminal Line wasn't just taking Robert to progressively more divergent realities—it was following a specific frequency pattern that mirrors quantum wave function collapse."

He grabbed a piece of chalk and began rapidly transcribing equations onto the board. "Each crossing represented a particular eigenstate in a seven-part quantum superposition. Together, they form a complete dimensional harmonic sequence—a mathematical expression of all possible Daybridges within a specific probability spectrum."

Noah struggled to follow the complex mathematics. "What does that mean for finding Robert?"

"It means we can predict exactly which threshold reality he's in." Jake completed the equation with a flourish. "And more importantly, we can calculate the precise dimensional coordinates needed to establish communication and eventually retrieval."

He returned to the quantum communicator, inputting settings based on his calculations. "If Gil has provided Robert with any form of dimensional stabilization, this should be able to reach him—even across the threshold boundary."

The device began to emit a soft, pulsing tone as Jake made final adjustments. "Now we wait. If Robert is in a position to receive, the quantum entanglement between this communicator and his fountain pen should establish a connection."

Noah watched the small screen on the device, which displayed shifting patterns of light that seemed to move in more dimensions than should have been possible on a flat surface.

"What was that thing the Station Master called Robert? A catalyst?"

Jake's expression darkened. "It's a term from the original 1943 documentation. The Daybridge Containment Initiative theorized that certain individuals possess unique quantum signatures that can amplify dimensional phenomena. They called these individuals 'catalysts'—people whose mere presence could accelerate or stabilize interdimensional effects."

"And they think Robert is one of these catalysts?"

"Evidently. Which explains the unprecedented rate of boundary deterioration following his crossings." Jake checked another instrument, which showed alarming spikes in its readings. "The dimensional instability is growing exponentially. We're seeing reality bleed-through across nearly seventy percent of Daybridge now."

As if to illustrate his point, the wall behind him briefly became transparent, revealing not the street beyond but a lush jungle with impossible plants and strange, glowing animals moving among the vegetation. The vision lasted only seconds before the solid wall returned.

"That's... not good," Noah said weakly.

"No, it's not. The convergence is accelerating." Jake returned to the quantum communicator, which had begun to emit a different tone—higher, more urgent. "Wait—we're getting something."

The patterns on the small screen coalesced into a recognizable image: a bearded man with intense blue eyes, his face partially obscured by static.

"... receive this... dimensional breach at coordinates..." The voice was broken, barely audible through bursts of interference.

Jake adjusted the settings frantically. "Gil! Gilbert Harmon! Can you hear me?"

The image stabilized slightly. "... Steinman? Margaret's protégé? How did you—"

"Quantum entanglement communicator. We have limited time. Is Robert North with you?"

The bearded man nodded, his image flickering. "... attempting dream navigation... find Central Nexus... Station Master's influence growing..."

"Dream navigation is too dangerous!" Jake leaned closer to the device. "The Station Master controls the dream realm in threshold reality. Tell Robert to abort immediately!"

"... only option... convergence imminent... need coordinates for..." The transmission deteriorated into unintelligible static.

Jake made further adjustments, but the image continued to break up. "Gil! You need to guide Robert to dimensional coordinates 7-3-9-Theta-Prime! Repeat: 7-3-9-Theta-Prime! It's a direct pathway back to his origin reality!"

The bearded face reappeared briefly. "... understood... 7-3-9-Theta... will attempt... wake him now..."

Then the transmission cut out completely, the screen returning to abstract patterns of light.

Jake sat back, concern evident on his face. "They're attempting something incredibly dangerous. Dream navigation in a threshold reality gives the Station Master direct access to Robert's consciousness."

"What's dream navigation exactly?" Noah asked.

"A technique for mapping interdimensional pathways through the subconscious mind. It allows travelers to perceive connections between realities that aren't visible in waking consciousness." Jake rubbed his temples. "But in a threshold state, where reality itself is unstable, the dream realm becomes a battleground for influence over the traveler's perceptions."

"And the Station Master has home field advantage," Noah guessed.

"Precisely. He exists partially in the dream realm at all times, able to manipulate perceptions and memories with ease." Jake returned to his instruments, making rapid adjustments. "We need to provide Robert with additional support—a dimensional anchor point strong enough to counter the Station Master's influence."

He turned to Noah. "That's where you come in. Your quantum entanglement with Robert—your friendship, your shared experiences—creates a natural resonance that transcends dimensional boundaries."

"What do I need to do?"

Jake retrieved a small device from a cabinet—a silver disc etched with concentric circles and strange symbols. "This is a quantum resonance amplifier. It will strengthen your natural connection to Robert across probability space."

He handed the disc to Noah. "Hold this in your dominant hand and concentrate on Robert—not just his appearance, but your emotional connection to him. Recall specific shared experiences, conversations, moments of significance between you."

Noah accepted the disc, which felt unexpectedly warm against his palm. "That's it? Just think about him?"

"Quantum entanglement between conscious beings is emotionally mediated. Your memories and feelings toward Robert create specific harmonic patterns in the probability matrix." Jake activated several more instruments. "I'll amplify those patterns and direct them along the coordinates we transmitted to Gil."

Noah closed his eyes, concentrating on his friendship with Robert. He recalled their first meeting as freshmen, their decision to room together in graduate school, late nights studying in their apartment. He remembered Robert's excitement when his quantum tunneling research was approved, his frustration when simulations failed, his methodical approach to solving complex problems.

As Noah focused on these memories, the silver disc grew warmer in his hand. A strange tingling sensation spread up his arm, reminiscent of a mild electric current but somehow deeper, as if it flowed through his thoughts rather than his nerves.

"Excellent," Jake said, monitoring the readings on his instruments. "Your quantum resonance is exceptionally strong.

Robert must be a significant anchor point in your personal probability matrix."

"Is that your scientific way of saying we're close friends?" Noah asked, eyes still closed.

"Friendship is merely our cultural framework for understanding quantum entanglement between conscious entities," Jake replied. "But essentially, yes."

The instruments around them began to emit harmonious tones, creating a complex chord that seemed to resonate with the silver disc in Noah's hand. The tingling sensation intensified, spreading throughout his body.

"The connection is establishing," Jake observed. "Your quantum signature is reaching across the probability spectrum, providing Robert with a directional beacon back to this reality."

Noah maintained his concentration, focusing even more intently on his memories of Robert. As he did, something unexpected happened—he began to perceive fragments of unfamiliar experiences. Brief flashes of locations he'd never visited, conversations he'd never had, versions of himself that felt simultaneously alien and familiar.

"I'm... seeing things," he said, disoriented but maintaining his focus. "Other versions of my life. Of Robert's life."

"Your consciousness is brushing against adjacent probability vectors," Jake explained. "The amplifier is creating a quantum superposition effect, allowing you to perceive multiple versions of your shared timeline simultaneously."

The visions intensified. Noah saw himself as a surgeon, as a pediatrician, as a forensic psychiatrist—all careers he had considered at various points. He saw Robert working in different laboratories, teaching classes he'd never taught, even performing music in a small club.

"So many possibilities," Noah murmured. "So many versions of us."

"All equally real within their own probability streams," Jake confirmed. "What you're experiencing is a glimpse of the multiverse—the infinite branching of possible outcomes from every decision point in your lives."

Among the kaleidoscope of possibilities, one image suddenly appeared with greater clarity than the others: Robert lying unconscious on a simple bed, a copper circlet on his forehead, while the bearded man from the communicator—Gil—monitored strange equipment nearby.

"I can see him!" Noah exclaimed. "Robert's unconscious, wearing some kind of metal headband. Gil is with him in what looks like... I don't know, some kind of lab with equations written all over the walls."

Jake moved quickly to Noah's side. "That's dream navigation equipment. Robert's consciousness is in the dream realm while his body remains in Gil's safe house." He checked his instruments. "Can you perceive any indicators of their dimensional coordinates? Any symbols or markings that might indicate their location within Threshold?"

Noah concentrated harder, trying to bring the vision into sharper focus. "There's a window... outside I can see three moons and buildings that keep changing shape. There's a map on one wall with a spiral pattern marked in red. One point on the spiral is glowing."

"The probability spiral," Jake said with evident excitement. "Gil has mapped the dimensional coordinates of Central Nexus. The glowing point must indicate its current location within Threshold reality."

He returned to his instruments, making rapid adjustments. "This is better than I hoped. If Gil has identified Central Nexus, he can guide Robert there once he awakens from dream navigation."

The vision began to fade, the connection weakening. Noah strained to maintain it, but the myriad possibilities were overwhelming his perception, creating a disorienting blur of alternate realities.

"I'm losing him," Noah said, the silver disc now almost painfully hot in his hand.

"You've done enough," Jake assured him. "The quantum resonance has been established. Robert now has a directional beacon back to this reality."

The disc cooled suddenly, the tingling sensation receding. Noah opened his eyes, finding himself back in Jake's office with no trace of the interdimensional visions.

"Did it work?" he asked, returning the silver disc to Jake.

"Better than expected. We've established a stable quantum resonance path between this reality and Robert's current location." Jake checked his readings. "Now we need to prepare for his potential return. If Gil can guide him to Central Nexus using the coordinates we transmitted, Robert might be able to transit back along the resonance path we've created."

"Might?"

"Interdimensional transit from a threshold state is... complicated. There are variables beyond our control." Jake moved to a cabinet and began removing equipment. "We need to establish a stabilized reception point—a dimensional anchor strong enough to pull Robert back to his origin reality once he reaches Central Nexus."

He placed several devices on his desk—a modified astrolabe, a compass with multiple needles, and what appeared to be a crystal housed in an intricate brass framework.

"These will help establish a fixed dimensional coordinate at this location—a beacon that will remain stable even as reality around us continues to fluctuate." Jake began assembling the components with practiced precision. "But we'll need more than equipment. We need to recreate the specific quantum state that defined Robert's connection to this reality before his first crossing."

"How do we do that?"

Jake gestured to the fountain pen. "That's a start. But we need more—objects with strong emotional resonance, people with significant quantum entanglement to Robert, locations where he spent considerable time."

"His apartment," Noah suggested. "His research lab at the university. Those are the places he spent most of his time."

"Good. We'll need to visit both, collect quantum resonance readings, and possibly retrieve additional anchor objects." Jake completed his assembly of the devices. "But first, we need to address the accelerating reality fluctuations across Daybridge. If the convergence progresses much further, even successful retrieval might not prevent catastrophic dimensional collapse."

As if to emphasize his point, the surrounding office briefly phased into multiple configurations simultaneously—books rearranging on shelves, furniture shifting position, walls changing color and texture. For a moment, they could see through the ceiling to an impossible sky filled with swirling, multicolored clouds.

"That's getting worse," Noah observed, shaken by the intensity of the fluctuation.

"The pattern in the noise is becoming the dominant signal," Jake said grimly. "Chaos overwriting order. We're running out of time."

He moved to his chalkboard, quickly sketching a map of Daybridge with several locations marked. "We need to establish dimensional stabilizers at key points throughout the city—locations where ley lines intersect and reality is naturally more resilient to fluctuation."

"What do these stabilizers look like?"

Jake opened another cabinet, revealing a dozen small devices resembling antique pocket watches. "Quantum anchors. They generate a field that reinforces local dimensional boundaries, creating pockets of stability amidst the growing chaos."

He handed several of the devices to Noah. "You'll need to place these at specific coordinates while I complete the retrieval preparations here."

"You want me to go out there? When reality itself is coming apart?"

"Someone must. I'm the only one who can calibrate the retrieval mechanism properly." Jake's expression was sympathetic but firm. "The anchors will protect you from the worst effects of the fluctuations. And as Robert's quantum-entangled friend, you have a natural resistance to dimensional displacement."

Noah looked at the devices in his hand, then at the increasingly unstable reality around them. Outside the shop's windows, the street scene flickered between multiple configurations—buildings changing style, vehicles transforming from cars to strange hovering craft and back again, pedestrians appearing and disappearing like ghosts.

"Okay," he said finally. "Tell me where to go and what to do."

Jake quickly marked specific locations on a map of Daybridge, explaining the activation procedure for each anchor. As Noah prepared to leave, Jake placed a hand on his shoulder.

"Be careful out there. Reality is becoming... negotiable. Trust your instincts more than your senses. When in doubt, focus on your connection to this specific reality—your memories, your experiences, your understanding of how things should be."

Noah nodded, pocketing the quantum anchors and the map. "And if I encounter the Station Master?"

"Run," Jake said simply. "No confrontation, no conversation. Just return here as quickly as possible."

As Noah moved toward the door, Jake added, "One more thing. If you notice people beginning to... change, to transform in response to the fluctuations, stay away from them. Some individuals are more susceptible to dimensional alteration than others. They become what we call 'probability sinks'—beings who absorb and reflect multiple reality states simultaneously."

"That sounds horrifying."

"It is. For them and anyone near them." Jake checked his watch. "You have approximately four hours to place all the anchors. After that, I expect the fluctuations will become too severe for safe navigation through the city."

Noah took a deep breath, steeling himself for the task ahead. "Four hours to help save reality. No pressure."

As he opened the door to leave, the bookshop around them stabilized momentarily—a brief pocket of normalcy amidst the growing chaos. But through the front windows, they could see the street outside shifting like a reflection in disturbed water, buildings rippling and reforming in endless variations.

The pattern in the noise was becoming the dominant reality. And their time to restore order was running out.

CHAPTER EIGHT: CONVERGENCE POINTS

Robert's consciousness drifted through landscapes of impossible geometry. The dream realm of Threshold Daybridge was unlike anything he had experienced in previous dreams—colors that existed beyond the visible spectrum, structures that folded in on themselves in ways that defied conventional physics, entities that seemed to be composed of pure mathematical concepts rather than matter.

The copper circlet on his forehead grew warm as his awareness expanded. Gil had explained that the device would help him maintain lucidity and purpose within the dream, preventing the natural disorientation that comes from navigating non-Euclidean mindscapes.

Focus, Robert reminded himself. *Central Nexus. Location. Direction. Nothing else.*

As he concentrated on this intention, the chaotic dreamscape began to coalesce into something more structured—a vast transit station with countless platforms extending in all directions, including several that seemed to run perpendicular to gravity. Trains of various designs arrived and departed continuously, some resembling the copper cars he had ridden, others entirely alien in concept—vehicles that moved through conceptual space rather than physical dimensions.

At the center of this impossible station stood the Station Master, his uniform now a deep crimson that seemed to absorb light rather than reflect it. He was speaking to a group of disoriented travelers—people from different eras and realities, all looking lost and confused.

"Your connecting trains await," the Station Master was saying, his voice resonating at frequencies that made the dream itself vibrate.

"Each of you has completed your designated sequence. Now you will be integrated into the system, becoming part of the grand convergence."

Robert remained at a distance, observing. The circlet allowed him to resist the natural pull toward the Station Master's authoritative presence—a gravitational effect that seemed to draw the other dreamers inexorably closer.

Just observe, he reminded himself. *Find the location of Central Nexus in physical reality. Don't engage.*

The Station Master suddenly paused in his address to the gathered travelers. His head turned with mechanical precision, eyes scanning the dream-space until they fixed directly on Robert's position.

"The catalyst awakens to deeper perception," he said, his voice carrying effortlessly across the vast station. "Welcome to the threshold of consciousness, Robert North. Your presence honors the system."

The other dreamers turned to look at Robert, their expressions uniformly blank, as if their individual personalities had already begun to fade.

Robert remained silent, focusing on his objective: *Central Nexus. Location. Direction.*

The Station Master smiled—a perfect, symmetrical expression that conveyed neither warmth nor malice. "You seek the hub of all probability paths. A commendable ambition for one so recently awakened to multiversal reality."

He gestured, and the dream-station around them transformed, becoming a three-dimensional map of Threshold Daybridge. Glowing lines represented streets, buildings appeared as translucent structures, and pulsing nodes indicated what Robert somehow knew were dimensional convergence points.

"The physical manifestation of Central Nexus currently resides here," the Station Master said, indicating a pulsing crimson node near the center of the map. "Though its location shifts in response to probability fluctuations and observer expectation."

Robert studied the location carefully, committing it to memory. The dream-map showed Central Nexus positioned at the intersection of three major boulevards, beneath what appeared to be a public plaza with a distinctive spiral pattern in its center.

"The Möbius Plaza," the Station Master continued, seemingly eager to share this information. "Where probability loops back upon itself in endless iteration. The ideal location for your integration into the system."

Robert remained focused on memorizing the exact coordinates, ignoring the Station Master's invitation. The copper circlet grew warmer against his forehead as he reinforced his purpose: *Central Nexus. Location. Direction. Nothing else.*

"Your resistance is unnecessary," the Station Master said, his tone unchanged despite Robert's silence. "Integration is not obliteration, but transcendence. You will maintain your identity while expanding beyond the limitations of singular reality."

He approached Robert, moving across the dream-space with that same unsettling precision—not walking so much as repositioning himself through conceptual rather than physical distance.

"Consider what you've already experienced," the Station Master continued. "The echo effect allows you to perceive multiple realities simultaneously—a glimpse of the consciousness that awaits you after integration. Imagine that awareness expanded exponentially, encompassing all possible variations of existence."

Despite his determination to remain detached, Robert found himself curious. "To what end? What purpose does this expanded awareness serve?"

The Station Master's expression shifted to something like satisfaction. "He speaks! Excellent. Dialogue facilitates understanding."

The dream-map around them expanded, showing not just Threshold Daybridge but hundreds of overlapping variations—each slightly different, each existing in its own probability space.

"The purpose is completion," the Station Master explained. "Since 1943, reality has been fragmented—splintered into countless variations by the breach. What was once whole became many. The convergence will restore unity, bringing all possibilities into harmonic alignment."

"By collapsing distinct realities into chaos," Robert countered, careful to maintain his focus despite the conversation.

"Not chaos—synthesis." The Station Master made another gesture, and the overlapping cities began to merge in the dream-map, forming a new configuration that somehow incorporated elements from all variations simultaneously. "A reality where all possibilities exist in quantum superposition, where nothing is lost because everything is realized."

Robert studied this representation of the Station Master's vision. It appeared beautiful in its complexity—a city where architectural styles from different eras coexisted, where contradictory historical events somehow occurred simultaneously, where the boundaries between what was and what might have been dissolved completely.

But he also saw the fundamental flaw in this vision: human consciousness, evolved to process singular linear reality, would be unable to comprehend such a state of existence. The echo effect he'd experienced was disorienting enough with just a few overlapping realities. A complete convergence would overwhelm any mind not fundamentally altered to perceive it.

"You would drive everyone insane," Robert said.

"Only temporarily. Consciousness adapts." The Station Master's expression remained serene. "Those who cannot adjust will experience a period of disorientation before their perception evolves. Those already sensitive to quantum fluctuations—like yourself—will transition more easily."

As they spoke, Robert became aware of a subtle change in the dream environment. The Station Master's influence seemed to be weakening, the dreamscape becoming less stable. Through the thinning fabric of the dream, he caught glimpses of other realities—including a brief image of Noah holding some kind of silver disc, his expression one of intense concentration.

The Station Master noticed this change as well, his perfect composure showing the first hints of concern. "Someone attempts to reach you across probability space. Your roommate, guided by the Guardian. Interesting."

Robert felt a surge of hope at this confirmation that Jake and Noah were working to help him. The copper circlet on his forehead grew suddenly hot, and he heard Gil's voice as if from a great distance:

"...7-3-9-Theta-Prime... direct pathway... wake now..."

Understanding that his time in the dream realm had served its purpose, Robert pressed his thumb against the sharp projection on the inner surface of the circlet. The pain was immediate and clarifying—a jolt of physical sensation that cut through the conceptual landscape of the dream.

The Station Master's expression shifted to alarm. "Wait! You cannot—"

But reality was already dissolving around them, the dream collapsing as Robert's consciousness returned to his physical body.

"—leave yet," the Station Master's voice faded as wakefulness rushed in.

Robert gasped awake, sitting up so abruptly that the copper circlet fell from his forehead. Gil was beside him immediately, steadying him with a firm hand.

"Easy," the older physicist cautioned. "Dream transition can be disorienting, especially from Threshold dreamscapes."

Robert blinked, his vision adjusting to physical reality after the impossible geometries of the dream. Gil's shelter looked solid and reassuringly normal, though the echo effect still overlaid multiple versions of their surroundings.

"I found it," Robert said, his voice hoarse. "Central Nexus. It's at something called Möbius Plaza—three boulevards intersecting around a spiral pattern."

Gil's expression brightened. "Möbius Plaza! Of course—the mathematical symmetry makes it a natural anchor point for interdimensional convergence." He moved to one of his wall maps, searching until he located the area Robert had described. "Here—approximately two miles east of our current location."

Robert stood carefully, testing his balance. "There's more. I heard your voice while I was in the dream—something about coordinates. 7-3-9-Theta-Prime?"

"Yes!" Gil's excitement was palpable. "I established brief contact with Jake Steinman—Margaret's successor. He transmitted dimensional coordinates for a direct pathway back to your origin reality."

"You can communicate across realities?"

Gil indicated a modified radio on one of his workbenches. "Quantum entanglement communicator. Highly unreliable, but occasionally functional during periods of dimensional alignment." He checked a device on his wrist. "We received the transmission just before you entered dream navigation. Jake and your roommate Noah have established a quantum resonance path between this reality and your origin point."

Robert felt a surge of hope. "So if we can reach Central Nexus..."

"We might be able to send you home, yes." Gil tempered his optimism with caution. "But the coordinates alone aren't enough. We need to understand the pattern—the specific sequence that will connect Central Nexus to your original Daybridge."

He led Robert to a table covered with calculations and diagrams. "While you were dream navigating, I analyzed the information in your journal entries combined with my decades of observation. The Liminal Line isn't random—it follows a mathematical progression based on quantum harmonic resonance."

Gil pointed to a spiral diagram that looked similar to the pattern Robert had seen in the dream. "Each crossing moves along this probability spiral, with the seventh completing a full cycle and returning to the origin point—but at a different level of the spiral."

"Like musical octaves," Robert observed.

"Precisely. The same note at a higher frequency." Gil traced the spiral with his finger. "The problem is that the 1943 breach distorted the natural pattern. Instead of returning travelers to their origin point, the seventh crossing diverts them to Threshold reality—a probability sink where the Station Master can harvest their perceptual energy."

"He mentioned integration," Robert recalled. "Becoming part of the system."

"That's how he maintains and expands the interdimensional transit network. Each integrated traveler adds their quantum consciousness to the infrastructure, strengthening the connections between realities." Gil's expression darkened. "And accelerating the progression toward complete convergence."

"Which would collapse all realities into one impossible configuration," Robert said, remembering the vision the Station Master had shown him.

"Exactly. A reality where all possibilities exist simultaneously—where causality itself becomes negotiable." Gil checked another instrument, which displayed alarming readings. "And based on these dimensional stability measurements, we're approaching critical threshold. The convergence could begin within hours."

Robert examined the spiral diagram more carefully. "But if we understand the pattern, we should be able to find the right train at Central Nexus—one that follows coordinates 7-3-9-Theta-Prime back to my original reality."

"That's the theory. The execution is considerably more challenging." Gil gathered several instruments into a worn leather bag. "We'll need to reach Möbius Plaza, locate the Central Nexus entrance, and identify the correct train—all while avoiding the Station Master's notice and navigating increasingly unstable reality fluctuations."

As if to emphasize this difficulty, the world outside Gil's shelter suddenly shifted—buildings briefly transforming into entirely different structures, the three moons in the sky merging into a single celestial body before separating again, the very color of reality cycling through impossible hues.

"The flux storms are intensifying," Gil observed grimly. "We should move quickly, while navigation is still possible."

He handed Robert the stone disk on a leather cord—the dimensional anchor he had provided before the dream navigation. "Wear this. It will help maintain your directional sense as reality becomes more fluid."

Robert slipped the cord around his neck, feeling the weight of the stone against his chest. Unlike Jake's pendant, which had stabilized his perception, this anchor seemed to provide a different kind of clarity—a sense of orientation within the shifting probabilities around them.

"What about you?" Robert asked, noticing Gil wasn't wearing a similar device.

"After forty years, I've developed my own internal compass." The older physicist smiled wryly. "One of the few benefits of prolonged interdimensional displacement."

Gil packed several additional instruments into his bag, then retrieved what looked like a modified compass from a drawer. "This will help us locate the exact position of Central Nexus once we reach Möbius Plaza. The entrance shifts in response to dimensional fluctuations, but always follows specific mathematical principles."

As they prepared to leave, Robert felt a strange doubling of his thoughts—as if another version of himself was thinking parallel thoughts just slightly out of sync. The echo effect was progressing despite the dimensional anchor.

"Gil," he said hesitantly, "I'm experiencing something new. Not just visual echoes, but... cognitive ones. Multiple thought processes occurring simultaneously."

Gil paused in his preparations, studying Robert with concern. "That's advanced dimensional dissolution. Your consciousness is beginning to exist across multiple probability states simultaneously." He checked a device that resembled an antique pocket watch. "The threshold effect is accelerating. We have less time than I thought."

"How much less?"

"Based on these readings... three hours, perhaps four, before your quantum coherence degrades beyond the point where targeted dimensional transit would be possible." Gil's expression was grave. "After that, even if we reach Central Nexus, you might not be able to maintain sufficient focus on a single reality to complete the journey."

The implications were clear: they were racing not just against the impending convergence of realities, but against the dissolution of Robert's very identity.

"Then let's not waste time," Robert said, moving toward the door with newfound determination.

Gil nodded, shouldering his bag of instruments. "Stay close to me. The streets of Threshold have never been predictable, and they're becoming less so by the hour."

Meanwhile, in Daybridge-Prime, Jake Steinman stood at the third convergence point identified in Robert's journal—the intersection of Thornfield Avenue and Riverside Drive. According to the detailed notes, Robert had encountered a particularly stable manifestation of the subway entrance at this location during his fourth crossing.

The surrounding area pulsed with dimensional instability. Buildings flickered between multiple architectural styles, pedestrians occasionally phased in and out of visibility, and the sky cycled through various weather conditions in rapid succession. Only the stabilizer devices Noah was currently placing throughout the city prevented complete chaos.

Jake removed an instrument from his case—a modified theodolite that detected variations in the quantum field rather than measuring angles. He adjusted the eyepiece and slowly scanned the intersection, measuring fluctuations in dimensional stability.

"There," he murmured, focusing on a particular spot between a coffee shop and a bookstore. The readings showed a significant thinning of reality—a point where the boundaries between dimensions had worn almost completely away.

He approached carefully, removing another device from his pocket—a brass sphere etched with intricate patterns that hummed softly when activated. This was a dimensional resonator, designed to amplify existing breaches in reality.

As he held the resonator toward the spot identified by the theodolite, the air began to shimmer. Gradually, the outline of a subway entrance materialized—ghostly at first, then gaining substance. Iron railings curved downward into warm light below, exactly as Robert had described in his journal.

Unlike Robert, Jake was not seeing this entrance by chance or quantum sensitivity. He was deliberately forcing it into manifestation, using tools developed by his mentor specifically for monitoring the interdimensional transit system.

The entrance wasn't stable—it flickered in and out of existence, sometimes appearing solid, other times fading to a mere outline. But it was unquestionably real, a physical manifestation of the breach created in 1943.

Jake set his instruments aside and approached the entrance cautiously. Unlike ordinary travelers, he knew better than to descend those stairs without preparation. The Liminal Line didn't respond to guardians the same way it did to travelers—it recognized them as foreign elements and often redirected them to randomized destinations.

Instead, Jake removed a small camera from his pocket—not a conventional photographic device, but a quantum imager that could capture dimensional signatures. He carefully documented the entrance from multiple angles, gathering data that would help him predict its materialization pattern.

As he worked, his quantum communicator vibrated in his pocket. Jake retrieved it quickly, hoping for another transmission from Gil.

The screen showed only static at first, then resolved into a pattern that Jake recognized as a directional vector—mathematical coordinates in probability space. Gil was too far into the threshold reality for voice communication, but had managed to transmit this critical information.

Jake quickly noted the coordinates in his ledger. They matched what Robert had seen in his dream navigation—the current location of Central Nexus within Threshold Daybridge. This confirmed that

Robert had successfully completed the first phase of their rescue plan.

Now Jake needed to establish a stable reception point—a dimensional anchor in Daybridge-Prime that could serve as a beacon for Robert's return journey. And for that, he needed to understand the exact pattern of the Liminal Line's probability path.

He turned his attention back to the flickering subway entrance, using his instruments to analyze its quantum frequency. Every interdimensional breach had a specific signature—a mathematical expression of its relationship to the multiverse. By identifying this signature, Jake could potentially calculate the precise sequence needed to navigate from Central Nexus back to Daybridge-Prime.

The subway entrance pulsed with energy as Jake measured it, the patterns revealing themselves in the readings from his instruments. It wasn't just a random tear in reality—it was a structured phenomenon following specific mathematical principles.

"Fibonacci sequence modified by prime number factorials," Jake muttered, recognizing the pattern. "Elegant and self-reinforcing."

He made rapid calculations in his ledger, the mathematics revealing a spiral progression through probability space—exactly what Gil had theorized. Each crossing moved the traveler along this spiral, with the seventh completing a full cycle.

But there was a distortion in the pattern—a deliberate manipulation introduced after the initial breach. Jake recognized the mathematical signature of human interference.

"Maxwell, what did you do?" he wondered aloud, studying the equations. The original designers of the Daybridge Containment Initiative had apparently modified the natural pattern of the breach, redirecting the seventh crossing to a specific probability coordinate rather than allowing it to complete its natural cycle.

This explained why travelers who completed the octave ended up in Threshold reality rather than returning to their origin point.

The system had been intentionally designed to harvest travelers, to collect quantum consciousness for some greater purpose.

But why? What goal could have been worth such deliberate manipulation of fundamental reality?

The answer came as Jake completed his calculations: convergence. The modified pattern created a gradual weakening of dimensional boundaries with each completed octave. Over decades, this would eventually lead to a complete collapse of the multiverse structure around Daybridge—a merging of all possible realities into a single, unified configuration.

"They were trying to force evolution," Jake realized. "To create a new type of reality where all possibilities exist simultaneously."

The hubris was staggering—scientists playing with forces they barely understood, attempting to accelerate the development of consciousness beyond its natural progression.

And Robert North, with his unique quantum sensitivity, had accidentally become the catalyst that would complete this decades-long process. His seven crossings had created the final instability needed to trigger complete convergence.

Jake quickly packed his instruments, his concern growing. The pattern was clear now—and it revealed that they had even less time than he had initially calculated. The dimensional instability was accelerating exponentially, with complete boundary collapse now likely within hours rather than days.

He needed to return to his shop immediately, to complete the preparations for Robert's potential return. But first, he had to verify one final aspect of the pattern.

Jake removed the brass resonator from his pocket once more, adjusting its settings based on his new understanding of the Liminal Line's mathematical structure. If his calculations were correct, he should be able to briefly stabilize the subway entrance—not enough to safely enter, but sufficient to confirm his theory about its connection to Central Nexus.

As the resonator activated, the flickering entrance solidified, becoming fully manifested for the first time. The iron railings gleamed in the sunlight, and the warm glow from below intensified. A sound emerged from the entrance—the distant rumble of an approaching train.

Jake peered down the stairs, careful not to descend. The station below matched Robert's description exactly—vintage design elements, constellation mosaics overhead, brass fixtures gleaming alongside worn marble tiles.

But the constellations depicted in those mosaics were wrong—star patterns that didn't exist in Earth's night sky. And as Jake watched, they seemed to move subtly, rearranging themselves into new configurations.

The rumble grew louder, and a warm breeze carrying the scent of ozone and brass polish wafted up from below. A train was approaching—one of the copper cars that had carried Robert between realities.

Jake stepped back quickly, deactivating the resonator. The entrance began to fade immediately, the stairs becoming transparent, then merely an outline, then vanishing completely. Within seconds, the solid brick wall had returned, with no indication that a subway entrance had ever existed there.

But Jake had seen enough to confirm his theory. The Liminal Line followed a consistent pattern, cycling through variations of Daybridge in a specific sequence determined by the mathematical properties of the original breach. And with this understanding came a realization: if Robert could identify the correct train at Central Nexus—one that followed coordinates 7-3-9-Theta-Prime—he might indeed find his way back to his original reality.

The quantum communicator vibrated again in Jake's pocket. This time, when he checked the screen, he found a simple message from Noah:

Anchors placed at seven locations. Reality fluctuations intensifying. Strange people gathering at Möbius Square. Returning to shop now.

Jake frowned. Möbius Square was the Daybridge-Prime equivalent of the Möbius Plaza in Threshold reality—the location Robert had identified as Central Nexus. If people were gathering there, it suggested the convergence was progressing faster than anticipated.

He quickly texted back: *Avoid Möbius Square. Return by alternate route. Prepare retrieval equipment.*

Then he packed his remaining instruments and hurried back toward his shop. The pattern was clear now, the noise resolved into a coherent signal. Robert North was their only hope of preventing complete dimensional collapse—if he could navigate the probability spiral correctly and return to Daybridge-Prime.

But first, Jake needed to establish a stable reception point—a beacon that would guide Robert along the correct probability path. And time was running out.

In Threshold Daybridge, Robert and Gil made their way cautiously through streets that grew increasingly fluid with each passing minute. Buildings rippled like reflections in disturbed water, streets occasionally rerouted themselves while pedestrians were mid-step, and the sky continued its unsettling color shifts.

"Reality degradation is accelerating," Gil observed, checking one of his instruments. "The convergence event has entered its preliminary phase."

Robert could feel the change in his own perception. The echo effect had intensified, overlaying not just multiple visual versions of their surroundings but multiple sensory experiences simultaneously. He could feel different textures underfoot with each step, smell contradictory scents on the same breath, hear conversations in languages that shifted mid-word.

More disturbing was the continued doubling of his thoughts—parallel cognitive processes that sometimes aligned and sometimes diverged wildly. One moment he would be focused on reaching Central Nexus, the next he would find himself contemplating quantum equations or remembering events that hadn't happened—at least not to him.

"Memory bleed-through," Gil explained when Robert described the sensation. "You're picking up experiences from other versions of yourself across the probability spectrum. It's a common symptom of advanced dimensional dissolution."

They turned onto a broad avenue that Gil identified as Schrödinger Boulevard—one of the three major thoroughfares that intersected at Möbius Plaza. The buildings here were taller, their architecture more dramatically unstable. Some structures appeared to exist in multiple configurations simultaneously, occupying contradictory spaces with impossible geometry.

The residents of Threshold seemed increasingly agitated as well. They moved with greater urgency, many wearing devices that Gil identified as "perception filters"—technology that helped them process the accelerating reality fluctuations.

"They sense the convergence approaching," Gil said quietly. "Most don't understand what's happening, but their instincts recognize the fundamental wrongness of dimensional collapse."

As they progressed down the boulevard, Robert noticed something disturbing: people were beginning to change. Some flickered between multiple appearances, their features and clothing shifting rapidly. Others seemed to merge with their surroundings, becoming partially transparent or incorporating elements of nearby architecture into their forms.

"Probability sinks," Gil explained grimly. "Individuals particularly susceptible to dimensional fluctuations. They're the first to absorb the effects of convergence."

They gave these unfortunate people wide berth, continuing toward their destination. As they approached Möbius Plaza, the dimensional instability intensified dramatically. The entire landscape seemed to pulse with energy, reality itself becoming thin and permeable.

And then, suddenly, they could see it—the plaza stretching before them, a vast circular space with a distinctive spiral pattern etched into its surface. Three major boulevards intersected here, just as Robert had seen in his dream navigation. But the plaza was not empty.

Hundreds of people had gathered in the space, standing in concentric circles around the central spiral. They stood perfectly still, facing inward, their expressions vacant and their outlines slightly blurred—as if they existed in multiple states simultaneously.

"Threshold residents drawn to the convergence point," Gil whispered, pulling Robert behind a flickering sculpture for cover. "The Station Master is gathering quantum consciousness to facilitate the process."

At the very center of the spiral pattern stood the Station Master himself, no longer in his transit uniform but wearing a suit of shifting, impossible colors. His hands were raised above his head, manipulating what appeared to be strings of pure light that extended outward to connect with each person in the gathering.

"He's binding them to the system," Gil explained, horror evident in his voice. "Integrating their perceptual energy to power the final phase of convergence."

Robert studied the plaza, looking for any sign of a subway entrance. "Where's Central Nexus? I don't see any station entrance."

Gil removed the modified compass from his bag, adjusting its settings as he aimed it toward the plaza. "It should be... there." He pointed to a spot near the edge of the spiral pattern, opposite from where they were hiding. "But it won't manifest until the dimensional frequencies align properly."

"When will that happen?"

"Based on these readings..." Gil checked another instrument. "Approximately twenty minutes. There will be a brief window—perhaps two minutes—when Central Nexus materializes before the convergence reaches critical mass."

Robert assessed their situation grimly. They needed to cross the plaza, avoid the Station Master's notice, locate the entrance when it appeared, and identify the correct train—all within a narrow window of opportunity, while reality itself was becoming increasingly unstable.

"We'll need a distraction," he said, thinking aloud. "Something to draw the Station Master's attention away from that section of the plaza when the entrance manifests."

Gil nodded, reaching into his bag. "I've prepared for this possibility." He removed what looked like a small silver sphere etched with complex patterns. "A dimensional resonance disruptor. It creates localized instability in the quantum field—essentially, a controlled reality fluctuation."

"Won't that make the convergence worse?"

"Temporarily, yes. But it might give us the window we need." Gil checked his watch-like device again. "We should position ourselves closer to the target area before the entrance manifests."

They began making their way around the perimeter of the plaza, staying hidden behind fluctuating architectural elements whenever possible. The gathered crowd remained motionless, focused entirely on the Station Master and his manipulations of the light-strings.

As they circled toward their destination, Robert became aware of another change in his perception. The echo effect was shifting, becoming less visual and more... conceptual. He was beginning to perceive not just multiple physical versions of his surroundings, but their underlying mathematical structures—the quantum probabilities that defined their existence.

"Gil," he whispered, "I'm seeing... equations. Probability functions underlying physical objects."

The older physicist glanced at him with concern. "Your quantum perception is evolving rapidly. It's both good and bad—useful for identifying the correct train, but a sign that your connection to singular reality is deteriorating."

As they reached a position near where Central Nexus would supposedly appear, Gil checked his instruments once more. "Ten minutes until manifestation. We should prepare the disruptor."

He began adjusting settings on the silver sphere, explaining as he worked: "When activated, this will create a localized probability storm approximately one hundred yards from our position—far enough to draw attention away from us, but close enough to be compelling."

Robert nodded, though his attention had shifted to the spiral pattern in the plaza's center. With his enhanced perception, he could now see that it wasn't merely a decorative element—it was a physical representation of the probability spiral Gil had shown him, a mathematical expression of the Liminal Line's interdimensional path.

And at its center, the Station Master was completing that pattern—using the quantum consciousness of the gathered crowd to stabilize the final configuration needed for complete convergence.

"He's using them to shape reality itself," Robert realized aloud. "To force the multiverse into a new configuration."

"Yes. The ultimate goal of the Daybridge Containment Initiative—not to seal the breach, but to exploit it. To force evolutionary change on reality itself." Gil's expression was grim as he finished preparing the disruptor. "Maxwell Hanover believed humanity was ready for the next stage of consciousness—perception across multiple realities simultaneously. He was wrong."

A sudden ripple passed through the gathered crowd, their forms briefly becoming even more translucent before solidifying again. The Station Master's manipulations of the light-strings grew more complex, the patterns shifting into new configurations.

"Five minutes," Gil whispered, checking his instruments. "The dimensional frequencies are beginning to align."

Robert touched the stone disk hanging around his neck, focusing on the coordinates Jake had transmitted: 7-3-9-Theta-Prime. With his evolved perception, he could almost visualize them as a specific vector through probability space—a path that led back to his original reality.

"How will we know which train is the right one?" he asked.

"Your dimensional anchor should resonate when the correct train arrives," Gil explained. "You'll feel a pull toward your origin reality—a quantum entanglement that transcends the probability spiral."

Another ripple passed through the crowd, stronger this time. Several of the gathered people seemed to merge briefly with their neighbors before separating again. The Station Master's form flickered, momentarily revealing something beneath the human appearance—a structure of pure mathematical relationships rather than physical matter.

"Two minutes," Gil said tensely. "Get ready."

He handed the silver disruptor to Robert. "When I give the signal, twist the top hemisphere clockwise until it clicks, then throw it toward the far side of the plaza. We'll have approximately thirty seconds of distraction."

Robert accepted the device, which felt unexpectedly heavy in his hand. As he waited for Gil's signal, he became aware of another presence in his perception—a familiar resonance that seemed to call to him across probability space.

Noah, he realized. *I can feel him reaching out to me.*

The sensation was faint but unmistakable—a connection that transcended the dimensional barriers, a quantum entanglement that had somehow remained intact despite his multiple crossings. And with it came a momentary clarity, a strengthening of his identity against the dissolution that threatened to scatter his consciousness across the multiverse.

"Now!" Gil hissed suddenly. "The entrance is beginning to manifest!"

Robert looked where Gil was pointing and saw a shimmer in the air—the ghostly outline of a subway entrance gradually taking form. Iron railings curved downward into warm light below, the structure becoming more solid with each passing second.

He twisted the disruptor as instructed and hurled it toward the opposite side of the plaza. The silver sphere arced through the air, landing with a soft click that belied the dramatic effect that followed.

Reality itself seemed to tear open at the impact point. A swirling vortex of contradictory matter and energy erupted, buildings and streets and even people caught in its radius shifting rapidly between multiple states of existence. Colors that shouldn't exist flashed in painful bursts, and geometries that defied comprehension twisted the very fabric of space.

The Station Master's head snapped toward the disturbance, his perfect composure faltering for the first time. The light-strings in his hands wavered as his attention diverted.

"Now!" Gil grabbed Robert's arm, pulling him toward the newly manifested subway entrance. "Before he realizes it's a distraction!"

They ran across the edge of the plaza; the crowd still focused on the Station Master despite the chaotic probability storm erupting behind them. The entrance had fully materialized now—a perfect replica of the stations Robert had used for his previous crossings.

They descended the stairs quickly, emerging into a station that dwarfed any Robert had seen before. The ceiling soared hundreds of feet overhead, supported by columns inscribed with mathematical formulas rather than conventional ornamentation. The platform extended seemingly infinitely in both directions, with dozens of tracks running parallel to each other.

"Central Nexus," Gil breathed, an expression of wonder breaking through his usual scientific detachment. "The hub of all probability paths."

Unlike the empty stations of Robert's previous experiences, Central Nexus bustled with activity. Travelers of all descriptions moved between platforms—some clearly human, others humanoid but with subtle differences, and some entities that defied conventional categorization entirely.

Most disturbing were the station attendants—identical copies of the Station Master in their navy uniforms and white gloves, moving with that same mechanical precision as they directed travelers to various trains.

"We need to find Platform 7-3-9," Gil said urgently, consulting his instruments. "The Theta-Prime line departs from there."

They moved quickly through the vast station, following signs in multiple languages and symbolic systems. Robert's evolved perception proved unexpectedly useful—he could somehow read all the signage regardless of its form, the information translating directly into understanding without conscious processing.

Above them, a massive departure board displayed hundreds of destinations in constantly shifting arrangements. Robert scanned it quickly, locating "DAYBRIDGE-PRIME (7-3-9-Theta)" among the listings.

"There!" he pointed. "Platform 24-B, departing in..." He squinted at the strange clock symbol next to the listing. "Three minutes!"

They hurried toward the indicated platform, weaving through crowds of interdimensional travelers. As they moved, Robert became aware of a growing commotion behind them—shouts and a sudden shift in the station's energy.

"He's realized we're here," Gil said grimly, not slowing his pace. "The Station Master has detected your presence in Central Nexus."

They reached Platform 24-B just as a copper train pulled into the station—identical to the one Robert had ridden on his first crossing, though this one gleamed with pristine newness, as if recently created.

The dimensional anchor around Robert's neck grew suddenly warm, vibrating against his chest. "This is it," he confirmed. "This train leads back to my original reality."

The doors slid open with that familiar pneumatic hiss. Unlike Robert's previous journeys, this train wasn't empty—several passengers waited to board, most appearing conventionally human though with the same subtle blurring that affected all residents of Threshold reality.

"You need to board quickly," Gil said, checking his instruments one last time. "The window of dimensional alignment won't last long."

Robert turned to the older physicist, suddenly realizing the implication. "You're not coming with me?"

Gil smiled sadly. "I can't. After forty years, my quantum signature is too diffuse to target a specific reality. I would destabilize your return trajectory."

"But the convergence—"

"If you successfully return to your origin point and Jake properly seals the breach, the convergence will be averted." Gil placed a hand on Robert's shoulder. "This is what I've worked toward for decades. The chance to prevent Maxwell's grand mistake from consuming all reality."

A commotion at the far end of the station drew their attention. Station attendants were converging on their position, moving with unnatural speed through the crowds. And behind them came the Station Master himself, his human disguise beginning to fail as his form flickered between his transit uniform and something else—something composed of mathematical relationships rather than matter.

"Go," Gil urged, pushing Robert toward the open train doors. "Complete the journey. Return to Daybridge-Prime."

Robert hesitated, reluctant to leave the man who had helped him understand the true nature of his situation. "There has to be a way to bring you back too."

"My journey took a different path long ago." Gil removed a small device from his pocket—another disruptor, this one larger than the first. "I'll delay them while you depart. When you reach Daybridge-Prime, tell Jake what we discovered about the convergence. Ensure this never happens again."

The dimensional anchor around Robert's neck grew hotter, pulling him toward the train with increasing urgency. The window of alignment was narrowing.

"Thank you," Robert said simply, knowing no words could adequately express his gratitude.

Gil nodded once, then turned to face the approaching Station Master and his duplicates. He activated the disruptor in his hand, which began to emit a high-pitched whine.

Robert boarded the train just as the doors began to close. Through the narrowing gap, he saw Gil standing defiantly before the Station Master, the disruptor glowing with increasing intensity between them.

"The cycle breaks," Gil called out, his voice barely audible as the doors sealed shut. "The pattern ends here!"

The train began to move, accelerating quickly away from the platform. Through the windows, Robert caught a final glimpse of Central Nexus—Gil surrounded by station attendants, the Station Master's form shifting erratically as the disruptor's effect intensified, and beyond them, the vast architectural impossibility of the interdimensional hub.

Then they entered the tunnel, and everything outside the train vanished into darkness.

Robert found a seat, clutching the dimensional anchor that now pulsed with warmth against his chest. The train moved with that same smooth acceleration he remembered from his first crossing, the rhythmic clacking of wheels on track the only sound.

But this journey felt different. Instead of the disconnected sensation of his previous trips, Robert could feel himself moving along a specific vector through probability space—following coordinates 7-3-9-Theta-Prime back toward his origin reality. The echo effect that had fragmented his perception began to simplify, multiple overlapping realities gradually resolving toward a single configuration.

His thoughts, too, became more coherent—the parallel cognitive processes merging back into a unified consciousness. Memories of his original Daybridge returned with increasing clarity: his apartment with Noah, his research with Professor Liang, the familiar campus and city he called home.

The train's velocity seemed to increase beyond normal physics, the darkness outside the windows occasionally broken by flashes of light that revealed glimpses of other realities—brief snapshots of Daybridges that might have been.

Robert closed his eyes, focusing on the dimensional anchor and the coordinates it contained: 7-3-9-Theta-Prime. His origin point. His home reality. The place where his journey had begun, and where—if Gil and Jake's plan succeeded—it would now end.

The train began to slow.

CHAPTER NINE: THE THINNING VEIL

Noah Thompson hurried through the increasingly unstable streets of Daybridge, the last quantum anchor clutched tightly in his hand. He had placed the previous seven devices at locations Jake had marked on his map—intersections of what the older man called "ley lines," points where reality naturally maintained greater stability.

But the surrounding city was changing more rapidly with each passing minute.

Buildings flickered between multiple architectural styles, sometimes becoming briefly transparent to reveal impossible interiors. Streets occasionally rerouted themselves mid-block, forcing pedestrians to adjust their paths with bemused expressions that suggested they weren't fully aware of the changes. Most disturbing were the people who appeared and disappeared seemingly at random—walking confidently along the sidewalk one moment, vanishing the next, leaving no indication they had ever existed.

As Noah approached Crescent Avenue—the location for the final anchor—he noticed a crowd gathering in the small park at the center of the roundabout. Dozens of people stood in concentric circles, facing inward, their expressions vacant and their outlines slightly blurred. At the center stood an elderly man in what appeared to be an old-fashioned transit uniform.

Noah froze, remembering Jake's warning about the Station Master. This had to be him—or some manifestation of him in Daybridge-Prime. And he was gathering people, just as Robert had described in his dream vision.

Keeping his distance, Noah circled around to the far side of the roundabout. The quantum anchor needed to be placed at the northeast corner of the park, according to Jake's instructions. He would need to approach within fifty yards of the gathering without drawing attention.

As he moved carefully around the perimeter, Noah noticed something unsettling about the gathered crowd. They weren't just standing still—they were slowly fading from view, becoming more translucent with each passing minute. And thin strands of light seemed to extend from each person toward the uniformed figure at the center.

"He's harvesting them," Noah realized with horror. "Taking their... what did Jake call it? Perceptual energy?"

The same process Robert had described from Threshold was happening here in Daybridge-Prime, though apparently at a slower rate. The boundaries between realities were thinning to the point where the Station Master could affect both sides simultaneously.

Noah reached the designated spot and quickly activated the quantum anchor as Jake had shown him—twisting the top section clockwise until it clicked, then pressing it firmly against the ground. The device hummed softly as it burrowed slightly into the earth, establishing its connection to the local dimensional fabric.

A faint blue glow emanated from the anchor, spreading outward in a circle approximately ten feet in diameter. Within this circle, reality seemed to stabilize—colors becoming more vivid, objects more solid, the subtle wavering of buildings and streets ceasing entirely.

Noah checked his map. All eight anchors were now in place, creating what Jake had called a "dimensional stabilization network" throughout Daybridge. It wouldn't prevent the convergence, but it might slow its progression long enough for Robert to return.

As he tucked the map back into his pocket, Noah's gaze returned to the gathering in the park. The Station Master had raised his hands above his head, manipulating the strands of light that connected him to the crowd. His form seemed to flicker between multiple versions of itself—sometimes an elderly transit official, sometimes something else entirely, something that hurt Noah's eyes to look at directly.

And the people connected to him were changing. Some had become almost completely transparent, while others seemed to merge with their neighbors, boundaries between individual forms breaking down.

Noah backed away slowly, not wanting to draw attention. He needed to return to Jake's shop immediately and report what he had seen.

As he turned to leave, his foot caught on an uneven section of sidewalk that hadn't been there seconds before. He stumbled, catching himself before falling, but the motion was enough to attract notice.

The Station Master's head turned with mechanical precision, his gaze fixing directly on Noah despite the distance between them. For a moment that seemed to stretch impossibly, they stared at each other across the park.

Then the Station Master smiled—a perfect, symmetrical expression devoid of warmth—and made a subtle gesture with one white-gloved hand.

Reality around Noah rippled like disturbed water. The stabilization field from the quantum anchor flickered, struggling to maintain coherence against whatever force the Station Master had directed toward him.

Noah didn't wait to see what would happen next. He turned and ran, heading back toward Merchant Street and Jake's bookshop.

Behind him, he heard a sound like tearing fabric—a high, thin noise that seemed to come from everywhere and nowhere simultaneously. Glancing back, he saw a distortion in the air where the Station Master had gestured, a warping of space itself that was spreading outward like a crack in glass.

The streets became increasingly difficult to navigate as Noah ran. Buildings shifted positions, sidewalks narrowed or widened unpredictably, street signs displayed names that changed mid-reading. Only his familiarity with Daybridge allowed him to maintain his bearings as reality itself became unreliable.

Other pedestrians seemed increasingly aware that something was wrong. Some stood frozen in confusion, watching as their surroundings transformed around them. Others moved with increasing urgency, as if fleeing some danger they couldn't articulate. A few had stopped completely, their forms beginning to blur at the edges in the same way as the crowd in the park.

Noah turned onto Merchant Street, relief washing over him as he spotted Steinman's Rare Editions ahead. The bookshop seemed more solid than surrounding buildings, its Victorian façade maintaining consistency despite the fluctuations affecting neighboring structures.

As he approached, the door opened before he could reach it. Jake stood in the entrance, his expression grim.

"Inside, quickly," he urged, pulling Noah through the doorway. "The convergence is accelerating faster than I anticipated."

Once inside, Jake locked the door and flipped the sign to "Closed." The interior of the bookshop seemed relatively stable compared to the chaos outside, though occasional ripples passed through the space, causing books to momentarily rearrange themselves on shelves.

"I placed all eight anchors," Noah reported, catching his breath. "But there's something happening at Crescent Park. The Station Master—or someone who matches your description—is gathering people in circles. They're becoming transparent, and he's collecting some kind of energy from them."

Jake's expression darkened further. "He's establishing convergence points in both realities simultaneously. The veil between worlds has thinned to the point where he can directly influence Daybridge-Prime."

He led Noah quickly through the maze of bookshelves to his back room, which had been further transformed in Noah's absence. The desk at the center had been cleared, replaced by a complex arrangement of devices surrounding a circular platform. Brass rings orbited the platform at various angles, driven by mechanisms that hummed with quiet intensity. Above it all, a crystal suspended in an intricate framework pulsed with soft blue light.

"The reception point," Jake explained, making final adjustments to the apparatus. "A dimensional anchor designed to provide Robert with a stable target for his return journey."

"Will it work?" Noah asked, eyeing the contraption with a mix of hope and skepticism.

"It should, assuming he successfully reaches Central Nexus and boards the correct train." Jake checked readings on several instruments. "The quantum resonance path you helped establish is holding steady, despite the increasing instability."

Noah moved to the window, looking out at Merchant Street. The reality fluctuations were visibly worse than when he had entered the shop. Pedestrians flickered in and out of existence, vehicles transformed between modern cars and strange alternatives mid-motion, and buildings briefly displayed impossible configurations before settling back into recognizable forms.

"What's happening to everyone out there? Do they understand what's going on?"

Jake joined him at the window, his expression somber. "Human perception naturally filters out quantum instabilities. Most people are experiencing this as a series of disorienting moments—déjà vu, brief confusion, sudden uncertainty about their surroundings. Their minds are attempting to maintain a coherent reality model despite contradictory sensory input."

"And when they can't maintain that model anymore?"

"Then they become susceptible to integration." Jake pointed to a woman on the street who stood motionless while other pedestrians moved around her. Her form had begun to blur at the edges, becoming slightly transparent. "The Station Master targets those individuals first—those whose perception has already begun to fragment. He harvests their quantum consciousness to fuel the convergence process."

Noah watched as another pedestrian approached the motionless woman, apparently concerned for her wellbeing. When he touched her shoulder, a strange connection formed between them—a thin strand of light similar to what Noah had observed in the park. Within seconds, the concerned citizen also became stationary, his outline beginning to blur.

"It's spreading," Noah realized with horror. "Like a contagion."

"Quantum entanglement propagating through direct contact," Jake confirmed. "The process accelerates as more individuals are integrated."

He turned away from the window, returning to his instruments. "We have perhaps thirty minutes before the convergence reaches critical mass. After that point, even if Robert successfully returns, we won't be able to seal the breach effectively."

Noah followed him back to the reception platform. "What can I do to help?"

Jake indicated Robert's fountain pen, which had been placed at the center of the platform. "Your quantum entanglement with Robert remains our strongest connection across realities. I need you to focus on that connection—to strengthen the resonance path we've established."

He handed Noah the same silver disc he had used earlier. "Hold this and concentrate on Robert. Recall your shared experiences, your emotional connection, the specific qualities that define him in your perception."

Noah accepted the disc, which felt warmer than before against his palm. He closed his eyes, focusing on his friendship with Robert as he had done previously. The familiar tingling sensation spread up his arm, but stronger this time—more directed, as if flowing along a specific channel rather than radiating outward.

"Excellent," Jake murmured, monitoring the instruments. "The quantum resonance is intensifying. Robert should be able to perceive this connection if he's aboard the correct train."

As Noah maintained his concentration, Jake moved around the room, activating additional devices and checking readings. The humming from the reception platform grew louder, the brass rings spinning faster as the suspended crystal pulsed with increasing brightness.

"The stabilization network is functioning as designed," Jake reported. "The anchors you placed are creating zones of relative dimensional coherence throughout Daybridge, slowing the convergence process. But the effect is temporary—the quantum anchors will eventually be overwhelmed by the increasing instability."

Outside, a sound like distant thunder rolled across the city. The floor trembled slightly beneath their feet, and the lights flickered. Books fell from shelves in the main shop, and somewhere glass shattered.

"What was that?" Noah asked, maintaining his grip on the silver disc despite his alarm.

"Dimensional shockwave," Jake said grimly. "The boundaries are beginning to collapse in specific locations. The convergence has entered its active phase."

He moved quickly to another instrument—a modified seismograph that recorded interdimensional disturbances rather than earthly tremors. The needle jumped erratically across the paper, creating a pattern of sharp peaks and valleys.

"The epicenter is Möbius Square," Jake noted, studying the readings. "The Daybridge-Prime equivalent of the location Robert identified as Central Nexus in Threshold reality. The Station Master is focusing the convergence energy there."

Another tremor shook the building, stronger than the first. The lights flickered again, then stabilized. Through the window, they could see buildings along Merchant Street briefly phase out of existence, replaced by alternative versions before returning to their original forms.

"Jake," Noah said carefully, "what happens if we fail? If Robert doesn't make it back in time, or if the convergence can't be stopped?"

Jake's expression was grave as he checked his pocket watch. "In approximately twenty-eight minutes, the dimensional boundaries will collapse completely. All versions of Daybridge within a specific probability radius will merge into a single, chaotic configuration—a reality where all possibilities exist simultaneously."

"And the people?"

"Those already integrated with the system will become part of its infrastructure—quantum consciousness redistributed across the new configuration. Those who maintain their individual perception will experience..." Jake hesitated. "Imagine suddenly perceiving dozens of contradictory realities simultaneously, without the ability to filter or prioritize the information. For most, it would mean madness. For some, eventually, a new form of consciousness might emerge—one capable of processing multiple realities as parallel streams of information."

"That's what the Station Master wants? To force some kind of... evolutionary leap?"

"Precisely. Maxwell Hanover believed humanity was limited by its perception of singular, linear reality. The Daybridge Containment

Initiative was his attempt to accelerate our evolution toward multiversal consciousness." Jake shook his head. "A hubristic goal, pursued without regard for the suffering it would cause or the natural development it would interrupt."

The tremors continued at irregular intervals, each slightly stronger than the last. The reception platform remained stable, protected by whatever fields Jake had established around it, but the rest of the shop showed increasing signs of dimensional instability—books changing titles mid-spine, furniture shifting between styles, windows briefly looking out onto entirely different streets.

Noah maintained his focus on the silver disc, drawing on every memory of Robert he could summon. As he concentrated, the tingling sensation intensified, spreading throughout his body. With it came that strange perception he had experienced earlier—glimpses of alternate realities, versions of himself and Robert that existed in different probability streams.

But this time, among the kaleidoscope of possibilities, one image emerged with startling clarity: Robert seated on a copper train, clutching a stone disc hanging from a leather cord around his neck. His expression was one of intense concentration, his body slightly blurred at the edges but growing more solid as Noah watched.

"I can see him!" Noah exclaimed. "He's on a train—one of the copper ones he described. He's wearing some kind of stone pendant and seems to be focusing on it."

Jake moved quickly to Noah's side. "That's Gil's dimensional anchor. Robert is following the coordinates I transmitted—attempting to navigate back to this specific reality."

He checked his instruments, excitement breaking through his usual reserve. "The quantum resonance is approaching harmonic alignment. He's on the correct probability vector!"

Another tremor shook the building, this one powerful enough to knock books from shelves throughout the shop. The lights went out completely, plunging the room into darkness except for the blue glow from the crystal above the reception platform.

"Emergency power," Jake explained, moving to a cabinet and removing several candles, which he quickly lit. "The convergence is affecting electrical systems throughout the city."

In the flickering candlelight, the reception platform took on an almost mystical quality—brass rings spinning in complex orbits around the central space where Robert's fountain pen rested, the crystal above pulsing with rhythmic intensity.

Through the window, they could see that Merchant Street had been transformed. Buildings shifted continuously between multiple configurations, sidewalks rippled like liquid, and the few pedestrians still visible moved with the jerky motion of film playing at the wrong speed. Above it all, the sky had taken on a greenish tinge reminiscent of Robert's description of Threshold Daybridge.

"We're running out of time," Jake said, checking his pocket watch again. "The convergence is approaching critical threshold faster than I calculated."

He moved to another instrument—one that resembled an antique radio but emitted no sound, only a pattern of lights that flickered in complex sequences. "The quantum communicator is detecting increasing activity at Central Nexus. Robert must be nearing the final stage of his journey."

Noah maintained his concentration on the silver disc, which had grown almost painfully hot against his palm. The vision of Robert on the train remained clear, but now he could see that the train was slowing, approaching what appeared to be a station platform.

"He's arriving somewhere," Noah reported. "The train is stopping at a station, but it doesn't look like any subway station I've ever seen. The ceiling is... impossibly high, with columns covered in mathematical formulas. There are multiple tracks, multiple platforms."

"Central Nexus," Jake confirmed, excitement and concern mingling in his voice. "The hub where all probability lines converge. If Robert can transition from there to the correct return vector, he should materialize on our reception platform."

Another, stronger tremor shook the building. Plaster dust rained from the ceiling, and a crack appeared in one wall, spreading slowly across the surface. Through the widening fissure, they could briefly glimpse another room entirely—not the bookshop next door, but what appeared to be a laboratory filled with strange equipment.

"Reality breach," Jake said grimly. "The dimensional boundaries are failing even here, despite our protections."

He moved quickly to the reception platform, making final adjustments to the brass rings and checking connections. "We need to establish the return vector immediately. Robert must have a clear path through the collapsing probability field."

Jake placed his hands on two brass nodes extending from the platform's base. Immediately, the spinning rings changed their orbital patterns, aligning along a specific axis that pointed toward the cracked wall. The crystal above pulsed more rapidly, its blue light intensifying.

"Noah, maintain your focus," Jake instructed. "Your quantum resonance with Robert is creating the path he needs to follow. Whatever happens, don't break that connection."

Outside, the sky had darkened further, the greenish tinge giving way to swirling patterns of colors that shouldn't exist in nature. Buildings along Merchant Street were no longer merely shifting between configurations—they were merging, architectural styles combining in impossible ways. Windows looked out onto different streets than the ones they faced, doors opened into locations that couldn't possibly connect to their buildings.

People who hadn't taken shelter had begun to change as well. Those who had already become stationary were now fully transparent, visible only as human-shaped distortions in the air. Others moved with increasing disorientation, their forms occasionally splitting into multiple overlapping versions before recombining.

"Seven minutes until critical threshold," Jake announced, checking his instruments. "After that point, dimensional collapse will be irreversible."

Noah strained to maintain his focus on Robert, the vision growing stronger as the silver disc heated in his hand. He could see Robert more clearly now—standing on a platform in Central Nexus, moving purposefully toward some kind of portal or gateway that pulsed with energy.

"He's approaching some kind of... door?" Noah reported, uncertain how to describe what he was seeing. "Not a normal door, but a vertical oval of light. Other people are moving away from it, but Robert is walking directly toward it."

Jake nodded, not looking up from his adjustments to the reception platform. "The probability portal. It forms when dimensional coordinates align perfectly between realities. If he passes through it, he should emerge here."

"Should?" Noah echoed, concerned by the uncertainty in Jake's voice.

"Interdimensional transit is never guaranteed, especially during convergence conditions." Jake made a final adjustment to the brass rings. "But we've done everything possible to establish a stable return vector. The rest depends on Robert's ability to maintain focus on his destination."

Another tremor rocked the building, this one accompanied by a sound like shattering glass amplified a thousandfold. Through the windows, they could see fragments of reality itself breaking apart and recombining in new configurations—buildings dissolving into component elements before reassembling in impossible architectures, streets flowing like rivers before solidifying in new patterns, the very sky fracturing into shards that revealed other skies beyond.

"The convergence has entered its final phase," Jake said, his voice tight with tension. "Three minutes until critical threshold."

Noah's vision of Robert intensified further. He could see him standing before the oval portal, the stone disc around his neck glowing with the same blue light as the crystal above their reception platform. Robert's expression showed determination mixed with fear as he reached toward the pulsing energy field.

"He's about to enter the portal!" Noah exclaimed.

In that moment, a new figure appeared in Noah's vision—the Station Master, no longer maintaining his human disguise but manifesting as something that defied comprehension. His form was composed of pure mathematical relationships rather than physical matter, extending in more dimensions than should be possible to perceive.

This impossible entity reached for Robert, attempting to intercept him before he could enter the portal.

"The Station Master is trying to stop him!" Noah warned, his voice rising with alarm.

Jake abandoned his instruments, moving to stand beside the reception platform. "We need to strengthen the return vector immediately. Place the silver disc on the platform, next to the fountain pen."

Noah did as instructed, carefully positioning the disc beside Robert's pen at the center of the spinning brass rings. As soon as he released it, the disc and pen both began to glow with the same blue light as the crystal above.

"Now place your hands on these," Jake directed, indicating two brass nodes opposite the ones he had used earlier. "Your quantum entanglement with Robert will complete the circuit, providing him with the additional energy needed to break free from the Station Master's influence."

Noah gripped the brass nodes, which vibrated slightly against his palms. Immediately, he felt a powerful connection forming—not just the tingling sensation from before, but a direct link that seemed to extend beyond physical space into the realm of pure probability.

In his vision, the blue glow around Robert intensified, forming a protective shell that repelled the Station Master's reaching tendrils of mathematical force. Robert looked momentarily surprised, then understanding dawned on his face. He turned back toward the portal with renewed determination.

"It's working!" Noah reported. "He's breaking free from the Station Master's hold!"

Another, more violent tremor shook the building. Books flew from shelves, furniture toppled, and the crack in the wall widened further, revealing glimpses of multiple alternative spaces existing simultaneously in the same location. The reception platform remained stable, protected by whatever fields Jake had established, but the rest of the room showed signs of imminent dimensional collapse.

"One minute," Jake said, his voice steady despite the surrounding chaos. "The return vector is stable. If Robert enters the portal now, he should materialize directly on the reception platform."

In Noah's vision, Robert had reached the portal. The stone disc around his neck pulsed in perfect synchronization with the crystal above their reception platform. He glanced back once at the Station Master, whose impossible form seemed to be shouting something—though no sound carried through Noah's perception.

Then Robert stepped through the portal and vanished from Noah's vision.

"He's entered the transit field!" Noah exclaimed. "He's coming through!"

The reception platform hummed with increasing intensity, the brass rings spinning so rapidly they became blurs of motion. The crystal above pulsed faster, its blue light expanding to encompass the entire platform in a spherical field of energy.

"Thirty seconds," Jake counted down, watching his instruments. "Quantum alignment at seventy percent and rising. Dimensional coordinates locked on return vector."

Outside, reality itself seemed to be tearing apart. The greenish sky had given way to a chaotic swirl of colors and patterns that hurt the eyes to look at directly. Buildings no longer maintained any consistent form, instead cycling through countless configurations too rapidly to track. The very structure of space appeared to be folding in on itself, dimensions intersecting at impossible angles.

"Twenty seconds. Quantum alignment at eighty-five percent."

The reception platform's humming rose to a near-deafening pitch. The blue energy field pulsed with increasing brightness, expanding and contracting in rhythmic waves.

"Ten seconds. Quantum alignment at ninety-two percent."

Noah maintained his grip on the brass nodes despite the pain in his hands from the vibration. His entire body tingled with the energy flowing through him, connecting him to the reception platform and, through it, to Robert somewhere in the interdimensional void.

"Five seconds. Quantum alignment at ninety-seven percent."

The blue field above the platform contracted suddenly, collapsing inward to a point of blinding intensity. Then, with a sound like a thunderclap, it expanded outward in a perfect sphere that momentarily filled the entire room.

When the light faded, a figure stood on the reception platform—Robert North, looking disoriented but undeniably present, the stone disc still hanging from his neck.

"Robert!" Noah released the brass nodes and rushed forward as the brass rings slowed their spinning.

Robert swayed slightly, his outline still showing a faint blur—the aftereffect of interdimensional transit. But he was solid, physically present in Daybridge-Prime for the first time in what had been, from his perspective, days of dimensional wandering.

"Noah?" Robert's voice sounded distant, as if coming from the bottom of a well. "Jake? Did it work? Am I home?"

"You're back," Jake confirmed, moving quickly to check Robert's condition. "Your quantum signature is realigning with this reality. The disorientation should pass within minutes."

Another violent tremor shook the building, this one strong enough to knock framed pictures from the walls. Through the window, they could see Merchant Street dissolving into a chaotic blend of multiple realities, buildings and streets and people merging and separating in impossible configurations.

"The convergence continues," Jake said grimly. "Your return hasn't stopped the process automatically as I'd hoped. We need to seal the breach manually, and quickly."

He turned to the reception platform, making rapid adjustments to the now-slowing brass rings. "Robert, I need the dimensional anchor you're wearing. It contains a quantum imprint of the probability path you followed—essential information for closing the breach properly."

Robert removed the stone disc from around his neck, handling it carefully. "Gil said to tell you that the Station Master modified the original pattern—redirected the seventh crossing to Threshold deliberately as part of the convergence plan."

"I suspected as much," Jake said, accepting the disc. "The mathematics were too precise to be accidental."

He placed the stone disc beside the fountain pen and silver disc at the center of the platform. All three objects began to glow with renewed intensity.

"What about Gil?" Noah asked. "Did he make it back with you?"

Robert shook his head, regret evident in his expression. "He couldn't. His quantum signature was too diffuse after forty years of dimensional transit. He stayed behind to delay the Station Master while I escaped."

"A brave choice," Jake said quietly. "Gilbert Harmon was a brilliant physicist. His sacrifice may have saved reality as we know it."

Another, stronger tremor shook the building. The crack in the wall had widened to the point where they could see clearly into multiple alternative spaces simultaneously—a laboratory, a storage room, a completely different bookshop with inverted layout.

"We have less than two minutes before dimensional collapse becomes irreversible," Jake said, returning to his instruments. "Robert, I need you at the western node position. Noah, remain at the eastern nodes. I'll take the southern position. Together, we can generate the quantum interference pattern needed to seal the breach."

They took their positions around the reception platform, each gripping a pair of brass nodes that extended from the base. As they did, the platform's humming intensified, and the brass rings began to spin again, though in different orbital patterns than before.

"Focus on this reality," Jake instructed. "Your memories of Daybridge as you know it, the physical details of familiar locations, the people you've known here. These collective perceptions will strengthen the quantum signature of this specific probability track, allowing us to designate it as the primary reality during the sealing process."

Robert and Noah concentrated as directed, calling to mind their experiences in Daybridge-Prime—their apartment, the university campus, their favorite coffee shops and study spots. As they focused, the blue energy field above the platform began to change, shifting from its previous spherical shape to a more complex configuration that resembled a many-pointed star.

"Quantum alignment at sixty percent," Jake reported, monitoring a dial on the platform's base. "We need at least eighty-five percent to generate sufficient interference for sealing."

Outside, the chaos had intensified. Reality itself seemed to be shattering, fragments of multiple Daybridges colliding and merging in impossible configurations. The sky had become a void filled with shifting geometric patterns that defied comprehension. People who hadn't been integrated into the Station Master's system moved like somnambulists through the chaos, their perceptions clearly unable to process what was happening around them.

"Seventy percent alignment," Jake announced as the brass rings spun faster. "Robert, focus specifically on your research—the quantum tunneling simulations that first connected you to the interdimensional breach. That quantum resonance is particularly important for the sealing process."

Robert nodded, closing his eyes to better concentrate on the details of his work. As he did, the star-shaped energy field above the platform grew more defined, its points extending outward toward the walls of the room.

"Eighty percent," Jake reported. "Almost there."

A final, devastating tremor shook the building. Books flew from shelves, furniture toppled, and the crack in the wall expanded dramatically, encompassing nearly the entire surface. Through it, they could see not just alternative versions of the room but glimpses of Threshold Daybridge itself—impossible architecture, entities that defied description, and at the center of it all, the Station Master in his true form, reaching toward them with tendrils of pure mathematical force.

"He's breaking through!" Noah warned, maintaining his grip on the brass nodes despite his alarm.

"Eighty-five percent," Jake reported, his voice steady despite the chaos. "Initiating sealing sequence."

He made a final adjustment to the controls at the base of the platform. The brass rings suddenly reversed their spin direction, creating a discordant harmonic that rose in pitch until it became almost painful to hear. The star-shaped energy field pulsed once, twice, then expanded outward with explosive force.

The wave of energy passed through the room, through the building, continuing outward to encompass the entire city. As it moved, it seemed to smooth the chaotic fluctuations of reality, forcing contradictory configurations to resolve into a single, coherent state.

The crack in the wall began to close, the alternative spaces beyond it fading from view. Through the window, they could see Merchant Street stabilizing—buildings settling into their familiar forms, the street itself becoming solid and fixed, the impossible sky returning to normal autumn twilight.

"Breach sealing at thirty percent," Jake reported, watching his instruments. "The quantum interference pattern is forcing dimensional realignment along the primary probability track."

The reception platform continued to generate pulses of energy that spread outward in concentric waves. With each pulse, reality seemed to become more solid, more definite—the echo effect that had plagued Robert's perception fading gradually.

"Sixty percent sealing," Jake continued. "The convergence is reversing. Dimensional boundaries are reestablishing themselves."

Through the nearly closed crack in the wall, they caught a final glimpse of the Station Master—his impossible form contorting in what might have been rage or pain as the connection between realities severed. Then the crack sealed completely, leaving only a faint line to mark where it had been.

"Ninety percent," Jake announced, his voice showing the first signs of fatigue. "Almost complete."

With a final, powerful pulse, the reception platform discharged its remaining energy. The brass rings slowed gradually to a stop, and the star-shaped field collapsed back into the crystal above, which gave one last bright flash before fading to a soft, steady glow.

"Sealing complete," Jake said, releasing his grip on the brass nodes. "The breach has been contained. Dimensional boundaries have been restored."

Robert and Noah also released their nodes, both showing signs of exhaustion from the intense energy channeling. Outside, Merchant Street had returned completely to normal—buildings solid and unchanging, pedestrians moving with natural motions, the sky a proper darkening blue of early evening.

"Is it over?" Noah asked, moving to the window to survey the restored reality. "Did we stop the convergence?"

"For now," Jake confirmed, checking his instruments. "The breach has been sealed according to the original containment protocols—the ones that should have been implemented in 1943. Interdimensional transit through the Liminal Line should no longer be possible."

Robert looked down at his hands, which had finally stopped showing the subtle blurring of dimensional displacement. "I can still feel echoes—memories of other realities, other versions of myself. Will that fade?"

"Eventually," Jake assured him. "Your consciousness was spread across multiple probability tracks for an extended period. It will take time for your quantum signature to fully realign with this specific reality."

He moved to his desk, opening his ledger to make notes on what had occurred. "Your experiences will remain—the knowledge you gained, the insights into multiversal structure. But the perceptual effects should diminish gradually until you're fully anchored in this reality."

Robert nodded, relief evident in his expression. "And the Station Master? Is he gone for good?"

Jake's expression grew more somber. "Not gone, but contained. The Maxwell Hanover who became the Station Master exists across all probability tracks simultaneously. We've severed his connection to this specific reality, but he continues to exist in the spaces between worlds."

"Could he find another way through? Another breach point?"

"Potentially, though it would require considerable time and energy to establish a new connection." Jake closed his ledger with a decisive motion. "Which is why the Guardians must remain vigilant. My work continues, as Margaret's did before me."

Robert moved to the window beside Noah, looking out at the restored Daybridge with new appreciation. "It looks so... normal. As if nothing happened."

"For most people, nothing did happen—at least nothing they'll consciously remember," Jake explained, joining them. "Human perception naturally filters out quantum anomalies. The events of the past few hours will be rationalized as power outages, minor earthquakes, perhaps unusual weather patterns."

"What about the people who were... integrated?" Noah asked hesitantly. "The ones the Station Master was harvesting energy from?"

Jake's expression grew troubled. "That's less clear. Some may have been fully reintegrated into this reality when the breach sealed. Others might remain partially displaced—existing here but with fragmented consciousness or memories. We'll need to monitor hospital reports for unusual cases in the coming days."

Robert thought of Gil, trapped in Threshold reality when the breach sealed. "And those on the other side? In Threshold?"

"Threshold reality exists at the convergence of all probability tracks. The sealing doesn't destroy it—merely disconnects it from this specific reality." Jake placed a hand on Robert's shoulder. "Gil knew what he was doing, Robert. He chose to remain there, to ensure you could return and the breach could be sealed."

Robert nodded, accepting this difficult truth. "He spent forty years trying to find a way to stop the convergence. At least he succeeded, even if he couldn't come back himself."

The three men stood in silence for a moment, looking out at the city that had so nearly been lost to interdimensional chaos. Pedestrians moved along the sidewalks, cars traveled the streets, lights came on in apartments and shops as evening settled over Daybridge. Normal life, continuing as if the very fabric of reality hadn't been on the verge of collapse just minutes earlier.

"So what happens now?" Noah asked finally.

"You return to your lives," Jake said simply. "Your studies, your research, your everyday routines. But with a deeper understanding of the nature of reality than most ever achieve."

He turned back to his instruments, beginning the process of powering them down. "I'll dismantle the reception platform and store the components. The quantum anchors Noah placed throughout the city will gradually deactivate over the next few days, allowing dimensional stability to maintain itself naturally."

"And you'll continue monitoring for new breaches?" Robert asked.

"Always. That is the Guardian's purpose." Jake smiled slightly. "Though I suspect Daybridge will enjoy a period of exceptional dimensional stability after this event. The sealing we performed was more thorough than anything attempted since the original breach."

Robert retrieved his fountain pen from the center of the now-inactive platform, turning it thoughtfully in his hands. "My research—the quantum tunneling simulations that showed particles existing in multiple states simultaneously. Was that real, or an effect of the breach?"

"Both, in a way," Jake replied. "Your research detected genuine quantum phenomena, but the results were amplified by your proximity to the interdimensional breach. The particles in your simulation were indeed existing across multiple realities simultaneously—you were just the first to develop instruments sensitive enough to detect it."

He picked up the silver disc and stone anchor, storing them carefully in a wooden box. "Your work has significant scientific value, even without its connection to interdimensional transit. I would encourage you to continue it, though perhaps with greater awareness of its potential implications."

Robert nodded, pocketing his pen. "I should probably revise my thesis slightly. 'Quantum Tunneling as Evidence of Interdimensional Bleed-Through' might raise too many questions."

Jake laughed—the first genuine expression of mirth they had seen from the serious guardian. "Indeed. Though I suspect Professor Liang would find it fascinating, if somewhat difficult to verify through conventional peer review."

Noah checked his watch, surprised to find it was barely 7:30 PM. The entire convergence crisis had unfolded in less than five hours, though it had felt like days.

"We should probably head home," he suggested to Robert. "You look like you could use about twenty hours of sleep in a reality that doesn't change every five minutes."

Robert smiled tiredly. "That sounds amazing. Though I'm not sure how easily I'll sleep after everything that's happened."

As they prepared to leave, Jake handed each of them a business card. "My private number. If you experience any unusual dimensional effects—echoes, memory bleed-through, perception shifts—contact me immediately. While the breach is sealed, your personal quantum signatures may take time to fully stabilize."

He shook their hands in turn, his expression serious once more. "Few people ever glimpse the true nature of reality as you have. It can be... challenging to readjust to conventional perception afterward. Don't hesitate to reach out if you need guidance."

Robert and Noah thanked him, promising to stay in touch, then made their way through the now-ordinary bookshop to the front door. Outside, Merchant Street was peaceful in the gathering darkness, streetlights creating pools of warm illumination along the sidewalks.

As they walked toward their apartment, Robert occasionally touched buildings or street signs they passed, as if confirming their solidity. Noah noticed but didn't comment, understanding his friend's need for tactile reassurance after days of shifting reality.

"It's strange," Robert said finally as they turned onto their own street. "Part of me already wonders if it really happened—if it wasn't some elaborate shared hallucination."

"The human mind prefers comfortable explanations," Noah replied. "Even ours, apparently, despite what we just experienced."

They reached their apartment building—the correct one, with the number 355 above the door, the familiar broken elevator, the same three flights of stairs to their unit. Inside, everything was exactly as it should be—living room straight ahead, kitchen to the left, bedrooms down the short hall to the right.

Robert stood in the center of the living room, turning slowly as he took in the familiar surroundings. "Home," he said quietly. "My actual, original home reality."

"Want some tea?" Noah offered, heading toward the kitchen. "I think we could both use something normal and comforting right now."

"That would be great," Robert agreed, moving to the window to look out at the night sky—a single moon, normal stars, no swirling impossible colors or geometric patterns that hurt the eyes to view directly.

As Noah filled the kettle, he watched his friend silently. Robert had been through an ordeal few humans had ever experienced—traversing multiple realities, witnessing the near-collapse of the multiverse, confronting entities that existed beyond conventional comprehension. Yet here he was, standing in their apartment, outwardly the same physics graduate student who had disappeared eight days ago.

But Noah knew he wasn't the same. No one could be, after what Robert had seen and learned. The veil between worlds had thinned for him in ways that could never be fully reversed, his perception forever altered by glimpses of the true structure of reality.

"Do you think we'll ever understand it all?" Robert asked suddenly, still gazing at the night sky. "The full nature of the multiverse, the mathematical principles that govern reality?"

Noah considered the question as he set mugs on the counter. "Probably not. At least, not with our current cognitive architecture. Like Jake said, human perception evolved to process singular, linear reality. Understanding the full complexity of multiple simultaneous realities might require a different kind of mind entirely."

"Maybe that's what the Station Master was trying to create," Robert mused. "A new form of consciousness that could perceive multiversal reality directly. He just chose a devastatingly traumatic way to get there."

The kettle whistled, and Noah poured hot water over tea bags. "Evolution through catastrophe. Not exactly an ethical approach."

"No," Robert agreed, turning from the window. "Though I wonder if a more gradual approach might someday be possible. Controlled expansion of perception rather than forced convergence of realities."

He accepted the mug Noah offered, inhaling the familiar scent of Earl Grey. "For now, though, I'm perfectly happy with this single, stable reality. Especially if it includes normal tea, a hot shower, and about twelve hours of uninterrupted sleep."

Noah smiled, relieved to hear his friend focusing on immediate, ordinary comforts. "That can definitely be arranged."

As they sat in their familiar living room, sipping tea and gradually unwinding from the day's extraordinary events, the city outside continued its normal evening routines. Traffic moved along predictable routes, people returned to unchanged homes, the physical laws of the universe remained comfortingly consistent.

The veil between worlds had thinned to the point of tearing, multiple realities nearly collapsing into chaotic convergence. But thanks to Robert's journey through the impossible subway, Gil's decades of research, Jake's guardian knowledge, and Noah's steadfast support, the breach had been sealed. Daybridge-Prime continued to exist as a singular, coherent reality—one probability track among countless possibilities, preserved in its unique configuration.

Yet somewhere in the spaces between worlds, in the threshold where all possibilities converged, the Station Master remained—waiting, planning, seeking another opportunity to complete his grand design. And in a bookshop on Merchant Street, a guardian continued his vigilance, monitoring the subtle fluctuations that might indicate new weaknesses in the dimensional boundaries.

The pattern in the noise had been resolved for now, the signal of chaos temporarily silenced. But the multiverse was vast, and the veil between worlds remained thin in places where reality itself had been wounded. The Liminal Line might be sealed, but other thresholds existed—other points where determined travelers might glimpse the true nature of a reality far more complex than most would ever comprehend.

Robert North had returned from his journey between worlds, but he carried with him knowledge that few humans had ever possessed—and the subtle echoes of experiences across multiple realities that would forever influence his perception of the world around him.

The subway that wasn't there had taken him on a journey beyond imagination. And though the entrance had vanished, sealed by Jake's interdimensional countermeasures, the memory of that impossible transit system would remain—a reminder that beneath the seemingly solid surface of reality lay mysteries still waiting to be discovered.

CHAPTER TEN: THE STATION MASTER

Two days after the sealing of the interdimensional breach, Robert sat in Professor Liang's office, attempting to explain his absence without mentioning parallel realities, quantum ghosts, or subway systems that traversed probability rather than physical space.

"Food poisoning," he repeated, maintaining eye contact despite his discomfort with the lie. "It hit me pretty hard. I should have contacted you sooner, but I was barely functional."

Professor Liang studied him over the rim of her silver-framed glasses, her expression skeptical. "For eight days? That would be quite serious, Robert. You should have gone to the hospital."

"I did, eventually," he improvised. "They gave me fluids, anti-nausea medication. I'm fully recovered now."

She tapped her pen against her notepad, clearly unconvinced but not pressing further. "Well, I'm glad you're back. Your research project has shown some interesting developments in your absence."

Robert straightened in his chair. "Developments?"

Professor Liang turned her computer monitor so he could see it. On the screen was a simulation result from his quantum tunneling experiment—the same one that had been failing repeatedly before his interdimensional journey began.

"The system ran a complete cycle two days ago," she explained. "The results are... unprecedented. The particles maintained quantum superposition even after multiple observation events, but then spontaneously collapsed into single states simultaneously at precisely 7:32 PM."

Robert felt a chill run down his spine. 7:32 PM—almost exactly when Jake had completed the sealing of the breach.

"That's... remarkable," he managed, trying to keep his voice steady.

"More than remarkable. It represents a fundamental challenge to Copenhagen principles." Professor Liang scrolled through the data. "It's as if the particles existed in multiple states simultaneously for an extended period, then received some external signal that forced them to align with a single probability track."

Robert nodded, understanding far better than he could admit. His experimental particles had been influenced by the same interdimensional instability that had allowed him to perceive and traverse multiple realities. When Jake sealed the breach, they had been forced back into conventional quantum behavior.

"I'd like to review the complete dataset," he said. "See if I can identify what caused the spontaneous collapse."

"Of course. I've already forwarded everything to your university account." Professor Liang leaned back in her chair. "This could be significant, Robert. Potentially publication-worthy, if we can determine the mechanism behind the observed phenomena."

Robert suppressed a wry smile at the irony. The mechanism was interdimensional breach sealing following near-catastrophic multiverse collapse—not exactly something they could replicate in the lab or explain in peer-reviewed literature.

"I'll get right on it," he promised, rising from his chair. "And thank you for being understanding about my absence."

"Just don't disappear again without notice," she cautioned. "Graduate advisers tend to worry when their students vanish without explanation."

Robert assured her it wouldn't happen again, then made his way across campus toward the library. The university grounds seemed almost supernaturally normal after his experiences in multiple versions of Daybridge. Students lounged on the grass enjoying the autumn sunshine, professors hurried between buildings clutching coffee cups and lecture notes, campus maintenance staff raked fallen leaves into neat piles.

No one showed any sign of remembering the reality fluctuations from two days ago—the buildings that had briefly phased between multiple architectural styles, the sky that had swirled with impossible colors, the moments when physical laws themselves had become negotiable. As Jake had predicted, human perception had filtered out these quantum anomalies, rationalizing them as power outages, minor earthquakes, or unusual weather patterns.

Robert entered the library, nodding to the security guard at the entrance. He had a specific purpose in mind—one that had nothing to do with his quantum tunneling research and everything to do with understanding what had happened to him.

The restricted collection was housed on the third floor, accessible only to faculty and graduate students with specific authorization. Robert swiped his ID card at the entrance, relieved when the system accepted it without issue. His credentials in this reality remained valid, despite his extended absence across multiple dimensions.

Inside, he moved directly to the section on theoretical physics, searching for the book Gil had mentioned and Jake had referenced: Dr. Eleanor Kwan's "Quantum Fractures: Theoretical Models of Multiversal Bleed."

To his surprise, he found it easily—a slim volume bound in blue leather, its spine decorated with subtle geometric patterns that seemed to shift slightly as he tilted it under the light. He checked it out using the automated system and found a quiet corner of the library to begin reading.

The book opened with a straightforward warning:

The theories presented herein represent speculative interpretations of observed quantum anomalies. Readers are cautioned that direct investigation of potential dimensional breaches without proper preparation may result in perceptual disruption, identity dissolution, or irreversible dimensional displacement.

"A bit late for that warning," Robert murmured to himself.

As he read further, he found that Dr. Kwan's theoretical models matched his experiences with remarkable accuracy. She described the exact symptoms of "reality slippage" he had experienced—the echo effect, memory bleed-through, cognitive doubling, and progressive dissolution of dimensional anchoring. She even referenced "transit anomalies" that manifested as hidden transportation systems connecting parallel reality configurations.

Most significantly, she detailed the mathematics of interdimensional breach mechanics—equations that described precisely how reality could fracture along probability lines and how such fractures might be contained or repaired.

Robert was so engrossed in the text that he didn't notice someone approaching until a shadow fell across his page. He looked up to find an unfamiliar woman standing beside his table—middle-aged, with short gray hair and penetrating dark eyes.

"Fascinating reading choice," she commented, nodding toward the book. "Kwan's work isn't exactly standard curriculum."

"It relates to some anomalous results in my research," Robert replied carefully, closing the book. "Professor Liang suggested I explore alternative theoretical frameworks."

The woman smiled slightly. "Did she? Interesting." She extended her hand. "Dr. Abigail Voss, Theoretical Physics. I don't believe we've met formally, though I've heard good things about your work from Professor Liang."

Robert shook her hand, noting that she didn't seem surprised to find him reading about interdimensional breaches. "Thank you. I wasn't aware my research had attracted attention outside our department."

"Quantum tunneling with persistent superposition? It's precisely the kind of work that interests those of us studying multiversal mechanics." Dr. Voss gestured to the chair opposite him. "May I?"

Robert nodded, increasingly curious about this unexpected encounter. Dr. Voss sat and glanced around to ensure no one was within earshot before continuing in a lower voice.

"Two days ago, at approximately 7:32 PM, every quantum measurement device in my laboratory registered a massive coherence event—a spontaneous alignment of probability vectors across what appeared to be the entire local reality framework." She studied his face carefully as she spoke. "The same evening, multiple witnesses reported unusual perceptual phenomena throughout Daybridge, though most now attribute these experiences to power fluctuations or mild earth tremors."

Robert maintained a neutral expression, though his heart rate accelerated. "That is unusual."

"More than unusual, Mr. North. In twenty years of monitoring quantum fluctuations in Daybridge, I've never recorded anything approaching that magnitude." She leaned forward slightly. "And then there's the curious fact that this event coincided precisely with your return to campus after an eight-day absence that neither your adviser nor your roommate can explain coherently."

"I was ill," Robert stated, sticking to his cover story. "Food poisoning."

Dr. Voss smiled—a knowing expression that made it clear she didn't believe him for a moment. "Of course. A common ailment, though rarely associated with dimensional displacement symptoms."

Robert tensed. "I'm not sure what you're implying."

"I'm not implying anything. I'm stating directly that you show clear signs of recent interdimensional transit—subtle visual echo effect, micro-hesitations when processing sensory input, occasional focus shifts consistent with memory bleed-through." She gestured to Kwan's book. "Hence your interest in quantum fractures and multiversal bleed theory."

Robert considered denying everything, but something in Dr. Voss's manner suggested she might be a potential ally rather than a threat. "You seem very familiar with these symptoms."

"I should be. I experienced them myself, twenty-two years ago, after my own encounter with what I believe you've come to know as the Liminal Line." She sat back, watching his reaction closely. "Though in my case, I only made three crossings before a guardian intercepted me."

"Margaret Steinman," Robert guessed, remembering what Jake had told him about his predecessor.

Dr. Voss nodded, looking impressed. "You've met her successor, then. Jake Steinman. A formidable guardian, by all accounts."

"He helped me return to my origin reality," Robert admitted, deciding to trust her. "After seven crossings and a brief sojourn in a threshold state."

Dr. Voss's eyebrows rose. "Seven crossings? And you maintained sufficient dimensional coherence to return? That's... unprecedented." She studied him with new interest. "You must have an unusually robust quantum signature."

"Or good help," Robert replied, thinking of Gil's guidance and Noah's quantum entanglement connection. "I wasn't alone in finding my way back."

"Even so, surviving seven crossings and threshold exposure without permanent perceptual distortion is remarkable." Dr. Voss tapped her fingers thoughtfully on the table. "Did you encounter the Station Master?"

The question caught Robert off guard. "Yes. Both in the transit system and in threshold reality. You know about him?"

"I've made it my life's work to understand the breach and its manifestations—including Maxwell Hanover's transformed state."

She glanced around again, ensuring their privacy. "What did he tell you about the system's origins?"

Robert hesitated, unsure how much to reveal. "That it was created during a wartime experiment in 1943. That the Daybridge Containment Initiative accidentally tore a hole in reality, splitting the city into countless parallel versions. That the subway system was an unintended consequence—a physical manifestation of the pathways between these fractured realities."

"Did he happen to mention why they were conducting such dangerous experiments in the first place?" Dr. Voss pressed. "The true purpose of the Containment Initiative?"

"Not specifically," Robert admitted. "Though I gathered they were researching weapons applications of quantum field manipulation."

Dr. Voss's expression darkened. "That was the official cover story. The actual goal was far more ambitious—and more disturbing." She lowered her voice further. "They were attempting to force human perceptual evolution through controlled exposure to multiple simultaneous realities. To create a new form of consciousness capable of perceiving and manipulating the multiverse directly."

"Forced convergence," Robert murmured, remembering the Station Master's ultimate goal. "Collapsing all realities into a single configuration where all possibilities exist simultaneously."

"Precisely. Maxwell Hanover believed humanity was limited by its perception of singular, linear reality. He saw this as an evolutionary bottleneck that could be overcome through technological intervention." Dr. Voss shook her head. "A catastrophically arrogant position, but not an uncommon one among certain scientific circles of that era."

"The experiment failed," Robert said. "Created the breach instead of controlled evolution."

"The initial experiment failed, yes. But Hanover—or the entity he became—never abandoned the original goal. For eight decades, the Station Master has been working toward the same objective: forced convergence of all probability tracks centered on Daybridge."

Robert processed this information, connecting it with what he had experienced. "He was using travelers like me—people who completed the seventh crossing—to weaken dimensional boundaries. Harvesting our 'perceptual energy' to power the convergence process."

"Yes. Though you were apparently more than just another traveler." Dr. Voss studied him intently. "Based on the quantum fluctuation readings from two days ago, you were somehow central to the process—a catalyst that accelerated the dimensional deterioration exponentially."

"That's what Gil called me," Robert said, surprised. "A catalyst. He said something about my specific dimensional signature amplifying the instability."

"Gilbert Harmon," Dr. Voss said, recognition in her voice. "The Wanderer. You met him in threshold reality?"

Robert nodded. "He helped me understand what was happening, guided me to Central Nexus. He stayed behind to delay the Station Master while I escaped."

"A brave choice," Dr. Voss said, echoing Jake's words. "Harmon was brilliant—one of the leading quantum field theorists of his generation before his disappearance. His sacrifice likely contributed significantly to the successful sealing of the breach."

She glanced at her watch, then stood. "I've taken enough of your time, Mr. North. And this isn't the proper venue for a complete discussion of these matters." She removed a business card from her pocket and placed it on the table. "If you're interested in understanding more about your experiences—and the broader implications of what you've witnessed—please contact me. My laboratory maintains comprehensive monitoring of Daybridge's dimensional stability, and your insights would be invaluable."

Robert picked up the card, which listed Dr. Voss as Director of the "Quantum Coherence Research Initiative," at the university. "Thank you. I do have questions that Kwan's book doesn't answer."

"I'm sure you do. Interdimensional transit leaves a lasting impression, both literally and metaphorically." She gestured to the book. "Keep that with you. It contains information you might find useful as you continue to process your experiences."

With a final meaningful look, Dr. Voss departed, leaving Robert to consider this unexpected development. He hadn't anticipated finding another person at the university who understood what he had experienced—someone who had made her own crossings through the Liminal Line and dedicated her career to studying its effects.

He returned his attention to Kwan's book, now even more interested in its contents given Dr. Voss's endorsement. The chapter on "Post-Transit Integration" seemed particularly relevant to his current situation:

Travelers who successfully return to their origin reality after multiple dimensional crossings typically experience a period of perceptual readjustment. This may include persistent echo effects, memory bleed-through from alternate reality versions, and occasional cognitive doubling where thought processes from different probability tracks occur simultaneously.

These symptoms gradually diminish as the traveler's quantum signature realigns with their origin reality, though complete restoration of pre-transit perception is rare. Most travelers retain some degree of multiversal awareness—an enhanced sensitivity to quantum fluctuations and probability shifts that conventional perception filters automatically.

This residual awareness can be both a gift and a burden. It allows travelers to perceive aspects of reality hidden from most observers but may also create difficulties in maintaining conventional social and professional functioning in a society that recognizes only singular reality as valid.

Robert closed the book, processing this information. He had indeed noticed continuing effects from his interdimensional journey—subtle visual echoes when he was tired, occasional memory fragments from other versions of himself, moments of déjà vu that felt more like genuine recognition of alternative possibilities than simple cognitive misfiring.

Rather than disturbing him, these lingering effects felt almost comforting—reminders that his experiences had been real, not hallucinations or delusions. They connected him to a broader understanding of reality that few ever glimpsed.

He gathered his belongings and left the library, deciding to walk to Jake's bookshop rather than returning to the lab. The questions raised by Dr. Voss's appearance deserved discussion with someone who had a deeper understanding of Daybridge's interdimensional history.

The autumn afternoon had turned golden, leaves drifting down from the massive oaks that lined the university paths. Students lounged on benches or hurried between classes, their concerns limited to assignments and social lives—blissfully unaware of the multiverse that surrounded them, the countless probability tracks where slightly different versions of themselves made slightly different choices with vastly different outcomes.

Robert found himself wondering which version of Daybridge this actually was. Jake had called it Daybridge-Prime, Variation 3.7—suggesting it was one of several closely related configurations that might all qualify as his "origin reality." How many Roberts had left their laboratories on rainy nights, discovered subway entrances on Thornfield Avenue, and embarked on journeys through parallel worlds? And how many had successfully returned?

These thoughts accompanied him as he made his way to Merchant Street, where Steinman's Rare Editions occupied its familiar Victorian townhouse. The bell above the door chimed softly as he entered, announcing his presence.

The shop appeared normal—no signs of the dimensional chaos that had transformed it two days earlier. Books filled shelves in orderly rows, comfortable reading chairs occupied quiet corners, and the scent of paper and leather binding created the distinctive atmosphere of a well-maintained collection.

Jake emerged from between two tall bookshelves, carrying a stack of volumes that he was apparently reshelving. He nodded in greeting, unsurprised by Robert's appearance.

"I was wondering when you'd visit," he said, placing the books on a nearby table. "How are you adjusting to singular reality again?"

"Better than expected," Robert replied. "Though I still experience echoes occasionally. And memory fragments from other versions of myself."

Jake gestured toward his office door. "That's normal. It should diminish gradually, though some awareness typically remains. Come through to the back—we can speak more freely there."

The office had been restored to its original configuration—desk returned to the center, monitoring equipment once again disguised as antique radios and measuring instruments along the walls. No sign remained of the reception platform that had allowed Robert's return from threshold reality.

"Tea?" Jake offered, moving to a small electric kettle in one corner.

"Please."

As Jake prepared two cups, Robert described his meeting with Dr. Voss and her apparent knowledge of the Liminal Line and the Station Master.

"Abigail Voss," Jake said, nodding. "Yes, she crossed three times in 2003 before Margaret intercepted her. Unusually perceptive, even before her transit experiences. She's been a valuable ally in monitoring Daybridge's dimensional stability."

He handed Robert a steaming cup. "Margaret chose to bring her into our confidence rather than simply redirecting her curiosity. It proved a wise decision—Dr. Voss's quantum coherence research has provided invaluable data on fluctuation patterns throughout the city."

"So she works with you? As another guardian?"

"Not precisely. She's more of an independent researcher with aligned interests." Jake sipped his tea thoughtfully. "She monitors, reports, occasionally assists with specific technical challenges. But the primary responsibility for containing breaches remains with the designated guardian."

Robert considered this information. "She mentioned that I was a 'catalyst' in the Station Master's convergence plan. That my specific dimensional signature somehow accelerated the process."

"Yes, we've confirmed that through analysis of the quantum fluctuation patterns." Jake moved to his desk and opened his ledger. "Your particular quantum signature resonates at a frequency that amplifies interdimensional effects—a characteristic present in perhaps one individual in ten million."

"Why me? What makes my quantum signature different?"

Jake studied his notes before answering. "It appears to be related to your research focus. Your work with quantum tunneling simulations created a self-reinforcing feedback loop—your consciousness became attuned to multiversal structures through prolonged exposure to quantum superposition models, which in turn enhanced your ability to perceive and traverse dimensional boundaries."

"So I essentially trained myself to see beyond conventional reality constraints?"

"In a manner of speaking, yes. Though there was likely an innate predisposition as well." Jake closed his ledger. "The Station Master would have recognized your potential immediately. It's why he directed the Liminal Line to manifest specifically on your route home that night."

This revelation startled Robert. "You mean it wasn't a coincidence? He deliberately placed the entrance in my path?"

"The Liminal Line doesn't appear randomly. It manifests in response to specific quantum signatures—individuals with the potential to serve the system's purpose." Jake's expression was grave. "You were selected, Robert. The Station Master had been monitoring your research for some time, waiting for the ideal moment to draw you into the transit network."

Robert set down his tea, disturbed by this information. "So everything that happened—my multiple crossings, the progressive reality shifts, even my arrival in threshold reality—was orchestrated?"

"Not entirely. The Station Master can influence probabilities but not control them absolutely. He created opportunities, but your choices determined the specific path you followed." Jake leaned forward, his tone reassuring. "Your resistance to integration, your determination to return home—those were genuine expressions of your autonomy, not predetermined outcomes."

Robert wasn't entirely comforted. The idea that he had been manipulated from the beginning—that his entire interdimensional journey had been part of the Station Master's grand design—left him feeling like a pawn in a game he hadn't known he was playing.

"What about Gil?" he asked after a moment. "Was his presence in threshold reality also part of the plan?"

"Unlikely. Gilbert Harmon has been a thorn in the Station Master's side for decades—a traveler who refused integration and dedicated himself to understanding the system rather than serving it." Jake smiled slightly. "Your encounter with him was probably one of those variables the Station Master couldn't control—a fortunate alignment of probability that provided you with the guidance you needed."

Robert nodded, taking some comfort in that assessment. "Dr. Voss mentioned that the original purpose of the 1943 experiment wasn't weapons development but forced perceptual evolution. Is that accurate?"

"Yes, though the distinction became somewhat academic once the military took interest." Jake rose and moved to a bookshelf, selecting a thin folder labeled "Daybridge Containment Initiative - Original Protocols." He placed it on the desk between them.

"Maxwell Hanover was a brilliant physicist with an unconventional perspective on human consciousness. He believed our perception of reality as singular and linear was an evolutionary limitation—a filtering mechanism that prevented madness but also restricted our potential." Jake opened the folder, revealing typewritten documents from the 1940s. "His research suggested that the human mind could potentially perceive multiple reality states simultaneously, given proper preparation and technological assistance."

Robert examined the documents, which outlined a theoretical framework for "expanded perceptual capacity through controlled quantum exposure." The technical language was dated, but the concepts remained cutting edge even by modern standards.

"The military saw the strategic applications immediately," Jake continued. "Soldiers who could perceive multiple probability outcomes simultaneously would have an insurmountable tactical advantage. Operatives who could move between parallel realities could gather intelligence or conduct operations without detection."

"But the experiment failed."

"Catastrophically. Instead of creating controlled quantum exposure, they tore a hole in the fabric of reality itself—a multiversal breach centered on Daybridge." Jake turned a page in the folder, revealing photographs of what appeared to be a laboratory in ruins, equipment twisted into impossible configurations. "The energy release collapsed the facility and fractured local reality into countless parallel versions."

"And Maxwell Hanover was at the epicenter," Robert said, remembering Gil's explanation. "He didn't die but became... integrated with the system itself. The Station Master."

"Yes. His consciousness expanded beyond his physical form, existing across all versions of Daybridge simultaneously." Jake's expression was somber. "In a twisted way, he achieved exactly what he had theorized—perception beyond singular reality constraints. But the process destroyed his humanity, transforming him into something neither fully human nor fully other."

Robert considered the implications. "And he's spent eight decades trying to complete his original objective—forcing humanity to evolve toward multiversal perception through convergence."

"Precisely. Each traveler who completes the seventh crossing and becomes integrated contributes to this goal—their quantum consciousness strengthening the connections between realities, gradually weakening the boundaries until complete convergence becomes possible."

"But we stopped him," Robert said. "Sealed the breach, prevented the convergence."

Jake closed the folder with a deliberate motion. "This time, yes. The sealing we performed was thorough—the most comprehensive containment since the original breach. The Liminal Line should no longer manifest in this specific reality."

Something in Jake's tone caught Robert's attention. "But?"

"But the Station Master exists across all probability tracks simultaneously. What we sealed was his connection to this particular version of Daybridge." Jake returned the folder to its shelf. "In other realities, other variations, his work continues."

"Could he find another way into this reality?"

"Eventually, perhaps. Though it would require considerable time and energy to establish a new connection point." Jake checked one of his monitoring instruments—a modified barometer that apparently measured dimensional pressure differentials. "For now, Daybridge-Prime remains secure. The quantum anchors Noah placed throughout the city have fully integrated with the local dimensional fabric, creating a stable network that should maintain boundary integrity for the foreseeable future."

Robert nodded, relieved but also sobered by the realization that their victory, while significant, was limited to their specific reality track. Somewhere in the multiverse, the Station Master continued his grand design, seeking convergence through other means, other travelers, other catalysts.

"What happens now?" he asked. "With me, I mean. Do I just... go back to normal life, pretending none of this happened?"

Jake studied him thoughtfully. "That depends entirely on you, Robert. Some travelers choose to compartmentalize their experiences—to return to conventional perception as completely as possible, filtering out the echoes and memory bleed-through until they fade to background noise."

"And the alternatives?"

"You could work with Dr. Voss, contributing your unique insights to her research while maintaining a connection to conventional academic frameworks." Jake paused before continuing.

"Or you could consider a more direct role in monitoring dimensional stability."

Robert raised an eyebrow. "You mean becoming a guardian?"

"Eventually, perhaps. The responsibility typically passes to those who have demonstrated both the perceptual capacity to recognize breaches and the commitment to containing them." Jake smiled slightly. "Though I have no plans to retire in the immediate future."

"I'm not sure I'm qualified for that kind of responsibility," Robert admitted. "I barely understood what was happening to me, even with Gil's guidance and your help."

"Few are prepared when they first encounter the multiverse," Jake assured him. "What matters is how you processed the experience, the choices you made when confronted with forces beyond conventional understanding."

He moved to the window, looking out at Merchant Street bathed in late afternoon sunlight. "For now, focus on reintegrating with your academic and personal life. The lingering effects of your transit experiences will continue to diminish, though some multiversal awareness will likely remain permanently—an enhanced sensitivity to quantum fluctuations that most people filter out automatically."

Robert joined him at the window, watching pedestrians move along the sidewalks, cars navigate the street, everyday life continuing in blissful ignorance of the multiverse that surrounded them, the countless probability tracks where slightly different versions of the same people made slightly different choices with vastly different outcomes.

"I'm not sure I want to lose that awareness entirely," he admitted. "As disorienting as it was, seeing beyond the conventional boundaries of reality was... illuminating. It changed my understanding of everything—not just physics, but consciousness itself, the nature of identity, the structure of existence."

Jake nodded, understanding in his expression. "That's the paradox of interdimensional transit. It traumatizes perception but expands it simultaneously. Few who have glimpsed the true nature of reality can ever be fully satisfied with the filtered version most humans experience."

They stood in companionable silence for a moment, watching the ordinary world outside—a world that had nearly dissolved into chaotic convergence just days earlier, saved by their combined efforts and Gil's sacrifice.

"I should get back to campus," Robert said finally. "Professor Liang is expecting me to analyze those anomalous simulation results."

"Of course. Though I suspect you understand the cause better than any conventional analysis could reveal." Jake walked him to the office door. "Feel free to visit anytime, Robert. And if you experience any unusual dimensional effects—anything beyond the expected echo and memory bleed-through—contact me immediately."

Robert promised he would, then made his way through the bookshop to the front entrance. As he reached for the door handle, he paused, noticing a book displayed prominently on a nearby table. The cover showed a subway station that looked remarkably similar to the ones he had traveled through—vintage design elements, constellation mosaics overhead, brass fixtures gleaming alongside worn marble tiles.

The title read: "Stations Beyond: A History of Abandoned Transit Projects in American Cities" by Maxwell Hanover, published in 1942—one year before the experiment that would transform the author into the Station Master.

Robert picked up the book, a chill running down his spine as he opened it to a random page. The text described conventional subway construction projects, but certain phrases seemed to carry double meaning when read with interdimensional awareness:

"Transit systems serve as physical manifestations of a city's connective tissue, linking not just locations but possibilities. Each station represents a node of potential—a nexus where travelers may choose between multiple trajectories, each leading to subtly different destinations despite identical route designations."

"Interesting choice," Jake said, suddenly beside him. "One of Hanover's last conventional publications before the Containment Initiative began."

"It seems... prescient," Robert observed. "As if he already understood the multiversal implications of transit systems."

"Hanover always straddled the boundary between theoretical physics and philosophical speculation." Jake took the book from Robert's hands and returned it to the display. "His insights were remarkable, even before his transformation. It's what makes the Station Master so dangerous—he combines genuine brilliance with multiversal perception and absolute conviction in his purpose."

Robert nodded, the encounter reinforcing his understanding of what they had faced—not a simple villain, but a complex entity pursuing what he genuinely believed was humanity's necessary evolution, regardless of the catastrophic means required to achieve it.

"I'll see you soon," Robert said, turning again toward the door.

"One last thing," Jake called after him. "Your roommate, Noah—he's handling this remarkably well for someone with no prior exposure to multiversal concepts. His quantum entanglement with you created a natural resistance to dimensional disorientation, but he might still experience delayed effects. Keep an eye on him."

"I will," Robert promised, making a mental note to check in with Noah more carefully than he had been.

Outside, Merchant Street bustled with late afternoon activity. Robert walked slowly toward campus, his mind processing everything he had learned from Dr. Voss and Jake. The world around him seemed simultaneously more solid and more provisional than before—a specific probability track made manifest through quantum observation, one reality among countless possibilities.

As he waited at a crosswalk, Robert noticed an elderly man in transit worker's clothing standing on the opposite corner. For a moment, his heart raced—the uniform looked remarkably similar to the Station Master's navy blue with gold buttons and trim.

But as the light changed and Robert crossed the street, he saw that it was just a regular city bus driver taking a break, his uniform similar but distinctly different from the Station Master's anachronistic attire. The echo effect playing tricks on his perception, nothing more.

Still, he found himself walking a little faster, putting distance between himself and the transit worker. Some caution was warranted, given what he now knew about the Station Master's ability to influence reality across dimensional boundaries.

As Robert approached the university campus, his phone chimed with a text from Noah:

Pizza and beer tonight? Need to talk about weird dreams I've been having. Involving subway stations that shouldn't exist.

Robert stopped mid-stride, reading the message twice to ensure he hadn't misunderstood. Noah was experiencing delayed effects from their interdimensional adventure—dream-state bleed-through from multiple reality tracks. Jake had warned this might happen, given Noah's direct involvement in the quantum resonance process that had facilitated Robert's return.

He quickly texted back: *Definitely. Home by seven. Save me a slice.*

Then, after a moment's hesitation, he added: *Has anything strange happened while you're awake? Seeing multiple versions of things, memories that don't quite fit?*

Noah's reply came almost immediately: *Not exactly. But sometimes buildings look wrong for a second before settling back to normal. And yesterday I could have sworn I saw a woman walking through Miller Hall who vanished when I blinked. Maybe we both got that food poisoning, huh?*

The attempt at humor didn't mask the underlying concern in Noah's message. Robert replied with reassurance that they'd talk it through that evening, then continued toward the science building with renewed purpose.

Noah's experiences confirmed what both Jake and Dr. Voss had suggested—that involvement in interdimensional events could leave lasting perceptual changes, even in someone who hadn't personally traversed the Liminal Line. The quantum entanglement between them had apparently created a bleed-through effect, allowing Noah to glimpse aspects of the multiverse that conventional perception filtered out automatically.

As Robert entered the science building and made his way to his laboratory, he found himself wondering how many others in Daybridge might be experiencing similar effects—subtle perceptual anomalies that they would likely dismiss as imagination or fatigue, never realizing they were actually glimpsing the true nature of a reality far more complex than most would ever comprehend.

The quantum tunneling simulation awaited his attention, its anomalous results now perfectly comprehensible to him, though he could never publish the true explanation. He would need to develop a conventional theoretical framework that could account for the observed phenomena without referencing interdimensional breaches or multiversal convergence.

But as he settled at his workstation and began reviewing the data, Robert felt a new sense of purpose beyond academic achievement. He had glimpsed the underlying structure of reality—had traveled through it, had helped prevent its collapse into chaotic convergence.

That knowledge changed everything, reshaping his understanding of his research, his future, and his place in a multiverse of infinite possibilities.

The subway that wasn't there had taken him on a journey beyond imagination. And though the entrance had vanished, sealed by Jake's interdimensional countermeasures, the memory of that impossible transit system would remain—a reminder that beneath the seemingly solid surface of reality lay mysteries still waiting to be discovered.

And somewhere in the spaces between worlds, in the threshold where all possibilities converged, the Station Master continued his patient work—waiting, planning, seeking another opportunity to complete his grand design. The pattern had been interrupted but not broken, the sequence delayed but not abandoned.

The veil between worlds had thinned, then been reinforced. But once glimpsed, the multiverse could never be unseen—its infinite branches extending through probability space in endless variation, a tree of possibilities with roots in quantum uncertainty and branches reaching toward futures not yet manifest.

Robert North had returned from his journey between worlds, but he carried with him knowledge that few humans had ever possessed—and the subtle echoes of experiences across multiple realities that would forever influence his perception of the world around him.

The adventure that had begun with a simple subway entrance on a rainy night had transformed him in ways that could never be reversed. And perhaps, in time, that transformation would lead him back to the threshold between worlds—not as an accidental traveler, but as someone with purpose and understanding, ready to face whatever mysteries the multiverse might reveal.

CHAPTER ELEVEN: RACING AGAINST TIME

One week after the sealing of the interdimensional breach, Robert stood at his apartment window, watching raindrops trace patterns down the glass. The weather matched his mood—contemplative, unsettled, caught between states.

His life had ostensibly returned to normal. He attended classes, worked in the laboratory, met with Professor Liang to discuss his research. He had even managed to develop a conventional theoretical framework that explained the anomalous quantum tunneling results without referencing interdimensional breaches.

But nothing felt truly normal anymore. The lingering awareness of the multiverse colored every experience, every interaction. He found himself constantly noticing probability branches—moments where reality could have diverged along different paths based on seemingly inconsequential choices or events.

Noah had been experiencing similar effects, though less intensely. His dreams continued to feature subway stations and copper trains, and occasionally while awake he would see brief overlays of alternative configurations—buildings that momentarily appeared in different architectural styles, people who flickered between multiple versions of themselves.

Jake had assured them both that these perceptual anomalies would gradually diminish as their quantum signatures realigned more completely with Daybridge-Prime. But Robert wasn't entirely sure he wanted them to fade. The expanded awareness, despite its occasionally disorienting effects, felt like a valuable insight into reality's true nature.

A knock at his bedroom door interrupted his thoughts.

"Come in," he called, turning from the window.

Noah entered, carrying two mugs of coffee. "Thought you might need this. You were up late again."

Robert accepted the mug gratefully. "Thanks. Just working through some calculations for the new theoretical model."

"At three in the morning?" Noah raised an eyebrow as he leaned against the doorframe. "Must be some calculations."

Robert shrugged, not wanting to admit he'd actually been awake because of increasingly vivid dreams featuring the Station Master—dreams where the enigmatic entity continued to offer him insights into multiversal mechanics while attempting to convince him that convergence was inevitable, merely delayed rather than prevented.

"How are your dreams?" he asked instead, changing the subject. "Still riding the quantum subway?"

"Less frequently," Noah admitted. "Though last night was... different." He hesitated before continuing. "I saw Gil. He was trying to tell me something important, but I couldn't quite hear him. The station was shaking, falling apart around him."

Robert felt a chill that had nothing to do with the rainy weather. "Gil? You're sure?"

"Bearded guy, intense blue eyes, wearing clothes that don't quite match? Yeah, I'm sure." Noah sipped his coffee. "I've never met him, but I've seen him clearly in these dreams. Last night he seemed... urgent. Desperate to communicate something."

This was troubling. Noah shouldn't be having detailed dreams about someone he'd never met, especially not with new content that suggested active communication rather than simple memory bleed-through.

"I should tell Jake about this," Robert said, reaching for his phone. "It could indicate ongoing dimensional permeability despite the sealing."

"Already texted him," Noah replied. "He wants us both to come by the shop this afternoon. Said he's detected some 'concerning fluctuation patterns' over the past forty-eight hours."

Robert nodded, both worried and oddly relieved. The persistent dreams might indicate problems with the dimensional sealing, but they also suggested Gil had survived in some form—that his sacrifice in Central Nexus hadn't resulted in complete obliteration.

"What time does he want to meet?"

"Three o'clock. I've got class until two-thirty, so I'll meet you there." Noah checked his watch. "Speaking of which, I should get going. Advanced Pathophysiology waits for no man."

After Noah left, Robert returned to the window, watching the rain intensify. Lightning flashed in the distance, followed seconds later by rumbling thunder—a proper autumn storm building over Daybridge.

The weather reminded him uncomfortably of the night he'd first discovered the Liminal Line's entrance on Thornfield Avenue. Was it coincidence, or did interdimensional phenomena correlate with certain meteorological conditions? Dr. Kwan's book had suggested that electrical storms could temporarily enhance dimensional permeability, creating natural alignment points between reality tracks.

Robert's phone chimed with a text from Dr. Voss:

Unusual quantum fluctuations detected at multiple monitoring stations. Similar to pre-convergence patterns but smaller amplitude. Available to discuss at my lab?

So Jake wasn't the only one detecting anomalies. Robert quickly replied that he would visit her laboratory after meeting with Jake, then gathered his research materials. If dimensional instability was recurring despite the sealing, he wanted to be prepared with the most current data from his quantum tunneling experiments.

The storm had intensified by the time Robert left for campus, rain falling in sheets that reduced visibility to mere yards. Lightning struck with increasing frequency, accompanied by thunder that seemed to shake the very air. Few pedestrians braved the downpour, and those who did hurried with heads down, seeking the nearest shelter.

As Robert passed the intersection of Maple and Fifth, a strange sensation washed over him—a momentary doubling of perception that was stronger than the usual echo effect he'd experienced since returning from threshold reality. For an instant, he saw the street as it existed in multiple configurations simultaneously: the current layout with the stoplight on the southwest corner, but also a version where the light stood on the northeast corner, and another where no light existed at all but a traffic circle occupied the center of the intersection.

The vision lasted only seconds before resolving back to normal, but it left Robert deeply unsettled. That level of perceptual overlay shouldn't be possible after the sealing of the breach. Something was weakening the dimensional boundaries again.

He quickened his pace, arriving at the science building just as another lightning strike illuminated the campus. Inside, he shook water from his coat and made his way directly to his laboratory, intending to check his quantum tunneling simulation before meeting with Dr. Voss.

The lab was empty at this hour, most graduate students sensibly avoiding campus during the storm. Robert powered up his equipment and initiated a standard measurement sequence, watching carefully as the system tracked the quantum states of his experimental particles.

The results were immediately concerning. The particles were once again showing signs of persistent superposition—maintaining multiple quantum states simultaneously even after repeated observation events. This was exactly the behavior they had exhibited just before the convergence crisis.

Robert documented the anomalous results, then shut down the equipment and headed to Dr. Voss's laboratory on the floor above. Her quantum coherence research occupied a significantly larger space than his modest experimental setup, filled with sophisticated monitoring equipment and detection arrays.

Dr. Voss herself stood before a wall-sized display showing a map of Daybridge overlaid with colored patterns that shifted constantly—a real-time visualization of quantum fluctuation intensity throughout the city.

"Ah, Robert," she said without turning, having somehow sensed his entrance. "Thank you for coming. The patterns are most concerning."

Robert approached the display, immediately recognizing similarities to the pre-convergence measurements Jake had shown him. "It looks like dimensional bleed-through, but less intense than before."

"For now," Dr. Voss agreed. "But the amplitude is increasing steadily. Compare the readings from this morning to those from forty-eight hours ago."

She tapped a command into the nearby console, and the display split to show a side-by-side comparison. The difference was striking—what had been barely perceptible fluctuations two days ago had intensified to significant dimensional instability, particularly around specific locations.

"These bright spots," Robert said, pointing to several intense concentrations of activity. "They're at the same locations as before—the convergence points where the boundaries were thinnest."

"Precisely. The quantum anchors at those locations are still functioning, but their effectiveness appears to be diminishing." Dr.

Voss adjusted the display to show a time-lapse of the past week. "The pattern suggests something is actively working to counter the sealing effect—not a natural deterioration of the dimensional boundaries but a deliberate attempt to reestablish connections."

"The Station Master," Robert murmured. "He's trying to reopen the breach."

"That would be my assessment as well." Dr. Voss turned to face him directly. "Your dreams have featured him recently, haven't they?"

Robert started, surprised by her perception. "Yes. How did you know?"

"Because mine have too, as have those of several other individuals I monitor who have had contact with the interdimensional transit system." She moved to another console, bringing up a series of brain scan images. "These show distinctive patterns of quantum entanglement within the neural structures of former travelers—patterns that intensify during dream states, creating a potential communication channel across dimensional boundaries."

"He's using our dreams to reestablish contact," Robert realized. "Weakening the sealing from multiple points simultaneously."

"With a particular focus on you." Dr. Voss highlighted one set of brain scans that showed significantly more intense activity than the others. "Your quantum signature remains especially resonant with the breach frequency. You're still a catalyst, Robert, even after returning to your origin reality."

The implications were disturbing. His very presence in Daybridge-Prime might be contributing to the weakening of dimensional boundaries, regardless of his conscious intentions.

"What can we do to counter this?" he asked.

"Jake Steinman has been implementing additional stabilization measures at the most vulnerable convergence points," Dr. Voss replied. "But permanent resolution may require more drastic intervention."

Before she could elaborate, a tremendous thunderclap shook the building, causing lights to flicker momentarily. Both scientists looked toward the windows, where rain lashed against the glass with increasing ferocity.

"This storm isn't natural," Dr. Voss observed. "The electrical discharge patterns show quantum characteristics consistent with interdimensional energy transfer."

As if to confirm her assessment, lightning struck the research building itself, the flash momentarily blinding even through the tinted windows. The lights went out completely, plunging the laboratory into darkness broken only by the emergency exit signs and the glow from battery-backed monitoring equipment.

"Backup generators should activate momentarily," Dr. Voss said calmly, moving to check her primary instruments.

But instead of the expected hum of generators coming online, a different sound filled the darkened lab—a familiar pneumatic hiss that sent chills down Robert's spine.

"That sounds like..." he began.

"A subway door opening," Dr. Voss finished, her voice tight with tension. "Impossible. There's no station entrance in this building."

Yet as their eyes adjusted to the darkness, both could see a faint glow emanating from what had been a solid wall moments earlier. The outline of a subway entrance gradually took form—iron railings curving downward, warm light spilling up from below.

"The Liminal Line is manifesting directly," Robert whispered. "I've never seen it create a new entrance point before."

"It shouldn't be possible with the quantum anchors still active," Dr. Voss agreed, moving cautiously toward the anomaly. "This represents a significant escalation in breach dynamics."

Robert followed her, both drawn and repelled by the impossible entrance. As they approached, the familiar scent of ozone and brass polish wafted up from below, accompanied by the distant rumble of an approaching train.

"We should contact Jake immediately," Robert said, reaching for his phone only to find it dead—all electronic devices apparently affected by the unusual lightning strike.

Dr. Voss nodded, keeping her distance from the entrance. "This manifestation is specifically targeted. The Station Master is reaching out directly, using the storm's electrical energy to temporarily override the sealing parameters."

The rumbling grew louder, and both scientists instinctively stepped back as the sound of a train arriving echoed up from the ghostly station below. The pneumatic hiss of doors opening carried clearly into the laboratory.

Then a voice called from within the entrance—not the Station Master's resonant tones, but a familiar gruff voice that Robert had never expected to hear again.

"North! Can you hear me? The connection is temporary—we need to communicate quickly!"

"Gil?" Robert moved closer to the entrance, peering down into the warm light. "Gil Harmon?"

"Yes!" The voice sounded strained, as if speaking required tremendous effort. "Listen carefully. The Station Master has found another approach. Instead of forcing convergence directly, he's attempting to create a cascade effect through parallel breaches in adjacent realities."

"Simultaneous breaches across multiple Daybridges," Dr. Voss murmured, understanding immediately. "Collapsing probability tracks sequentially rather than simultaneously."

"Exactly," Gil confirmed. "The sealing you performed was effective for your specific reality track, but he's working around it by initiating convergence in neighboring probability vectors. When those collapse, the quantum pressure on your reality will increase exponentially."

"Like dominoes," Robert said. "Each collapsing reality increases the instability in adjacent tracks."

"Precisely. He's already triggered the process in three neighboring realities. Their dimensional boundaries are failing rapidly." Gil's voice grew more urgent. "You need to reinforce your sealing parameters immediately, focusing on probability insulation rather than simple breach containment."

"The quantum anchors," Dr. Voss said. "They're configured for local stability, not cross-dimensional reinforcement."

"Yes. They need recalibration to create a probability shield around your entire reality track." Gil's voice began to fade, the connection clearly weakening. "The adjustment sequence is epsilon-theta-prime-seven-three..."

His voice cut out as the entrance flickered, the outlines becoming less distinct as the dimensional connection deteriorated.

"Gil!" Robert called. "We didn't get the full sequence!"

The entrance stabilized momentarily, but instead of Gil's voice, they heard another sound—a rhythmic, mechanical clicking accompanied by the measured tread of formal shoes on marble stairs.

"The Station Master," Robert whispered, backing away. "He's detected the connection."

The clicking grew louder, and a white-gloved hand appeared on the iron railing, followed gradually by the familiar figure in his navy uniform with gold buttons and trim. The Station Master ascended partially into view, remaining on the steps rather than fully entering the laboratory.

"Catalyst," he greeted Robert, his perfect symmetrical smile unchanged despite the dimensional boundaries between them. "Our connection persists despite the guardian's efforts. Most satisfactory."

His gaze shifted to Dr. Voss, recognition evident in his expression. "Dr. Abigail Voss. We meet at last, though I have observed your work with interest for many years. Your quantum coherence research has proven unexpectedly useful to my purposes."

Dr. Voss maintained a composed expression despite the unsettling encounter. "Maxwell Hanover. Or what remains of him."

"What transcended him," the Station Master corrected smoothly. "As all consciousness must eventually transcend its initial limitations."

He turned his attention back to Robert. "The Wanderer attempts to interfere again, I see. Gilbert Harmon never understood that delay merely increases the inevitable disruption when probability tracks realign. The convergence cannot be prevented—only postponed at increasing cost."

"You're triggering collapses in adjacent realities," Robert said. "Sacrificing entire probability tracks to force convergence in ours."

"Not sacrifice—transformation. Those realities are not being destroyed, merely evolved into their next configuration." The Station Master adjusted his white gloves with mechanical precision. "The process you interrupted required recalibration, but proceeds according to essential parameters."

Lightning flashed again outside the windows, and the subway entrance flickered in response. The Station Master glanced upward, momentary concern crossing his perfect features.

"Our connection window closes," he observed. "But before it does, I offer you the same choice as before, Catalyst. Join me willingly. Accept your role in the probability matrix. Your consciousness has already begun the transformation—the persistent awareness of multiple states simultaneously, the dreams that transcend dimensional boundaries, the growing dissatisfaction with filtered perception."

Robert felt a chill at how accurately the Station Master had assessed his internal experience since returning to Daybridge-Prime. He had indeed found conventional perception increasingly limited, frustratingly narrow compared to the expanded awareness he had glimpsed.

"The convergence will proceed with or without your conscious participation," the Station Master continued. "But willing integration would be significantly less traumatic for you—and for those quantum entangled with you."

The implied threat to Noah was unmistakable. Robert felt a surge of anger, stepping forward despite Dr. Voss's warning hand on his arm.

"You can't reach us directly anymore," he challenged. "The breach is sealed. The quantum anchors maintain dimensional stability throughout Daybridge."

The Station Master's smile remained unchanged, but something cold entered his eyes. "For now. But anchors can be uprooted, seals broken, stability undermined. Particularly when the catalyst himself harbors growing resonance with multiversal reality."

Another lightning strike, closer this time, caused the lights to flicker back to life momentarily before failing again. The subway entrance began to fade, the connection weakening rapidly.

"Consider your position carefully, Catalyst," the Station Master said, his form becoming translucent as the entrance deteriorated. "The guardian cannot maintain your reality's isolation indefinitely. When probability pressure from collapsing adjacent tracks reaches a critical threshold, you will face the convergence regardless of preparation."

His voice faded to an echo as the entrance dissolved completely, leaving only a solid laboratory wall where the ghostly staircase had been.

In the sudden silence, emergency generators finally activated, bringing low-level lighting back to the laboratory. Dr. Voss moved immediately to her monitoring equipment, checking readings with focused intensity.

"The quantum fluctuations have intensified by thirty percent just during that brief manifestation," she reported grimly. "The Station Master was able to directly influence our local dimensional fabric despite the sealing parameters."

Robert joined her at the console, studying the patterns with growing concern. "The convergence points are showing particularly high instability. If what Gil said is accurate, we're experiencing bleed-through effects from adjacent realities that are already beginning to collapse."

"We need to contact Jake immediately," Dr. Voss said, moving to a landline phone that had remained functional through the power outage. "The quantum anchors must be recalibrated for cross-dimensional reinforcement before the cascade effect reaches critical threshold."

As she dialed, Robert reviewed the fluctuation data more carefully, noticing a pattern he hadn't initially recognized. "The instability isn't uniform. It's concentrating specifically around locations where I crossed between realities during my journey through the Liminal Line."

"Your transit points maintain quantum entanglement with your specific signature," Dr. Voss explained as she waited for Jake to answer. "They're naturally more susceptible to resonance effects targeted toward you."

She spoke briefly into the phone, explaining the situation in technical terminology that suggested long familiarity with interdimensional breach mechanics. After a moment, she held the receiver out to Robert.

"Jake wants to speak with you directly."

Robert took the phone. "Jake? We've just had direct contact with both Gil and the Station Master. A temporary breach formed directly in Dr. Voss's laboratory during the storm."

"I detected the energy spike," Jake replied, his voice tense. "This represents a significant escalation. The Station Master shouldn't be able to manifest connections through the quantum anchor network."

"Gil said something about adjacent realities collapsing—creating a cascade effect that will eventually overcome our dimensional stability regardless of local sealing measures."

"Yes, I've detected evidence of that process beginning. Three neighboring probability tracks are showing critical instability patterns." Jake's tone grew more urgent. "Did Gil provide recalibration parameters for the quantum anchors?"

"He started to, but the connection failed before he could complete the sequence. He said 'epsilon-theta-prime-seven-three' before cutting out."

Jake was silent for a moment, and Robert could hear pages turning rapidly. "That's a partial interdimensional insulation protocol. I can extrapolate the remainder based on standard guardian sequences, but implementation will be challenging under current conditions."

"What do you need us to do?"

"Meet me at Möbius Square immediately. It's the focal point of the quantum anchor network and the location where dimensional pressure will manifest most intensely when adjacent realities begin to collapse."

"Möbius Square is miles from campus," Robert pointed out. "With this storm and the power outages, transportation will be difficult."

"Dr. Voss has emergency protocols for precisely this situation," Jake replied. "Implement Protocol Threshold immediately. I'll meet you at the convergence point in thirty minutes."

The line went dead, and Robert returned the phone to Dr. Voss. "He said to implement 'Protocol Threshold' and meet him at Möbius Square as soon as possible."

Dr. Voss nodded grimly, moving to a cabinet secured with both electronic and mechanical locks. She deactivated the electronic system using her security credentials, then entered a complex mechanical combination.

"Protocol Threshold was established after my own encounters with the Liminal Line," she explained as the cabinet opened. "It provides emergency transit capabilities in case of dimensional instability events that prevent conventional transportation."

From within the cabinet, she removed what appeared to be two silver discs identical to the one Noah had used during the previous convergence crisis. She handed one to Robert.

"Quantum resonance transporters," she explained. "They allow directed dimensional sliding within a single reality track—essentially, short-range teleportation utilizing the same principles that govern the Liminal Line, but constrained to prevent cross-reality transit."

Robert accepted the disc, which felt unexpectedly warm against his palm. "I didn't know such technology existed."

"It's experimental and extremely limited in application. The energy requirements are prohibitive for anything beyond emergency use, and the process is... unpleasant." Dr. Voss removed two additional devices from the cabinet—small cylinders that resembled oversized pills. "Stabilizers. Swallow this before transport. It helps maintain physical coherence during the process."

Robert accepted the stabilizer, examining it dubiously. "Is this safe?"

"Safer than remaining here while reality collapses around us," Dr. Voss replied pragmatically. "The storm is intensifying, and conventional transportation routes will be increasingly unreliable as dimensional bleed-through accelerates."

As if to emphasize her point, another massive lightning strike hit nearby, the thunder immediate and deafening. Through the laboratory windows, they could see that the campus was now completely dark, emergency lighting providing the only illumination in surrounding buildings.

"How exactly does this transport system work?" Robert asked, studying the silver disc.

"Focus on your destination—Möbius Square—while maintaining physical contact with the disc. The quantum resonance field will align your molecular structure with the corresponding location, essentially moving you through probability space rather than physical space." Dr. Voss swallowed her stabilizer without hesitation. "The process takes approximately thirty seconds of subjective time, though external observation would register it as instantaneous."

Robert followed her example, swallowing the stabilizer despite his reservations. It dissolved immediately upon contact with his tongue, spreading a cool numbness throughout his body.

"That's the preliminary molecular stabilization taking effect," Dr. Voss explained. "It prevents cellular disruption during quantum realignment."

She moved to the center of the laboratory, holding her silver disc at chest level with both hands. "We should transit simultaneously. Focus completely on Möbius Square—visualize it in as much detail as possible. The more precise your mental image, the more accurate the spatial targeting."

Robert joined her, holding his disc as she demonstrated. He closed his eyes, concentrating on his memory of Möbius Square—the distinctive spiral pattern in the pavement, the three boulevards that intersected there, the central fountain with its abstract sculpture.

"On my mark," Dr. Voss said quietly. "Three... two... one... initiate."

Robert felt the silver disc grow suddenly hot against his palms. A tingling sensation spread rapidly from his hands throughout his entire body, reminiscent of the echo effect but far more intense—as if every cell were vibrating at a frequency just beyond perception.

The sensation intensified, becoming momentarily uncomfortable as the vibration increased. Then came a disorienting shift in his awareness of space—a feeling of simultaneously expanding beyond his physical boundaries and contracting to a singular point of consciousness.

For a subjective eternity that probably lasted mere seconds, Robert existed as pure quantum potential—a probability wave rather than a physical entity, spread across a limited spectrum of spatial coordinates all centered on his targeted destination.

Then, with a sensation like reality snapping back into focus, he rematerialized. The process was not gentle—he fell to his knees on hard pavement, nausea and disorientation overwhelming him momentarily as his consciousness realigned with his physical form.

"Breathe deeply," Dr. Voss advised beside him, looking only slightly less affected by the transport. "The disorientation passes quickly."

Robert followed her suggestion, taking slow, deliberate breaths as his perception stabilized. They had indeed arrived at Möbius Square, though the elegant urban plaza barely resembled its normal appearance.

The storm raged with supernatural intensity here, lightning striking repeatedly around the perimeter of the square. The distinctive spiral pattern in the pavement glowed with an eerie blue luminescence, pulsing in rhythm with the lightning strikes. Most disturbing, the air itself seemed unstable—rippling like the surface of disturbed water, occasionally showing glimpses of other configurations of the same location as seen from different reality tracks.

"Dimensional bleed-through has progressed further than anticipated," Dr. Voss observed, helping Robert to his feet. "The quantum anchor at this location is barely maintaining coherence."

She pointed to a small device installed at the center of the spiral pattern—one of the quantum anchors Noah had placed during the previous crisis. It glowed with the same blue luminescence as the pavement, but the light flickered erratically, suggesting failing power or effectiveness.

"Where's Jake?" Robert asked, scanning the deserted square. The storm had driven away any pedestrians who might normally have been present, leaving the space eerily empty except for themselves.

"He'll be coming from his shop on Merchant Street. Even with quantum transport, the precision targeting decreases with distance." Dr. Voss checked a device on her wrist that resembled a watch but displayed incomprehensible symbols rather than time. "Probability fluctuations are intensifying. We have perhaps twenty minutes before adjacent reality collapse begins affecting local dimensional stability."

As they moved toward the center of the spiral pattern, Robert noticed something disturbing—ghostly figures occasionally visible around the perimeter of the square. They resembled pedestrians but appeared translucent, their movements jerky and unnatural, as if viewed through a failing video connection.

"Bleed-through entities," Dr. Voss explained, following his gaze. "Echoes of people from adjacent realities already experiencing convergence effects. They're not physically present in our reality—merely quantum impressions pushing through weakened dimensional boundaries."

The ghostly figures seemed unaware of Robert and Dr. Voss, moving in patterns that suggested normal urban activities from their original reality tracks. Some walked in groups, others alone, occasionally passing directly through solid objects in the square without apparent awareness.

"They look like the residents of Threshold reality," Robert observed. "Partially transparent, existing in multiple states simultaneously."

"In a sense, that's exactly what they're becoming," Dr. Voss agreed. "As their home realities collapse, they're transitioning toward the threshold state—existing across multiple probability tracks simultaneously as distinct reality frameworks break down."

They reached the quantum anchor at the center of the spiral. Up close, Robert could see that the device was indeed failing—its housing had developed hairline fractures through which blue energy leaked like luminous smoke, dissipating into the storm-charged air.

"Can we repair it?" he asked, kneeling to examine the damage more closely.

"Not without Jake's specialized equipment. This is merely a symptom of the larger problem." Dr. Voss consulted her wrist device again. "The anchor network was designed for localized dimensional stabilization within a single reality track. It's not configured to withstand cross-dimensional pressure from collapsing adjacent realities."

A flash of blue light near the northern entrance to the square caught their attention. Jake Steinman materialized from the quantum transport effect with considerably more grace than they had managed, maintaining his balance despite the disorienting transition.

He carried a leather case that Robert recognized as containing guardian equipment and wore an expression of grim determination as he approached them through the storm.

"The cascade effect has accelerated beyond my initial calculations," he said without preamble. "Three adjacent reality tracks have already collapsed completely. Their probability energy is transferring to neighboring tracks, including ours."

"Can the quantum anchor network be recalibrated to withstand the pressure?" Dr. Voss asked.

"Potentially, with the proper adjustment sequence." Jake knelt beside the failing anchor, opening his case to reveal an array of specialized tools and components. "Gil provided the beginning of the necessary protocol. I've extrapolated the remaining parameters based on standard guardian sequences, but implementation carries significant risks."

"What kind of risks?" Robert asked.

"The recalibration creates a probability shield around our entire reality track—essentially isolating us from the multiverse temporarily while adjacent realities collapse and restabilize." Jake selected several tools from his case. "But complete isolation has consequences. Some probability functions might be permanently altered, changing subtle aspects of our reality in unpredictable ways."

"Better than complete convergence," Dr. Voss noted pragmatically.

"Agreed. But there's another, more immediate concern." Jake looked up from the quantum anchor, his expression grave. "The recalibration requires simultaneous adjustment of all eight anchors in the network. One person must remain here at the central node to coordinate the process, but the other anchors need physical adjustment as well."

"We'll split up," Dr. Voss said immediately. "How many locations can we cover with three people?"

"Not enough. We need eight simultaneous adjustments, precisely coordinated." Jake removed a device from his case that resembled an antique telegraph key attached to a small brass box.

"This will control the central node and synchronize the network, but the other seven anchors require direct manipulation at their specific locations."

Robert understood the problem immediately. "We need more help."

"Yes. I've contacted Noah, who's already en route to the anchor at Crescent Park. And I've reached out to several other individuals in Daybridge who have had contact with the Liminal Line and maintain sufficient quantum awareness to assist." Jake began connecting his device to the failing anchor. "But communication is difficult under current conditions. I can't confirm they've received the message or understand what's required."

The storm intensified around them, lightning now striking continuously around the perimeter of the square. The ghostly figures of bleed-through entities had increased in number and definition, some now appearing almost solid enough to interact with physical objects.

More disturbing, the reality fluctuations had worsened. The buildings surrounding the square shifted between multiple architectural configurations, streets visible through the gaps between them rearranged themselves continuously, and even the sky above showed patches where other atmospheric conditions bled through—glimpses of sunshine, snowfall, and strange colored mists all visible simultaneously through rifts in the storm clouds.

"How much time do we have?" Robert asked, watching as a section of pavement briefly transformed into grass before returning to concrete.

"Less than fifteen minutes before cascade failure begins affecting our reality irreversibly," Jake replied, focused on his adjustments to the central anchor. "The dimensional pressure is building exponentially as each adjacent track collapses."

Dr. Voss consulted her wrist device again, her expression growing more concerned. "The probability curve is steepening faster than projected. We may have even less time."

Jake completed his connection to the central anchor, the telegraph key now glowing with the same blue luminescence as the device itself. "I need to remain here to coordinate the network recalibration. Dr. Voss, can you take the eastern node at Riverside Junction?"

"Yes. I know the location and the necessary adjustments." She accepted a small tool that resembled a tuning fork from Jake's case.

"Robert, you'll need to take the western node at Thornfield Avenue—the location where you first encountered the Liminal Line." Jake handed him an identical tool and a small device that resembled a pocket watch. "This will indicate when to make the adjustment. When the needle reaches the red mark, turn the resonator key clockwise until it clicks three times, then counterclockwise until the blue light stabilizes."

Robert accepted the tools, trying to memorize the instructions despite the chaotic conditions around them. "What about the other five locations?"

"Noah has Crescent Park. I've sent messages to Dr. Eleanor Kwan for the university node, Marcus Chen for the hospital location, and several others who've shown quantum sensitivity in the past." Jake checked his own timepiece. "We initiate in exactly twelve minutes, regardless of confirmation from all locations. Partial network recalibration is better than none at all under current circumstances."

As Robert prepared to depart for the western node, a particularly violent lightning strike hit the center of the square, the bolt connecting directly with the failing quantum anchor. Blue energy surged through the spiral pattern in the pavement, momentarily stabilizing the reality fluctuations before fading again.

In that brief moment of dimensional clarity, a figure appeared at the southern entrance to the square—not a bleed-through entity but a solid, physically present individual. Robert recognized him immediately despite the distance.

"Gil?" he called, shock and hope mingling in his voice.

The bearded physicist staggered slightly as he entered the square, his form occasionally blurring at the edges but undeniably present in their reality. He wore the same tattered clothes Robert remembered from threshold reality, though they appeared partially burned or damaged.

Jake turned sharply at Robert's exclamation, equal surprise evident in his expression. "Gilbert Harmon? That's impossible. He remained in threshold reality when the breach was sealed."

"The cascade effect," Dr. Voss suggested, already moving toward the newcomer. "Collapsing adjacent realities are creating temporary bridges between dimensional states."

Gil spotted them and changed direction, moving with obvious effort toward the central spiral. As he drew closer, Robert could see that his condition was poor—his face gaunt, his movements pained, his entire being seeming to require tremendous effort to maintain coherence in this reality.

"The sequence," he gasped as he reached them, his voice ragged. "Epsilon-theta-prime-seven-three-omega-delta-sigma.   Full probability insulation requires all eight parameters in precise order."

"Gil," Robert said, still struggling to believe the physicist had somehow returned from threshold reality. "How did you get here? We sealed the breach."

"Dimensional pressure from collapsing adjacents created temporary transit opportunities," Gil explained, each word clearly requiring effort. "I've been tracking the cascade effect from threshold, attempting to identify intervention points before total convergence manifests."

Jake had already incorporated the complete sequence into his control device, making rapid adjustments based on Gil's information. "This completes the protocol. With all eight parameters properly sequenced, the probability shield should maintain integrity despite adjacent collapse."

"Not without simultaneous activation at all nodes," Gil cautioned, leaning heavily against the central sculpture to remain upright. "The shield generates from intersection points in the dimensional fabric. All eight must transition simultaneously or the effect fails."

"We're still missing confirmed operators at three locations," Jake said grimly.

Gil straightened with visible effort. "I can take the southern node at Central Hospital. My quantum signature is already diffuse enough to withstand the transition effects."

"You're barely maintaining coherence in this reality," Dr. Voss objected. "The strain of additional dimensional manipulation could—"

"Is irrelevant," Gil interrupted firmly. "My physical form has limited remaining duration regardless of current actions. Better to utilize it constructively while possible."

The practical fatalism in his tone silenced further objections. Jake nodded once, accepting Gil's decision, and handed him the necessary tools from his case.

"That still leaves two locations without confirmed operators," Robert pointed out.

"I'll take a second location," Dr. Voss decided. "With quantum transport, I can activate the eastern node, then immediately transit to the northern position at Veterans Park."

"The timing would be exceptionally tight," Jake cautioned. "Even with instantaneous transport, the adjustment process requires at least thirty seconds of precise manipulation."

"Then we adjust the sequence timing accordingly," she replied. "Delay the network synchronization by thirty seconds after my first activation to allow for the secondary positioning."

Jake considered this, then nodded reluctantly. "It could work, though with reduced effectiveness. The probability shield would form with a minor structural weakness at the junction point."

"Better than catastrophic failure at two nodes," Gil noted, already checking the tools Jake had provided him.

"That still leaves the southeastern node at Alexander Plaza without an operator," Robert said.

Before anyone could propose a solution, another figure materialized at the eastern entrance to the square—not through quantum transport but by a conventional approach, running through the storm with determination. As the figure drew closer, Robert recognized Noah, soaked from the rain but moving with purpose.

"Jake!" Noah called as he reached them. "Crescent Park anchor is completely non-functional. The housing has cracked open, and the internal components are melting down."

Jake's expression grew even more concerned at this news. "That leaves two non-operational nodes, creating a dangerous asymmetry in the probability shield."

"What about reconfiguring the network to function with six nodes instead of eight?" Robert suggested. "Adjusting the resonance pattern to compensate for the missing points?"

Gil shook his head. "Impossible with current equipment. The network geometry is fixed by the underlying dimensional structure of Daybridge itself. Eight points or none."

The situation seemed increasingly desperate. Without all eight nodes functioning properly, the probability shield would fail to form completely, leaving their reality vulnerable to the cascade effect from collapsing adjacent tracks.

Then Noah spoke up again. "What about the Station Master?"
Everyone turned to him in surprise.

"Explain," Jake prompted.

"In my dreams recently, he's been... different. Less focused on convergence, more concerned with maintaining some form of structured reality." Noah looked uncomfortable under their collective gaze but continued. "He keeps saying that 'uncontrolled collapse serves no purpose' and that 'evolution requires stability within transformation.'"

"He's recognizing that complete multiversal collapse would destroy the system itself," Gil said thoughtfully. "Including his own existence across probability tracks."

"Could we use that?" Robert asked. "Appeal to his self-preservation instinct?"

"It's a significant risk," Jake warned. "Any direct communication with the Station Master creates an opportunity for interdimensional manipulation."

"But he exists across all probability vectors," Dr. Voss pointed out. "If anyone can stabilize multiple nodes simultaneously, it would be him."

They all exchanged uncertain glances, weighing the desperate circumstances against the danger of involving an entity that had previously attempted to force catastrophic dimensional convergence.

"I can reach him," Robert said finally. "He's been appearing in my dreams consistently, attempting to reestablish a connection. If I open that channel deliberately, I might be able to communicate our proposal."

"It's too dangerous," Jake objected. "Your quantum signature is still highly resonant with the breach frequency. Direct connection could trigger premature collapse or allow the Station Master access to our reality despite the sealing."

"We don't have alternatives," Gil countered, checking a device on his wrist similar to Dr. Voss's. "Dimensional pressure is approaching critical threshold. In approximately nine minutes, cascade failure will begin affecting our reality irreversibly, with or without the probability shield."

Jake considered this grim assessment, then nodded reluctantly. "Very well. But we establish strict parameters for the communication. Robert, you'll remain here at the central node with me. Your connection to the Station Master must be carefully controlled and terminated immediately after the necessary agreement is secured."

He removed another device from his case—a circlet of copper wire similar to the one Gil had provided for dream navigation in threshold reality.

"This will allow directed communication across dimensional boundaries without full transit of consciousness," Jake explained, handing the circlet to Robert. "It creates a limited connection that I can monitor and terminate if necessary."

Robert accepted the device, recognizing both the opportunity and danger it represented. Deliberately establishing contact with the Station Master after their previous confrontations carried significant risk, but the alternative—allowing reality to collapse around them—was unquestionably worse.

"What exactly am I offering him?" Robert asked as he placed the circlet on his head.

"Structured transition rather than chaotic collapse," Gil suggested. "The probability shield won't prevent all changes to our reality, but it will maintain basic coherence through the cascade effect. That serves his long-term goal of perceptual evolution better than uncontrolled dimensional failure."

Jake made final adjustments to the circlet, connecting it to the central anchor control device with a thin wire. "You'll have approximately three minutes of connection time before the strain becomes dangerous to your neural structure. Make them count."

With the parameters established, the team prepared to move to their respective positions. Dr. Voss would take both the eastern and northern nodes, Gil the southern node, and Noah would attempt to repair the damaged anchor at Crescent Park if possible, or else serve as backup for another location.

"Synchronize timepieces," Jake instructed, checking his pocket watch against the others' devices. "Initial activation in eight minutes, seventeen seconds. Robert's communication attempt begins immediately. If successful, network recalibration will proceed as planned. If not, we implement the asymmetrical shield configuration and hope for minimal reality distortion in the uncovered sectors."

As the others departed for their assigned locations, Robert sat cross-legged beside the central quantum anchor, the copper circlet cool against his forehead. Jake knelt opposite him, one hand on the telegraph key that would control the network recalibration, the other holding a device that would monitor Robert's neural activity during the connection attempt.

"Focus on the Station Master," Jake instructed quietly. "Not just his appearance but his essential nature—the mathematical relationships that define his existence across probability tracks. The circlet will amplify that focus into a directed communication channel."

Robert closed his eyes, concentrating as instructed. He visualized the Station Master as he had appeared in both physical encounters and dreams—the elderly transit worker with his perfect symmetrical features, navy uniform with gold buttons and trim, and white gloves maintained with mechanical precision. But beyond that surface appearance, he focused on what he had glimpsed in threshold reality—the underlying structure of pure mathematical relationships that defined the Station Master's true nature.

The copper circlet grew warm against his forehead as the connection established. Unlike the dream navigation in threshold reality, this process felt more controlled, more directed—creating a specific channel rather than opening his consciousness to the entire dream realm.

Gradually, Robert became aware of another presence—not physically present but distinctly perceptible across dimensional boundaries. The Station Master's consciousness touched his own, the contact feeling like mathematical equations unfolding directly in his mind rather than conventional communication.

"Catalyst," the familiar voice resonated, not in his ears but in his thoughts. *"You initiate contact willingly. A significant development."*

"Out of necessity," Robert replied, unsure if he was speaking aloud or merely thinking the words. "Adjacent reality collapse threatens the integrity of the entire system, including your existence across probability tracks."

"Indeed. The cascade effect proceeds more rapidly than anticipated. Unstructured convergence serves no purpose in the evolutionary framework."

Robert sensed an opening in this acknowledgment. "We're implementing a probability shield to maintain basic coherence through the cascade effect. It requires simultaneous activation of eight-dimensional nodes throughout Daybridge."

"The guardian's quantum anchor network. A primitive but potentially effective approach to temporary dimensional insulation."

"Two nodes are non-functional or unattended," Robert continued, aware of the limited connection time. "Without complete network activation, the shield will fail asymmetrically, causing unpredictable reality distortions throughout our probability track."

The Station Master's consciousness seemed to consider this information, mathematical equations flowing through Robert's mind as the entity analyzed the implications.

"And you propose collaboration to ensure complete network functionality," the Station Master concluded. *"Interesting. Your adaptation to multiversal awareness progresses more rapidly than standard parameters would suggest."*

"Will you help stabilize the missing nodes?" Robert pressed, sensing both curiosity and calculation in the Station Master's response.

"Intervention in your reality track contradicts the guardian's sealing parameters. Direct manifestation would require significant energy expenditure and create additional dimensional instability."

"But it's possible," Robert insisted. "You exist across all probability tracks simultaneously. You can influence specific locations within our reality without full manifestation."

Another flow of equations passed through Robert's mind as the Station Master analyzed this assertion.

"Correct, though with limitations. I can establish temporary quantum resonance with the non-functional nodes, creating sufficient dimensional alignment to participate in the shield formation."

Robert felt a surge of hope at this confirmation. "Then you'll help?"

"Conditional participation may be arranged," the Station Master replied, his mathematical thought patterns shifting toward more complex structures. *"In exchange for specific considerations regarding future dimensional boundary parameters."*

Jake, monitoring the conversation through Robert's neural patterns, leaned forward slightly. "Ask for specifics," he whispered. "No open-ended agreements."

"What considerations?" Robert asked cautiously.

"The probability shield will temporarily isolate your reality track from the multiverse. When dimensional pressure normalizes and connections naturally reestablish, certain modifications to the sealing parameters would be appropriate."

"What kind of modifications?"

"Limited permeability rather than absolute separation. Controlled observation channels rather than complete dimensional isolation. Evolution requires exposure to expanded possibilities, even if gradual and structured."

Robert understood what the Station Master was requesting—not unrestricted access to their reality or the ability to force convergence, but rather the maintenance of limited connections that would allow continued influence over perceptual evolution. It was both less and more than he had expected—a scaled-back approach to the same fundamental goal.

"Jake?" Robert murmured, uncertain how to respond to this proposal.

"Clarify the limitations," Jake instructed quietly. "Specifically, regarding transit capabilities and integration protocols."

Robert relayed these questions through the connection, receiving another complex flow of mathematical concepts in response.

"No physical transit between realities would be permitted under modified parameters. Observational channels only, allowing perception of alternative probability tracks without direct interaction. Integration would remain voluntary rather than systematic—individuals choosing expanded awareness rather than having it imposed through convergence events."

"A compromise approach," Robert realized. "Gradual perceptual evolution through voluntary exposure rather than forced convergence."

"Evolution proceeds most effectively when chosen rather than imposed," the Station Master acknowledged. *"Recent events have demonstrated the limitations of the original methodology. Adaptation of approach is appropriate."*

Robert was surprised by this apparent shift in the Station Master's position—from forcing catastrophic convergence to accepting gradual, voluntary perceptual evolution. Had their previous confrontation and the sealing of the breach actually changed the entity's fundamental approach? Or was this merely a tactical adjustment in service of the same ultimate goal?

"Jake?" Robert asked again, aware that their connection time was growing short.

Jake seemed equally uncertain about this unexpected development. "We need his immediate assistance with the probability shield. Future parameter modifications can be negotiated more thoroughly after the current crisis is resolved."

Robert relayed this position through the connection. "We propose a two-phase agreement. Immediate assistance with the non-functional nodes during shield formation, followed by structured negotiation regarding future boundary parameters after dimensional stability is restored."

The Station Master's consciousness seemed to withdraw slightly, analyzing this counter-proposal through another complex series of mathematical operations that flickered through Robert's awareness.

"Acceptable, with one additional condition," he finally responded. *"The Catalyst must participate personally in future boundary parameter negotiations. Your unique quantum signature provides essential resonance for optimal communication across dimensional frameworks."*

This specific request for Robert's continued involvement made him uneasy, but time was running critically short. The copper circlet had grown uncomfortably warm against his forehead, indicating the connection was approaching its safe duration limit.

"Agreed," Robert replied after a brief hesitation. "Assistance now, negotiation later, with my participation in the process."

"Configuration accepted. I will establish quantum resonance with the non-functional nodes at Crescent Park and Alexander Plaza when the network activation sequence initiates."

"How will we know you've successfully connected?" Robert asked, aware that Jake would require confirmation.

"The guardian will detect my signature in the network energy pattern. It will be unmistakable."

The connection began to fade, the Station Master's consciousness withdrawing from the communication channel as the circlet reached its operational limits.

"Until our next communication, Catalyst. Your perceptual evolution continues to progress most satisfactorily."

With those final words, the connection terminated completely. Robert opened his eyes, finding himself back in the storm-lashed reality of Möbius Square, the copper circlet now cool against his forehead as its energy dissipated.

"Did you get all that?" he asked Jake, who was studying readings on his monitoring device with intense concentration.

"Yes. An unexpected development, but potentially advantageous under current circumstances." Jake removed the circlet from Robert's head, checking for any signs of neural damage from the extended dimensional communication. "The question remains whether he will actually assist as promised or use this opportunity to attempt another breach of the sealing parameters."

"I think he will help," Robert said, somewhat surprised by his own certainty. "The cascade effect threatens his existence across probability tracks. Uncontrolled dimensional collapse would destroy the system he's spent decades creating and maintaining."

Jake nodded, accepting this assessment as they both checked the time. Less than two minutes remained before the scheduled network activation.

"The others should be in position by now," Jake said, adjusting the telegraph key connected to the central quantum anchor. "Dr. Voss will have completed her first adjustment at the eastern node and transported to the northern position. Gil should be at the southern node, and Noah attempting repairs at Crescent Park."

"And the Station Master will supposedly handle the southeastern node and potentially assist at Crescent Park if Noah's repairs are unsuccessful," Robert added, still uncertain whether to trust the entity's commitment.

Around them, reality continued to deteriorate at an accelerating rate. The ghostly figures of bleed-through entities had become more numerous and defined, some now appearing almost completely solid. Buildings around the square cycled through architectural configurations more rapidly, and sections of the pavement occasionally transformed into completely different materials—grass, water, strange crystalline structures—before returning to concrete.

Most concerning was the sky above, which had developed visible fractures like a breaking eggshell, through which other atmospheric conditions could be seen—swirling colors, geometric patterns, and occasionally glimpses of the three moons Robert remembered from threshold reality.

"Thirty seconds to network activation," Jake announced, his hand poised over the telegraph key. "The probability shield will create significant sensory disruption as reality parameters temporarily reconfigure. Maintain physical contact with the central anchor to prevent spatial displacement during the transition."

Robert placed his hand on the quantum anchor beside Jake's, feeling the device vibrate with increasing intensity as the activation moment approached. The blue luminescence had spread throughout the spiral pattern in the pavement, pulsing in rhythm with what appeared to be heartbeat-like fluctuations in the dimensional fabric itself.

"Ten seconds," Jake counted down, watching his timepiece with unwavering focus. "Nine... eight... seven..."

The storm reached a crescendo of intensity, lightning now striking continuously around the perimeter of the square, creating a cage of electrical energy that seemed to isolate them from the surrounding city.

"Six... five... four..."

Robert could feel reality itself growing thin around them, the boundaries between worlds stretching to near-breaking point as the pressure from collapsing adjacent tracks reached its peak.

"Three... two... one..."

Jake pressed the telegraph key with deliberate precision. Immediately, the central quantum anchor emitted a pulse of blue energy that traveled outward along invisible pathways, connecting to the other nodes throughout Daybridge.

For a breathless moment, nothing seemed to happen. Then, with startling suddenness, a dome of blue energy expanded outward from the central spiral, encompassing first the square, then the surrounding blocks, continuing to grow until it presumably covered the entire city.

Within this dome, reality itself seemed to solidify—the fluctuations ceasing, the ghostly bleed-through entities fading, the architectural shifting of buildings halting as everything settled into a single, coherent configuration.

Most dramatically, the fractured sky above repaired itself, the glimpses of other atmospheric conditions disappearing as a normal stormy sky reasserted itself over Daybridge.

"Network synchronization achieved," Jake reported, monitoring readings on his control device. "All eight nodes responding, including..." He paused, studying a particular pattern with intense concentration. "Yes, including quantum resonance signatures at Crescent Park and Alexander Plaza that match the Station Master's dimensional frequency. He fulfilled his part of the agreement."

"Is it working?" Robert asked, watching as the blue energy dome began to fade from visibility, though its effects on reality stabilization remained evident.

"The probability shield is forming correctly," Jake confirmed. "Our reality track is being temporarily insulated from the dimensional pressure of collapsing adjacent worlds. We should maintain coherence through the cascade effect."

As the shield completed its formation, becoming invisible but functionally complete, the storm began to diminish rapidly—the unnatural lightning ceasing, the rain reducing to a gentle shower, the wind calming to occasional gusts rather than continuous gales.

"The meteorological anomalies were symptoms of dimensional pressure," Jake explained, seeing Robert's questioning look. "With the shield in place, natural weather patterns are reasserting themselves."

Robert relaxed slightly, cautiously optimistic that their desperate plan had succeeded. "How long will the shield remain active?"

"Approximately seventy-two hours—sufficient time for the cascade effect to complete its progression through adjacent reality tracks and for dimensional pressure to normalize." Jake began carefully disconnecting his control device from the central anchor, which now glowed with steady blue light rather than erratic flickering. "After that, the quantum anchors will gradually reduce their insulation effect, allowing controlled reintegration with the multiverse."

"And then we negotiate new boundary parameters with the Station Master," Robert added, remembering his agreement.

"Yes, though on much more favorable terms than would have been possible during crisis conditions." Jake packed his equipment carefully back into its case. "The probability shield gives us time to prepare a comprehensive approach to multiversal relations rather than merely reacting to imminent catastrophe."

Robert nodded, understanding the strategic advantage they had gained. The desperate crisis had somehow transformed into an unexpected opportunity—a chance to establish a more balanced relationship with the interdimensional transit system and its enigmatic caretaker.

"We should check on the others," he suggested, rising from his position beside the central anchor. "Especially Gil. His physical condition seemed precarious even before the shield activation."

"Agreed. Dr. Voss and Noah should return here once they've confirmed their nodes are functioning properly." Jake closed his case and stood. "Gil's position at Central Hospital is closest. We should start there."

As they prepared to leave Möbius Square, Robert looked back at the central spiral pattern, now glowing with steady blue light that symbolized the temporary stability they had achieved. The probability shield had saved their reality from immediate collapse, but fundamental questions remained unanswered.

What would happen when the shield inevitably came down? Could they actually negotiate sustainable boundary parameters with an entity that had previously attempted to force catastrophic convergence? And what role would Robert himself play in this new chapter of Daybridge's interdimensional history?

The journey that had begun with a simple subway entrance on a rainy night had transformed into something far more complex and consequential than he could have imagined. And despite the temporary resolution of the immediate crisis, Robert suspected that his adventures between worlds were far from over.

The Station Master's final words echoed in his mind as he and Jake left the square, heading toward Central Hospital to find Gil: *"Your perceptual evolution continues to progress most satisfactorily."*

Whatever happened next, one thing was certain—Robert North would never see reality the same way again.

CHAPTER TWELVE: DIMENSIONAL COLLAPSE

Three days after the activation of the probability shield, Robert sat in Jake's office at Steinman's Rare Editions, watching the guardian make final adjustments to a complex array of monitoring equipment. The shield was scheduled to begin its automated dissolution process in less than six hours, gradually reintegrating their reality with the broader multiverse after temporarily isolating it from the cascade effect.

"The adjacent reality collapse has completed its progression through the nearest probability tracks," Jake explained, checking readings on what appeared to be an antique seismograph modified with quantum sensors. "Seven complete dimensional failures, three partial collapses with residual stability, and twelve reality tracks showing significant alteration but maintaining basic coherence."

"How many people lived in those collapsed realities?" Robert asked quietly, the scale of the catastrophe difficult to comprehend despite his expanded awareness.

"Millions in each, though 'lived' may not be the appropriate term." Jake adjusted a dial, bringing a different set of readings into focus. "Reality collapse doesn't necessarily equate to death in the conventional sense. Consciousness appears to redistribute across remaining probability tracks, often integrating with corresponding versions of the same individuals."

"Like what happened to Gil," Noah suggested from his position by the window. He had insisted on being present for the shield dissolution preparations, his own involvement in the interdimensional crisis having left him with a personal stake in its resolution.

"Similar, though Gilbert Harmon's case is unique in many respects," Jake replied. "His prolonged exposure to threshold reality before the original collapse altered his quantum signature in ways we don't fully understand."

Robert's thoughts turned to Gil, now recovering under Dr. Voss's care at her specialized medical facility. His condition had stabilized after the shield activation, but his physical form remained compromised—occasionally transparent, sometimes shifting between multiple states simultaneously. Dr. Voss had described him as "probability fluid"—existing partly in their reality and partly across multiple adjacent tracks simultaneously.

"Has there been any communication from the Station Master?" Robert asked, returning to the more immediate concern.

"Nothing direct, though the quantum anchors have registered periodic energy signatures consistent with observational scanning from outside our dimensional boundaries." Jake closed the panel on one of his instruments, apparently satisfied with its calibration. "He's monitoring our shield dissolution preparations, but not attempting to interfere."

"Yet," Noah added skeptically.

Jake acknowledged this caution with a nod. "Indeed. Which is why we've implemented additional safeguards around the dissolution process."

He moved to a large map of Daybridge mounted on the wall, where eight glowing points indicated the quantum anchor locations throughout the city. "Each anchor has been modified with a dimensional circuit breaker—a mechanism that will immediately halt the dissolution and reinstate full shielding if unauthorized interdimensional transit is detected."

"And if the Station Master honors our agreement?" Robert asked. "Limited observational channels rather than physical transit or forced convergence?"

"Then the shield dissolution will proceed as scheduled, creating carefully calibrated permeability rather than either complete isolation or unrestricted access." Jake checked his pocket watch. "Dr. Voss should be arriving shortly with the final calibration parameters based on Gil's equations."

As if on cue, the bell above the shop's front door chimed, announcing a visitor. Moments later, Dr. Voss entered the office, carrying a leather portfolio and looking tired but determined.

"The calculations are complete," she announced without preamble, opening the portfolio on Jake's desk to reveal pages of complex mathematical formulas and diagrams. "Gilbert believes these parameters will create precisely controlled dimensional permeability—allowing observational connection without physical transit capabilities."

Jake studied the equations with intense concentration. "These are considerably more sophisticated than standard guardian protocols. The harmonization sequence for the anchor network is particularly elegant."

"Gil's understanding of interdimensional mathematics is exceptional," Dr. Voss agreed. "Even in his current condition, his insights into quantum resonance patterns exceed our most advanced theoretical models."

"Will these parameters satisfy the Station Master's requirements?" Robert asked, examining the equations despite being able to comprehend only portions of the advanced mathematics.

"They should," Dr. Voss replied. "They create exactly what was agreed upon—observational channels without physical transit capabilities. The Station Master will be able to monitor developments in our reality track and communicate across dimensional boundaries under controlled conditions but not directly manifest or force convergence events."

Jake transferred the key equations to his ledger, making additional notations as he worked. "These will need to be implemented at all eight anchor points simultaneously during the dissolution initiation. We'll need to coordinate our efforts precisely."

"Gil has prepared simplified instruction protocols for each location," Dr. Voss said, removing additional documents from her portfolio. "I've reviewed them with Noah and the other volunteers who'll be assisting with the network adjustments."

Robert examined the instruction sheet designated for his assigned location at Thornfield Avenue—the convergence point where he had first encountered the Liminal Line. The technical complexity had been reduced to a specific sequence of adjustments, each clearly illustrated and explained.

"This seems straightforward enough," he acknowledged. "Even for those of us without advanced degrees in quantum mechanics."

"Gil designed the procedures specifically for implementation by non-specialists," Dr. Voss confirmed. "The underlying mathematics remain complex, but the physical adjustments have been simplified to essential parameters."

Jake finished his review of the equations, closing his ledger with a decisive motion. "These should work. We'll begin final preparations immediately."

As the others discussed implementation logistics, Robert moved to the window, looking out at Merchant Street bathed in late afternoon sunshine. The city appeared entirely normal—pedestrians strolling along sidewalks, vehicles navigating the street, buildings solid and unchanging in their familiar configurations. No sign remained of the dimensional chaos that had nearly consumed Daybridge just days earlier.

Yet beneath this apparent normality, Robert knew, fundamental changes had occurred. The probability shield had preserved their reality's basic coherence, but subtle alterations were evident to those with sufficient awareness—small variances in architectural details, minor shifts in street layouts, occasional unfamiliar faces among otherwise known populations.

"Reality reconfiguration," Jake had explained when Robert first noticed these changes. "The shield prevented catastrophic collapse but couldn't maintain absolute stasis during extreme dimensional pressure. Our reality track has adapted slightly, incorporating elements from adjacent tracks that partially collapsed."

Most residents of Daybridge remained blissfully unaware of these alterations, their perceptions automatically adjusting to accept the reconfigured reality as normal and unchanged. Only those with direct exposure to interdimensional phenomena—Robert, Noah, Jake, Dr. Voss, and the few others who had assisted with the shield activation—retained awareness of the subtle differences between the Daybridge that had existed before the cascade effect and the one that emerged after shield implementation.

"Robert?" Noah's voice pulled him from his contemplation. "You've gone quiet. Everything okay?"

"Just thinking about how different everything is while appearing exactly the same," Robert replied, turning back to the group. "It's strange to walk past buildings that have subtly changed overnight and watch everyone else treat them as if they've always been that way."

"Quantum perception dissonance," Dr. Voss nodded sympathetically. "Your awareness encompasses both the previous and current configurations simultaneously, creating a cognitive overlay effect that can be disorienting."

"It's getting easier to manage," Robert admitted. "Though I still occasionally turn down the wrong street when I'm not paying attention, expecting a layout that no longer exists."

"Your mind will eventually establish new neural pathways that prioritize current reality configuration," Jake assured him. "Though some awareness of the previous arrangement will likely remain permanently."

Their discussion was interrupted by a subtle vibration that ran through the building—not a conventional earthquake, but a rippling effect that seemed to momentarily distort spatial relationships within the room. Books on shelves briefly shifted positions before settling back, and the air itself appeared to waver like heat shimmer over hot pavement.

"Probability fluctuation," Jake said sharply, moving quickly to his monitoring equipment. "The shield is experiencing harmonic interference at multiple nodes."

Dr. Voss joined him at the instruments, checking readings with practiced efficiency. "Significant energy buildup along the dimensional boundaries. Something is applying pressure against the shield from outside."

"The Station Master?" Noah suggested, concern evident in his voice.

"No," Jake replied, studying the pattern on one of his displays. "This signature doesn't match his dimensional frequency. It's something else... something more fundamental."

Another, stronger fluctuation rippled through the room, causing furniture to momentarily shift positions and the windows to briefly display different views before returning to normal. The monitoring equipment responded with alarming increases in activity—needles jumping erratically, lights flashing in irregular patterns, audible tones rising in pitch.

"The shield is experiencing critical resonance disruption," Jake announced, his normally calm voice tight with tension. "Something is forcing harmonic destabilization across all eight nodes simultaneously."

"Could it be backlash from the collapsed adjacent realities?" Robert asked, steadying himself against the desk as another, more violent fluctuation shook the building.

"Possible," Dr. Voss acknowledged, checking her own specialized instruments. "The dimensional energy released during multiple reality collapses could be creating a pressure wave that's only now reaching our insulated track."

Jake moved to his communication device—a modified radio that could transmit messages to the other quantum anchors through the dimensional fabric rather than conventional electromagnetic signals.

"Attention all anchor monitors," he broadcast. "We're experiencing shield instability. Implement emergency stabilization protocol immediately. Adjust resonance keys to frequency delta-seven and maintain until further instructions."

As the others responded to Jake's instructions, Robert moved back to the window, drawn by a strange quality to the light outside. The previously sunny afternoon had taken on an unsettling cast—shadows appearing to fall at impossible angles, colors shifting subtly toward unfamiliar spectra, the very air seeming to thicken with visual distortions.

"Jake," he called, not turning from the window. "You need to see this."

The guardian joined him, his expression growing more concerned as he observed the changes occurring outside. Pedestrians had stopped in confusion, looking around with disoriented expressions as reality fluctuations became visible even to conventional perception. Vehicles had pulled to the curb, drivers emerging to stare at the increasingly unstable surroundings.

Most alarming was the sky above Daybridge, which had begun to fracture along jagged lines, revealing glimpses of other atmospheric conditions behind the breaks—swirling colors, geometric patterns, and occasional views of multiple celestial bodies where only the sun should be visible.

"The shield is failing," Jake said grimly. "Not dissolving in a controlled fashion as planned, but experiencing catastrophic harmonic disruption."

"Can we reinforce it?" Noah asked, joining them at the window.

"Not against this level of dimensional pressure. The stabilization protocols might buy us time, but the fundamental resonance pattern is breaking down." Jake returned to his instruments, making rapid adjustments in an attempt to counter the growing instability. "We need to understand what's causing this disruption before we can effectively address it."

Dr. Voss had connected her specialized equipment to Jake's monitoring array, creating an enhanced detection system that displayed more detailed analysis of the dimensional fluctuations.

"The disruption pattern is centered on the original breach location," she reported, studying the readings intently. "Thornfield Avenue, precisely where Robert first encountered the Liminal Line."

"That can't be a coincidence," Robert said, moving to examine the data himself. "Could the original tear be reopening despite the shield?"

"Not reopening," Jake corrected, his expression growing increasingly troubled as he analyzed the patterns. "The original breach never fully healed—we simply contained its effects and sealed off its manifestations. What we're seeing now suggests the fundamental tear in reality has become unstable in new ways."

Another, more violent fluctuation shook the building, this one accompanied by a sound like tearing fabric amplified to deafening levels. Through the windows, they could see buildings along Merchant Street briefly phase out of existence, replaced by alternative versions before returning to their original forms—though now partially transparent, as if their reality had become less substantial.

"The shield harmonics are approaching critical failure," Dr. Voss announced, checking her instruments. "Estimated complete collapse in less than thirty minutes based on current degradation rate."

"And when the shield fails?" Noah asked, though his expression suggested he already anticipated the answer.

"Dimensional collapse," Jake replied grimly. "Not just the controlled dissolution we planned, but catastrophic boundary failure across our entire reality track. The cascade effect we temporarily avoided will resume with even greater intensity, accelerated by the accumulated pressure against our insulated reality."

"We need to reach the origin point," Robert said suddenly, a realization forming as he processed this information. "The disruption is centered on Thornfield Avenue because that's where everything began—my first crossing, the initial destabilization that eventually led to the convergence crisis."

Jake considered this, then nodded sharply. "You may be right. If the original breach is the source of the current instability, we need to examine it directly to determine appropriate countermeasures."

"I'm coming too," Noah insisted as Jake and Robert prepared to depart.

"It's too dangerous," Jake began, but Noah cut him off.

"I've been part of this from the beginning," he said firmly. "Besides, you might need my quantum entanglement with Robert again. It helped create the resonance path for his return last time."

Jake conceded this point with a reluctant nod, then turned to Dr. Voss. "Can you coordinate the anchor network from here? Maintain the stabilization protocols as long as possible to buy us time?"

"Yes, though I can't guarantee how long the shields will hold under current conditions." She was already connecting additional equipment to the communication system. "I'll establish direct links with all monitor stations and implement emergency reinforcement sequences if the degradation accelerates."

With responsibilities assigned, Jake collected essential equipment from his cabinets—devices Robert now recognized as specialized tools for dimensional analysis and manipulation. He placed these in his leather case alongside his guardian ledger, which contained the accumulated knowledge of interdimensional breach mechanics passed down from Margaret Steinman.

"Quantum transport would be too risky under current conditions," Jake decided, checking his pocket watch. "The dimensional instability could cause serious spatial displacement. We'll need to use conventional transportation to reach Thornfield Avenue."

This proved easier said than done. When they emerged from the bookshop onto Merchant Street, the reality fluctuations had intensified visibly. Buildings rippled like reflections in disturbed water, streets occasionally rerouted themselves mid-block, and pedestrians moved with growing disorientation through an environment that refused to maintain consistent configuration.

Jake's vintage automobile, normally parked behind the bookshop, had partially merged with a completely different vehicle—the front half remaining his familiar black sedan, while the rear had become a station wagon of unfamiliar design and color.

"That's unfortunate but not unexpected," Jake observed with remarkable composure. "We'll proceed on foot. Thornfield Avenue is approximately fifteen blocks from here. If we maintain a direct route despite the spatial fluctuations, we should arrive within twenty minutes."

They set out immediately, moving with purpose through the increasingly unstable cityscape. The reality fluctuations made navigation challenging—landmarks shifted positions, streets changed configurations, and occasionally entire blocks briefly transformed into completely different urban arrangements before returning to something approximating their original form.

Other residents of Daybridge appeared increasingly distressed by these impossible changes. Some stood frozen in confusion, others moved with growing panic, and a few had begun to exhibit the same partial transparency Robert remembered from the previous convergence crisis—the first sign of quantum consciousness beginning to separate from conventional physical reality.

"They're experiencing dimensional dissolution," Jake explained as they passed a group of particularly affected individuals. "Their perceptual filters can no longer reconcile the contradictory sensory information they're receiving."

"Can we help them?" Noah asked, his medical training instinctively prompting concern for their condition.

"Not individually. Stabilizing the original breach is their only hope—and ours." Jake checked his pocket watch again, his expression growing more troubled. "The shield degradation is accelerating. We have perhaps twenty minutes before complete failure."

They quickened their pace, taking shortcuts through alleyways and parks when streets became too unstable for direct passage. The sky above continued to fracture along increasingly wide breaks, revealing glimpses of what Robert recognized as threshold reality—the strange atmospheric conditions and multiple celestial bodies he had experienced during his time in that interdimensional state.

As they approached the university district where Thornfield Avenue intersected with Riverside Drive, the dimensional instability intensified dramatically. Entire buildings cycled rapidly between multiple architectural configurations, streets flowed like rivers before temporarily resolidifying in new arrangements, and people flickered in and out of existence as if reality itself couldn't decide which version of them should manifest.

Most disturbing was the growing transparency of everything around them—as if their entire reality track was becoming less substantial, fading toward a ghost-like state that would eventually dissolve completely into the interdimensional void.

"There," Robert pointed ahead to where Thornfield Avenue should be, though the street sign currently displayed a completely different name that shifted between multiple alternatives every few seconds. "That's the convergence point—where I first saw the subway entrance."

The location was immediately recognizable despite the dimensional instability affecting the surrounding area. A swirling vortex of energy had formed at the precise spot where Robert had discovered the Liminal Line entrance during that rainy night that now seemed a lifetime ago. The vortex pulsed with chaotic patterns of light, occasionally emitting shock waves that rippled outward, intensifying the reality fluctuations with each release.

"The original breach point has become completely unstable," Jake observed, removing instruments from his case to take measurements. "The dimensional barriers are failing at an accelerating rate, creating a cascading breakdown effect that's overwhelming the shield network."

"Can we reseal it?" Noah asked, watching as another shock wave emanated from the vortex, causing nearby buildings to momentarily phase out of existence before reappearing in altered configurations.

"Not with conventional containment methods," Jake replied, studying his readings with growing concern. "The breach characteristics have fundamentally changed. This isn't simply a tear in reality anymore—it's becoming a dimensional singularity, drawing multiple reality tracks toward a convergence point."

"The Station Master's original goal," Robert realized. "Convergence of all possibilities into a single configuration. But happening chaotically rather than in a controlled fashion."

"Precisely. Unstructured convergence accelerated by the cascade effect from adjacent reality collapses." Jake continued his analysis, using multiple instruments to examine different aspects of the growing singularity. "The probability pressure has exceeded the critical threshold. We can't prevent the convergence process now, only potentially influence its configuration."

"What does that mean exactly?" Noah asked, steadying himself as another, stronger shock wave passed through them.

Before Jake could answer, the vortex at the center of the convergence point pulsed with blinding intensity, then expanded dramatically, engulfing the entire intersection in swirling energy. When the light receded, the streetscape had transformed completely.

Instead of the Thornfield Avenue intersection they knew, they found themselves standing at the entrance to a massive transit station that had impossibly manifested in the middle of Daybridge. Broad marble steps led down to brass doors embellished with intricate geometric patterns. Above the entrance, a sign in flowing script simply read "CENTRAL STATION" without further explanation or identification.

"The physical manifestation of Central Nexus," Robert whispered, recognizing elements from his previous experience in threshold reality. "It's breaking through into our reality track directly."

"The dimensional boundaries have deteriorated beyond the point where separate realities can maintain distinct configuration," Jake confirmed, his instruments now displaying readings that appeared to exceed their measurement capabilities. "The convergence has entered its final phase."

As they stood before this impossible manifestation, pedestrians who had been caught in the transformation stared in confusion at the station that had materialized around them. Some backed away in alarm, while others seemed drawn toward the entrance with expressions of curious wonder.

"We need to go inside," Robert said with sudden certainty. "The answers we need are in there—at the center of the convergence."

Jake nodded grimly, packing away his instruments. "You're right. If there's any possibility of influencing the convergence configuration, it would be from within Central Nexus itself."

"Is that safe?" Noah asked, eyeing the station entrance with understandable caution.

"Nothing about our current situation is safe," Jake replied. "But remaining here as reality collapses around us guarantees failure. Within Central Nexus, we might at least find options not available from outside."

With that sobering assessment, they approached the station entrance together. As they descended the marble steps, Robert experienced a powerful sense of déjà vu—though this manifestation of Central Station appeared more substantial, more permanently anchored to physical reality than the threshold version he had visited previously.

The brass doors swung open automatically as they approached, releasing a wave of warm air carrying that familiar scent of ozone and brass polish. Inside, the station opened into a vast space that shouldn't have been possible within the physical constraints of Daybridge's urban geography—a cavernous hall with soaring ceilings supported by columns inscribed with mathematical formulas rather than conventional ornamentation.

Unlike the bustling interdimensional hub Robert had experienced in threshold reality, this manifestation of Central Station was eerily quiet. No crowds of travelers moved between platforms, no trains arrived or departed, no station attendants directed passengers to their correct routes. Only a profound silence filled the impossible space, broken occasionally by distant sounds like the groaning of metal under extreme pressure.

"The convergence is still forming," Jake observed, his voice echoing slightly in the vast empty hall. "This physical manifestation represents the initial framework upon which multiple realities will eventually merge."

They moved deeper into the station, their footsteps echoing on the marble floor. Multiple platforms extended in various directions, each with tracks leading into tunnels that seemed to curve away into impossible geometries. Signage above these platforms displayed continuously shifting destinations—names of places that existed in various versions of Daybridge across different reality tracks.

As they reached the central concourse, a massive departure board dominated the space, displaying hundreds of destinations in constantly changing configurations. Unlike conventional transit information, these listings showed not just locations but reality designations—"Daybridge-Prime," "Daybridge-Theta," "Daybridge-Epsilon," each with coordinates that resembled the dimensional parameters Jake and Gil had discussed during the shield implementation.

"The full transit network," Jake said, studying the board with professional interest despite their dire circumstances. "Every probability track connected to the original breach, mapped according to dimensional coordinates within the multiverse framework."

Robert scanned the listings, locating "DAYBRIDGE-PRIME (3.7)" among the entries. Unlike the other destinations, which showed various arrival and departure times, their reality track displayed only "TERMINAL CONVERGENCE" in pulsing red letters.

"That can't be good," Noah observed, following Robert's gaze to their reality's listing.

"It confirms what we already knew," Jake said grimly. "Our reality track has reached the end of its distinct existence. The convergence will incorporate it into a new configuration that merges multiple probability vectors simultaneously."

As they contemplated this confirmation of their reality's imminent transformation, a rhythmic clicking sound became audible from one of the adjoining corridors—the measured tread of formal shoes on marble flooring accompanied by the tapping of what might have been a walking stick or ceremonial baton.

Robert recognized the sound immediately. "The Station Master."

They turned toward the approaching footsteps, watching as the familiar figure emerged from the corridor—the elderly transit worker in his navy uniform with gold buttons and trim, white gloves maintained with mechanical precision, and an air of absolute authority despite his seemingly benign appearance.

The Station Master approached unhurriedly, his movements displaying that unsettling mechanical precision Robert remembered from their previous encounters. When he reached them, he nodded in formal acknowledgment, his perfect symmetrical smile revealing nothing of his thoughts or intentions.

"Guardian," he greeted Jake first, then turned to the others. "Catalyst. Anchor." This last was directed at Noah, apparently referencing his role in establishing the quantum resonance path during Robert's previous return from threshold reality.

"Maxwell," Jake responded with equal formality. "Or do you prefer 'Station Master' in this context?"

"Titles are irrelevant at convergence threshold," the Station Master replied, his resonant voice carrying that same unsettling quality that seemed to vibrate at frequencies beyond normal human hearing. "Identities themselves become negotiable when probability tracks merge."

He gestured toward the vast empty station around them. "Central Nexus manifests physically when reality boundaries deteriorate beyond sustainable separation. The framework for dimensional reconfiguration establishes itself in preparation for complete convergence."

"You promised controlled observation channels, not physical convergence," Robert reminded him, anger cutting through his apprehension. "Was that agreement merely a delaying tactic?"

The Station Master's expression remained unchanged, but something like regret entered his voice. "The agreement was genuine, Catalyst. This unstructured convergence represents system failure rather than designed implementation. The cascade effect from adjacent reality collapses created dimensional pressure beyond calculated parameters."

"You're saying this isn't your doing?" Noah asked skeptically.

"Direct causation is complex within multiversal frameworks," the Station Master replied. "My original actions established conditions for potential convergence, but current manifestation exceeds intended configuration parameters significantly."

He turned to Jake. "The Guardian understands. Dimensional systems, once destabilized beyond a critical threshold, proceed according to fundamental quantum mechanics rather than conscious intention."

Jake nodded reluctantly. "He's telling the truth, at least partially. What we're experiencing is uncontrolled dimensional collapse accelerated by cascading reality failures throughout adjacent probability tracks. Even the Station Master can't direct convergence once systemic breakdown reaches this level."

The station shuddered around them, marble columns momentarily becoming transparent before resolidifying. The vast ceiling above briefly displayed multiple configurations simultaneously—some showing constellation mosaics Robert remembered from the Liminal Line stations, others revealing open sky with impossible celestial arrangements, still others manifesting geometric patterns that hurt the eyes to look at directly.

"Structural integrity diminishes as reality frameworks continue to degrade," the Station Master observed, glancing upward. "Complete dimensional collapse approaches terminal phase."

"Can it be stopped?" Robert asked directly. "Is there any way to halt the convergence process at this point?"

The Station Master considered him for a moment before responding. "Not halted, no. Reality boundaries have deteriorated beyond restoration threshold. However, convergence configuration remains potentially malleable—the specific parameters of the resulting merged reality could be influenced by sufficiently significant intervention."

"What kind of intervention?" Jake asked, professional interest overriding his natural caution toward the entity.

Instead of answering immediately, the Station Master turned and gestured toward one of the platforms, where a figure was approaching from the shadows of an adjoining corridor. As the newcomer emerged into the light, Robert recognized him with a mixture of surprise and relief.

"Gil!"

Gilbert Harmon looked substantially better than when Robert had last seen him at Central Hospital. His form had stabilized, no longer flickering between multiple states, though a subtle translucency remained—as if he existed partially in their reality and partially elsewhere. He wore his familiar tattered clothing, but moved with greater strength and purpose than during the shield activation crisis.

"The dimensional mathematics suggested you'd be here," Gil said by way of greeting, nodding to each of them in turn. "Central Nexus always manifests physically at terminal convergence threshold."

"Dr. Voss said you were still recovering," Noah remarked, clearly surprised by Gil's appearance.

"Recovery is relative when one's quantum signature spans multiple reality tracks simultaneously," Gil replied with a wry smile. "My condition stabilized enough to allow limited transit once the dimensional boundaries began to fail."

He turned to the Station Master, his expression becoming more serious. "You've explained the situation?"

"Partial exposition only," the Station Master replied. "Fundamental parameters established, specific intervention mechanics pending."

Gil nodded as if this cryptic response made perfect sense, then addressed the others directly. "The convergence can't be prevented, but it can be reconfigured. Rather than a chaotic merging of multiple reality tracks, we might be able to implement a controlled reset—essentially returning the local dimensional framework to its pre-breach configuration."

"A reset?" Robert questioned. "You mean like... undoing everything that's happened?"

"More precisely, creating a structured loop in local spacetime that returns to the point of original divergence," Gil explained. "The 1943 experiment created a fracture in reality that split Daybridge into countless parallel versions. If we can return to that exact moment and alter the outcome, we might be able to prevent the fracture from occurring in the first place."

"Time travel?" Noah asked incredulously. "Is that even possible?"

"Not conventional temporal displacement," Jake clarified, understanding dawning in his expression. "Gil is suggesting a dimensional loop that connects our current convergence point back to the original divergence point—essentially collapsing the probability branches back to their root."

"Precisely," Gil confirmed. "The mathematics are complex but theoretically sound. As realities converge, the dimensional barriers between not just space but time become increasingly permeable. At the moment of complete convergence, a properly calibrated quantum resonance field could redirect the collapse energy toward the original breach point, essentially healing the fracture rather than allowing chaotic merger."

The station shuddered again, more violently this time. Sections of the walls and floor briefly phased out of existence, revealing glimpses of other spaces beyond—some recognizable as versions of Daybridge, others entirely alien in configuration. The departure board flickered erratically, listings changing too rapidly to read as reality itself became increasingly unstable.

"Time grows short," the Station Master observed. "Dimensional collapse accelerates toward critical threshold."

"What exactly would this 'reset' mean for us?" Robert asked, trying to understand the implications of Gil's proposal. "For everyone in Daybridge?"

Gil exchanged a glance with the Station Master before answering. "If successful, the reset would essentially rewrite the timeline from the moment of the original breach. Reality would reconfigure along a single primary probability track rather than fragmenting into countless parallel versions."

"Everyone would still exist," Jake added, seeing Robert's concerned expression. "But in a single, coherent reality rather than spread across multiple variations. Experiences would consolidate, memories would integrate, identities would merge into composite versions that incorporate elements from across probability tracks."

"And the Liminal Line?" Robert asked. "The interdimensional transit system?"

"Would never have existed," the Station Master replied, something like resignation in his normally emotionless voice. "The subway system manifested as a physical expression of pathways between fractured realities. In a singular, unfractured reality, no such pathways would be necessary or possible."

The implications of this struck Robert forcefully. Without the Liminal Line, he would never have experienced multiple versions of Daybridge, never have met Gil in threshold reality, never have glimpsed the true nature of the multiverse that existed beneath the seemingly solid surface of conventional perception.

"You're willing to sacrifice the transit system you've maintained for decades?" he asked the Station Master directly. "Your own existence across multiple realities?"

"Existence is negotiable at convergence threshold," the Station Master replied cryptically. "The Maxwell Hanover who initiated the 1943 experiment sought expanded consciousness through dimensional manipulation. The entity that process created has witnessed the ultimate outcome of that ambition."

He gestured toward the increasingly unstable station around them. "Unstructured convergence benefits no consciousness, individual or collective. A reset to singular reality, while limiting in some respects, preserves coherent existence for all involved."

Another, more violent tremor shook the station. Massive cracks appeared in the marble columns, and sections of the ceiling collapsed, revealing swirling chaotic energy beyond rather than conventional sky or building structure. The very air seemed to thicken with visual distortions as reality itself struggled to maintain any coherent configuration.

"We're running out of time," Gil warned, checking a device on his wrist. "Dimensional collapse has entered the terminal phase. If we're going to implement the reset protocol, we need to move immediately."

"What exactly does this protocol involve?" Jake asked, professional guardian instincts focusing on practical implementation despite the extraordinary circumstances.

"We need to reach the central convergence point—the exact dimensional coordinates where all probability tracks intersect during collapse," Gil explained. "From there, we can establish a quantum resonance field calibrated to redirect the convergence energy toward the original breach point in 1943."

"And where is this central convergence point?" Noah asked.

In answer, Gil pointed toward the most distant platform visible from their position. Unlike the others, which extended straight into tunnels, this platform appeared to curve upward at an impossible angle, defying conventional physics as it spiraled toward what looked like a swirling vortex of energy suspended in mid-air above the tracks.

"That doesn't look particularly safe," Noah observed with considerable understatement.

"Dimensional collapse is inherently hazardous," the Station Master noted. "Conventional physical laws become increasingly negotiable as reality frameworks deteriorate."

"We'll need to take the last train," Gil said, checking his wrist device again. "It should be arriving momentarily, if my calculations are correct."

As if on cue, a distant rumbling became audible from the spiraling tracks, growing steadily louder until it clearly indicated an approaching train. Unlike the copper cars Robert remembered from his journeys on the Liminal Line, the vehicle that gradually came into view seemed to be composed of translucent material that shifted constantly between multiple configurations—sometimes appearing as a conventional subway car, other times as something far more exotic in design.

"The final configuration remains unstable," the Station Master explained, seeing their reactions to the unusual vehicle. "It reflects the malleable nature of reality at convergence threshold."

The train slowed as it approached the platform, eventually coming to a complete stop with doors aligning perfectly despite its constantly shifting form. These doors opened with that familiar pneumatic hiss, releasing a wave of air that carried not just the usual scent of ozone and brass polish but hints of countless other environments—ocean spray, forest pine, desert heat, mountain snow—as if the vehicle had traveled through innumerable realities before arriving at this final destination.

"We must board quickly," the Station Master urged, already moving toward the open doors. "Dimensional stability continues to deteriorate. The platform itself may not maintain coherence much longer."

To emphasize his warning, another violent tremor shook the station. Large sections of the ceiling collapsed completely, revealing a chaotic void beyond where multiple versions of Daybridge seemed to overlap and intersect in impossible configurations. The marble floor beneath their feet began to crack along jagged lines, blue energy pulsing from within these fissures as the dimensional fabric itself started to tear.

"Go," Jake ordered, ushering Robert and Noah toward the train. "I'll be right behind you."

As Robert boarded, he found the interior of the train as unstable as its exterior—seating arrangements shifting between multiple configurations, windows sometimes looking out onto the station and sometimes revealing glimpses of other locations entirely, lighting alternating between various technologies from different eras and realities.

The Station Master moved to what appeared to be a control panel at the front of the car, though its design changed continuously between various interface styles. He placed his white-gloved hands on what momentarily stabilized as a brass lever, apparently preparing to operate the vehicle manually.

Gil joined him, removing several small devices from his pockets and beginning to assemble what Robert recognized as a quantum resonance generator similar to the one Jake had used during the shield activation. The two worked with coordinated precision despite the unstable environment, suggesting they had discussed this plan previously.

Noah entered next, looking around with a mixture of scientific curiosity and understandable apprehension at the constantly shifting interior. "This is... something else," he managed, finding a seat that remained relatively stable despite the transformations occurring around it.

Jake was the last to board, pausing briefly at the threshold to look back at the disintegrating station. Central Nexus was breaking apart rapidly now, massive sections of architecture dissolving into swirling energy as reality itself struggled to maintain any coherent form.

As he finally stepped aboard, the doors closed behind him with that same pneumatic hiss, sealing them inside the unstable vehicle. The Station Master activated the control mechanism, and the train began to move immediately, accelerating with surprising smoothness despite the chaotic environment outside.

"The reset protocol requires specific preparations," Gil explained as they gained speed, the train beginning to climb the impossibly curved track that spiraled upward toward the energy vortex. "Each of us has a particular role based on our quantum signatures and dimensional experiences."

He turned to Robert first. "As the catalyst whose journey initiated the current convergence sequence, you form the primary resonance anchor. Your connection to both the original breach and multiple subsequent reality tracks creates a natural harmonic that can be amplified to redirect the collapse energy."

"What do I need to do?" Robert asked, determined to contribute whatever was necessary despite not fully understanding the complex interdimensional mechanics involved.

"Maintain focus on your origin point—the exact moment and location where you first encountered the Liminal Line," Gil instructed. "Your quantum signature still resonates strongly with that specific coordinate in spacetime. We'll use that resonance to establish the primary vector for the reset field."

He turned to Noah next. "Your quantum entanglement with Robert creates a stabilizing influence that prevents resonance dispersion. Essentially, you're the ground wire that keeps the energy focused rather than scattering across multiple probability vectors."

Noah nodded, accepting this responsibility without hesitation. "Like when we established the return path during the first convergence crisis."

"Precisely, though amplified significantly." Gil handed him a small device that resembled the silver disc he had used previously. "This will help maintain your connection despite the dimensional turbulence we'll experience as we approach the convergence point."

To Jake, Gil provided a more complex apparatus—a brass sphere etched with intricate patterns that hummed softly when activated. "The guardian's role is perhaps most critical. Your training with dimensional breach mechanics allows you to shape the reset field according to specific parameters, ensuring it targets the original fracture point rather than creating additional instabilities."

Jake accepted the device with professional focus, already examining its configuration and making minor adjustments based on his guardian knowledge.

"What about you and the Station Master?" Robert asked, noticing that Gil had kept several components of the quantum resonance generator for himself.

"We provide the mathematical framework and energetic direction," Gil explained. "My understanding of interdimensional transit mechanics combined with the Station Master's direct connection to the original breach creates the necessary computational structure for the reset protocol."

The train continued its impossible spiral upward, now moving at tremendous speed along a track that curved at angles that should have been physically unattainable. Outside the windows—when they briefly stabilized enough to show consistent views—they could see Central Station collapsing beneath them, dissolving into swirling energy that was gradually being drawn upward toward the same vortex they were approaching.

"We're witnessing the final phase of dimensional collapse," the Station Master observed, his mechanical precision seemingly unaffected by the chaos around them. "All probability tracks converging toward a singular point in dimensional space-time."

"Which we're going to redirect back to 1943," Robert said, still trying to fully comprehend the extraordinary plan they were attempting to implement.

"Not redirect the convergence itself, but rather the energy it releases," Gil clarified, continuing to assemble his portion of the resonance generator. "That energy, properly focused, can essentially cauterize the original wound in reality—healing the fracture before it splinters into countless parallel tracks."

The train had nearly reached the vortex now, the spiral track leading directly into the swirling energy that seemed to contain glimpses of innumerable versions of Daybridge simultaneously. The vehicle's unstable nature had intensified, its form shifting more rapidly between configurations, occasionally becoming almost completely transparent before resolidifying in yet another variation.

"We're approaching the convergence threshold," the Station Master announced. "Preparation for resonance field generation should commence immediately."

Gil nodded, activating his portion of the equipment. Blue energy began to flow between the components, creating a network of luminous connections that gradually expanded to encompass all five of them.

"Each focus on your designated function," he instructed as the energy field strengthened. "Robert, concentrate on your origin point at Thornfield Avenue. Noah, maintain your quantum entanglement focus. Jake, shape the field according to guardian protocols for breach sealing."

Robert closed his eyes, concentrating as directed on his precise memory of that rainy night on Thornfield Avenue—the streetlight reflecting off wet pavement, the unexpected subway entrance appearing between buildings, his decision to descend those iron steps into warm light below. He could feel the quantum resonance building around him, his connection to that specific point in space-time strengthening as the energy field amplified his natural dimensional signature.

Noah held the silver disc in both hands, focusing on his friendship with Robert—their shared experiences, conversations, the quantum entanglement that had formed between them through years of close association. The disc grew warm against his palms, pulsing in rhythm with the larger energy field as it stabilized the connections between disparate elements of the system.

Jake manipulated the brass sphere with practiced precision, shaping the developing resonance field according to dimensional mathematics evolved over decades of guardian experience. The sphere responded to his adjustments, emitting patterns of light that interacted with the larger field, creating specific geometric configurations that would direct the convergence energy along precisely calculated vectors.

Gil and the Station Master worked in unexpected harmony, their combined understanding of interdimensional mechanics creating the fundamental framework upon which the others' contributions built. Despite their historically opposed objectives, they now collaborated with perfect coordination—the wanderer physicist and the quantum ghost united in their final purpose.

The train reached the edge of the vortex, the track disappearing into swirling energy that contained fragments of countless realities simultaneously. For a moment, the vehicle paused at this threshold, as if gathering itself for the final transit.

"When we enter the convergence point, conventional reality parameters will cease to apply," the Station Master warned. "Maintain absolute focus on your designated functions regardless of perceptual distortions you may experience."

"What happens to us if this works?" Noah asked, the practical question that others might have overlooked in the extraordinary circumstances. "If reality resets to 1943, do we just... cease to exist?"

"Not cease, but transform," Gil replied. "Our consciousness will integrate with the reset timeline, merging with our corresponding selves in the new singular reality. Memories may persist partially, like echoes or dreams, but primary identity will reconfigure according to the new probability track."

"And if it doesn't work?" Robert asked.

"Then unstructured convergence proceeds," the Station Master said simply. "All realities collapse into a chaotic configuration where coherent existence becomes impossible for most consciousness structures."

With these sobering alternatives established, the train resumed its forward motion, entering the vortex with a sound like reality itself tearing open. The vehicle's structure immediately began to break down, walls becoming transparent, floors insubstantial, the entire conveyance gradually dissolving as it penetrated deeper into the convergence point.

Around them, fragments of countless Daybridges swirled in kaleidoscopic confusion—buildings from different eras and architectural styles, streets in various configurations, people frozen in moments of time across multiple probability tracks. The effect was both beautiful and terrifying, a glimpse of the entire multiversal structure collapsing into a single point of infinite density.

"Resonance field approaching critical amplitude," Gil announced, his voice sounding distant despite his physical proximity. "Prepare for final synchronization."

The blue energy connecting them intensified dramatically, becoming almost painfully bright as it reached full power. Robert could feel his quantum signature vibrating at frequencies that seemed to extend beyond physical reality, connecting him simultaneously to his origin point on Thornfield Avenue and to countless other versions of himself across the probability spectrum.

"Catalyst signature locked," the Station Master confirmed, his form becoming increasingly transparent as the train dissolved completely around them, leaving them suspended within the vortex itself. "Anchor connection stable. Guardian field configuration optimized."

"Initiating reset protocol," Gil called, making a final adjustment to his equipment. "Dimensional mathematics aligned with original breach coordinates. Targeting 1943 divergence point in three... two... one..."

With a sound beyond description—something felt rather than heard, a vibration that resonated through consciousness itself rather than physical senses—the energy field expanded explosively outward. The blue luminescence engulfed the swirling fragments of reality around them, imposing structure on chaos, direction on randomness, purpose on dissolution.

Robert felt his perception expanding beyond normal constraints, his awareness encompassing not just his current self but countless versions simultaneously—every Robert North who had ever encountered the Liminal Line, every probability track where he had experienced some variation of the journey that had led to this extraordinary moment.

Then his focus narrowed abruptly, concentrating with laser precision on that specific point in space-time where everything had begun—Thornfield Avenue on a rainy night, a graduate student heading home from his laboratory, an unexpected subway entrance appearing between familiar buildings.

The blue energy coalesced around this singular focus point, drawing the scattered fragments of multiple Daybridges toward it like metal filings to a magnet. Reality itself seemed to bend, folding inward toward that crucial moment of first divergence—not just in Robert's personal timeline but in the broader history of Daybridge itself.

Images flashed through his consciousness with increasing speed—the 1943 laboratory where Maxwell Hanover and his team had conducted their fateful experiment, the moment when dimensional boundaries first fractured, the cascade of probability lines emerging from that single point of divergence, spreading outward like branches from a tree root.

And then, with startling clarity, Robert understood what they were attempting to do—not just reset reality to a previous configuration, but heal the original fracture at its source, prevent the splintering of Daybridge into countless parallel versions, restore the singular reality that should have existed all along.

The vortex around them began to contract, reality fragments accelerating toward the central focus point with increasing velocity.

The blue energy field pulsed with rhythmic intensity, guiding this process with mathematical precision toward its intended conclusion.

"Reset sequence initiated," the Station Master announced, his form now barely visible within the swirling energy. "Probability tracks converging toward original divergence point."

"Maintain focus," Gil urged, his own form similarly transparent. "The process is inherently unstable. Any deviation in the resonance field could create additional fractures rather than healing the original breach."

Robert concentrated with every ounce of his being on that rainy night on Thornfield Avenue, anchoring the reset protocol to that specific coordinate in space-time. Noah's quantum entanglement provided the stability this focus required, preventing dispersion across multiple potential targets. Jake's guardian knowledge shaped the energy field according to precise dimensional mathematics, ensuring it would cauterize rather than exacerbate the original reality wound.

The vortex contracted further, compressing innumerable versions of Daybridge toward a single unified configuration. The pressure of this compression became almost unbearable—not physically painful but perceptually overwhelming, as if consciousness itself was being squeezed beyond its natural parameters.

"Critical threshold approaching," Gil called, his voice now seeming to come from everywhere and nowhere simultaneously. "Prepare for temporal displacement."

The blue energy field reached maximum intensity, becoming so bright that it transcended visual perception entirely, manifesting instead as pure mathematical concepts unfolding directly in consciousness. Reality compression accelerated toward its ultimate conclusion—countless probability tracks merging into a singular timeline centered on that crucial moment in 1943 when everything had first diverged.

"Reset protocol engaged," the Station Master's voice resonated through the mathematical landscape their perception now inhabited. "Dimensional reconfiguration commencing."

With those final words, the energy field imploded, collapsing inward with impossible force. Robert felt his consciousness compressed to a singular point, then stretched across time and space simultaneously—connecting him to every version of himself that had ever existed across the probability spectrum, then gradually consolidating these infinite variations into a coherent whole.

His last coherent thought before awareness itself transformed was a profound realization: they weren't just resetting reality to a previous configuration, but evolving it to an entirely new state—one that incorporated the wisdom gained from experiencing multiple dimensions while restoring the stability of singular, coherent existence.

Then thought itself dissolved as the reset protocol completed its function, reality reconfiguring around the healed breach point, probability tracks merging into a singular timeline that flowed forward with renewed purpose and direction.

The subway that wasn't there had taken Robert North on a journey beyond imagination. And now, that journey was coming full circle—returning to its beginning point transformed by the extraordinary path it had followed, forever changed by glimpses of a multiverse that would now exist only in the echoes of dreams and the whispers of quantum possibility.

Reality reset. The fracture healed. The journey completed.

And somewhere in the newly singular Daybridge, a graduate student named Robert North paused on his way home from the laboratory, looking up at the rain-washed street with an inexplicable sense of déjà vu—a fleeting impression of countless other possibilities that had once existed, now merged into this one precious, coherent reality that continued onward, whole and complete at last.

CHAPTER THIRTEEN: THE LAST RIDE

Robert North stood at the window of his apartment, watching rainfall trace familiar patterns down the glass. Something about the storm stirred an odd sense of déjà vu—not the vague feeling of having experienced something before, but a more specific sensation, as if multiple memories were attempting to overlay themselves simultaneously.

He'd been experiencing these strange moments with increasing frequency over the past few weeks. Occasional flashes of recognition when passing certain street corners, brief disorientation when entering familiar buildings, dreams filled with copper trains and impossible stations. His doctor had suggested stress from his graduate studies might be causing minor dissociative episodes, but Robert suspected something else entirely.

His phone chimed with a text from Noah: *Heading home. Pizza tonight?*

Robert smiled, typing back: *Already ordered. Should be here in 30.*

He returned his attention to the rain-slicked streets below, watching pedestrians navigate the weather with varying degrees of success. An elderly man in what appeared to be an outdated transit uniform caught his eye—standing perfectly still amid the hurrying crowds, looking up directly at Robert's window with an enigmatic expression.

When Robert blinked, the man was gone.

Shaking his head, he turned from the window and surveyed his apartment. Everything was exactly as it should be—research papers spread across the coffee table, half-empty coffee mug perched precariously atop journal articles, Noah's medical textbooks stacked beside the sofa. Normal, familiar, consistent.

Yet something felt... incomplete. As if there were gaps in the fabric of his reality that his mind kept trying to fill with impossible alternatives.

His gaze fell on a fountain pen he didn't remember purchasing—an elegant antique piece with intricate brass accents. When he picked it up, a powerful wave of familiarity washed over him, accompanied by fragmented images that vanished before he could fully grasp them: a spiral pattern etched into pavement, swirling colors in an impossible sky, a station with constellation mosaics overhead.

The apartment door opened, breaking his reverie as Noah entered, shaking water from his umbrella.

"Man, it's coming down out there," Noah remarked, hanging his coat on the rack. "Feels like it's been raining for weeks."

"Forty-three days," Robert replied automatically, then frowned, unsure where that specific number had come from.

Noah gave him a curious look. "You've been counting?"

"No, I just..." Robert shook his head. "Weird feeling, that's all."

Noah studied him for a moment before speaking again. "More déjà vu stuff?"

"Something like that." Robert placed the fountain pen back on the table, trying to dismiss the strange sensation it had triggered. "Different this time, though. More like... memories that don't quite fit."

"Like what?"

Robert hesitated, reluctant to voice the bizarre impressions that had been haunting him. "Like I've lived multiple versions of the same events. Or that I've been to places that don't exist." He laughed self-consciously. "Sounds crazy when I say it out loud."

Noah didn't laugh. Instead, he sat on the arm of the sofa, his expression unusually serious. "What if I told you I've been having similar experiences?"

Robert stared at him. "What kind of experiences?"

"Dreams about subway stations. Glimpses of buildings that look wrong for a second before snapping back to normal." Noah ran a hand through his damp hair. "And this constant feeling that we've forgotten something important—something we both experienced but can't quite remember."

The apartment suddenly seemed very quiet, the sound of rainfall against the windows the only interruption to a silence heavy with unspoken recognition.

"There's a bookshop on Merchant Street," Robert said finally. "Steinman's Rare Editions. I've never been there, but I know exactly what it looks like inside—right down to the creaky third step and the smell of old leather bindings."

Noah nodded slowly. "The owner has silver-streaked hair and always wears a waistcoat with a pocket watch."

"Jake," they said simultaneously, then looked at each other in startled recognition.

"How do we know that name?" Robert whispered.

Before Noah could respond, a knock at the door made them both jump. They exchanged uncertain glances before Robert moved to answer it, checking the peephole first.

Standing in the hallway was an older man with silver-streaked hair and a formal waistcoat, complete with pocket watch chain visible across his midsection.

Robert opened the door with a strange sense of inevitability. "Jake Steinman."

The man nodded, unsurprised that Robert knew his name. "May I come in? There are matters we need to discuss—matters concerning quantum resonance, dimensional stability, and the increasingly thin veil between memory and reality."

Robert stepped aside to let him enter, closing the door behind their unexpected visitor. Jake surveyed the apartment with a knowing expression, his gaze lingering on the antique fountain pen Robert had been examining earlier.

"You've been experiencing temporal echo effects," Jake stated rather than asked. "Memories from probability tracks that no longer exist asserting themselves into your current consciousness."

"We reset reality," Robert said suddenly, the words emerging before he fully understood their meaning. Images flashed through his mind—a train spiraling upward toward a swirling vortex, blue energy enveloping multiple versions of Daybridge, a final convergence point where countless realities merged into one.

Jake's expression showed both concern and approval. "You remember more than you should. Both of you do." He glanced at Noah. "The quantum entanglement between you created a mnemonic resonance that persisted through the reset protocol. Highly unusual, but not entirely unexpected given your unique circumstances."

"The Liminal Line," Noah said, another fragment of memory surfacing. "The subway system that connected different versions of Daybridge."

"That never existed in this reality," Jake corrected gently. "The reset protocol healed the original breach before it could fracture Daybridge into multiple probability tracks. The interdimensional transit system was never needed because reality remained singular rather than fragmenting."

Robert sat heavily on the sofa, trying to reconcile these impossible memories with the world he knew. "But we remember it. Parts of it, anyway."

"Memory exists partially outside conventional spacetime constraints," Jake explained, taking a seat in the armchair opposite them. "The reset changed reality's configuration but couldn't completely erase the quantum imprint your experiences left on your consciousness. What you're experiencing are echoes from probability tracks that were integrated into the current singular timeline during the convergence event."

"The last ride," Robert murmured, another fragment surfacing. "We were on a train heading toward... something. The Station Master was there. And Gil."

Jake nodded, removing a familiar leather-bound ledger from his coat pocket. "Perhaps it would be helpful if I explained what actually happened—both in the probability tracks that no longer exist and in the reset timeline we now inhabit."

He opened the ledger, revealing pages of handwritten notes and complex diagrams that seemed to shift slightly when viewed from different angles.

"In 1943, a research project called the Daybridge Containment Initiative conducted experiments with quantum field manipulation. In the original probability track, these experiments created a catastrophic breach in reality, fracturing Daybridge into countless parallel versions across the multiverse."

Jake turned a page in his ledger. "The lead physicist, Maxwell Hanover, was transformed by direct exposure to the interdimensional energies released during the breach event. He became what you knew as the Station Master—an entity existing across multiple reality tracks simultaneously, maintaining the interdimensional transit system that manifested as a physical expression of the pathways between fractured realities."

"The subway that wasn't there," Robert said, the phrase triggering a cascade of additional memories—copper trains, stations with constellation mosaics, journeys between increasingly divergent versions of Daybridge.

"Precisely." Jake continued his explanation. "For eight decades, dimensional guardians like myself monitored these breaches, attempting to contain their effects and prevent catastrophic convergence of multiple reality tracks. Margaret Steinman, my predecessor, dedicated her life to this work, as did I after her."

He turned another page. "Then you, Robert, with your unique quantum sensitivity, encountered the Liminal Line. Your repeated crossings between realities accelerated a process that had been building for decades, eventually leading to a convergence crisis that threatened to collapse all versions of Daybridge into a chaotic, impossible configuration."

Noah leaned forward. "I remember parts of this. The quantum anchors we placed throughout the city, the shield we created to prevent dimensional collapse."

"That was merely a temporary solution," Jake explained. "The fundamental instability remained, eventually leading to a more severe crisis when adjacent reality tracks began to collapse sequentially, creating a cascade effect that overwhelmed even our enhanced containment measures."

Robert's fragmented memories were coalescing into a more coherent narrative. "The final convergence. Central Station manifested physically in our reality as dimensional boundaries failed completely."

"Yes. At that point, conventional containment became impossible. The only option remaining was a complete reset—redirecting the convergence energy to heal the original breach in 1943 before reality fractured into multiple tracks."

Jake closed his ledger. "Which brings us to our current situation. The reset protocol succeeded. Reality reconfigured around the healed breach point, creating a singular timeline where Daybridge never fractured into parallel versions. The Daybridge Containment Initiative still conducted their experiments, but with a crucial difference—they succeeded in their original objective of controlling quantum field effects rather than creating catastrophic dimensional destabilization."

"So none of it happened?" Noah asked, struggling to reconcile these impossible memories with the world he knew. "The Liminal Line, the different versions of Daybridge, the convergence crisis—it was all just... undone?"

"Not undone," Jake corrected. "Transformed. The reset didn't erase history but rather created a new singular timeline that incorporated elements from across the probability spectrum. People, places, events—all were integrated into a coherent whole rather than remaining fragmented across multiple realities."

"What about the Station Master?" Robert asked. "And Gil? What happened to them in this reset timeline?"

Jake's expression grew more solemn. "Maxwell Hanover completed his research successfully in this timeline. He made significant contributions to quantum field theory before retiring to write several influential books on theoretical physics. He passed away in 1972, having never transformed into the interdimensional entity you knew."

"And Gilbert Harmon became one of his most prominent students," Jake continued. "He extended Hanover's work into practical applications of quantum field manipulation, eventually developing technologies that revolutionized our understanding of reality without creating dangerous instabilities. He's currently professor emeritus at Daybridge University's Institute for Quantum Studies."

Robert sat back, processing this information. "So everyone got better lives in this reset timeline."

"Different lives," Jake clarified. "Neither better nor worse, necessarily, just coherent within a singular reality framework rather than fragmented across multiple probability tracks."

"But you remember everything," Noah observed. "You still have your guardian ledger, even though there was never a breach to guard against in this timeline."

Jake smiled slightly. "The guardian function transcends conventional reality constraints. Someone must maintain awareness of the multiverse's true nature, even in a singular timeline, to prevent similar breaches from occurring in the future."

"And us?" Robert asked. "Why do we remember fragments of probability tracks that never existed in this timeline?"

"As I mentioned, your quantum entanglement created a mnemonic resonance that persisted through the reset protocol." Jake studied them thoughtfully. "But there may be another factor involved. You both played crucial roles in the convergence event—catalyst and anchor for the reset protocol. That level of direct involvement leaves quantum imprints that even reality reconfiguration cannot completely erase."

He leaned forward, his expression growing more serious. "Which brings me to the purpose of my visit. These memory fragments you're experiencing aren't simply curiosities—they represent potential instability in the reset timeline. If they continue to strengthen, they could eventually create new fracture points in reality's coherence."

"We're destabilizing reality by remembering things that never happened?" Noah asked incredulously.

"In a manner of speaking, yes. Quantum consciousness can influence reality at fundamental levels. Your memories of multiple probability tracks create resonance patterns that could potentially reintroduce dimensional instability to the reset timeline."

Robert understood the implication immediately. "You're saying we need to forget."

Jake nodded gravely. "For the stability of this singular reality, yes. The memory fragments need to be properly integrated into your current timeline consciousness rather than remaining as disruptive echoes from probability tracks that no longer exist."

"And how exactly do we do that?" Noah asked skeptically.

In response, Jake removed two small devices from his pocket—silver discs identical to those they had used during the shield activation crisis in the now-nonexistent probability track.

"These will help realign your quantum signatures with the current timeline, essentially integrating the fragmented memories into coherent forms that won't disrupt dimensional stability." He placed the discs on the coffee table between them. "The process isn't about erasing but harmonizing—allowing these experiences to become part of your singular timeline consciousness without creating reality discordance."

Robert reached for one of the discs, experiencing immediate recognition as his fingers touched the cool metal surface. Images flashed through his mind—holding a similar device while focusing on dimensional coordinates, feeling quantum resonance flow through his body, establishing connections across reality boundaries that shouldn't have been possible.

"This will help us forget?" he asked, studying the device with mixed emotions.

"Not forget entirely," Jake clarified. "Rather, it will transform direct memories of interdimensional experiences into something your current reality consciousness can process without disruption—intuitive understanding, déjà vu, perhaps dreams or creative inspiration. The knowledge remains, but in forms that won't create dimensional instability."

Noah picked up the second disc, turning it thoughtfully in his hands. "Do we have a choice?"

"There is always a choice," Jake replied. "But continuing on your current trajectory risks creating new fracture points in reality—essentially reintroducing the very instability the reset protocol was designed to heal."

Robert and Noah exchanged glances, a wordless communication passing between them that transcended ordinary understanding—a resonance of their quantum entanglement that had persisted through reality reconfiguration.

"What do we need to do?" Robert asked finally.

"Hold the discs and focus on integration rather than separation," Jake instructed. "Visualize your fragmented memories merging with your current timeline consciousness, becoming coherent aspects of a singular experience rather than disruptive echoes from probability tracks that no longer exist."

As Robert and Noah positioned the silver discs in their palms, Jake continued with gentle guidance: "The process works best if you focus on a specific memory from your interdimensional experiences—something meaningful that can serve as an anchor point for the integration process."

Robert closed his eyes, considering which memory to focus on. After a moment, he settled on the image of the copper train arriving at that first station—the beginning of his journey through multiple realities, the moment when his understanding of existence fundamentally changed.

Noah's choice was different—he concentrated on the moment they had activated the quantum anchors together, establishing the shield that temporarily protected Daybridge from dimensional collapse. That experience of shared purpose and connection across reality boundaries felt most significant to him.

"Now visualize these memories transforming," Jake's voice continued soothingly. "Not disappearing but evolving into forms that belong within your current timeline consciousness—intuitive understanding, creative insight, emotional resonance without dimensional disruption."

The silver discs grew warm in their hands, vibrating slightly as quantum resonance established between their consciousness and the reset timeline's fundamental structure. Robert felt his fragmented memories beginning to shift—not vanishing but changing form, becoming less literal and more metaphorical, transitioning from disruptive echoes to integrated aspects of his singular reality experience.

The process wasn't entirely comfortable. There was a sense of loss as direct recollections of interdimensional transit became more impressionistic, more dream-like. The Liminal Line stations with their constellation mosaics, the copper trains that traveled between realities, the threshold world with its impossible architecture—all were transforming into something his current consciousness could process without creating reality discord.

Yet something essential remained—not the literal memories of traveling between multiple Daybridges, but the expanded awareness those journeys had created. An understanding of reality's underlying flexibility, an appreciation for existence's precious coherence, a recognition of consciousness's remarkable adaptability.

As the integration process neared completion, the silver discs cooled in their hands. Robert opened his eyes to find the apartment unchanged yet somehow different—as if he were seeing it with new appreciation for its solid, consistent reality after glimpsing what might have been in probability tracks now transformed into mere potential.

"How do you feel?" Jake asked, studying them with professional interest.

Robert considered the question carefully. "Like I've had an incredibly vivid dream that's fading the more I try to hold on to it. I still know something extraordinary happened, but the specifics are... shifting."

"Similar," Noah agreed. "I remember feelings more than details now. A sense of purpose, of connection to something larger than myself, but the actual events are becoming more abstract."

Jake nodded, satisfied with their responses. "The integration is proceeding correctly. Over the next few days, the process will complete naturally. Your quantum signatures will fully align with the reset timeline, and the disruptive echo effects will cease."

He collected the silver discs, which had fulfilled their purpose, and returned them to his pocket. "You may experience occasional dreams or intuitive insights related to your interdimensional experiences, but they won't create the reality discord that threatened dimensional stability."

"Will we remember you?" Robert asked suddenly. "After the integration is complete?"

Jake smiled slightly. "You'll remember meeting me, certainly. Steinman's Rare Editions exists in this timeline as well, after all. But our conversation today will likely transform into something your consciousness can more easily reconcile with singular reality—perhaps a discussion about rare books or theoretical physics rather than interdimensional transit and reality reset protocols."

He rose to leave, gathering his guardian ledger and returning it to his coat pocket. "I'll check on you both in a few days, though you may not recognize the significance of my visit by then."

"Thank you," Robert said, rising to walk him to the door. "For everything—not just today, but for all you did across probability tracks that no longer exist. For helping save reality itself."

Jake nodded in acknowledgment. "The guardian function continues, even in a singular timeline. Though the nature of the work has changed somewhat."

"No more interdimensional subway to monitor," Noah observed with a faint smile.

"No, but quantum field stability requires ongoing attention, nonetheless. Reality may be singular now, but it remains fundamentally malleable at certain levels." Jake's expression became momentarily distant, as if looking beyond conventional perception. "The multiverse still exists as potential, even in a timeline where probability tracks haven't physically manifested."

With those cryptic words, he bid them farewell and departed, leaving Robert and Noah to contemplate their transforming memories and the singular reality they now fully inhabited.

The pizza delivery arrived minutes later, providing a welcome return to ordinary concerns. As they ate, they found their conversation gradually shifting away from interdimensional phenomena and toward everyday topics—classes, research projects, upcoming exams. The integration process was already working, helping them align more completely with their current timeline consciousness.

Later that evening, Robert stood at the window again, watching as the rain finally began to ease. The city lights reflected off wet pavement, creating patterns that seemed momentarily significant before resolving into mere illumination. A familiar sense of déjà vu washed over him, but gentler now—less disruptive, more contemplative.

He understood that something profound had happened, something that had fundamentally changed his perception of reality. The specifics were becoming increasingly abstract, transforming into intuitive understanding rather than literal memory, but the essence remained—a recognition that existence was both more complex and more precious than most people ever realized.

Across the apartment, Noah had fallen asleep on the sofa, a medical textbook open on his chest. Robert noticed with a faint smile that his roommate appeared perfectly, solidly real—no longer showing the subtle quantum echo effects that had briefly manifested during their most intense recall of interdimensional experiences.

The integration was working. They were becoming fully present in this singular timeline, their consciousness aligning with the reset reality while retaining the wisdom gained from glimpsing the multiverse beyond.

Robert turned back to the window, his gaze drawn to a particular intersection several blocks away—Thornfield Avenue and Riverside Drive. Something about that location still resonated with special significance, though the specific memory was becoming increasingly dreamlike.

A subway entrance that wasn't there. Copper trains that traveled between realities. A journey beyond imagination that had ultimately led back home—to this singular, precious reality where existence maintained coherent form rather than fracturing into countless parallel versions.

He didn't need to remember the details. The understanding remained, transformed into something his current consciousness could integrate without creating dimensional discord. And perhaps that was enough—to know that reality was both more malleable and more miraculous than most ever suspected, to appreciate the remarkable coherence of existence after glimpsing what happened when that coherence failed.

Robert turned from the window, ready to wake Noah and suggest they both get proper sleep after their strange and transformative day. As he did, he noticed the antique fountain pen on the coffee table—the one that had triggered such powerful recognition earlier.

Without thinking, he picked it up, feeling its familiar weight in his hand. For a moment, something flickered at the edges of his perception—a sense of other possibilities, other timelines, other selves existing across a probability spectrum now collapsed into a singular reality.

Then the sensation faded, leaving only an elegant writing instrument with brass accents that caught the light just so. Robert smiled, placing the pen carefully in his shirt pocket. Some connections transcended even reality reconfiguration—quantum resonance patterns that persisted through dimensional reset, linking him to experiences now transformed but never truly forgotten.

Outside, the rain stopped completely, stars becoming visible through breaks in the clouds. A single timeline continued forward, whole and coherent, carrying within it the integrated wisdom of countless probability tracks that had once existed and now remained only as potential—as dreams, as intuition, as the whispered recognition that reality was both simpler and more extraordinary than most would ever know.

Three months later, Robert North hurried across campus toward the physics building, running late for a meeting with his adviser. The winter afternoon was already fading toward evening, campus lights beginning to illuminate paths between buildings where students moved with end-of-semester urgency.

His quantum tunneling research had taken an unexpected turn in recent weeks, yielding results that challenged conventional models of particle behavior in ways he couldn't entirely explain. Professor Liang was intrigued by his findings, particularly his novel approach to measuring superposition states without triggering immediate wave function collapse.

As he approached the physics building, Robert noticed an elderly man sitting on a bench nearby, feeding pigeons with methodical precision. Something about the scene triggered a moment of déjà vu—a sense of recognition that extended beyond ordinary familiarity.

The man looked up as Robert passed, fixing him with a penetrating gaze that seemed to see beyond conventional perception. "Interesting weather we're having," he remarked casually. "Single pattern but multiple potential configurations, wouldn't you say?"

Robert slowed, studying the stranger more carefully. He appeared to be in his eighties, with intelligent blue eyes and a neatly trimmed white beard. Something about him seemed vaguely familiar, though Robert was certain they had never met.

"I suppose that's true of most weather systems," Robert replied. "Chaotic dynamics with multiple potential outcomes determined by initial conditions."

The old man smiled, seemingly pleased with this response. "Precisely. Though some initial conditions prove more influential than others, particularly at dimensional intersection points."

The phrasing triggered another wave of déjà vu, stronger this time. "Dimensional intersection points?"

"Nexus locations where probability density functions achieve maximum overlap," the man clarified, scattering more bread crumbs for the eager pigeons. "Your quantum tunneling research touches on similar principles, I believe."

Robert stared at him in surprise. "How do you know about my research?"

"I make it my business to follow promising work in quantum field theory," the man replied casually. "Particularly when it exhibits resonance patterns consistent with expanded probability frameworks."

He extended his hand. "Gilbert Harmon. Professor Emeritus at the Institute for Quantum Studies. Though most people just call me Gil."

Robert shook his hand, experiencing a powerful sense of connection that transcended their brief acquaintance. "Robert North. But you already knew that, apparently."

"Indeed." Gil's eyes twinkled with something that might have been private amusement. "Your approach to quantum measurement without observer-induced collapse is particularly interesting. Reminds me of work I did decades ago on probability track maintenance across potential reality configurations."

"That sounds... theoretical," Robert remarked, trying to place the terminology within conventional quantum mechanics and finding no exact match.

"Most significant breakthroughs begin as theoretical frameworks before finding practical application," Gil observed. "Maxwell Hanover's early work was dismissed as philosophical speculation until experimental verification demonstrated its fundamental accuracy."

The name triggered another flicker of recognition in Robert's mind, though he couldn't immediately place it. "Hanover... the physicist who developed alternative interpretation models for quantum field behavior in the 1940s?"

"The same. His most significant contribution was recognizing that reality maintains coherence through continuous quantum observation across probability density functions." Gil scattered the last of his bread crumbs. "In simpler terms, the universe observes itself to maintain singular timeline configuration rather than fracturing into multiple parallel versions."

Something about this explanation resonated deeply with Robert, as if connecting with an intuitive understanding he possessed but couldn't quite articulate. "That's similar to what my research suggests about particle behavior in quantum tunneling experiments."

"Not coincidental, I suspect." Gil rose from the bench with surprising agility for his age. "Your quantum signature shows distinctive resonance patterns consistent with expanded probability awareness, even within singular timeline constraints."

Before Robert could ask what exactly that meant, Gil glanced at his watch. "You're late for your meeting with Professor Liang. She values punctuality, as I recall from our collaborative work some years ago."

"Right." Robert checked his own watch, surprised to find he was now more than ten minutes late. "It was interesting meeting you, Professor Harmon."

"Gil, please." The older physicist smiled. "And I suspect we'll meet again soon. Your research is approaching a critical threshold that may benefit from historical context regarding quantum field stabilization techniques."

He reached into his pocket and produced a business card, which he handed to Robert. "My contact information. When you're ready to discuss expanded applications of your measurement protocols, particularly those relating to probability track analysis, please don't hesitate to reach out."

Robert accepted the card, noticing it displayed only Gil's name, title, and a phone number—no email address or institutional affiliation. "Thank you. I might take you up on that."

"I expect you will." Gil's expression became momentarily distant, as if perceiving something beyond conventional awareness. "Probability configurations suggest a 93.7% likelihood of significant collaboration within the next three months."

With that cryptic prediction, he nodded farewell and walked away, his gait showing the same peculiar precision Robert had noticed in his bread-scattering technique—movements that seemed somehow measured against standards beyond ordinary physical parameters.

Robert watched him go, feeling as if something important had just occurred, though he couldn't articulate exactly what. The encounter had left him with a strange sensation of reconnecting with something he hadn't realized was missing—a quantum resonance that extended beyond conventional interaction.

Shaking his head to clear it, he hurried into the physics building for his meeting, tucking Gil's business card carefully into his wallet. Something told him their conversation had been more significant than it appeared on the surface—a connection that would prove important to his research and perhaps to his understanding of reality itself.

As he rushed down the corridor toward Professor Liang's office, Robert passed a display case containing historical artifacts from the department's past. A particular item caught his eye—a photograph from 1943 showing a research team gathered around experimental equipment. The caption identified Maxwell Hanover at the center, with several colleagues arranged around him.

Robert paused, drawn by unexpected recognition. One of the younger researchers standing slightly apart from the main group looked remarkably like Gil Harmon, though the photograph had been taken decades before their bench encounter could have occurred.

More interesting was the experimental apparatus itself—a configuration of equipment that seemed strangely familiar despite its obvious antiquity. Something about the arrangement triggered intuitive understanding in Robert's mind, as if he could perceive the quantum field manipulations it had been designed to measure and control.

For a brief moment, Robert experienced a strange perceptual shift—as if seeing beyond the photograph to the experiment itself, to the moment when reality's fundamental nature had been probed in ways that could have fractured existence into countless parallel versions but instead had established the coherent singular timeline he now inhabited.

Then the moment passed, leaving only a photograph in a display case and a graduate student already late for his advisory meeting. Robert continued down the corridor, the encounter with Gil and the strange recognition of the historical photograph filing themselves in his mind as curious but not immediately significant.

Yet something had changed—a subtle alignment between intuitive understanding and conscious awareness, a bridge forming between knowledge that transcended conventional memory and his current research into quantum field behavior. As if pieces of a puzzle he hadn't realized he was solving had suddenly connected, revealing glimpses of a larger pattern previously hidden.

Robert arrived at Professor Liang's office and knocked, putting aside these philosophical speculations to focus on the immediate concerns of his quantum tunneling experiments. But the business card in his wallet and the memory of Gil's penetrating gaze remained present in his awareness—reminders that reality might be both simpler and more extraordinary than conventional physics had yet determined.

The journey continued, though its nature had transformed. The subway that wasn't there had given way to pathways of understanding that existed within singular reality rather than crossing between multiple versions. And somewhere within this coherent timeline, the wisdom gained from probability tracks now integrated into potential rather than manifestation remained accessible to those with quantum signatures attuned to such expanded awareness.

The story wasn't ending but evolving—from interdimensional transit to deeper comprehension of reality's fundamental nature, from fragmented existence across multiple Daybridges to meaningful collaboration within a singular, precious timeline that contained within it the infinite potential of what might have been and what might yet become.

Reality itself was the ultimate journey—singular yet infinitely complex, coherent yet endlessly malleable, one path containing unlimited possibility for those who learned to perceive beyond conventional constraints. And Robert North, without fully understanding how or why, had somehow been granted a ticket for that extraordinary voyage of discovery.

His adviser was waiting. His research contained breakthroughs he hadn't yet recognized. And somewhere in Daybridge, an elderly physicist with remarkable insight into probability configurations was feeding pigeons while calculating the likelihood of significant collaboration.

The journey continued, transformed but undiminished, within a reality both more coherent and more miraculous than most would ever comprehend.

CHAPTER FOURTEEN: FULL CIRCLE

Professor Liang studied the readouts from Robert's latest quantum tunneling experiment with growing excitement. "These results are extraordinary, Robert. The particles maintain superposition despite multiple measurement events, only collapsing when specific resonance parameters are introduced."

"It's as if they exist in multiple states simultaneously until receiving a precise signal to align with a singular configuration," Robert explained, pointing to the most anomalous data points. "Almost like reality itself maintaining coherence through selective quantum observation."

The professor looked up sharply. "That's remarkably similar to Maxwell Hanover's theoretical work from the 1940s. Have you been researching historical quantum field theories?"

"Not specifically," Robert admitted. "Though I recently met Gilbert Harmon, who mentioned Hanover's research on probability density functions and reality coherence."

"Gil Harmon?" Professor Liang's expression showed surprise and respect. "He rarely engages with graduate students directly. You must have impressed him somehow."

"We had an... unusual conversation," Robert replied, remembering his strange encounter with the elderly physicist three weeks earlier. "He seemed to know about my research already, and suggested my approach to measurement without observer-induced collapse had connections to his work on 'probability track maintenance.'"

Professor Liang nodded thoughtfully. "Harmon's theoretical frameworks extend conventional quantum mechanics in fascinating directions. His mathematics suggests reality naturally maintains singular coherence despite inherent quantum potential for multiple configurations."

She tapped Robert's experimental data displayed on her computer screen. "And your results appear to demonstrate aspects of his theoretical model at the particle level. This could represent a significant breakthrough in understanding quantum observation effects."

"I've been considering reaching out to him," Robert said. "He gave me his contact information and mentioned potential collaboration."

"I would strongly encourage that," Professor Liang replied. "Gil Harmon doesn't offer his time lightly. If he's expressed interest in your work, it represents a remarkable opportunity."

The conversation shifted to practical aspects of continuing the experiments, but Robert's thoughts kept returning to his strange encounter with Gil and the intuitive understanding it had awakened—a sense that his research touched on fundamental aspects of reality maintenance that extended beyond conventional quantum mechanics.

Later that afternoon, Robert finally decided to call the number on Gil's business card. The phone rang several times before being answered by a voice he recognized immediately.

"Gilbert Harmon speaking."

"Professor Harmon, this is Robert North. We met on campus a few weeks ago—"

"Robert, yes. Precisely on schedule, according to probability projections." Gil's tone held that same peculiar mix of scientific precision and cryptic amusement Robert remembered. "Your quantum tunneling experiments have produced increasingly anomalous results, I presume?"

Robert blinked in surprise. "Yes, actually. How did you know?"

"Probability configurations suggested a 97.3% likelihood of a significant breakthrough within twenty-one days of our initial encounter." Gil spoke as if predicting experimental outcomes was perfectly ordinary conversation. "Are you familiar with Steinman's Rare Editions on Merchant Street?"

The non sequitur caught Robert off guard. "I've... heard of it, but never visited." Though as he said this, an inexplicable sense of familiarity contradicted his statement—as if he knew exactly what the bookshop looked like despite never having been there.

"Excellent location for discussing expanded applications of quantum field theory," Gil continued. "The owner maintains an extensive collection of historical scientific texts, including original manuscripts from the Daybridge Containment Initiative. Tomorrow at 3 PM would be optimal, if your schedule permits."

Robert found himself agreeing before fully processing the invitation. Something about the proposed meeting location triggered that same sense of déjà vu he'd been experiencing intermittently since his strange dreams began months earlier.

"Perfect. I'll inform Jake to expect us," Gil said, then added cryptically: "Bring your fountain pen. Certain artifacts maintain quantum resonance patterns that facilitate expanded awareness during theoretical discussions."

Before Robert could ask how Gil knew about his antique fountain pen—the one he didn't remember purchasing but felt inexplicably attached to—the call ended. He stared at his phone for a moment, wondering what exactly he had just agreed to and why it felt simultaneously bizarre and inevitable.

The next day, Robert found himself approaching Steinman's Rare Editions with a growing sense of anticipation mixed with that persistent déjà vu. The Victorian townhouse on Merchant Street looked exactly as he had somehow expected—three stories of weathered brick with large bay windows displaying antique books and curiosities.

The bell above the door chimed softly as he entered, announcing his presence to the shop's single visible occupant—a middle-aged man with silver-streaked hair and a formal waistcoat, complete with pocket watch chain visible across his midsection. He looked up from the ledger he was writing in, fixing Robert with a penetrating gaze that seemed to assess far more than physical appearance.

"Robert North," the man said, closing his ledger. "Right on schedule. I'm Jake Steinman. Gil is waiting in the back room."

No introduction had been necessary, apparently. Robert nodded, that sense of familiarity intensifying as he followed Jake through the maze of bookshelves toward the rear of the shop. Everything about the space felt known to him—the creaky third floorboard, the particular smell of leather bindings and old paper, even the specific arrangement of books on certain shelves.

The back room proved to be a comfortable office lined with more bookshelves, these containing volumes that looked considerably rarer and more esoteric than those in the main shop. Gil Harmon sat in an armchair by the window, examining what appeared to be ancient manuscripts spread across a small table.

"Ah, Robert, excellent," Gil looked up, showing no surprise at his arrival. "Right on schedule, as probability configurations suggested."

Jake closed the door behind them, then moved to a cabinet from which he retrieved an antique tea service. "Earl Grey, if I recall your preference correctly," he said to Robert, who had never mentioned his tea preferences to either man but was indeed particularly fond of Earl Grey.

As Jake prepared the tea with practiced efficiency, Gil gestured to the manuscripts before him. "Original research notes from the Daybridge Containment Initiative, 1943. Maxwell Hanover's quantum field manipulation experiments that laid the foundation for modern understanding of observer effects on reality coherence."

Robert took the seat opposite Gil, drawn to the yellowed pages covered in handwritten equations and diagrams. Something about the mathematical formulations seemed instantly comprehensible to him, despite their complexity and antiquated notation.

"These describe quantum observation networks," he said, pointing to a particular set of equations. "Systems for maintaining coherent reality configuration through distributed observation points."

Gil's eyebrows rose slightly. "Most physicists require considerable time to decipher Hanover's notation system. Your quantum signature clearly resonates with the underlying concepts."

"Quantum signature?" Robert questioned, accepting the cup of tea Jake handed him.

The two older men exchanged glances before Jake spoke. "Each consciousness maintains a specific quantum resonance pattern that influences its interaction with reality at fundamental levels. Yours displays unusual characteristics—a harmonic structure suggesting awareness that extends beyond conventional probability constraints."

Gil nodded agreement. "In simpler terms, you perceive reality differently than most. Your consciousness naturally recognizes the potential for multiple configurations while maintaining coherent experience within a singular manifestation."

Robert sipped his tea, considering this assessment. It aligned with his recent experiences—the dreams of multiple Daybridges, the déjà vu moments where he seemed to recognize places he'd never visited, the intuitive understanding of quantum field theories beyond his formal education.

"This relates to my research," he said slowly. "The particles in my tunneling experiments exhibit similar behavior—maintaining potential for multiple states while demonstrating coherent existence within measured parameters."

"Precisely!" Gil's eyes lit with scientific enthusiasm. "You've independently rediscovered aspects of Hanover's quantum coherence theory through empirical observation. Your measurement techniques allow particles to maintain superposition despite observation events—essentially demonstrating at a microscopic scale how reality preserves singular coherence while containing multiversal potential."

Jake placed his teacup on the desk and opened the ledger he had brought from the front of the shop. "What Gil is approaching somewhat circuitously is that your research has significant implications beyond conventional quantum mechanics. You're essentially documenting the mechanisms by which reality maintains singular configuration despite inherent quantum potential for multiple manifestations."

Robert looked between the two men, sensing they were gradually working toward something beyond theoretical physics discussion. "Why does this matter so specifically? Quantum mechanics has acknowledged superposition and probability wave functions for decades."

Gil and Jake exchanged another meaningful glance before Gil spoke again. "Because approximately eight months ago, certain monitoring instruments detected unusual quantum fluctuations centered on specific locations throughout Daybridge—fluctuations suggesting temporary thinning of what we might call reality coherence parameters."

"In less technical terms," Jake continued, "locations where the singular reality configuration briefly displayed characteristics consistent with potential alternate manifestations. These fluctuations corresponded precisely with unusual dream reports and déjà vu experiences among individuals with heightened quantum sensitivity."

Robert felt a chill of recognition. "Like my dreams of subway stations that don't exist and different versions of Daybridge."

"Exactly." Gil leaned forward. "Your consciousness was registering echo effects from probability configurations that exist as potential rather than manifestation within our singular reality framework."

Jake turned his ledger toward Robert, revealing pages of handwritten notes and complex diagrams that documented these fluctuation events. "The most significant event occurred approximately six months ago—a temporary but dramatic intensification of quantum instability throughout Daybridge, centered on Thornfield Avenue and Riverside Drive."

Robert's pulse quickened at the mention of that specific intersection—the location that featured prominently in his most vivid dreams. "What happened there?"

"Reality briefly displayed characteristics consistent with multiple simultaneous configurations," Gil explained. "For approximately 3.7 minutes, quantum observation frameworks registered overlapping probability manifestations before singular coherence reasserted itself."

"In simplified terms," Jake added, "the fundamental mechanisms that maintain our singular reality timeline experienced temporary disruption, allowing potential alternate configurations to partially manifest before being reintegrated into coherent form."

Robert sat back, processing this extraordinary information. "And you think this connects to my research somehow?"

"Not just connects—derives from identical fundamental principles," Gil confirmed. "Your measurement techniques that allow particles to maintain superposition despite observation events mirror the larger quantum mechanisms that maintain reality coherence across probability potentials."

Jake closed his ledger with deliberate care. "We believe your unique quantum signature and research focus make you particularly valuable for understanding these fluctuation events and potentially helping prevent more significant disruptions to reality coherence."

The conversation had moved far beyond ordinary scientific discussion into territory that should have seemed absurd. Yet Robert found himself accepting these concepts with that same strange intuitive recognition he'd experienced when examining Hanover's equations.

"You're suggesting reality itself occasionally... glitches?" he asked, searching for a simpler formulation. "Showing multiple possible versions before settling back into singular form?"

"An imprecise but not inaccurate analogy," Gil nodded. "Though 'glitches' implies malfunction, when in fact these fluctuations represent natural quantum behavior at reality-scale parameters. The remarkable aspect isn't that they occur but that they remain so rare despite the inherent indeterminacy of quantum systems."

"Reality maintenance requires continuous observation networks operating at quantum levels," Jake explained. "Maxwell Hanover's greatest insight was recognizing that consciousness itself forms part of this network—that awareness helps collapse probability waves into coherent manifestation."

Robert touched the fountain pen in his shirt pocket without thinking, drawing Gil's immediate attention.

"You brought it," the elderly physicist observed with evident satisfaction. "Certain objects maintain quantum resonance patterns that transcend conventional temporal constraints. Your pen appears to be one such artifact."

"I don't even remember where I got it," Robert admitted, removing the pen for closer examination. "It just appeared among my possessions months ago, and I felt... connected to it somehow."

Jake extended his hand. "May I?"

Robert passed him the pen, watching as Jake examined it with professional interest, turning it carefully to study markings near the clip that Robert had never noticed before.

"Manufactured in 1943," Jake noted. "Part of a limited production series commissioned by the Daybridge Containment Initiative for documenting quantum field experiments. The brass components contain specific metallic alloys selected for their quantum resonance characteristics."

He handed the pen back to Robert. "Such artifacts often find their way to individuals with compatible quantum signatures across probability configurations. The resonance creates a natural attraction that transcends conventional causality."

"You're saying this pen somehow... chose me?" Robert asked incredulously.

"More accurately, your quantum signature and the pen's resonance pattern established mutual attraction across probability configurations," Gil clarified. "In potential alternate manifestations, you might have acquired it through different means, but the connection would establish itself regardless due to harmonic compatibility."

Robert turned the pen in his fingers, noticing how the brass accents caught the light in ways that occasionally created unusual optical effects—brief prismatic patterns that seemed to contain more colors than should be possible.

"Why are you telling me all this?" he asked finally, looking up at the two men. "What do you want from me?"

Jake and Gil exchanged another significant glance before Jake answered. "We'd like your assistance with a specific research project related to quantum coherence maintenance. Your unique perspective and experimental approach could prove invaluable for understanding the fluctuation events we've been monitoring."

"More directly," Gil added, "we believe your quantum tunneling experiments have inadvertently demonstrated mechanics directly relevant to reality coherence at fundamental levels. With proper adaptation, your measurement techniques could potentially help stabilize quantum fluctuations if they recur with greater intensity."

The offer was simultaneously flattering and unsettling. Robert sensed there was more to their interest than they were directly stating, yet he felt an inexplicable trust toward both men despite their unusual assertions.

"What would this research project involve exactly?" he asked.

"Initially, adapting your experimental protocols to measure quantum fluctuations at specific locations throughout Daybridge," Jake explained. "Particularly focusing on sites where previous reality coherence variations have been detected."

"We've established monitoring stations at eight key locations," Gil continued. "Your quantum measurement approach could significantly enhance their sensitivity to probability configuration variations."

Robert considered the proposal, finding himself intrigued despite the extraordinary nature of their claims. His recent dreams and déjà vu experiences had left him with questions conventional physics couldn't answer—perhaps this unusual collaboration might provide explanations.

"I'd need to discuss this with Professor Liang," he said. "My graduate research is under her supervision."

"Dr. Liang has collaborated with me previously on quantum field projects," Gil replied with a knowing smile. "I suspect she would support your involvement, particularly given the potential applications to your current research focus."

Jake retrieved a folder from his desk drawer and handed it to Robert. "Review these materials when you have time. They provide additional context regarding the fluctuation events and our current monitoring approaches."

Robert accepted the folder, noting its unusual weight and the faint vibration he felt when touching it—as if the contents somehow resonated with his own quantum signature, as Gil might say.

"There's one location in particular we'd like you to visit with us," Gil added, his expression becoming more serious. "The intersection of Thornfield Avenue and Riverside Drive—the center point of the most significant fluctuation event. Your quantum signature might register aspects of residual probability resonance not detectable by our conventional instruments."

The mention of that specific intersection triggered another powerful wave of déjà vu. In Robert's dreams, that location had featured a subway entrance that didn't exist in waking reality—a station with brass fixtures and constellation mosaics overhead.

"When?" he asked, already knowing he would agree despite the rational part of his mind suggesting caution.

"Tonight would be optimal," Gil replied promptly. "Quantum fluctuation patterns suggest an increased probability of resonance detection between 11 PM and midnight. Similar temporal parameters to the original event."

Robert nodded, that sense of inevitability growing stronger. "I'll meet you there."

As he prepared to leave, Jake handed him a small device that resembled an antique pocket watch. "This monitors quantum signature variations. Keep it with you today—it might register interesting patterns as you move through locations with residual probability resonance."

Robert accepted the device, noticing that its face displayed not time but a complex pattern of shifting symbols that somehow seemed partially comprehensible to him despite their unfamiliarity.

"Thornfield and Riverside, 11 PM," Jake confirmed as he showed Robert to the door. "And bring your fountain pen. Its quantum resonance characteristics may prove useful during our investigation."

As Robert left the bookshop and stepped onto Merchant Street, he felt as if he had crossed some invisible threshold—moving from conventional reality into something more complex and mysterious. The pocket watch device in his hand hummed softly, its display shifting in response to his movement through the city.

Whatever awaited him at Thornfield Avenue that night, he sensed it would answer questions he hadn't even fully formulated—explaining the dreams, the déjà vu, and the strange intuitive understanding that had been growing within him for months.

At 10:45 PM, Robert approached the intersection of Thornfield Avenue and Riverside Drive with mounting anticipation. The night was clear but cool, autumn having fully established itself across Daybridge. Street lights created pools of illumination at regular intervals, with darker spaces between where shadows gathered in layered patterns.

Jake and Gil were already waiting at the designated meeting point, both carrying equipment cases that suggested sophisticated monitoring technology. As Robert joined them, he noticed additional devices had been positioned around the intersection—small silver discs placed at precise intervals that occasionally emitted soft blue pulses of light.

"Right on schedule," Gil greeted him with that now-familiar phrase. "Your quantum signature is registering increased resonance already, precisely as probability configurations predicted."

Jake opened one of the equipment cases, revealing an array of instruments Robert didn't recognize despite his extensive laboratory experience. "We've established a monitoring perimeter to track quantum fluctuations throughout the intersection. The readings already show unusual patterns consistent with probability resonance."

Robert removed the pocket watch device Jake had given him earlier, noting that its display had changed significantly as he approached the intersection—the shifting symbols now pulsing with increased intensity and forming patterns that seemed almost linguistically coherent, as if trying to communicate specific information.

"It's responding to this location," he observed, showing the device to Gil.

"Quantum signature harmonization," the elderly physicist confirmed. "Your personal resonance pattern is aligning with residual probability configurations from the fluctuation event. This suggests you maintain a specific connection to the alternative manifestations that briefly surfaced here."

Jake had finished setting up his equipment and now stood in the center of the intersection, holding a device that resembled an antique theodolite modified with unusual components. "Probability density measurements indicate increasing quantum instability throughout the location. The coherence parameters are thinning precisely as they did during the previous event."

Robert felt it too—a subtle vibration in the air, a quality of light that seemed to shift between various spectrum configurations, occasional visual echoes where objects momentarily displayed multiple potential states before settling back into singular form.

"What exactly happened here?" he asked, watching as the silver discs positioned around the intersection pulsed with increasing frequency.

Gil and Jake exchanged another of their significant glances before Gil answered. "Six months ago, at approximately 11:17 PM, reality coherence parameters at this intersection experienced significant disruption. For 3.7 minutes, multiple probability configurations manifested simultaneously before singular coherence reasserted itself."

"In less technical terms," Jake added, "the quantum mechanics that maintain our reality as a singular coherent timeline temporarily faltered, allowing glimpses of potential alternate configurations to manifest physically."

"Like what?" Robert pressed, sensing they were still withholding specific details.

Gil adjusted one of his monitoring devices before responding. "Architectural variations, altered street configurations, and most significantly, manifestation of structures that don't exist in our current reality configuration—including what appeared to be a subway entrance between those buildings." He pointed to the exact location that had featured in Robert's most vivid dreams.

A chill ran down Robert's spine. "There's no subway in Daybridge."

"Not in this reality configuration," Jake confirmed. "But in potential alternate manifestations, different urban development decisions might have resulted in subterranean transit systems rather than the surface trolley network historically implemented here."

"I've dreamed about it," Robert admitted, staring at the space between buildings where his dreams had shown an entrance with iron railings curving downward into warm light. "A subway station with constellation mosaics overhead and brass fixtures that gleamed like they were polished daily. Copper trains that traveled between... between different versions of Daybridge."

Gil nodded, unsurprised by this revelation. "Your quantum signature demonstrates resonance with these potential configurations. In your dreams, your consciousness accesses probability patterns that exist as potential rather than manifestation within our current reality framework."

"But it felt so real," Robert insisted. "Not like ordinary dreams—more like actual memories, experiences I really had but somehow forgot."

"The distinction between memory, dream, and probability resonance becomes philosophically complex at quantum consciousness levels," Jake observed, checking readings on his theodolite-like device. "What we experience as 'real' ultimately derives from quantum observation collapsing probability waves into specific configurations. When this observation networks experience fluctuation, reality coherence itself becomes temporarily negotiable."

The pocket watch device in Robert's hand suddenly emitted a high-pitched tone, its display shifting to a solid blue illumination. Similar responses came from the monitoring equipment Gil and Jake had positioned around the intersection.

"Quantum fluctuation intensifying," Gil announced, checking his instruments. "Probability resonance approaching parameters consistent with potential coherence variation."

Jake moved quickly to one of his equipment cases, removing what appeared to be an antique brass disc etched with intricate patterns. "Stabilization may be required if fluctuation continues to intensify. This artifact helps maintain reality coherence during probability resonance events."

Robert felt the change in the surrounding air—a thickening of atmosphere, a quality of light that seemed to bend around objects in subtle but impossible ways, an auditory effect where sounds echoed slightly before they occurred. The buildings surrounding the intersection occasionally shimmered, briefly displaying alternative architectural configurations before settling back into familiar forms.

"What's happening?" he asked, watching as a street sign momentarily displayed three different street names simultaneously before returning to "Thornfield Avenue."

"Reality coherence experiencing temporary fluctuation," Gil explained, monitoring his instruments with intense concentration. "Quantum observation networks adjusting to probability resonance intensification."

Jake placed the brass disc on the ground at the precise center of the intersection, where it began to emit a soft blue glow similar to the smaller silver discs positioned around the perimeter. "This will help stabilize local coherence parameters if fluctuation exceeds natural adjustment capacity."

Robert's attention was repeatedly drawn to the space between buildings where his dreams had shown a subway entrance. As he watched, the solid brick wall there occasionally rippled like disturbed water, briefly becoming transparent to reveal what appeared to be iron railings and steps leading downward before solidifying again.

"You see it, don't you?" Gil asked quietly, observing Robert's focused gaze. "The entrance manifesting through probability resonance."

"It's like it's trying to exist," Robert replied, struggling to articulate the strange visual effect. "Pushing through from... somewhere else."

"Potential alternate configurations exerting quantum pressure against current reality coherence," Jake confirmed, checking his pocket watch. "It's 11:15. The fluctuation event six months ago initiated at precisely 11:17."

The surrounding air continued to change, developing a quality that made conventional perception increasingly difficult. Objects left visible trails when moved, light sources created prismatic effects that shouldn't have been possible, and occasionally the entire intersection seemed to shift slightly out of alignment with itself, as if multiple versions were trying to occupy the same space simultaneously.

"Two minutes to potential coherence fluctuation," Gil announced, his instruments now emitting continuous tones of varying pitch that somehow corresponded to the visual distortions affecting the intersection.

Jake removed another device from his case—a copper circlet similar to those used in early electroencephalography experiments, though modified with components Robert didn't recognize.

"If significant fluctuation occurs, we may need to establish direct quantum resonance monitoring," Jake explained, handing the circlet to Robert. "This allows consciousness to maintain coherent perception despite reality configuration variations."

Robert accepted the device with mounting apprehension, the situation having progressed far beyond theoretical discussion into phenomena that challenged fundamental understanding of reality itself.

"One minute," Gil called, checking multiple instruments simultaneously. "Quantum fluctuation intensifying beyond previous measurement parameters."

The brass disc at the center of the intersection now pulsed with rhythmic blue light, each wave temporarily stabilizing the visual distortions before they resumed with increased intensity. The brick wall between buildings where the subway entrance kept trying to manifest had developed a continuous rippling effect, occasionally becoming completely transparent to reveal a fully formed station entrance before solidifying again.

"Thirty seconds," Jake announced, moving to stand beside Robert. "If significant coherence fluctuation occurs, maintain physical contact with your fountain pen. Its quantum resonance characteristics will help stabilize your personal perception regardless of reality configuration variations."

Robert removed the pen from his pocket, feeling it vibrate slightly against his palm—responding to the changing quantum parameters around them like a tuning fork to specific frequencies.

"Ten seconds," Gil called, his expression showing scientific fascination despite the extraordinary circumstances. "Probability configurations approaching critical resonance threshold."

As if responding to some unheard signal, all the monitoring devices activated simultaneously—the silver discs around the perimeter, the brass disc at the center, the instruments in Gil and Jake's equipment cases. Blue light pulsed outward in concentric waves from multiple sources, creating a complex interference pattern throughout the intersection.

"Now," Jake said quietly, checking his pocket watch as it displayed 11:17 PM.

For a moment, nothing seemed to happen beyond the continuing visual distortions and monitoring equipment activity. Then, with startling suddenness, reality itself appeared to fracture.

The intersection split into multiple overlapping versions simultaneously—different architectural configurations, altered street layouts, various lighting technologies, even different weather conditions all manifesting in the same physical space. Through these overlapping realities, Robert could see countless versions of themselves standing in essentially the same positions but with subtle variations in clothing, posture, and accompanying equipment.

Most dramatically, the brick wall between buildings disappeared completely, replaced by a fully manifested subway entrance—iron railings curving downward into warm light below, exactly as Robert had seen in his dreams. But this wasn't a single entrance; it was dozens of slightly different versions overlapping, each leading to a similar but distinct station below.

"Complete coherence fluctuation," Gil announced, his voice echoing strangely as if coming from multiple sources simultaneously. "Multiple probability configurations manifesting concurrently."

Jake activated additional equipment, creating a stable zone around them where the overlapping realities remained visible but didn't cause physical disruption to their immediate environment. "Containment field established. We can observe without direct interaction."

Robert stared in astonishment at the manifested subway entrance and the multiple overlapping versions of reality throughout the intersection. "This is... impossible."

"Improbable rather than impossible," Gil corrected, checking readings on his instruments. "Quantum mechanics allows for such configurations theoretically. The remarkable aspect is that reality normally maintains singular coherence despite inherent probability potential for multiple manifestations."

As they observed the extraordinary phenomenon, Robert noticed something even more unsettling—figures emerging from the various subway entrances. Not conventional pedestrians, but ghostly, transparent forms that moved with strange fluidity between the overlapping reality configurations.

"Station attendants," Jake identified them, noticing Robert's focused attention. "Consciousness constructs that maintain transit functionality between probability configurations in realities where the subway system manifested."

The ghostly figures moved throughout the intersection, seemingly unaware of Robert, Gil, and Jake within their containment field. They performed what appeared to be routine maintenance tasks—adjusting signs, polishing brass fixtures, occasionally directing equally transparent "passengers" toward specific entrances.

"This is what I've been dreaming about," Robert whispered, recognition flooding through him. "The subway system that connects different versions of Daybridge. The Liminal Line."

Jake and Gil exchanged another significant glance at this specific terminology.

"You recall the designation," Gil noted with interest. "That suggests deeper probability resonance than initially calculated."

"Recall? How could I recall something that doesn't exist?" Robert asked, confused by the phrasing.

Before either could answer, a new figure appeared at the central subway entrance—an elderly man in a precise transit uniform with gleaming brass buttons and immaculate white gloves. Unlike the other ghostly attendants, this figure moved with mechanical precision and seemed to survey the intersection with conscious awareness.

"The Station Master," Robert said automatically, the name emerging before he consciously recognized the figure.

Jake moved quickly to adjust the containment field parameters. "He's detecting our observation. Reality coherence fluctuation is intensifying beyond anticipated parameters."

The elderly transit worker turned slowly, his gaze fixing directly on their position despite the containment field that should have prevented such perception. His expression showed neither surprise nor confusion, but rather a calm recognition that suggested he had expected their presence.

"Catalyst," the Station Master said, his voice somehow audible despite the spatial separation and containment field. "The probability cycle reasserts itself despite reality reconfiguration. Some patterns transcend even singular timeline protocols."

"He's addressing you," Gil told Robert, surprise evident in his voice. "Your quantum signature must maintain a specific resonance with the Liminal Line configuration despite reality coherence restoration."

Robert felt the fountain pen grow warm in his hand, vibrating at increasing frequency as if responding to the Station Master's presence. The pocket watch device Jake had given him emitted a high-pitched tone, its display shifting to patterns that somehow corresponded to the Station Master's precise movements.

"What does he mean, 'catalyst'?" Robert asked, instinctively gripping the fountain pen tighter as reality fluctuations intensified around them.

Instead of answering directly, Jake removed an artifact from his case—a stone disc on a leather cord, etched with geometric patterns similar to those on the brass stabilization disc at the intersection's center.

"Dimensional anchor," he explained, handing it to Robert. "If coherence fluctuation continues to intensify, this will help maintain your quantum signature alignment with our primary reality configuration."

Robert accepted the disc, feeling immediate resonance between it, the fountain pen, and some essential aspect of his own consciousness—as if these objects were extensions of himself across quantum probability patterns.

The Station Master remained focused on Robert, his unnaturally perfect features displaying what might have been recognition. "The sequence realigns despite parameter adjustments. Some journeys cannot be prevented, merely postponed."

With those cryptic words, he turned and descended into the central subway entrance, disappearing into the warm light below. As he vanished, the reality fluctuations intensified dramatically—buildings cycling through multiple configurations with increasing speed, streets rearranging themselves continuously, the very air seeming to shatter and reform in kaleidoscopic patterns.

"Coherence parameters approaching critical instability," Gil announced, his instruments now emitting continuous alarm tones. "Containment field limitations exceeded by fluctuation intensity."

Jake moved quickly to the brass disc at the intersection's center, making adjustments to its configuration. "We need to implement secondary stabilization protocols immediately. The quantum resonance is amplifying beyond sustainable parameters."

Robert felt himself becoming increasingly disoriented as reality fluctuations intensified. The overlapping versions of the intersection seemed to be merging and separating in complex patterns, making it impossible to determine which configuration represented their original reality.

"What's happening?" he asked, clutching the dimensional anchor and fountain pen as his only points of stability in the chaos.

"Reality coherence experiencing cascading resonance effect," Gil explained, though his form now occasionally blurred as if existing in multiple states simultaneously. "The probability configurations are approaching convergence parameters similar to the original event."

"Original event?" Robert repeated, another wave of déjà vu washing over him. "You mean this has happened before? Not just six months ago?"

Jake and Gil exchanged yet another significant glance, this one containing clear concern about how much to reveal.

"We need to tell him," Gil said finally, his voice distorting slightly as reality fluctuations affected even sound propagation. "The quantum resonance patterns suggest he already maintains partial awareness despite reality reconfiguration."

Jake nodded reluctantly, then turned to Robert. "The event six months ago wasn't the first fluctuation, but rather the completion of a reset protocol initiated during catastrophic coherence failure. What you're experiencing now are echo effects from probability configurations that existed before reality reconfiguration."

This explanation should have been incomprehensible, yet Robert found himself nodding with intuitive understanding. "The reset. We reset reality to heal the original breach."

The words emerged automatically, triggering a cascade of fragmented memories—a train spiraling upward toward a swirling vortex, blue energy enveloping multiple versions of Daybridge, countless realities merging into one coherent configuration centered on a specific point in 1943.

"His quantum signature maintains configuration memory despite timeline adjustment," Gil observed with scientific fascination despite the increasingly dangerous situation. "Consciousness transcending reality reconfiguration parameters."

Jake moved quickly between his monitoring devices, attempting to stabilize the escalating fluctuations. "We need to implement full containment protocols before coherence failure reaches the critical threshold. The reset timeline itself is experiencing instability due to residual probability resonance."

The subway entrances were now fully manifested, no longer flickering between existence and non-existence but maintaining stable configuration despite their impossibility within conventional Daybridge geography. More concerning, they had begun to emit a rhythmic humming sound accompanied by warm air carrying the scent of ozone and brass polish—signs that Robert somehow recognized as indicating approaching trains.

"The Liminal Line is reactivating," he said, certainty filling him despite the impossibility of knowing such things. "The system is reconnecting probability tracks that were merged during the reset."

Gil checked his instruments, alarm evident despite his scientific detachment. "Quantum signatures throughout the intersection show harmonic alignment with transit system parameters. The probability configurations are approaching resonance patterns consistent with pre-reset manifestation."

Jake returned to them, carrying what appeared to be an antique telegraph key connected to a small brass box. "We need to establish a quantum interference pattern to counteract the resonance effect. This device can generate dimensional harmonics that reinforce reality coherence against probability fluctuation."

He placed the device on the ground near the brass disc, making rapid adjustments to both artifacts. "Robert, your quantum signature may be inadvertently amplifying the fluctuation due to residual resonance with the transit system. The dimensional anchor should help counteract this effect if you focus on current reality configuration."

Robert clutched the stone disc, feeling it grow warmer against his palm. "How do I focus on 'current reality configuration' when everything is fluctuating?"

"Concentrate on fixed points in your personal timeline," Gil suggested. "Experiences unique to this reality that maintain quantum consistency regardless of probability variations."

Before Robert could attempt this, a new development caught their attention—the central subway entrance had begun to emit increasingly bright light, accompanied by the unmistakable sound of an approaching train. Unlike the other entrances, which remained in flux between multiple configurations, this one had stabilized into a single, solid manifestation.

"Probability convergence initiating at primary nexus point," Gil announced, checking his instruments. "Transit system attempting to reestablish interdimensional connectivity through residual quantum resonance."

Jake abandoned his stabilization attempts, instead moving quickly to his equipment case and removing what appeared to be a copper rod etched with similar patterns to the brass disc. "We need to seal the breach before complete resonance alignment occurs. This coherence wand can generate a localized quantum interference field directly at the manifestation point."

As he approached the subway entrance, reality fluctuations intensified around him—his form occasionally blurring as if existing in multiple states simultaneously. The copper rod in his hand emitted pulses of blue light that temporarily stabilized the space immediately surrounding him but couldn't prevent the larger coherence breakdown occurring throughout the intersection.

Gil turned to Robert, his expression grave despite the scientific fascination he clearly felt. "Your quantum signature shows direct resonance with the transit system manifestation. You may be inadvertently functioning as a catalyst for the probability realignment process."

"What does that mean?" Robert asked, the dimensional anchor now almost painfully hot against his palm.

"In simplified terms, your consciousness maintains a connection to probability configurations that existed before the reality reset," Gil explained. "This connection is strengthening the quantum resonance patterns necessary for the transit system to rematerialize in current reality."

The rumbling of an approaching train grew louder, and the light from the central subway entrance intensified to near-blinding levels. Jake had reached the manifestation point and was using the copper rod to generate a containment field around the entrance, but the energy emanating from below clearly exceeded his equipment's capacity.

"Probability convergence approaching critical threshold," Gil warned, his instruments now emitting continuous alarm tones. "Dimensional breach imminent at primary manifestation point."

Jake returned to them quickly, his containment attempts having proven insufficient. "We need to implement the contingency protocol immediately. The probability resonance is too intense for conventional stabilization methods."

He turned to Robert, his expression showing both concern and determination. "There's something we haven't fully explained. Your quantum signature isn't merely resonating with the transit system—it maintains specific configuration memory because you personally experienced the original probability tracks before the reset protocol."

"What are you saying?" Robert asked, though a growing certainty was filling him, fragments of memory coalescing into coherent understanding despite their impossibility.

"You were the catalyst for both the convergence crisis and the subsequent reality reset," Gil stated directly. "Your journeys through the Liminal Line across multiple versions of Daybridge eventually led to catastrophic coherence failure that necessitated complete reality reconfiguration."

As these words registered, Robert experienced a sudden, overwhelming cascade of memories—discovering the subway entrance on a rainy night, traveling between increasingly divergent versions of Daybridge, meeting Gil in a threshold reality where normal physics didn't apply, working with Jake to prevent dimensional collapse, and finally participating in the reset protocol that merged countless realities into the singular timeline they now inhabited.

"I remember," he whispered, staggered by the implications. "All of it. The seven crossings. The Station Master. The convergence point where reality itself began to fold inward."

Jake nodded grimly. "The reset protocol was successful in healing the original breach and creating a stable singular timeline. But your quantum signature maintained configuration memory despite reality reconfiguration, creating residual resonance that's now reactivating the transit system."

"We need to implement secondary containment immediately," Gil urged, checking his instruments. "The probability convergence is approaching parameters similar to the pre-reset crisis."

Jake opened another equipment case, removing what appeared to be three silver discs identical to those positioned around the intersection perimeter, though larger and etched with more complex patterns.

"These quantum resonance stabilizers can generate an interference pattern that should prevent complete breach manifestation," he explained, handing one disc to Gil and another to Robert. "We need to position them at precise coordinates around the central entrance while maintaining quantum harmonization through conscious intent."

Robert accepted the disc, feeling immediate resonance between it, the dimensional anchor, and his fountain pen—as if these objects formed a connected system responding to his specific quantum signature.

"What do I need to do?" he asked, the memories of his previous interdimensional experiences now fully accessible despite their impossibility within current reality parameters.

"Focus on stability—on singular coherent reality rather than multiple overlapping configurations," Jake instructed. "Your quantum signature naturally resonates with probability variation due to your previous experiences. We need to reverse that resonance to reinforce current reality coherence."

The three men moved quickly toward the central subway entrance, now fully manifested as a solid structure between buildings where no such entrance should exist. The sound of an approaching train had intensified to an unmistakable imminence, accompanied by warm air carrying that familiar scent of ozone and brass polish.

Jake positioned himself at what appeared to be a precisely calculated point north of the entrance, while Gil took a similar position to the east. Robert completed the triangle on the western side, each man holding his silver disc at chest level with both hands.

"On my mark, activate your resonance disc by turning the outer ring clockwise until it clicks into position," Jake instructed. "Then focus completely on current reality configuration—singular coherent Daybridge rather than multiple overlapping versions."

Robert nodded, positioning his disc as instructed. Around them, reality continued to fluctuate with increasing intensity—buildings cycling through multiple architectural styles, streets rearranging themselves, the sky above displaying impossible atmospheric conditions as probability configurations overlapped and merged in chaotic patterns.

"Three," Jake began counting down, checking his pocket watch. "Two. One. Activate!"

Robert turned the outer ring of his disc as instructed, feeling it click into position with surprising resistance, as if fighting against powerful opposing forces. Immediately, the disc began to vibrate intensely, emitting a blue glow that extended outward to connect with similar energy fields emanating from Jake and Gil's positions.

"Maintain focus," Gil called, his voice distorting slightly as reality fluctuations affected sound propagation. "Quantum resonance stabilization requires continuous conscious reinforcement."

Robert concentrated as instructed, visualizing singular coherent reality rather than multiple overlapping configurations. He focused on specific details of his daily life in this version of Daybridge—his apartment with Noah, his laboratory at the university, the coffee shop where he studied each Thursday afternoon.

The three energy fields strengthened, forming a triangular containment pattern around the subway entrance. The reality fluctuations began to diminish within this perimeter, overlapping configurations gradually resolving toward singular coherence.

For a moment, it seemed the containment protocol was succeeding. The impossible subway entrance began to fade, the sound of the approaching train diminishing, the scent of ozone and brass polish dissipating from the air.

Then, with startling suddenness, the Station Master appeared at the entrance—no longer a ghostly manifestation but fully present, his navy uniform with gold buttons and white gloves crisp and perfect despite the quantum chaos surrounding him.

"The probability cycle cannot be indefinitely postponed," he stated, his voice carrying that same unsettling quality Robert now remembered from previous encounters—resonating at frequencies that seemed to vibrate reality itself. "Some journeys must complete their designated patterns regardless of timeline configuration."

As he spoke, the quantum stabilization field generated by their silver discs began to falter, blue energy flickering erratically as the Station Master's presence somehow disrupted the interference pattern.

"He's generating counter-resonance," Gil called, checking readings on a wrist device while maintaining his position. "His quantum signature transcends conventional reality parameters."

Jake activated additional functions on his stabilization disc, temporarily strengthening the containment field. "We need to complete the protocol before the train arrives. Once direct interdimensional transit manifests, containment becomes exponentially more difficult."

The Station Master observed their efforts with that same mechanical precision Robert remembered from his journeys through the Liminal Line—his perfect symmetrical features displaying neither concern nor alarm, merely calm observation of probability patterns unfolding according to some incomprehensible calculation.

"The catalyst's quantum signature maintains configuration memory despite timeline adjustment," he noted, his gaze fixing on Robert. "Some connections transcend even reality reconfiguration protocols."

The rumbling of the approaching train intensified again, and light from the entrance grew blindingly bright. The stabilization field continued to weaken despite their concentrated efforts, reality fluctuations resuming with increased intensity throughout the intersection.

"We need to implement the final containment measure," Jake called over the growing noise. "The probability resonance is too intense for conventional stabilization methods."

Gil nodded grimly, understanding something Robert didn't yet comprehend. "Full circle protocol?"

"Yes. It's the only option remaining." Jake turned to Robert, his expression grave. "There's something we need to tell you. The reset protocol was never meant to be permanent—merely a temporary stabilization measure until a more comprehensive solution could be implemented."

"What does that mean?" Robert asked, struggling to maintain his focus on the stabilization disc as reality fluctuations intensified around them.

"It means we need to complete the circle," Gil explained, his scientific detachment giving way to emotional directness. "Reality reset created a temporal loop that must be closed properly to achieve permanent stability."

Before Robert could ask for clarification, the Station Master spoke again, his voice somehow audible despite the deafening rumble of the approaching train.

"The journey begins and ends at the same point," he stated cryptically. "Probability configurations maintain fundamental patterns despite surface variation."

Jake moved quickly to Robert's side, maintaining his stabilization disc in one hand while removing the dimensional anchor from his pocket with the other.

"You need to wear this," he instructed, placing the stone disc on its leather cord around Robert's neck. "It will help maintain your quantum coherence during the final phase of the containment protocol."

"What final phase?" Robert asked, increasingly concerned by their grave expressions and cryptic explanations.

Gil had joined them, forming a tight triangle of stabilization energy that temporarily strengthened the containment field despite the Station Master's disruptive presence.

"To permanently heal the breach, we need to close the temporal loop created during the reset protocol," Gil explained. "This requires returning to the precise point of original divergence—the moment when you first discovered the Liminal Line entrance."

"But that never happened in this reality," Robert objected. "The reset protocol created a singular timeline where the subway system doesn't exist."

"Not exactly," Jake corrected. "The reset created a temporal loop where the original discovery still occurs, but leads to different outcomes through guided intervention. That's why your quantum signature maintains configuration memory despite reality reconfiguration—you're an essential component of the loop itself."

The subway entrance had fully stabilized now, no longer flickering between existence and non-existence but maintaining solid physical form despite its impossibility within conventional Daybridge geography. The approaching train sound had reached its peak, suggesting imminent arrival at the platform below.

"What exactly do you need me to do?" Robert asked, sensing that events had progressed beyond theoretical discussion into crucial practical action.

Jake and Gil exchanged one final significant glance before Jake answered. "You need to enter the station, board the arriving train, and complete a journey that will take you back to the precise moment and location where everything began."

"You want me to use the interdimensional subway system that shouldn't exist to travel back in time?" Robert asked incredulously.

"Not back in time in the conventional sense," Gil clarified. "Rather, to a specific nexus point in the temporal loop where probability configurations can be permanently realigned through conscious quantum intervention."

The Station Master, who had been observing their conversation with mechanical patience, now approached their stabilization triangle. The blue energy field rippled but didn't break as he stopped precisely at its perimeter.

"The Catalyst must complete the designated sequence," he stated, his perfect symmetrical features displaying what might have been satisfaction. "The probability cycle maintains fundamental coherence despite timeline adjustment."

"Why should I trust any of this?" Robert demanded, the situation having progressed far beyond reasonable scientific inquiry into what seemed like reality-bending madness. "Why should I trust him?" He nodded toward the Station Master.

"Because your quantum signature already recognizes the necessity," Gil replied, indicating Robert's fountain pen, which had begun to glow with the same blue luminescence as their stabilization discs. "Some understanding transcends conscious thought, operating at fundamental consciousness levels where quantum resonance directly influences perception."

Jake removed one final device from his pocket—a small silver sphere etched with patterns similar to those on their stabilization discs.

"This quantum resonance key will guide you to the precise nexus point required for loop closure," he explained, handing it to Robert. "When you reach Central Station, give this to the Gil Harmon you'll find there. He'll know how to use it."

"The Gil Harmon I'll find there?" Robert repeated, looking at the elderly physicist standing beside him. "But you're here."

Gil smiled sadly. "Quantum consciousness exists partially outside conventional spacetime constraints. In the nexus point you're traveling to, a version of me has been waiting to complete the containment protocol since the original convergence crisis."

The sound of a train arriving echoed up from the impossible subway entrance, accompanied by that familiar pneumatic hiss of doors opening. The stabilization field around them pulsed erratically, struggling to maintain coherence against the fully manifested interdimensional breach.

"You need to go now," Jake urged, adjusting his stabilization disc to strengthen the field temporarily. "We can maintain containment for approximately 3.7 minutes—enough time for you to board the train before probability resonance exceeds sustainable parameters."

Robert looked between the two men, then at the Station Master still waiting patiently at the perimeter of their energy field. "What happens when I reach this nexus point? How do I close the temporal loop?"

"You'll understand when you arrive," Gil assured him. "Your quantum signature contains the necessary configuration memory to recognize the required actions when presented with the appropriate context."

The Station Master inclined his head slightly, that perfect symmetrical smile revealing nothing of his thoughts or intentions. "The Catalyst returns to origin coordinates. The probability cycle maintains fundamental coherence."

With those cryptic words, he turned and descended back into the subway entrance, disappearing into the warm light below.

Jake placed his hand on Robert's shoulder. "We've been preparing for this moment since the reset protocol was implemented. Your quantum signature maintained configuration memory for precisely this purpose—to complete the temporal loop and permanently stabilize reality coherence."

"The dimensional anchor will maintain your quantum alignment throughout the journey," Gil added, indicating the stone disc around Robert's neck. "The fountain pen provides continuous connection to your origin point, and the resonance key will guide you to the proper nexus coordinates."

Robert clutched these objects, feeling their strange resonance with his own consciousness—as if they were extensions of himself across quantum probability patterns. Despite the extraordinary circumstances and seemingly impossible task before him, he felt an inexplicable certainty that this journey was both necessary and inevitable.

"What about you?" he asked, looking between Jake and Gil. "What happens to you while I'm gone?"

"We'll maintain the stabilization field as long as possible," Jake replied. "But once you depart, reality fluctuations will probably intensify beyond our containment capacity. What happens after that depends entirely on whether the temporal loop is successfully closed at the nexus point."

"In simplified terms," Gil added with a hint of his scientific detachment returning, "we're betting everything on your ability to complete this journey correctly. The entire probability configuration of our reality track depends on it."

No pressure, then, Robert thought wryly. Just the small matter of maintaining reality coherence through interdimensional subway travel to a temporal nexus point.

The stabilization field pulsed erratically, weakening despite their concentrated efforts. Reality fluctuations resumed throughout the intersection—buildings cycling through architectural variations, streets rearranging themselves, the sky displaying impossible atmospheric conditions.

"It's time," Jake said quietly, checking his pocket watch. "The train will depart in approximately forty-seven seconds. You need to board it before the probability resonance exceeds containment parameters."

Robert nodded, a strange calm settling over him despite the extraordinary circumstances. "How will I know which train to take when I reach Central Station?"

"The one that feels right," Gil replied simply. "Your quantum signature will recognize the correct probability vector when presented with appropriate options."

Jake made a final adjustment to the stabilization field, creating an opening directly aligned with the subway entrance. "Go now. We'll maintain containment as long as possible."

Robert took a deep breath, clutching the dimensional anchor around his neck, the fountain pen in his pocket, and the silver resonance key in his hand. With a final nod to Jake and Gil, he stepped through the opening in the stabilization field and approached the impossible subway entrance between buildings.

The iron railings curved downward exactly as he remembered from his dreams—or rather, from his actual experiences across probability tracks now reintegrated into the current timeline. Warm light spilled upward from below, accompanied by that familiar scent of ozone and brass polish.

As he descended the steps, reality seemed to solidify around him—the fluctuations ceasing, the overlapping configurations resolving into a single, coherent environment. The station below matched his memories precisely—vintage design elements,

RAE STONEHOUSE

constellation mosaics overhead, brass fixtures gleaming alongside worn marble tiles.

A copper train waited at the platform; its doors open invitingly. Unlike the ghostly manifestations he had glimpsed earlier, this vehicle appeared completely solid and real—more real, somehow, than the fluctuating reality he had just left behind.

The Station Master stood beside the open doors, his perfect symmetrical features displaying that same mechanical precision Robert remembered from his previous journeys.

"The Catalyst returns to designated transit parameters," he observed as Robert approached. "Probability configurations maintain fundamental coherence despite timeline adjustment."

"Where does this train go?" Robert asked, though he already suspected the answer.

"To where all journeys ultimately lead," the Station Master replied cryptically. "The nexus point where probability tracks converge and diverge simultaneously."

Robert boarded the train without further hesitation, feeling an inexplicable rightness to this action despite its apparent impossibility. The dimensional anchor around his neck hummed softly against his chest, the fountain pen glowed gently in his pocket, and the silver resonance key pulsed with blue light in his palm.

The doors closed behind him with that familiar pneumatic hiss, sealing him inside the copper car. Through the windows, he caught a final glimpse of the platform—empty now, the Station Master having disappeared as suddenly as he had manifested.

The train began to move with that same smooth acceleration he remembered from his previous journeys, quickly entering a tunnel that plunged the car into momentary darkness before soft lighting activated along the ceiling.

Robert found a seat, trying to process everything that had happened and what might await him at the journey's end. The dimensional anchor continued to hum against his chest, its vibration maintaining a steady rhythm that somehow calmed his racing thoughts.

The silver resonance key in his hand pulsed in a complementary pattern, its blue glow intensifying and diminishing in waves that seemed to correspond with the train's movement through the tunnel. These artifacts were clearly more than simple objects—they contained quantum properties that transcended conventional physical limitations.

As the train continued its journey, Robert noticed subtle changes in its environment. The copper walls occasionally displayed shifting patterns that resembled mathematical equations, the windows sometimes showed glimpses of locations that couldn't possibly exist along any conventional route, and the air itself seemed to thicken with visual distortions that suggested movement through more than just physical space.

Time became difficult to track, with minutes seemingly stretching into hours or compressing into seconds without clear delineation. The dimensional anchor maintained its steady vibration throughout these temporal fluctuations, providing the only reliable constant in an increasingly fluid environment.

Eventually, the train began to slow. Through the windows, Robert could see they were approaching a station vastly larger than the one he had departed from—a cavernous space with a ceiling that soared hundreds of feet overhead, supported by columns inscribed with mathematical formulas rather than conventional ornamentation.

"Central Station," he whispered, recognition flooding through him as the train pulled alongside a platform that extended seemingly infinitely in both directions. This was the interdimensional hub he remembered from the convergence crisis—the nexus point where all probability tracks intersected before the reality reset had merged them into a singular timeline.

The doors opened with that familiar pneumatic hiss, releasing him into an environment that shouldn't have existed yet felt more real than the fluctuating reality he had left behind. Unlike his previous experience of Central Station during the convergence crisis, when the hub had bustled with travelers from countless reality variations, this manifestation appeared eerily empty—as if waiting specifically for his arrival.

Robert stepped onto the platform, the dimensional anchor, fountain pen, and resonance key all vibrating in perfect harmonic alignment. As Jake had predicted, he somehow knew exactly which direction to take—a certainty that operated at levels deeper than conscious thought, guided by quantum resonance patterns within his very consciousness.

He moved through the vast empty station, footsteps echoing on marble flooring that occasionally displayed shifting patterns like ripples in disturbed water. The columns supporting the impossible ceiling seemed to adjust their mathematical inscriptions as he passed, equations transforming to reflect his specific quantum signature.

At the center of the concourse, he found what he had somehow known would be waiting—Gil Harmon, though not the elderly physicist he had left behind in fluctuating Daybridge. This version appeared younger, perhaps in his sixties rather than eighties, though his eyes contained the same intensity and his bearing the same precise scientific focus.

"Right on schedule," Gil greeted him with that familiar phrase. "Your quantum signature maintained temporal alignment despite probability fluctuations. Most impressive."

"Jake said to give you this," Robert replied, holding out the silver resonance key, which pulsed with increased intensity as Gil approached.

"Excellent. The final component required for complete loop closure." Gil accepted the key, which responded to his touch by shifting its illumination pattern to complement rather than match the blue glow emanating from similar devices positioned around the central concourse—devices Robert hadn't noticed until that moment.

"What exactly is happening here?" Robert asked, surveying the vast empty station with its impossibly high ceiling and infinitely extending platforms. "Jake mentioned a temporal loop that needs closing, but didn't explain what that actually means."

Gil smiled slightly as he integrated the resonance key into a larger apparatus positioned at the precise center of the concourse—a complex arrangement of brass rings orbiting a central platform upon which rested what appeared to be a perfect replica of the fountain pen Robert carried in his pocket.

"The reset protocol created a temporary solution to catastrophic coherence failure," Gil explained as he worked. "It merged countless probability tracks into a singular timeline centered on the original breach point in 1943. But that merger wasn't perfect—residual quantum resonance patterns remained, creating potential for renewed probability divergence."

"Like what happened at the intersection tonight," Robert suggested. "Reality starting to fracture into multiple configurations again."

"Precisely. The reset created a temporal loop that must be properly closed to achieve permanent stability." Gil made final adjustments to the apparatus, which had begun to emit a soft humming sound as the brass rings spun with increasing speed. "This requires returning to the precise origin point—the moment when you first discovered the Liminal Line entrance—and implementing specific quantum interventions to prevent probability divergence."

"But that never happened in the reset timeline," Robert objected. "The subway system doesn't exist in our current reality."

"Not as physical infrastructure, no," Gil agreed. "But the quantum potential remains—probability configurations that exist as possibility rather than manifestation. Your consistent dreams and déjà vu experiences demonstrate this persistent potential despite reality reconfiguration."

The apparatus at the center of the concourse had reached full activation, the brass rings spinning so rapidly they appeared as solid spheres rather than separate components. The blue glow from the central platform intensified, creating a field of energy that extended outward in concentric waves.

"The temporal loop requires precise closure parameters," Gil continued, checking readings on devices integrated into the apparatus. "Your quantum signature must return to origin coordinates with specific modifications that prevent probability divergence while maintaining essential causal relationships."

"You're saying I need to go back to the beginning," Robert said slowly, understanding gradually forming despite the extraordinary complexity. "To the rainy night when I first found the subway entrance."

"Yes, but not to repeat the same journey. Rather, to implement a specific quantum intervention that redirects probability flow toward stable singular configuration rather than multiple divergent tracks."

As Gil spoke, the energy field from the central apparatus expanded to encompass the entire concourse. The station around them began to shift subtly—walls becoming partially transparent, ceiling heights adjusting, architectural details transforming between multiple configurations before settling into new arrangements.

"Reality frameworks adjusting to temporal loop requirements," Gil explained, noticing Robert's concern at these transformations. "Central Station exists partially outside conventional spacetime constraints, allowing direct access to various nexus points within the probability matrix."

The transformations continued until the vast interdimensional hub had reconfigured into a much smaller, more specific station—one Robert recognized immediately from his first journey on the Liminal Line.

"Thornfield Station," he whispered, taking in the familiar details—the constellation mosaics overhead, the brass fixtures along the walls, the worn marble tiles underfoot. "Where everything began."

"The origin point of your journey across probability tracks," Gil confirmed. "And now the nexus point where the temporal loop must be closed to achieve permanent reality stabilization."

The apparatus at the center had transformed as well, the complex arrangement of brass rings resolving into a simple copper train waiting at the platform—identical to the one Robert had boarded on that first rainy night months ago, or years ago, or perhaps in a probability configuration that technically never existed at all.

"You need to board this train," Gil instructed, gesturing toward the open doors. "It will take you to the precise temporal coordinates where the loop closure must occur."

"And then what?" Robert asked, the dimensional anchor around his neck vibrating with increasing intensity as he approached the waiting train. "What exactly am I supposed to do when I arrive?"

"The quantum resonance patterns within your consciousness will recognize the required actions when presented with appropriate context," Gil replied, the same explanation Jake had given earlier. "Your fountain pen, dimensional anchor, and personal quantum signature contain all necessary configuration data to implement proper loop closure."

Robert hesitated at the train doors, a final question occurring to him. "What happens to you? And to Jake? If I successfully close this temporal loop, what becomes of the reality we just left?"

Gil smiled—a genuine expression rather than the mechanical precision of the Station Master, though containing similar certainty about probability configurations and quantum resonance patterns.

"Consciousness exists partially outside conventional spacetime constraints," he replied. "When the temporal loop closes properly, quantum signatures realign according to coherent probability patterns rather than fragmented configurations. Nothing is lost, merely reconfigured into more stable arrangements."

This cryptic answer wasn't entirely satisfying, but Robert sensed it was the best explanation possible given the extraordinary circumstances and fundamental limitations of language when describing quantum consciousness phenomena.

"Good luck, Catalyst," Gil said, using the Station Master's designation but with genuine emotion rather than mechanical precision. "Though probability configurations suggest success parameters exceeding 93.7%, so perhaps luck is superfluous."

With those final words of scientific encouragement, he stepped back from the train. The doors began to close automatically, sealing Robert inside the copper car that would take him to the nexus point where everything had begun—and where, apparently, everything needed to end properly to achieve permanent reality stabilization.

The train began to move immediately, accelerating smoothly into a tunnel that plunged the car into momentary darkness. When subtle lighting activated along the ceiling, Robert noticed this journey felt different from his previous experiences on the Liminal Line—the movement seemed to affect more than just physical location, creating sensations that suggested transit through temporal as well as spatial dimensions.

The dimensional anchor around his neck vibrated with increasing intensity, establishing a rhythm that somehow corresponded to both the train's movement and something deeper—perhaps the fundamental quantum resonance patterns Gil had mentioned that would guide him to proper loop closure actions when he reached his destination.

Through the windows, Robert occasionally glimpsed strange landscapes that couldn't exist in conventional reality—cities with impossible architecture, environments where physical laws seemed negotiable rather than fixed, locations where time itself appeared to flow in multiple directions simultaneously. These weren't separate realities like the different Daybridges he had visited during his original journeys, but rather probability configurations that existed as potential rather than manifestation—quantum possibilities compressed into visual representations.

After what might have been minutes or hours or some temporal duration that transcended conventional measurement, the train began to slow. Through the windows, Robert could see they were approaching a station that seemed simultaneously familiar and new—Thornfield Avenue, but not exactly as he remembered it from either his original journey or the fluctuating reality he had recently left behind.

This manifestation existed at the precise nexus point between probability configurations—the exact temporal coordinates where reality had first begun to diverge into multiple tracks following his initial discovery of the Liminal Line. It represented both what had happened in probability configurations that technically no longer existed and what needed to happen for proper temporal loop closure.

The train stopped with that familiar subtle precision, doors opening with a pneumatic hiss that released him onto a platform identical to the one he had first encountered months ago, or years ago, or perhaps in a reality that had been reset into mere potential rather than manifestation.

As Robert stepped off the train, he noticed immediately that this station was unstable—walls occasionally becoming transparent to reveal glimpses of ordinary Thornfield Avenue above, constellation mosaics overhead shifting between multiple configurations, brass fixtures along the walls fluctuating between polished brilliance and tarnished neglect.

"Reality frameworks adjusting to temporal loop parameters," he murmured, unconsciously adopting Gil's technical terminology to describe the quantum phenomena surrounding him. The dimensional anchor around his neck vibrated with increasing intensity, guiding him toward the station exit—the iron staircase leading up to the intersection where his journey had originally begun.

As he approached the stairs, Robert noticed something extraordinary—multiple transparent versions of himself descending from above, each slightly different in clothing or posture or expression, all converging on this specific nexus point from various probability configurations that had once existed as separate reality tracks before the reset protocol.

"Quantum echoes from probability configurations integrated during reality reconfiguration," he realized, again finding himself naturally adopting technical terminology that seemed to emerge from levels of understanding beyond conventional consciousness.

These transparent duplicates didn't acknowledge him or each other, moving with predetermined patterns that suggested fixed probability sequences rather than conscious awareness. They descended the stairs, approached the platform, boarded trains identical to the one that had brought Robert to this nexus point, and departed along probability tracks that technically no longer existed except as quantum potential.

Robert began ascending the stairs, the dimensional anchor guiding him upward toward the intersection above where temporal loop closure needed to occur. As he climbed, the surrounding station became increasingly unstable—walls fading to transparency, ceiling height fluctuating, the very substance of reality seeming to thin to the point where multiple configurations showed through simultaneously.

He emerged onto Thornfield Avenue in the midst of a rainstorm identical to the one he had experienced on that first night—water cascading from dark skies, streetlights reflecting off wet pavement, occasional lightning illuminating buildings momentarily before returning them to shadow. But unlike conventional reality, this manifestation showed multiple overlapping versions simultaneously—different architectural configurations, altered street layouts, various lighting technologies all existing in the same space.

More unsettling were the countless transparent versions of himself visible throughout the intersection—some approaching the subway entrance he had just exited, others walking in various directions toward different destinations, all existing as quantum echoes from probability configurations integrated during reality reconfiguration.

The dimensional anchor around his neck now pulsed with rhythmic intensity, directing his attention to a specific version among these many duplicates—a Robert North hurrying through the rain with a backpack slung over one shoulder, looking tired after a long evening in the laboratory, taking a shortcut across Thornfield Avenue toward his apartment.

This particular duplicate didn't see the subway entrance that had manifested between buildings, his attention focused on reaching home quickly through the downpour. Robert recognized this specific version immediately—it was himself from that original night, before any awareness of multiple realities or interdimensional transit systems, before everything changed with one simple decision to investigate an unexpected subway entrance on a street that shouldn't have had one.

The fountain pen in Robert's pocket began to glow with blue luminescence, complementing the vibration from the dimensional anchor around his neck. Together, these artifacts seemed to be guiding him toward a specific action—an intervention at this precise nexus point that would redirect probability flow toward stable singular configuration rather than multiple divergent tracks.

As his original self approached the point where he would notice the subway entrance, Robert understood intuitively what needed to happen. He moved quickly to intercept this quantum echo from the original probability configuration, positioning himself directly in its path.

The dimensional anchor pulsed with confirmation, and the fountain pen glowed brighter in his pocket. This was the nexus point where probability configurations would either diverge into multiple reality tracks or maintain singular coherence, depending on specific quantum interventions implemented at this crucial moment.

As his original self drew nearer, seemingly unaware of his presence despite their proximity, Robert removed the fountain pen from his pocket. It now glowed with intense blue luminescence, responding to the specific quantum parameters of this temporal nexus point.

When his duplicate was just steps away from the spot where he would have noticed the subway entrance, Robert made the quantum intervention that intuition and artifact guidance suggested was necessary for proper temporal loop closure.

He clicked the fountain pen.

The simple action generated a pulse of blue energy that expanded outward in concentric waves, encompassing both versions of himself and the entire intersection. Reality itself seemed to pause momentarily, probability configurations suspended in perfect balance between divergence and coherence.

In that suspended moment, Robert felt his consciousness expanding beyond conventional constraints—connecting simultaneously to every version of himself across probability configurations, accessing awareness that transcended singular identity to encompass quantum consciousness in its more fundamental form.

Through this expanded awareness, he understood completely what the temporal loop closure required—not preventing his original journey entirely, but redirecting it along parameters that maintained essential causal relationships while preventing catastrophic probability divergence.

The blue energy pulse continued expanding outward, reaching the limits of the intersection before reversing direction, flowing back inward toward the nexus point where both versions of Robert North stood in quantum resonance alignment. As the energy reconverged, reality itself began to reconfigure—not fracturing into multiple tracks as it had originally but flowing into a singular coherent manifestation that incorporated essential elements from across probability configurations.

The duplicate version of himself that represented his original pre-awareness state began to fade, not disappearing entirely but merging with his current consciousness—quantum signatures realigning according to coherent probability patterns rather than fragmented configurations, just as Gil had described.

Robert felt this integration occurring within his own awareness—memories reconfiguring, experiences realigning, consciousness itself adjusting to new temporal parameters that maintained singular coherence while preserving essential understanding gained through probability exploration.

As the blue energy completed its reconvergence, reality solidified around him in singular coherent form. The rain continued falling, streetlights still reflected off wet pavement, buildings maintained consistent architectural configuration—but the subway entrance between buildings had vanished completely, leaving only a solid brick wall where interdimensional transit had once been possible.

The dimensional anchor around his neck had stopped vibrating, its purpose apparently fulfilled. The fountain pen in his hand no longer glowed with blue luminescence, returning to the appearance of an elegant antique writing instrument with no obvious extraordinary properties.

Robert stood alone at the intersection of Thornfield Avenue and Riverside Drive, rain soaking through his clothing as he tried to process what had just occurred. The temporal loop had closed successfully, probability configurations redirected toward stable singular manifestation rather than multiple divergent tracks.

Reality had been fundamentally reconfigured, yet maintained essential continuity. He still remembered everything—his journeys through multiple Daybridges, meeting Gil in threshold reality, working with Jake to prevent dimensional collapse, the convergence crisis and subsequent reset protocol, and now this final temporal loop closure that had apparently stabilized everything permanently.

But these memories now existed within a coherent singular framework rather than fragmented across probability configurations. The Liminal Line no longer existed as physical infrastructure, only as quantum potential integrated into more stable arrangements within unified reality.

As Robert contemplated these extraordinary developments, he noticed a familiar figure approaching through the rain—Jake Steinman, carrying an umbrella and wearing the same formal waistcoat with pocket watch chain visible across his midsection.

"Right on schedule," Jake greeted him with the phrase Robert had come to associate with predetermined quantum alignment. "The temporal loop closure parameters appear to have implemented correctly. Reality configurations show stable singular coherence throughout monitored sectors."

"You remember everything?" Robert asked, surprised that Jake maintained complete awareness despite the fundamental reality reconfiguration that had just occurred.

"The guardian function transcends conventional reality constraints," Jake replied with a slight smile. "Someone must maintain awareness of the multiverse's true nature, even in a singular timeline, to prevent similar breaches from occurring in the future."

He glanced around the intersection, which now displayed perfectly normal rainy evening characteristics with no hint of the quantum fluctuations or overlapping probability configurations that had existed minutes earlier.

"The loop closure was executed with remarkable precision," Jake observed. "Your quantum signature established perfect resonance alignment at the nexus point, redirecting probability flow exactly as required for stable singular configuration."

"What about Gil?" Robert asked, suddenly concerned about the physicist who had guided him through so much of this extraordinary journey across realities both manifest and potential.

"Professor Harmon is currently giving a lecture at the university's Institute for Quantum Studies," Jake replied. "His consciousness integrated successfully into the reconfigured reality framework, though he maintains partial awareness of probability configurations that technically no longer exist except as quantum potential."

He opened his umbrella wider, offering Robert shelter from the continuing downpour. "We should leave this intersection now that temporal loop closure is complete. Your apartment is approximately twelve blocks from here, I believe."

Robert accepted the offered shelter, falling into step beside Jake as they left Thornfield Avenue behind. "So that's it? Reality is fixed permanently? No more interdimensional subway or multiple Daybridges or probability divergence?"

"'Fixed' implies previous dysfunction, when in fact reality has simply reconfigured according to more stable quantum parameters," Jake corrected gently. "The multiverse still exists as potential, even in a timeline where probability tracks haven't physically manifested. But the specific breach that created the Liminal Line has been permanently sealed through proper temporal loop closure."

They walked in silence for several blocks, Robert processing the extraordinary events he had experienced and the even more extraordinary reality reconfiguration that had apparently resolved everything into stable singular coherence.

"Will I remember all this tomorrow?" he asked finally. "Or will my consciousness integrate these experiences into the reconfigured reality framework until they seem like dreams or imagination?"

Jake considered this question carefully before answering. "Your quantum signature maintains unusual resonance characteristics that transcend conventional reality constraints. I suspect you'll retain more awareness than most would under similar circumstances, though the experiences may gradually transform into forms your consciousness can process without creating reality discord."

"Like intuitive understanding rather than literal memory," Robert suggested.

"Precisely. The knowledge remains, but in forms that won't disrupt dimensional stability." Jake checked his pocket watch. "Your roommate Noah will be wondering where you are. The reconfigured reality framework establishes that you left the laboratory approximately ninety-seven minutes ago."

Robert nodded, another question occurring to him. "Does Noah remember anything? He was quantum entangled with me during the original convergence crisis and reset protocol."

"To some degree, yes. His consciousness shows residual resonance patterns consistent with probability awareness beyond conventional parameters. But his integration into the reconfigured reality appears more complete than yours—memories transforming more thoroughly into intuitive understanding rather than direct recollection."

They had reached Robert's apartment building now—the correct one, with the number 355 above the door, the familiar broken elevator, the same three flights of stairs leading to his unit.

"Thank you," Robert said sincerely as they paused at the entrance. "For everything—the guidance, the explanations, helping save reality itself from whatever catastrophic convergence might have happened without proper temporal loop closure."

Jake nodded in acknowledgment. "The guardian function continues, even in a singular timeline. Though the nature of the work has changed somewhat."

"No more interdimensional subway to monitor," Robert noted with a faint smile.

"No, but quantum field stability requires ongoing attention, nonetheless." Jake's expression became momentarily distant, as if perceiving aspects of reality beyond conventional awareness. "I'll check on you in a few days, though you may find your memories of recent events gradually transforming into less literal forms as your consciousness fully integrates with reconfigured reality parameters."

With those words, he bid Robert farewell and departed, walking back into the rainy night with measured steps that somehow suggested movement calibrated against standards beyond ordinary physical parameters.

Robert entered his apartment building, climbing the three flights to his unit with a strange mixture of exhaustion and exhilaration. The extraordinary journey that had begun with an unexpected subway entrance on Thornfield Avenue had finally come full circle, concluding with quantum intervention at that same nexus point to establish a stable singular reality.

He unlocked his apartment door, finding Noah inside watching television with a half-eaten pizza on the coffee table.

"There you are!" Noah greeted him. "I was about to send a search party. Your phone kept going straight to voicemail."

Robert checked his pocket, finding his phone battery completely drained—perhaps a side effect of the quantum energies involved in temporal loop closure, or simply the result of forgetting to charge it before leaving the laboratory earlier.

"Sorry, long night at the lab," he replied, the explanation technically accurate despite omitting extraordinary interdimensional journeys and reality reconfiguration events. "My quantum tunneling experiment finally showed consistent results."

"That's great," Noah said with genuine enthusiasm. "Professor Liang will be thrilled. There's pizza if you're hungry."

Robert joined him on the sofa, accepting a slice of now-lukewarm pizza with unexpected appreciation for such ordinary comforts after experiencing reality fluctuations and temporal loop closure.

As they ate and Noah filled him in on his day at the medical school, Robert noticed his roommate occasionally displaying subtle signs of residual probability awareness—brief pauses mid-sentence as if experiencing déjà vu, moments where his gaze seemed to track visual effects that shouldn't be visible in conventional perception, occasional use of terminology that suggested quantum understanding beyond his formal education.

Jake had been right—Noah maintained some resonance with probability configurations that technically no longer existed except as quantum potential, though his consciousness had integrated these experiences more thoroughly into reconfigured reality parameters.

Later that night, Robert stood at his bedroom window, watching raindrops trace familiar patterns down the glass. The storm was finally easing, clouds beginning to break apart to reveal glimpses of stars between their dark masses.

He still remembered everything—the multiple Daybridges, the Station Master with his mechanical precision, Gil's guidance through threshold reality, Jake's guardian knowledge that had ultimately led to proper temporal loop closure. But these memories had already begun transforming, becoming less literal and more intuitive, shifting toward forms his consciousness could process without creating reality discord.

The fountain pen sat on his desk, no longer glowing with blue luminescence but still somehow maintaining quiet resonance with his quantum signature. The dimensional anchor hung from his bedpost, its stabilization purpose fulfilled but its connection to extraordinary journeys across probability configurations preserved as a quiet reminder.

Reality had reconfigured into stable singular coherence; the temporal loop properly closed through precise quantum intervention at the crucial nexus point. The Liminal Line no longer existed as physical infrastructure, only as quantum potential integrated into more stable arrangements within unified reality.

Yet something essential remained—not the literal ability to travel between multiple Daybridges, but the expanded awareness these journeys had created. An understanding of reality's underlying flexibility, an appreciation for existence's precious coherence, a recognition of consciousness's remarkable adaptability.

Robert turned from the window, ready for sleep after what had been perhaps the most extraordinary day of his life—or lives, considering the multiple probability configurations he had experienced before reality reconfiguration established stable singular coherence.

Tomorrow would bring ordinary concerns—classes, research, everyday interactions within conventional reality parameters. His quantum signature would maintain the unusual resonance Jake had mentioned—an awareness transcending conventional constraints, allowing him to recognize the multiverse existing as potential even within singular timeline manifestation.

The subway that wasn't there had taken him on a journey beyond imagination. And though the entrance had vanished, sealed by proper temporal loop closure that established stable reality coherence, the memory of that impossible transit system would remain—transformed but not forgotten, integrated but not erased, a reminder that beneath the seemingly solid surface of reality lay mysteries still waiting to be discovered.

Full circle. The journey complete. Reality stable.

But awareness forever expanded beyond what had been possible before that rainy night when a graduate student noticed an unexpected subway entrance on a street that shouldn't have had one—a discovery that technically never happened in current reality configuration yet somehow changed everything permanently through the quantum miracle of probability, possibility, and consciousness itself.

CHAPTER FIFTEEN: ECHOES AND AFTERMATHS

On a crisp autumn morning six weeks after the temporal loop closure at Thornfield Avenue, Robert North woke to sunlight streaming through his bedroom window. He stretched, feeling thoroughly rested after a dreamless night—a welcome change from the vivid, disorienting dreams that had plagued him for months.

Those strange dreams had gradually diminished over the past weeks, fading from sharply detailed experiences of impossible subway journeys to vague impressions that dissolved upon waking. This morning, he remembered nothing of his sleeping mind's wanderings—only the pleasant sensation of deep, untroubled rest.

His room appeared exactly as it should: research papers stacked on his desk, quantum mechanics textbooks arranged by frequency of use rather than any conventional organizational system, coffee mug from yesterday perched precariously atop journal articles he'd been reviewing before bed.

Robert showered and dressed, his thoughts already turning to the day's schedule—a meeting with Professor Liang to discuss his quantum tunneling research, lunch with Noah between classes, laboratory time to continue his experiments on observer effects and probability wave functions.

In the kitchen, he found Noah already awake, making coffee and toast while reviewing medical terminology flashcards.

"Morning," Noah greeted him without looking up. "Sleep okay? You were talking in your sleep again last night."

"Was I?" Robert poured himself coffee from the freshly brewed pot. "I don't remember dreaming at all."

"Something about constellation patterns and brass fixtures," Noah replied with a shrug. "Sounded like some kind of architectural design discussion."

Robert frowned slightly, the words triggering a momentary sense of familiarity that vanished before he could grasp it. "Weird. Maybe I've been spending too much time in the physics building. Those old brass light fixtures in the main hall are pretty distinctive."

Noah nodded absently, focused on his flashcards. "Your quantum tunneling presentation is today, right? The one Professor Liang is so excited about?"

"Tomorrow. Today's just final preparation and one last data review." Robert buttered a piece of toast, his thoughts already shifting to the equations he needed to verify before the presentation. "You working at the hospital tonight?"

"Yeah, evening shift in the ER. Don't wait up." Noah gathered his flashcards and textbooks, stuffing them into his backpack. "Dinner's on you tomorrow, by the way. I covered the last three takeout orders."

"Fair enough." Robert checked his watch. "I should get moving too. I want to stop by the library before meeting with Professor Liang."

They parted ways outside their apartment building, Noah heading toward the medical campus while Robert turned in the direction of the university's main library. The autumn day was pleasantly cool, trees along the sidewalk displaying vibrant oranges and reds that seemed particularly vivid against the clear blue sky.

As Robert walked, he experienced a strange moment of disorientation when passing the intersection of Maple and Fifth—a brief sensation that the surrounding buildings were somehow in the wrong places, or perhaps the right places but wrong configurations. The feeling lasted only seconds before reality reasserted itself, everything appearing exactly as it should.

He'd been experiencing these occasional perceptual hiccups for weeks now—brief moments where the world seemed slightly out of alignment with his expectations before settling back into proper arrangement. His doctor had suggested they might be related to his intense focus on quantum mechanics, theorizing that studying probability wave functions and superposition states all day might occasionally affect how his brain processed visual information.

The explanation seemed reasonable enough, though it didn't quite account for the specific nature of these episodes. They always occurred at particular locations throughout Daybridge—certain street corners, specific buildings, and most noticeably, near the city's transit stations.

Daybridge had no subway system, only a network of electric trolleys that had served the city since the early twentieth century. Yet Robert often experienced the strongest disorientation when passing locations where subway entrances might logically have been placed had the city developed different transportation infrastructure.

He had mentioned this pattern to his doctor, who had simply added "transit-focused architectural interest" to his notes and recommended regular sleep schedules and occasional breaks from quantum mechanics research.

The university library came into view, its imposing stone facade catching the morning sunlight. Robert climbed the broad steps and entered the main hall, nodding to the security guard who monitored the entrance.

He had a specific purpose in mind—locating articles about Maxwell Hanover, a physicist whose work on quantum observation effects had recently captured his interest. Hanover's theories from the 1940s had been largely overlooked until recent developments in quantum field theory had suggested his unconventional models might have merit after all.

The reference librarian directed him to the physics archives on the third floor, where historical scientific journals were maintained in their original print editions. As Robert searched through the collection, he found himself drawn to a particular volume from 1943 containing Hanover's most controversial paper: "Quantum Observation Networks and Reality Coherence."

The article described theoretical frameworks for how consciousness itself might function as part of the quantum observation system that collapsed probability waves into specific reality configurations. Hanover had proposed that reality maintained coherence through continuous quantum observation across distributed networks—a concept that had seemed philosophically interesting but scientifically unfalsifiable in the 1940s.

What struck Robert now, reviewing the paper with a modern understanding of quantum mechanics, was how precisely Hanover's theoretical models aligned with his own experimental results. The quantum tunneling phenomena he had observed in his laboratory demonstrated exactly the kind of observer-influenced probability wave behaviors that Hanover had predicted decades earlier.

As he made photocopies of the article, Robert noticed a small photograph accompanying the text—Maxwell Hanover himself, an unsmiling man in formal attire, standing before experimental equipment at what was identified as the Daybridge Containment Initiative laboratory.

Something about the photograph triggered another moment of disorientation—a sense that he recognized not just the physicist but the specific equipment arranged behind him. The feeling was so strong that Robert found himself reaching out to touch the image, as if physical contact might explain this inexplicable familiarity.

"Interesting choice of research material."

The voice startled him from his contemplation. Robert turned to find an elderly man with intelligent blue eyes and a neatly trimmed white beard observing him from the adjacent reading table.

"Maxwell Hanover's work is rarely studied by contemporary physicists," the man continued. "His theories were considered too speculative for serious consideration during his lifetime."

"You're familiar with Hanover's research?" Robert asked, somehow unsurprised by this unexpected conversation despite the unusual circumstances.

"Intimately." The old man smiled slightly. "Gilbert Harmon. Professor Emeritus at the Institute for Quantum Studies. I wrote my dissertation on Hanover's quantum observation networks theory back when everyone considered it philosophical speculation rather than serious physics."

The name triggered immediate recognition. "Professor Harmon! I've read your papers on probability track analysis and quantum resonance patterns. Your work on observer effects in tunneling experiments directly influenced my current research."

"Did it now?" Harmon's blue eyes twinkled with something that might have been private amusement. "And what specifically captured your interest?"

"Your mathematical models for measuring superposition states without triggering immediate wave function collapse," Robert replied enthusiastically. "I've adapted your probability resonance equations for my quantum tunneling experiments, and the results are extraordinary—particles maintaining superposition despite multiple observation events, only collapsing when specific resonance parameters are introduced."

"Fascinating." Harmon studied him with increased interest. "Your name?"

"Robert North. I'm a graduate student in the physics department, working under Professor Liang."

"Ah, Mei Liang. An excellent physicist with appropriately flexible thinking regarding quantum mechanics." Harmon nodded approvingly. "She wouldn't dismiss experimental results merely because they challenge conventional models."

He gestured to the chair opposite his own. "May I see what you've found in Hanover's paper that connects to your research?"

Robert joined him, spreading out the photocopied article and his own research notes. For the next hour, they discussed quantum observation networks, probability resonance patterns, and the mathematical frameworks that connected Hanover's theoretical models to Robert's experimental results.

Throughout their conversation, Robert experienced occasional moments of déjà vu—a sense that he had discussed these exact topics with Professor Harmon before, in circumstances he couldn't quite recall. The feeling was particularly strong when they examined Hanover's equations for reality coherence maintenance through distributed quantum observation.

"These mathematical relationships essentially describe how consciousness itself participates in collapsing probability waves into specific reality configurations," Harmon explained, tracing a particular equation with his finger. "Hanover proposed that reality maintains coherence through continuous observation across networks that include both conscious entities and certain quantum-sensitive inanimate objects."

"Like measurement devices in quantum experiments," Robert suggested.

"Among others." Harmon smiled slightly. "Hanover believed certain materials and artifacts naturally maintained quantum sensitivity that transcended conventional physical properties—objects that resonated with probability patterns in ways that contributed to reality coherence."

As they continued their discussion, Robert noticed Professor Harmon occasionally checking his watch—an unusual timepiece with a face that displayed complex symbols rather than conventional numbers. When he commented on it, Harmon merely described it as "a prototype that tracks probability configurations rather than linear time," without further explanation.

Eventually, Robert realized he was running late for his meeting with Professor Liang. As he gathered his materials, Harmon removed a business card from his pocket and handed it to him.

"Your research shows remarkable alignment with certain aspects of quantum field theory I've been developing for decades," the elderly physicist said. "If you're interested in discussing potential applications beyond conventional laboratory parameters, please contact me."

Robert accepted the card, noting it displayed only Harmon's name, title, and a phone number—no email address or institutional affiliation. "Thank you, Professor. I'd be very interested in continuing our discussion."

"Excellent. Probability configurations suggest significant collaborative potential." With that cryptic comment, Harmon nodded farewell and returned to his own research materials.

Robert left the library, the business card tucked carefully into his wallet. The conversation had been unexpectedly stimulating, connecting his experimental work to theoretical frameworks he hadn't previously considered. Yet something about the encounter left him with that same strange sense of familiarity—as if he and Professor Harmon had discussed these topics many times before in circumstances he couldn't quite remember.

Shaking off this peculiar feeling, he hurried across campus to Professor Liang's office, arriving several minutes late for their scheduled meeting.

"Sorry for the delay," he apologized as he entered. "I was in the library researching Maxwell Hanover's quantum observation networks theory and ended up in a fascinating discussion with Professor Harmon."

Professor Liang looked up from her computer with raised eyebrows. "Gil Harmon? He rarely engages with graduate students directly. You must have impressed him somehow."

"We discovered some interesting connections between Hanover's theoretical models and my experimental results," Robert explained, setting his materials on her desk. "The quantum tunneling phenomena I've been observing seem to demonstrate precisely the kind of observer-influenced probability behaviors that Hanover predicted in the 1940s."

"Fascinating." Professor Liang examined the photocopied article and Robert's notes with evident interest. "Hanover's work was largely dismissed during his lifetime, but recent developments in quantum field theory have suggested his models might have had merit after all."

Their discussion shifted to Robert's upcoming presentation, reviewing the experimental data and theoretical frameworks he would present to the department. Throughout their meeting, Robert occasionally experienced those same brief moments of déjà vu—a sense that certain phrases or concepts triggered recognition beyond what his conscious memory could explain.

After leaving Professor Liang's office, Robert headed to his laboratory to continue his quantum tunneling experiments. The physics building was relatively quiet that afternoon, most students attending classes or working in the library rather than conducting laboratory research.

His experimental setup occupied a small room filled with specialized equipment for measuring quantum behaviors in controlled environments. At the center was an apparatus designed to track particles through potential barriers, measuring their quantum states before, during, and after tunneling events.

As Robert activated the equipment and began calibrating the measurement parameters, he experienced another powerful wave of déjà vu—a sense that he had performed these exact actions countless times before, not just in his daily research routine but in some broader context he couldn't quite grasp.

The feeling intensified as the experiment ran, displaying results on his monitoring screens that showed particles maintaining superposition states despite multiple observation events—exactly the kind of quantum behavior that conventional models suggested should be impossible.

Robert documented these results carefully, noting the specific resonance patterns that seemed to allow observation without wave function collapse. Something about these patterns triggered yet another flash of recognition—mathematical relationships that seemed familiar beyond his formal education or research experience.

When he finally left the laboratory that evening, the sun had already set, campus lights illuminating paths between buildings where a few students hurried toward dormitories or evening classes. Robert decided to walk home rather than taking the trolley, wanting time to process the day's developments and prepare for tomorrow's presentation.

His route took him past Merchant Street, a charming area of small shops and cafes that catered to the university community. As he walked, his attention was drawn to a Victorian townhouse with large bay windows displaying antique books and curiosities—Steinman's Rare Editions, according to the discreet sign above the door.

Something about the bookshop triggered such a powerful sense of familiarity that Robert stopped walking entirely, staring at the building with the uncanny feeling that he knew exactly what the interior looked like despite never having visited it. He could almost picture the layout—bookshelves arranged in precise configurations, comfortable reading chairs in quiet corners, a back office with unusual monitoring equipment disguised as antique radios and measuring instruments.

The shop appeared closed for the evening, lights dimmed except for a single lamp visible in what must be that back office. Robert could make out a silhouette moving behind the partially drawn blinds—someone working late among the books and artifacts.

Without conscious decision, he found himself approaching the door. A small sign indicated the shop was indeed closed, but as he peered through the glass, the interior lights suddenly brightened. Moments later, the door opened to reveal a middle-aged man with silver-streaked hair and a formal waistcoat, complete with pocket watch chain visible across his midsection.

"Robert North," the man said, sounding neither surprised nor confused by his presence after hours. "I've been expecting you. Please, come in."

Startled by this greeting from a stranger who somehow knew his name, Robert hesitated. "I'm sorry, have we met? I was just passing by and noticed your bookshop..."

"Not formally, no. But probability configurations suggested our paths would intersect this evening." The man stepped back, holding the door open. "I'm Jake Steinman. I believe you've already encountered Gilbert Harmon today."

This reference to his earlier meeting with Professor Harmon was sufficiently intriguing that Robert decided to enter despite the unusual circumstances. The bookshop interior matched his inexplicable expectations with unsettling precision—the exact arrangement of shelves, the reading chairs positioned exactly where he had imagined them, even the particular smell of leather bindings and old paper.

"How did you know I met Professor Harmon?" Robert asked as Jake led him through the maze of bookshelves toward the back office.

"Gil and I maintain regular communication regarding quantum sensitivity patterns throughout Daybridge," Jake replied cryptically. "Your interaction with him registered particularly distinct resonance signatures."

Before Robert could ask what that meant, they had reached the office door. Jake opened it to reveal a comfortable space lined with more bookshelves, these containing volumes that looked considerably rarer and more esoteric than those in the main shop. A large desk occupied the center, covered with what appeared to be antique measuring instruments and a leather-bound ledger.

"Please, sit." Jake gestured to a chair opposite the desk before moving to a cabinet from which he retrieved a tea service. "Earl Grey, if I recall correctly."

Robert sat, increasingly puzzled by this strange encounter. "How would you know my tea preference? We've never met."

"Probability resonance suggests certain patterns with high consistency across configuration variants," Jake replied, preparing the tea with practiced efficiency. "Your preference for Earl Grey registers with 93.7% probability, according to Gil's calculations."

This cryptic explanation did nothing to clarify the situation. Robert accepted the offered teacup, noting with increasing unease that it was prepared exactly as he preferred—moderate strength with precisely one sugar cube and no milk.

"Mr. Steinman, I don't understand what's happening here. You seem to know things about me that you shouldn't, and this entire shop feels impossibly familiar despite my never having visited before."

Jake regarded him thoughtfully as he took the seat behind his desk. "What you're experiencing are echo effects from probability configurations that exist as potential rather than manifestation within our current reality framework. Your quantum signature maintains resonance with these alternatives despite timeline reconfiguration."

These terms should have been meaningless, yet Robert found himself nodding with an intuitive understanding that transcended his conscious knowledge. "Timeline reconfiguration. You're talking about the reset protocol and temporal loop closure."

The words emerged automatically, triggering a cascade of fragmented memories—a train spiraling upward toward a swirling vortex, blue energy enveloping multiple versions of Daybridge, countless realities merging into one coherent configuration, and finally, a quantum intervention at Thornfield Avenue that closed a temporal loop and established stable singular reality.

Jake's expression showed both concern and approval. "You remember more than you should. The integration process appears incomplete despite optimal probability parameters."

"Integration process?" Robert repeated, struggling to reconcile these impossible memories with his understanding of reality.

In response, Jake opened the leather-bound ledger on his desk, revealing pages of handwritten notes and complex diagrams that seemed to shift slightly when viewed from different angles.

"Six weeks ago, reality experienced significant reconfiguration following what we might call a dimensional convergence event," he explained, turning the ledger toward Robert. "Multiple probability tracks that had previously existed as separate manifestations were integrated into a singular coherent timeline through a process that involved your direct participation as quantum catalyst."

Robert studied the diagrams in the ledger, which depicted mathematical relationships he somehow recognized despite their extraordinary complexity. They showed what appeared to be multiple reality configurations converging toward a singular framework through precisely calculated quantum resonance patterns.

"The Liminal Line," he whispered, the term emerging from some deeper level of awareness. "The subway system that connected different versions of Daybridge across probability tracks."

Jake nodded, watching him carefully. "The interdimensional transit system manifested as a physical expression of pathways between fractured realities. In our current singular timeline, it exists only as quantum potential rather than physical infrastructure, following successful implementation of the reset protocol and temporal loop closure."

"But I remember it," Robert said slowly, fragmented images coalescing into more coherent recollections. "Copper trains that traveled between different versions of Daybridge. Stations with constellation mosaics overhead and brass fixtures that gleamed like they were polished daily."

"Memory exists partially outside conventional spacetime constraints," Jake explained. "The reset changed reality's configuration but couldn't completely erase the quantum imprint your experiences left on your consciousness. What you're experiencing are echoes from probability tracks that were integrated into the current singular timeline during the convergence event."

Robert sipped his tea, trying to process this extraordinary information. "If what you're saying is true, why don't I remember everything clearly? Why just fragments and feelings of déjà vu?"

"The integration process is designed to transform direct memories of interdimensional experiences into forms your current reality consciousness can process without disruption," Jake replied. "Complete, literal memory of multiple probability tracks would create significant quantum discord within singular timeline parameters."

He turned another page in his ledger, revealing a diagram that depicted consciousness itself as a quantum system capable of existing across multiple probability configurations simultaneously.

"Your quantum signature is unusually resonant with probability variation, which is why you maintain greater awareness than most would under similar circumstances. But even your consciousness must integrate these experiences into forms compatible with singular reality framework to prevent dimensional instability."

This explanation should have seemed absurd, yet Robert found himself accepting it with that same intuitive recognition he'd experienced when examining Hanover's equations. It aligned with his fragmented memories and explained the persistent déjà vu he'd been experiencing since... since when, exactly? His chronological sense of these events remained frustratingly unclear.

"When did this 'convergence event' happen?" he asked, trying to establish some temporal framework for these impossible memories.

"From your perspective, approximately six weeks ago," Jake replied. "Though 'when' becomes somewhat ambiguous regarding events that fundamentally reconfigured temporal parameters."

Robert focused on the ledger before him, noticing that certain diagrams depicted specific locations throughout Daybridge—including the intersection of Thornfield Avenue and Riverside Drive where his disorientation episodes were most pronounced.

"That's where it happened, isn't it? Thornfield and Riverside. Where I first found the subway entrance that shouldn't have existed."

Jake nodded, impressed by this specific recollection. "The origin point of your journey across probability tracks, and ultimately the nexus point where temporal loop closure was implemented through your direct quantum intervention."

Another fragment surfaced in Robert's memory—standing in pouring rain at that same intersection, holding a glowing fountain pen that somehow redirected probability flow toward stable singular configuration rather than multiple divergent tracks.

"The pen," he said suddenly. "A fountain pen with brass components that contained specific metallic alloys selected for their quantum resonance characteristics."

Jake smiled slightly, opening a drawer in his desk and removing an object wrapped in silk cloth. "Some artifacts maintain quantum resonance patterns that transcend conventional temporal constraints."

He unwrapped the cloth to reveal an elegant antique fountain pen with intricate brass accents—identical to the one in Robert's fragmentary memory of the temporal loop closure.

"You've had it all this time," Robert observed, not reaching for the artifact despite feeling its resonance with his quantum signature. "Since the reset protocol and temporal loop closure."

"The guardian function requires maintaining certain artifacts that facilitate monitoring of dimensional stability," Jake confirmed. "This particular object served as your quantum intervention tool during temporal loop closure, establishing probability redirection toward singular coherent reality."

Robert studied the pen without touching it, recognizing its significance while understanding that direct contact might trigger more complete memory recovery than current reality parameters could safely accommodate.

"There's something else," he said, another fragment surfacing. "A journal. I kept notes during my journeys between probability tracks—observations about different versions of Daybridge, the stations I visited, the people I encountered."

Jake nodded, removing another item from his drawer—a leather-bound notebook that showed signs of considerable use, its pages slightly warped as if it had been soaked in rain and then dried.

"Your interdimensional transit log," he confirmed. "Another artifact I've maintained as part of the guardian record. It contains detailed documentation of your journeys through seven different probability configurations of Daybridge before the convergence crisis necessitated reality reset."

He placed the journal beside the fountain pen but didn't open it. "These artifacts maintain quantum resonance with your experiences across probability tracks that technically no longer exist except as potential rather than manifestation. Direct interaction might trigger memory recovery beyond what current reality parameters can safely integrate."

Robert nodded, understanding the implicit warning while feeling irresistibly drawn to these physical connections to experiences his conscious mind could only partially access.

"Why show me these things if I'm not supposed to remember completely?" he asked. "Why risk triggering 'memory recovery beyond what current reality parameters can safely integrate'?"

Jake closed his ledger before answering. "Because your quantum signature continues to display unusual resonance characteristics that suggest incomplete integration with singular timeline parameters. These occasional disorientation episodes you've been experiencing—particularly at specific locations throughout Daybridge—indicate residual probability awareness that requires proper contextualization."

"You're saying I need to understand what happened to stop feeling like reality occasionally glitches around me?"

"In simplified terms, yes. Conscious contextualization of quantum resonance patterns can facilitate more complete integration without requiring literal memory of events that technically never occurred within current timeline parameters."

Robert considered this explanation, finding it aligned with his experiences over the past six weeks. The disorientation episodes had been most intense immediately following what must have been the temporal loop closure, gradually diminishing in frequency and intensity as his consciousness adjusted to singular reality parameters.

"What about Noah?" he asked suddenly. "My roommate. He was involved somehow, wasn't he? He mentions my sleep-talking about constellation patterns and brass fixtures."

"Noah was quantum entangled with you during certain critical phases of the interdimensional transit sequence," Jake confirmed. "This created residual resonance patterns in his consciousness as well, though his integration with singular timeline parameters appears more complete than yours."

"Because his quantum signature isn't as 'unusually resonant with probability variation'?"

"Precisely. His consciousness maintained less direct connection to multiple probability configurations, making integration less complex following reality reconfiguration."

Robert sipped his now-cooling tea, processing these extraordinary revelations. "And Professor Harmon? Gil? He was my guide through... through threshold reality. The Wanderer who'd been exploring the Liminal Line for decades."

Jake nodded, unsurprised by this specific recollection. "Gilbert Harmon's quantum signature maintains unique characteristics resulting from prolonged exposure to threshold parameters before reality reconfiguration. In our current timeline, he exists as Professor Emeritus at the Institute for Quantum Studies but maintains significant awareness of probability configurations that technically never manifested."

"That's why he approached me in the library today," Robert realized. "He recognized my quantum signature somehow."

"Gil's consciousness operates partially outside conventional reality constraints," Jake explained. "He perceives quantum resonance patterns most people filter out automatically, allowing him to identify individuals with similar sensitivity."

Robert's gaze returned to the journal and fountain pen resting on Jake's desk—physical connections to experiences his consciousness could only partially access despite having lived through them in probability configurations now integrated into potential rather than manifestation.

"May I?" he asked, gesturing toward the journal without reaching for it.

Jake hesitated briefly before nodding. "Limited interaction should remain within safe integration parameters. But I wouldn't recommend reading extensive sections or handling the fountain pen directly at this stage of your consciousness realignment."

With careful movements, Robert opened the journal to a random page near the middle. The handwriting was unmistakably his own, though the content described experiences he remembered only in fragments:

Day four of transit exploration. The third Daybridge differs significantly from the previous two. Architecture shows strong Art Deco influence throughout downtown, and the university campus has been relocated to the western hills rather than its central location in my home reality. The Liminal Line station beneath Crescent Park displays unusual constellation configurations in its ceiling mosaics—stellar arrangements that don't match any recognized patterns from astronomy texts I've consulted.

Most notably, this version of Daybridge developed extensive underground transit following what locals refer to as the "Great Reconfiguration" of 1943—apparently a major urban renewal project implemented under Maxwell Hanover's guidance as city engineer. The locals find nothing unusual about their subway system, though station attendants give me curious looks when I ask about connections to other versions of the city.

Gil's theory about "dimensional anchoring" through consistent elements across probability tracks seems validated by certain buildings maintaining identical placement and function despite architectural variations. The public library, central hospital, and Steinman's Rare Editions all occupy exactly the same coordinates as in my home reality, though their specific designs reflect this timeline's aesthetic preferences.

Robert turned to another page, finding a carefully drawn map that appeared to show transit connections between different versions of Daybridge. The diagram used unfamiliar symbols to indicate what might be dimensional coordinates or probability variation parameters alongside more conventional geographical markings.

"The pattern," he murmured, recognizing something significant in the transit lines' arrangement. "It's not arbitrary. The Liminal Line followed specific mathematical relationships between probability configurations."

"Indeed," Jake confirmed. "The interdimensional transit system manifested along quantum resonance pathways that naturally formed between probability variations of the same geographical location. In simplified terms, the subway connected points where reality fabric was thinnest between different versions of Daybridge."

Robert carefully closed the journal, sensing that prolonged exposure might indeed trigger memory recovery beyond what his consciousness could currently integrate without creating reality discord.

"The Station Master," he said, another significant fragment surfacing. "The entity that maintained the transit system. He existed across all probability tracks simultaneously, perceiving multiple realities as a single integrated framework."

Jake nodded, returning the journal and fountain pen to his drawer. "Maxwell Hanover was transformed during the original reality fracture event in 1943—the experiment that split Daybridge into countless parallel versions across the probability spectrum. His consciousness expanded beyond conventional constraints to encompass multiple configurations simultaneously."

"But in this timeline, that experiment never created a catastrophic breach," Robert noted, understanding forming despite fragmentary memories. "The reset protocol healed the original fracture point, creating a singular coherent reality where Daybridge never split into multiple probability tracks."

"Precisely. In our current timeline, Maxwell Hanover completed his research successfully without dimensional disruption. He made significant contributions to quantum field theory before retiring to write several influential books on theoretical physics, eventually passing away in 1972 as a respected if somewhat unconventional scientist."

Robert finished his tea, placing the empty cup on Jake's desk. "And the guardian function? Your role monitoring dimensional stability? That continues even in a singular timeline where no catastrophic breach occurred?"

"Reality coherence requires ongoing maintenance even without active interdimensional transit," Jake confirmed. "The quantum mechanics that prevent probability divergence operate continuously across observation networks that include both conscious entities and certain resonant artifacts."

He gestured to the antique measuring instruments arranged on his desk—devices Robert now recognized as sophisticated quantum monitoring equipment disguised as vintage collectibles.

"I maintain awareness of probability configurations that technically never manifested in our current timeline to prevent similar breaches from occurring in the future. The multiverse still exists as potential, even in a reality where probability tracks haven't physically diverged."

Robert nodded, finding this explanation aligned with both his fragmentary memories and his intuitive understanding of quantum mechanics. "And my role in all this now? Do I just... continue my research and gradually forget these probability configurations that technically never manifested?"

"Your consciousness will continue integrating these experiences into forms compatible with singular reality framework," Jake replied. "The disorientation episodes should diminish further as integration progresses. Eventually, your awareness of alternate probability configurations will transform completely into intuitive understanding rather than fragmentary memory."

"But some connection remains," Robert suggested. "My quantum signature still resonates with these potential alternatives even as they integrate into my consciousness."

"Yes. Some quantum resonance patterns transcend even reality reconfiguration protocols. Your particular signature maintains unusual sensitivity to probability configurations that exist as potential within our singular timeline."

Jake checked his pocket watch—a device Robert now recognized as more than a simple timepiece. "It's getting late. Your roommate will be at the hospital until morning, but you have your presentation tomorrow. Adequate rest would be advisable for optimal cognitive function."

Robert stood, recognizing the polite dismissal while feeling there was still much more to discuss. "Will I remember this conversation tomorrow? Or will it integrate into something my consciousness can process without creating reality discord?"

"Some aspects may transform into more abstract understanding," Jake acknowledged. "But our interaction has been carefully calibrated to remain within safe integration parameters. The conscious contextualization should actually help diminish your disorientation episodes by providing a framework for your quantum resonance experiences."

He walked Robert to the shop's front door. "Feel free to visit again if you experience significant disorientation or require additional contextualization. The guardian function includes assisting those with unusual quantum sensitivity to maintain coherent consciousness within singular reality parameters."

As Robert prepared to leave, a final question occurred to him. "The fountain pen. Will I ever... should I ever handle it again? It seems significant to my quantum signature somehow."

Jake considered this carefully before answering. "Perhaps, eventually. When your consciousness has completed its integration process, direct interaction with resonant artifacts might be possible without triggering excessive probability awareness. For now, I'll maintain it as part of the guardian collection."

With that qualified promise, they said their farewells. Robert stepped out onto Merchant Street, now quiet in the evening darkness except for occasional pedestrians and passing cars. The bookshop behind him looked exactly as it should—a Victorian townhouse with large bay windows displaying antique books and curiosities, nothing to suggest it contained quantum monitoring equipment or artifacts from probability configurations that technically never manifested.

As Robert walked home through the autumn night, he found the disorientation episodes that had plagued him for weeks notably absent. Streets maintained consistent configuration, buildings remained in their proper locations and architectural styles, reality itself seemed more solidly coherent than it had since... since the temporal loop closure he now partially remembered implementing six weeks earlier at the intersection of Thornfield Avenue and Riverside Drive.

Over the following months, Robert's consciousness continued integrating his interdimensional experiences as Jake had predicted. The disorientation episodes diminished until they occurred only rarely, usually when he passed specific locations with particularly strong quantum resonance—the intersection of Thornfield and Riverside, the university physics building where Maxwell Hanover had once conducted his experiments, and occasionally Steinman's Rare Editions itself.

His quantum tunneling research progressed remarkably well, earning recognition throughout the physics department and eventually leading to publication in prestigious scientific journals. Professor Liang marveled at his intuitive understanding of probability wave functions and observer effects—knowledge that seemed to transcend his formal education and research experience.

"It's as if you somehow know how particles will behave before they do," she commented during one laboratory session, watching as Robert predicted complex quantum behaviors with uncanny accuracy. "Your models for measurement without observer-induced collapse represent a genuine breakthrough in quantum mechanics."

Robert collaborated occasionally with Professor Harmon, whose theoretical frameworks for "probability track analysis" provided mathematical foundations for his experimental observations. Their discussions never directly referenced interdimensional transit or multiple Daybridges yet sometimes contained terminology and concepts that triggered momentary recognition from those experiences now integrated into intuitive understanding rather than literal memory.

Noah completed his medical studies and began residency at Daybridge Central Hospital, maintaining their shared apartment despite his irregular schedule. He occasionally mentioned Robert's sleep-talking about "subway stations" or "copper trains," but these episodes gradually diminished as Robert's consciousness completed its integration process.

Jake Steinman continued his guardian function from the bookshop on Merchant Street, monitoring quantum resonance patterns throughout Daybridge with his collection of disguised equipment. Robert visited occasionally, sometimes browsing the rare books but more often sitting in the back office discussing quantum mechanics over Earl Grey tea prepared exactly as he preferred.

During one such visit nearly a year after their first meeting, Jake removed Robert's journal from his drawer and placed it on the desk between them.

"I believe your consciousness has sufficiently integrated your interdimensional experiences to safely interact with this artifact," he said, sliding the leather-bound notebook toward Robert. "Your disorientation episodes have ceased entirely, and your quantum signature shows stable resonance patterns consistent with singular timeline parameters."

Robert accepted the journal cautiously, opening it to find his own handwriting documenting journeys through multiple versions of Daybridge—experiences now transformed into intuitive understanding rather than literal memory. Reading these accounts triggered recognition but not disorientation, confirming Jake's assessment of his completed integration process.

Near the end of the journal, he found several pages containing meticulously drawn maps of the Liminal Line system, showing connections between different stations across probability configurations. The final diagram particularly caught his attention—a complex pattern that seemed to change slightly when viewed from different angles.

"This is unusual," Robert commented, turning the page to examine the pattern from various perspectives. "The transit connections seem to reconfigure themselves depending on how you look at them."

"Try folding it," Jake suggested. "Some information transcends two-dimensional representation."

Following this cryptic instruction, Robert carefully folded the page along what appeared to be intentional crease marks. The diagram transformed through this manipulation, revealing a three-dimensional pattern that couldn't have been properly represented on flat paper.

"It's a quantum resonance matrix," he realized, recognition flowing from intuitive understanding rather than literal memory. "The Liminal Line followed natural harmonic patterns in the dimensional fabric—connections that existed independently of the physical infrastructure that manifested along them."

"Indeed." Jake studied the folded diagram with professional interest. "And do you notice anything familiar about this pattern?"

Robert examined the three-dimensional configuration more carefully, suddenly recognizing its significance. "It matches the ley line system beneath Daybridge—the geomagnetic anomalies mapped by archaeological surveys in the 1930s."

"Precisely. The interdimensional transit system manifested along pathways that existed within the geographical and geological structure of Daybridge itself—quantum resonance channels that predated human settlement in the region by millennia."

This revelation connected numerous fragments in Robert's integrated understanding—why certain buildings maintained identical placement across probability configurations, why specific locations triggered stronger disorientation during his integration process, why the Liminal Line stations had appeared in consistent locations despite architectural variations between different Daybridges.

"Reality coherence utilizes existing structural patterns within geographical locations," he murmured, the understanding emerging from levels deeper than conscious thought. "The quantum observation networks Hanover described align with natural resonance channels in the physical environment."

"A sophisticated insight," Jake acknowledged. "The guardian function has documented such alignments across numerous locations globally, though Daybridge represents a particularly strong convergence of natural resonance channels—which explains why the original breach occurred here rather than elsewhere."

As Robert carefully refolded the diagram and continued examining the journal, a small object fell from between the final pages—a business card that had apparently been tucked into the back cover. He picked it up, finding it displayed Professor Harmon's name, title, and a phone number, similar to the card he had received in the library a year earlier.

"Interesting," Jake commented, examining the card with unusual intensity. "May I see that briefly?"

Robert handed it over, watching as Jake studied the simple card with the focused attention he usually reserved for quantum monitoring equipment.

"Remarkable," Jake murmured, turning the card over several times. "The phone number changes each time I look at it—cycling through what appears to be a sequence of probability variations."

He returned the card to Robert, who observed the same phenomenon—digits rearranging themselves subtly between observations, never displaying the same complete sequence twice though certain numbers remained consistent.

"And the address," Robert noted, finding small text on the card's reverse side that he hadn't initially noticed. "It's for the Institute for Quantum Studies, but..."

"But the location doesn't quite exist in our current reality configuration," Jake finished for him. "The coordinates correspond to a probability variation of Daybridge where urban development followed different parameters."

Robert carefully placed the card back in the journal, understanding its significance without requiring explicit explanation. Gilbert Harmon's quantum signature maintained connections to probability configurations that technically never manifested in their current timeline—his consciousness operating partially outside conventional reality constraints even after successful implementation of the reset protocol and temporal loop closure.

"Some connections transcend even reality reconfiguration," Robert observed, echoing Jake's words from their first meeting a year earlier.

"Indeed." Jake accepted the journal as Robert returned it, carefully rewrapping it in silk cloth before placing it back in his drawer alongside the fountain pen. "Consciousness exists partially outside conventional spacetime constraints. Certain quantum signatures maintain resonance patterns that persist through dimensional adjustments and timeline integration."

As their conversation shifted to more conventional topics—Robert's recent research publications, upcoming conferences on quantum mechanics, rare books Jake had acquired for his collection—Robert felt a profound sense of completion. His consciousness had successfully integrated experiences from probability configurations that technically never manifested in their current timeline, transforming literal memories into intuitive understanding that enhanced his perception of reality rather than creating discord with singular coherence parameters.

Later that evening, walking home through streets that maintained perfect coherence despite his awareness of potential alternative configurations, Robert passed the intersection of Thornfield Avenue and Riverside Drive. For the first time since the temporal loop closure, he felt no disorientation at this location—only a quiet recognition of its significance in probability configurations that existed now as potential rather than manifestation.

The subway entrance that had once appeared between buildings remained solid brick wall, as it had always been in this singular timeline where Daybridge developed surface trolleys rather than underground transit. Yet Robert could perceive, not with physical senses but with quantum awareness that transcended conventional perception, the subtle resonance patterns that still flowed beneath the city—natural channels along which probability configurations aligned, and reality maintained coherent manifestation through continuous quantum observation.

In his apartment, he found a note from Noah indicating he'd be working overnight at the hospital again. Robert made himself tea—Earl Grey, prepared exactly as he preferred—and stood at his window watching the city lights against the night sky.

Somewhere across Daybridge, Jake Steinman maintained his guardian function, monitoring quantum resonance patterns through disguised equipment in his Victorian bookshop. Professor Gilbert Harmon likely worked late in his office at the Institute for Quantum Studies, his consciousness perceiving aspects of reality most filtered out automatically. And countless residents moved through their evening routines, blissfully unaware that their coherent singular reality had once fractured into multiple probability configurations before being carefully reintegrated through precise quantum intervention at a specific nexus point.

The subway that wasn't there had taken Robert North on a journey beyond imagination. And though the entrance had vanished, sealed by proper temporal loop closure that established stable reality coherence, the memory of that impossible transit system remained—transformed but not forgotten, integrated but not erased, a reminder that beneath the seemingly solid surface of reality lay mysteries still waiting to be discovered.

He sipped his tea, quantum awareness perceiving subtle resonance patterns flowing through the city along ancient channels that predated human settlement. Reality maintained its coherence through continuous observation across networks that included both conscious entities and certain resonant artifacts—exactly as Maxwell Hanover had theorized in 1943, in a singular timeline where catastrophic dimensional breach had been prevented through successful implementation of the reset protocol and temporal loop closure.

Echo effects from probability configurations that technically never manifested. Aftermaths of journeys across realities now integrated into potential rather than separate manifestation. A quantum signature that maintained unusual resonance with possibility beyond conventional perception.

Robert North had returned from his journey between worlds, but he carried with him knowledge that few humans had ever possessed—and the subtle echoes of experiences across multiple realities that would forever influence his perception of the world around him.

Reality itself was the ultimate journey—singular yet infinitely complex, coherent yet endlessly malleable, one path containing unlimited possibility for those who learned to perceive beyond conventional constraints.

And Robert North, without fully remembering how or why, had somehow been granted a ticket for that extraordinary voyage of discovery.

Copyright:

First Edition

Published by Live For Excellence Productions

ISBNs:

E-book: 978-1-997784-42-5

Paperback: 978-1-997784-43-2

Audiobook: 978-1-997784-44-9

About the Author

Rae Stonehouse turned to fiction writing after establishing himself as a prolific author of self-development and professional growth books.

With over fifty published works helping readers navigate personal and professional challenges, he embarked on a new creative path with the Ethan Reeves Werewolf Detective Series.

When not weaving tales of supernatural sleuthing, Stonehouse continues to share his expertise in personal development through workshops and speaking engagements from his home in British Columbia.

The Ethan Reeves series marks his debut in fiction writing, blending his understanding of human nature with a newfound passion for urban fantasy.

The story doesn't end here. Scan for more books in the Daybridge Chronicles, part of the Ethan Reeves Werewolf Detective Series: https://my.linkpod.site/daybridgechronicles

www.ingramcontent.com/pod-product-compliance
Lightning Source LLC
Chambersburg PA
CBHW022147010726
47493CB00002B/373